Praise for the Dragon Diaries Novels

Flying Blind

"This is a YA book but with just the right amount of action, suspense, humor, and just a touch of romance. I think fans of both YA and adult fantasy books will enjoy [this] dragon tale." —Paranormal Haven

"This story crosses the boundaries. It will appeal to both teens and adults across the board. The story is engaging and fun. It's bringing to life a world of dragons and magic that appeals to all."

—Night Owl Reviews (top pick, 5 stars)

"Whether you're young or just young at heart, you will equally enjoy this brand-new series by Ms. Cooke. . . . It's entertaining, it's exciting, and it's adventurous." —The Reading Frenzy

"This. Book. Rocks . . . *Flying Blind* has everything a dragon-loving, shape-shifting romantic girl who loves adventure, fun, and epic tales could want in a book." —One a Day Y.A.

"A fantastic offshoot of her *Pyr* universe. [Cooke] has hit exactly the right tone and cadence for a young-adult novel while still keeping all the fantasy and mystery of the ancient *Pyr* woven through the story line. . . . After turning the final page, I sat for a moment with a sense of excitement I haven't felt since I finished my first of Anne McCaffrey's Pern books." —Fresh Fiction

"I dare any reader to start this book and not get caught up in the story immediately. The first of the new series about the next generation of dragons, *Flying Blind* is a story of coming of age, of finding one's true worth, and of trusting in one's self." —Romance Reviews Today

continued . . .

Praise for the Dragon Fire Novels

Darkfire Kiss

"Deborah Cooke's Dragonfire novels are impossible to put down. *Darkfire Kiss* is no exception. I dare any reader to skim any part of this terrific story!" —Romance Reviews Today

Whisper Kiss

"Cooke introduces her most unconventional and inspiring heroine to date. . . . The sparks are instantaneous. . . . Cooke aces another one!"

—*Romantic Times* (4½ stars)

Winter Kiss

"A beautiful and emotionally gripping fourth novel, *Winter Kiss* is compelling and will keep readers riveted in their seats and breathing a happy sigh at the love shared between Delaney and Ginger. . . . Sizzling-hot love scenes and explosive emotions make *Winter Kiss* a must read!" —Romance Junkies

Kiss of Fate

"An intense ride. Ms. Cooke has a great talent. . . . If you love paranormal romance in any way, this is a series you should be following."

—Night Owl Romance (reviewer top pick)

Kiss of Fury

"Epic battles, suspense, ecological concerns, humor, and romance are highlights that readers can expect in this tale. Excellent writing, a smart story, and exceptional characters earn this novel the RRT Perfect 10 Rating. Don't miss the very highly recommended *Kiss of Fury*."

—Romance Reviews Today

Kiss of Fire

"Wow, what an innovative and dazzling world Ms. Cooke has built with this new Dragonfire series. Her smooth and precise writing quickly draws the reader in and has you believing it could almost be real. . . . I can't wait for the next two books."

—Fresh Fiction

THE DRAGON DIARIES NOVELS

Flying Blind

THE DRAGONFIRE NOVELS

Kiss of Fire

Kiss of Fury

Kiss of Fate

Winter Kiss

Whisper Kiss

Darkfire Kiss

Winging It

THE DRAGON DIARIES

DEBORAH COOKE

NEW AMERICAN LIBRARY
Published by New American Library, a division of
Penguin Group (USA) Inc., 375 Hudson Street,
New York, New York 10014, USA
Penguin Group (Canada), 90 Eglinton Avenue East, Suite 700, Toronto,
Ontario M4P 2Y3, Canada (a division of Pearson Penguin Canada Inc.)
Penguin Books Ltd., 80 Strand, London WC2R 0RL, England
Penguin Ireland, 25 St. Stephen's Green, Dublin 2,
Ireland (a division of Penguin Books Ltd.)
Penguin Group (Australia), 250 Camberwell Road, Camberwell, Victoria 3124,
Australia (a division of Pearson Australia Group Pty. Ltd.)
Penguin Books India Pvt. Ltd., 11 Community Centre, Panchsheel Park,
New Delhi - 110 017, India
Penguin Group (NZ), 67 Apollo Drive, Rosedale, Auckland 0632,
New Zealand (a division of Pearson New Zealand Ltd.)
Penguin Books (South Africa) (Pty.) Ltd., 24 Sturdee Avenue,
Rosebank, Johannesburg 2196, South Africa

Penguin Books Ltd., Registered Offices:
80 Strand, London WC2R 0RL, England

First published by New American Library,
a division of Penguin Group (USA) Inc.

First Printing, December 2011
10 9 8 7 6 5 4 3 2 1

REGISTERED TRADEMARK—MARCA REGISTRADA

LIBRARY OF CONGRESS CATALOGING-IN-PUBLICATION DATA:

Cooke, Deborah.
Winging it/Deborah Cooke.
p. cm.—The dragon diaries)
ISBN 978-0-451-23489-6
1. Supernatural—Fiction. 2. Dragons—Fiction. 3. Shape-shifting—Fiction.
4. Secrets—Fiction. 5. Fantasy. I. Title.
PZ7.C774347Win 2011
Fic—dc23 2011031881

Set in Janson Text STD

Printed in the United States of America

For Diana Trohdahl and Debbie Haupt,
with many thanks
for their continued enthusiasm and support.

ACKNOWLEDGMENTS

It may not take a village to produce a work of fiction, but bringing a book into the world certainly does require the efforts of a great many people.

As always, I am impressed by the talents of the team at NAL. Special thanks go to my editor, Kerry Donovan, and her assistant, Jhanteigh Kupihea, who have been so fantastic about making Zoë's books all that they can be. Alexandra Israel in Publicity has been fabulous to work with, and I appreciate her deft organization of review copies and blog stops. The copy editor on this book, Jan McInroy, did a wonderful and gracious job of correcting my inevitable inconsistencies and errors. (Those that remain are entirely mine.)

I want to specifically thank Ginger Legato at NAL for such a wonderful interior layout on Zoë's books. A work that includes lists and book excerpts and text messages makes for a particular challenge in terms of interior design—but a great design makes all the elements and their roles perfectly clear. Thank you, Ginger, for sharing your expertise and magic here.

I'd like to also thank my agent, Dominick Abel, for being so consistently wise, practical and enthusiastic. My husband, Konstantin, deserves great credit for putting up with me when I'm lost in a story. Finally, I want to thank the Points West Writers for a monthly dose of laughter, good conversation, gossip—and maybe just one more warm buttered scone.

Thank you all.

Winging It

Chapter 1

October 24, 2024

The black envelope fell out of my locker when I unlocked the door before lunch.

I distrusted that envelope on sight.

Not because it was black. Not because it looked like an invitation. Not because I couldn't think of anyone who would invite me anywhere.

Because it was the first weird thing to happen in six months.

I watched it fall, reluctant to touch it.

Why would someone shove an envelope into my locker instead of just talking to me? I couldn't think of one good reason.

I'm not *that* scary.

And if I am, courtesy of my ability to shift into a dragon at will, no one at school knows it. I'm all about managing information these days. I'd been cut slack as a newbie for letting humans see me shift shape—twice—when my Wyvern powers had made their debut in April, but it wouldn't happen again.

My dad, leader of the *Pyr*, had made that perfectly clear.

The envelope landed right side up, my name printed on the front in sparkly gold ink. Not a case of mistaken identity, then. I glanced up and down the corridor but no one was paying any attention to me, just like usual.

The envelope looked more like an invitation the longer I studied it. I lifted it with the toe of my boot, still skeptical. It didn't look thick enough to hold a practical joke.

Suspicious, me? You bet. And with good reason. In April, we younger dragon shifters had discovered that our old enemy the Mages had concocted an evil plan—to eliminate all shifters, one species at a time. We'd found out because they'd targeted us *Pyr*, invading the boot camp held for teenage dragons in Minnesota. The apprentice Mage Adrian had turned us against each other with his nasty magic spells, keeping us busy while the superior Mages tricked and trapped the older *Pyr*. The Mages must have been thinking they could take us dragons down easily, but my friends Liam and Nick and Garrett and I had (ultimately) saved the day.

With—it must be said—the help of two humans in the know. Jared and Isabelle.

All humans know dragons exist, of course—that's why there are so many stories about us—and many humans know about the *Pyr*, dragon shape shifters on a quest to save Earth. The Covenant was designed by my father for our protection, to keep our identities as secret as possible. We have pledged to use the utmost discretion in shifting—to make sure that very few humans know any *Pyr* in both dragon and human form, yada yada yada.

The thing was, the *Pyr* hadn't known until last spring that there still were other kinds of shifters in the world. Call us isolationist. Kohana—the Thunderbird shifter who'd tried to sell us to the Mages to save his own kind—had told me that there were four varieties of shape shifters left. Wolves, jaguars, dragons, and Thunderbirds. The Mages, he'd told me, had eliminated all the rest and claimed their shapes.

Like a right of conquest: exterminate a species, snag its second skin.

I still have no idea whether this is true, or whether he'd left out some important detail(s). He has an unfortunate tendency to manipulate information. I do know that the Mages somehow get a power boost once they've exterminated an entire race of shifters, and they also become able to assume their forms.

Without having been exterminated ourselves—and thus having actual data from the experience—details are fuzzy.

The adult *Pyr* had been predictably, well, adult about the whole crisis—after we'd saved them from certain death. My dad had negotiated a treaty with the Mages. They all thought that was that.

Please. I didn't buy it. The *Pyr* were still in the hot seat, so to speak, at least as far as I could see. Just because we'd foiled the Mages once didn't persuade me that they had abandoned their scheme.

That they had been completely quiet since April just made me more suspicious. (In contrast, it made my dad sure that he was right, plus persuaded a whole bunch of other *Pyr* who'd had their doubts that he was right, too.) But lying low was exactly the kind of thing Mages would do to make us believe they were reconciled to keeping the treaty.

Never mind that Trevor Wilson, the hot guy in my school who played the sax like he was making love to it, was one of them. He was an apprentice Mage, although I didn't exactly know their education process, much less how close to graduation he was. I'd been watching him so carefully this fall that my best friend, Meagan, was convinced that I had a crush on him.

That couldn't be further from the truth.

It also complicated things because *she* had a crush on him.

Not that anything was simple between me and Meagan these days. She has a best friend's radar for knowing when she isn't being told the whole truth—and I can't confide in her, thanks to the restrictions of the Covenant.

As if that wasn't enough, I hadn't heard a thing from the hot motorcycle-riding rebel rocker Jared—yes, the guy who had melted my synapses with one kiss. Last summer I'd finally worked up my nerve to contact him, and he'd sent me only a short reply.

Two sentences, then silence.

Even after that kiss.

I told myself I didn't care, that my only interest in him was that he had the one copy of the only book about the *Pyr* that I knew existed. I needed to talk to him for the sake of the *Pyr*.

Even I knew that was a lie.

The thing is, Jared has the ability to read minds, as well as being a spellsinger who had once been recruited by the Mages because of his innate musical abilities. He'd turned down the Mages, and I had to wonder whether he'd read my thoughts, not liked the view, and decided to turn me down, too.

So, back to the envelope. I was cautiously picking it up just as Meagan appeared beside me. Her timing was perfect.

Perfectly awful, that is.

"What's that?"

"I don't know."

She tilted her head to read the front. "Then maybe you should open it and find out. It looks like an invitation."

Which just reminded me of another issue I wanted to avoid with Meagan. My birthday was coming up in two weeks, my sixteenth, and my dad wanted to invite all of the *Pyr*. That meant my human friends—specifically, my very best friend, Meagan—couldn't be invited, in case she saw something she shouldn't.

I was really starting to hate the Covenant.

I hadn't yet figured out how I'd tell Meagan about the party she wasn't invited to attend.

I ripped open the envelope, avoiding the inevitable.

"It *is* an invitation," Meagan said, reading over my shoulder. "To Trevor Wilson's Halloween party!" She was amazed and impressed. "Lucky you. It's like a dream come true."

Uh, no. In fact, there was a shiver of dread running down my spine. Trevor's party was the last place I'd be on October 31. It'd be thick with Mages of all experience levels. Nuh-uh. The invitation had to be a trick, or a trap, and I wasn't going to walk right into it—like the heroine in a scary movie who goes down to the basement by herself to check out the strange noise, despite the creepy organ music.

I read the invitation again and had a feeling Trevor wasn't going to take no for an answer without a fight. Funny that I'd been itching all summer for something to happen but now that it *was* happening, I wanted it to stop.

Meagan poked me with one finger. "You must have known!"

"I didn't."

"Oh, come on. You've been talking to him, haven't you? He doesn't invite just anybody."

"No, I haven't talked to him at all. You're the one who tutors him in math."

Meagan opened her own locker with obvious optimism.

No envelope fell out.

She rummaged a little, then gave me a look. "I thought we were friends. Forever." Her voice was quiet and I knew she was hurt.

And I'd done the hurting. Inadvertently, but still. "We are."

"So, why don't you tell me what's going on?"

"There's nothing going on that you don't know about."

Have I mentioned that I'm the world's worst liar? Well, I am and Meagan has my number. One of the hazards of having known someone most of your life.

She leaned in really close and said something completely uncharacteristic. "Bullshit."

I blinked.

"Something happened on spring break, and you've been holding out on me ever since. You never even told me what you said to scare Suzanne so much in the locker room, when she picked on me. That was right before you went to Minnesota. Something's changed. Don't think I don't know it."

Something *had* changed. I had changed. In coming to Meagan's defense, I'd started to shift shape for the first time. My eye and my nail had been the only things that changed, but Suzanne had seen both and freaked.

The only good thing was that it was so weird no one believed her.

Meagan took a deep breath and I saw a shimmer of tears on her lashes. Her next words were tight. "If you don't want to be friends anymore, maybe because you suddenly know all kinds of cool people, then at least have the guts to say so."

"That's not true!"

Her lips tightened. "Okay, then. Promise me that you've told me everything."

Trust the math queen to put me in a logical corner. "Well, I haven't and you know it, but that's because I can't, not because I don't want to."

"Why can't you?"

"Because I promised not to tell anyone."

"Promised who?"

I fidgeted. There was no way to make this better. "I can't tell you that."

"Sounds like the same excuse to me." She folded her arms across her chest and leaned against the lockers beside mine. "You think I didn't notice that you haven't mentioned your birthday party?"

Here it came. "My dad wants me to have a family party."

"For your sixteenth? I don't believe it. Your dad isn't a jerk."

"Well, he's determined this time."

"Your mom would never put up with it. If he wanted you to have a family party, she'd let you have another one with your friends." Meagan was on a roll and it wasn't one that made me look good. My mom and I had talked about a friends party. Problem was that most of my friends were also dragon shifters. Except Meagan. Which kind of brought us back to the same place of my dad worrying about what she might see. "You know what I think? I think you're having a party and you're just not inviting me."

She stared at me, daring me to correct her.

And I couldn't hold her gaze.

Because she was right.

"Nice, Zoë," she said, her tone more bitter than I'd ever heard it. Meagan is not a bitch—that I've made her sound this way said more about me than about her. "Really nice. Here's hoping that your new friends are more worth keeping than your old ones." She closed her locker and started to walk away.

"But, Meagan, it's not like that. . . ."

She paused to look back at me. "You can tell me anytime how it is," she said. "But I know already that you won't."

I looked down at the stupid invitation, wishing I'd never gotten it. As much as I liked my new *Pyr* powers, it really sucked to have to keep everything secret from my best friend.

"Have fun at Trevor's party," Meagan added. "And don't worry about me. I've got a new friend of my own."

She slung her pack over one shoulder and marched down the hall, and I knew I couldn't change her mind. I watched as she stopped beside the locker of the new girl, the one who had switched to our school earlier that year.

The one I really didn't like, although I couldn't have said why.

Jessica has dark hair and dark eyes. She's slim and pretty and quiet. She's another math whiz, so she and Meagan bonded in the land where calculating derivatives is as easy as pie. (Pi, maybe. As in, recalling the first hundred digits of. So not my territory. Never mind citizenship: I don't even have a visitor's visa to that place.) The thing is, I should have liked Jessica; there was no reason why I shouldn't.

But she gave me the creeps.

Big-time.

I was pretty sure it wasn't just jealousy. I just had this sense that she was hiding something. As someone who has a pretty hefty secret myself, I think I know something about keeping secrets. It wasn't because she wore really baggy clothes—like she'd raided her brother's closet—or even that she kept a baseball hat jammed on her head all the time.

Maybe my Wyvern sense was tingling. There's only one female dragon shifter at a time, and she's the Wyvern. *I'm* the Wyvern. And the Wyvern is supposed to have mystical powers. The ability to see the future. The power to give prophecies. Lots of seriously cool stuff.

So far I couldn't do any of it.

But Jessica creeped me out.

And I didn't know why.

Maybe it *was* a Wyvern thing.

I watched as Jessica smiled at Meagan now and hugged her, then looked over Meagan's shoulder at me. She held my gaze for a minute, like she was daring me, then looked away. A sly smile stole over her lips.

That smile sent a shudder right down my spine.

And gave me the worst feeling I've ever had in my life.

Then it was gone.

Precognition?

Jealousy?

Overactive imagination? You choose. I have no idea.

Jessica and Meagan walked toward the cafeteria, their heads bent together as they talked. I noticed the new guy at school, Derek Black, leaning against the lockers, watching me. He looked after Jessica and Meagan, then back at me, and shrugged.

I was embarrassed to have been caught staring at them—like a pathetic loser, not invited to have lunch with two math whizzes. Which I was, but still. I was used to not being noticed by anyone at school. I felt myself blush—no surprise there. A smile tugged at the corner of Derek's mouth and I turned to my locker, apparently fascinated by its contents.

I had the sense that the slightest encouragement from me would have brought him right to my side, but I wasn't in the mood to look for new friends. I had enough issues with my current ones. I kicked my locker shut, jammed the invitation into my backpack, and headed out to the bleachers to eat my lunch.

Alone.

I had no idea how to fix things with Meagan, and no one to ask. An older sibling, even one who found me annoying and tedious, could have been helpful. At least he or she would have dealt with the Covenant's restrictions in the past.

But I have no brothers or sisters. My mom is human. My dad is a dragon shifter, but he's hundreds of years old. I doubt he even remembers being a teenager—I doubt he remembers being a frisky young dragon of three centuries. The guys, who are roughly my contemporaries and also dragon shifters—Liam, Garrett, and Nick—always tell me I worry too much about it.

They are not much help.

I WAS SITTING ON THE bleachers, debating the merits of asking one of the guys for help anyway, when Derek came out of the school.

No, that's not how it was. I was alone one minute, and the next, he was there.

Just as if he'd been sitting at the other end of the bleachers all along.

I didn't hear him coming, not at all. That might not seem like much of a big deal, but I *should* have heard him. No matter how quiet he was. We dragons have sharp senses, sharper than human senses, but I didn't hear him come outside. I'm not used to having people sneak up on me—because it never happens.

Was I losing the *Pyr* powers that I had?

Or had I just been really, really lost in my thoughts?

I thought for a minute that Derek had followed me, but he didn't glance my way. His back was toward me as he unpacked his lunch. Courtesy of my extra-keen vision, I could check it out. His lunch looked a lot like mine—homemade sandwich, piece of fruit, granola bar. Except he had two sandwiches, and he'd bought a carton of milk.

I studied him as he ate, pretending not to. He was a bit stocky, solidly built but not fat. Dark hair, and he wore dark clothes. I'd guess that he was an inch or two taller than me, and I'm the tall skinny type. Not sure because I'd never been that close to him. He was the kind of quiet guy people overlooked. He slid in and out of English class like a shadow and never said much. Even when he got called on, his answers were always short and gruff. He could have used a haircut—I'd noticed before that his hair hung over his eyes. It made him look a little wild. Or just scruffy.

He seemed to spend a lot of time alone, which made me wonder whether we had something in common. The fact that we were the only two outside having lunch on a snowy day just reinforced that sense. In a few hours, the bleachers would be crowded for the big football game against Central, but I liked it better quiet. It was snowing lightly, a bit cold for a picnic, but a little frigid solitude suited my mood.

Which was bleak, in case you weren't sure.

I decided not to send messages to the guys. I wasn't ready to be told that I was being a dope. They're good friends, but they're *guys.* I would have loved to talk to Meagan.

But she was with Jessica.

Which brought me right back to square one.

I could have used a confidence boost, the kind I get from shifting shape, but Derek was too close. He would notice the sudden appearance of a dragon in the bleachers and he'd guess that the dragon and I were one and the same. (He didn't seem to be stupid.) That was Covenant-breaking territory again. I shoved my hands into my pockets and tried to content myself with shifting my thumbnail to a talon instead.

It was no substitute.

I didn't eat my granola bar, even though it was chocolate-dipped. That tells you everything you need to know about the state of the world in Zoë terms.

LIKE I SAID, it was nearly my sixteenth birthday. There were three things I wanted for the big day:

1. A grudge match against Kohana, the Thunderbird shifter who'd lied to me, plus worked with the Mages to nearly wipe me and the rest of the *Pyr* off the map
2. A tattoo
3. A chance to see Jared again, if only to find out that I was never going to see him again.

Of the above, I had a remote chance of achieving only #3. Even with it being my birthday. I knew what my dad thought about me fighting anyone, and I knew what my mom thought of tattoos. But they both knew Jared, and they knew I knew him. And his band was playing a concert right in town, on Saturday (thus not a school night) at a co-op club downtown that didn't serve alcohol.

The way I saw it, Jared had chosen the venue because he *expected* me to come.

Or he was daring me.

He's like that. Irreverent. Challenging.

Hot.

Whether it was to deliver the flight on Dragon Air that I owed him, to snag another kiss—just to verify that the first one had, in fact, been amazing and of the bone-melting variety—or to barter for another peek at the book he had on my kind, didn't really matter.

I wanted to go.

I *needed* to go.

Which meant that I needed to persuade my mom that going was a good idea. And do it without beguiling her. Beguiling is kind of like hypnosis and it's a dragon trick I mastered pretty early. We conjure flames in our eyes; the humans look closer; we make suggestions. That's beguiling. As you might expect, it works best when it's a suggestion the person already wants to take—which meant that beguiling my mom wasn't a good plan on a whole bunch of fronts. She'd likely catch me—she's not stupid, either—and then I'd be toast.

Better to go with plain old begging.

Negotiating.

Shameless groveling.

Even being a dragon girl didn't make me think that sneaking out to go to the concert without parental approval would end well.

So, I *had* to convince my mom.

I was running out of time—it was Thursday and the concert was Saturday. This had to be the day.

I figured I was due for *something* to go right.

DURING ART CLASS I SENT a message to Nick, asking his advice about Meagan (and nearly had my fabulous shiny new messenger confiscated in the process. My mom says kids used to have cell phones which were plenty good enough, that they didn't need messengers with all their apps and computing powers, right in their hands all the time. Wrong. Mine is my umbilical cord to the world). He told me—predictably—that I was making too big of a deal about it.

> Talk to her. Hang out with her. Just don't talk about THAT. You can be friends and still have ONE secret.

Right.

Meagan was at her locker when I got out of science class at the end of the day. She was alone, which had to be a good sign for making up, and tugging on her coat.

I decided to make a valiant effort.

"Hi," I said as I unlocked my locker. She glanced up but didn't say anything. Then she started to rummage in her locker.

At least she hadn't left.

"Going to the game?" I asked, even though I could guess the answer.

She shook her head. "I've got two hours of piano practice to finish before dinner." She shoved a couple of books into her bag and zipped it up.

She didn't ask me if I was going, which would have been a nice opening, but I'd make my own.

"So, I was thinking, maybe I could have lunch with you and Jessica one day. Maybe tomorrow. You know, so I could get to know her a bit."

Meagan looked at me. She tended to be very serious, but even if she hadn't been, her glasses made her look that way.

I smiled. "I don't want to fight with you," I said, feeling that it was impossibly lame. "Maybe we can hang out."

Meagan sighed. She glanced down the hall, then back at me. She looked me right in the eye. "Will you tell me what's going on when you can?"

"I'd tell you everything right this minute if I could."

She smiled a little then, a bit of a sad smile, but anything she might have said was cut short.

By guess who.

"Meagan!" Jessica shouted. "You'll never believe what I got on that math test! Woo-HOOO!"

Meagan turned toward her new friend, and I stared at my boots. They squealed together about Jessica's perfect score—how either of them could be surprised by that was a mystery—and I felt completely excluded from the discussion. Forgotten.

"Going to the game?" a guy asked, from my other side.

I nearly jumped out of my skin.

It was Derek. How long had he been there? I was surprised that he'd done that silent approach thing again, but there was no disputing it—I hadn't heard him.

I looked him up and down. He *was* just a bit taller than me. He was watching me closely. His eyes were a very pale blue, almost icy, and he didn't seem to blink much.

That made me feel awkward, too. I got interested in my books. Dropped three.

He reached for them when I reached for them and our hands brushed. I pulled mine back like I'd been burned. He picked up my books and handed them to me. If I'd been blushing before, I had to be as red as a beet then.

"Sorry," he said. "Didn't mean to surprise you." He shrugged and hefted his bag of gear. "Just thought I'd ask."

"You're on the team?" The fact that he had a bag of football gear made that a stupid question, but it was too late to pretend I hadn't said it.

He glanced at the bag, then back at me, and almost smiled. "So?"

I liked that he didn't make a big deal of my stupid question. Or about me being awkward and flustered. He was still giving me a shy smile, like he would wait all week for me to answer. I was a bit disconcerted by how steadily he watched me.

"Um, I'm not sure." I turned to Meagan as if I would ask her, but she had already moved down the hall, hauling her backpack onto her shoulders and laughing with Jessica. They hugged and then Jessica headed for the far doors. Meagan turned toward the bathroom, her coat swinging open and her gloves in her hands.

In that moment, I saw my nemesis, Suzanne, and her followers coming down the corridor toward us. They were already in their cheerleader uniforms, the four of them cutting a path through the kids in the hallway like they were royalty. Suzanne was—naturally—in the lead. She swung her hips hard as she walked, making the pleats of her little skirt flip up. Every guy in the vicinity was watching her thighs. Probably salivating. Suzanne knew it—and she loved it. She had buckets of confidence and seemed to expect to be the center of attention.

All the time.

I swear she was taking inventory of who was looking.

But her smile dimmed when she saw Meagan. She watched Meagan go into the bathroom—oblivious—and her expression turned mean. She waved off her minions and strolled in after Meagan.

I had a really bad feeling about that.

"Good luck in the game, then," I said brightly to Derek, remembering a bit late that he was still there, waiting. I smiled at him, grabbed my stuff, slammed my locker, and headed down the hall.

"Thanks." His single word seemed to follow me.

Like old-speak, almost.

That caught my attention. Old-speak is dragon stuff, speech uttered at a lower frequency than humans can hear. It slides into your thoughts, mingles with them, starts to seem like your own idea.

But only dragons can do it (yes, some better than others) and Derek wasn't *Pyr.*

By the time I looked back, Derek was striding toward the guys' locker room.

As if he'd forgotten me, too.

At that moment, though, I had bigger mysteries to solve than guys and their presto-chango interest.

Meagan. No coincidence that the first time I'd made even a partial shift to dragon form had been in defense of Meagan.

When Suzanne had picked a fight in gym.

I wasn't going to let Suzanne bully my friend again.

I opened the door to the bathroom silently, freezing when I overheard Suzanne's words.

"Listen, Jameson." There was menace in Suzanne's tone, a menace I would have heard even if I hadn't had sensitive hearing. The sound of it made me shiver. "We're going to come to an understanding right here and right now."

"B-b-but I—I—I—," Meagan stammered, the way she always does when she's nervous. I closed the bathroom door quietly behind myself. I turned the dead bolt—silently—so no one else could join us, then stood completely still as I listened.

Lucky for me the bathroom was designed to provide some privacy. There was a short wall opposite the door, one that hid the stalls from the hallway even when the door was open. I lurked in that space, invisible to Meagan and to Suzanne, too.

And I eavesdropped.

I could almost hear Meagan sweat.

"I need to pass this trig test or they're going to cancel my extracurricular activities," Suzanne whispered.

"Th-th-that's too bad."

"It would be, if it happened, but nobody takes cheerleading away from me." I heard Suzanne take a step. "So, you're going to help me."

"Are you c-c-coming to the math lab for t-t-tutoring?"

Suzanne laughed. "No. You already sit in front of me in math. Tomorrow, during the test, you're going to pass me the answers."

"I can't do that!" Meagan was too horrified even to stammer.

"Can't you?" Suzanne's voice was low and silky. Trouble. "Maybe I haven't made myself clear. This isn't optional."

"I t-t-told you last year, I wouldn't help you ch-ch-cheat." Now there were shuffling footsteps—Meagan retreating.

"Maybe I can change your mind."

"N-n-no . . ." I heard Meagan gasp, then something smash.

That was followed by a muffled thump and a moan.

Something heavy fell to the floor.

I peeked around the wall to see Meagan doubled over and Suzanne aiming another punch at her gut. Meagan's bag was on the ground where she'd dropped it. Her glasses were shattered against the far wall, where Suzanne had thrown them.

So Meagan couldn't see the blow coming.

Suzanne had always been a contender on my Incinerate Now list, but with this move she zoomed right to the number one slot.

I wasn't going to stand aside and let my friend get thumped for doing the right thing.

It was dragon time.

I summoned the shimmer, let it rip through my body, and shifted shape with a dull roar.

I'VE GOT TO TELL YOU that it feels amazing to shift shape. It's kind of spooky at first, because the sensation is so powerful. Your instinct is to try to control it, to manage the transition, but that's not really possible. You have to go with it.

You have to abandon control and trust your body.

Maybe it's like surfing. You have to get on the wave the right way, but then you just ride and ride and ride. Over time, the getting-on-the-wave bit becomes instinctive and you just look forward to the ride.

It's exhilarating stuff.

It was no different this time, even in a plain old taupe and white high school bathroom. The change ripped through me with lightning speed, surging through my veins and filling me with ferocious power. One minute, I was zitty Zoë of the virtually nonexistent breasts, and the next, I was an enormous white dragon, my talons stretching for Suzanne before she had any clue what was happening.

She took one look at me and screamed. I did enjoy that. She fell back against the metal wall of the cubicles, shrieking. She apparently didn't dare look away from me—she slid her hands along the edges of the cubicles, feeling her way as she put distance between us.

I heard her cronies—Trish and Anna probably—bang on the door. "Suzanne! You okay? Let us in!"

Suzanne couldn't even answer them, she was so shocked. Her mouth was opening and closing, but just a little whimper was coming out.

She crossed herself then, which made me laugh.

I breathed fire as I laughed, which made her turn even more pale. I did ensure that the plume of flame roared right over her head. I wanted to scare her, not hurt her. Not really—mostly because I didn't want to deal with repercussions. I slashed in her general direction with one claw. I sent a playful little plume of flame to burn her skirt and she screamed again.

She stumbled over her own feet in her anxiety to get away. She grabbed the door to the next stall, and it swung open suddenly beneath her weight. She lost her balance, shouted, and fell.

She landed sprawling on the toilet, then covered her face with her hands. She looked so graceless that I nearly laughed out loud.

I took a step closer and smiled, letting her see all my sharp dragon teeth. She peeked through her fingers and trembled.

"Don't hurt me!" she whispered.

I reared back, showing off my full dragon-scaled magnificence. I gripped the walls of the cubicles and gave them a mighty shake, ripping them loose from their moorings.

I was just warming up, but Suzanne fainted.

Her eyes rolled back in her head and she slumped against the wall. Her elbow hit the lever and the toilet flushed, getting her cute little skirt wet.

"Suzanne! Are you all right?" Trish shouted, as the banging on the door grew louder.

I had one minute to think I had done something right, and then I glanced toward Meagan. She'd retrieved her glasses and was peering through the broken lenses at me.

I knew that look.

I called it her Einstein look.

She got it when she was figuring something out, connecting the dots, finding the key to the universe. My heart clenched, because Meagan is pretty much the smartest sixteen-year-old I've ever met.

"Open this door, right this minute!" someone shouted sternly. It sounded like the principal. I heard the jingle of keys.

Meagan turned to the door, panic in her expression. The Einstein look was gone so fast that I wondered whether I'd imagined it. "I'm c-c-coming," she said, sparing one last look at me.

I had to get out of there ASAP—and without Meagan seeing more than she had.

No pressure.

I raged fire at the ceiling, a great orange plume of crackling fire. I heard the paint blister and crack. Meagan covered her eyes against the brightness of the flames, which was all I needed. I conjured the image of exactly where I wanted to be and willed myself to be there.

And when I opened my eyes, I was on the roof of the building where my family's loft took up most of the top floor.

In salamander form.

My heart thundering.

I took a shaky breath, crawled into the shadows by the air-conditioning units to give myself cover, then shifted to my human form.

As usual, it felt good to just be a skinny chick again.

And it felt awesome to have frightened Suzanne.

She'd deserved no less.

Being a dragon shifter completely rocks.

Just in case I haven't mentioned it.

I grinned as I rummaged in my pocket for that granola bar. I needed a sugar hit before I could figure out whether I had technically broken the Covenant again or not.

THE COVENANT IS A CREED all we dragon shifters have to swear. Essentially we are forbidden from revealing ourselves in both human and dragon form to humans, and when some human does know us in both forms, my dad—as leader of the *Pyr*—adds that person's name to his list.

Those people-in-the-know are not always trusted, and he makes decisions on a case-by-case basis, but this theoretically creates a Go To list in case one of us gets targeted or stalked. My dad remembers our kind being hunted almost to extinction in the Middle Ages. He likes us staying under the radar, so to speak.

He'd let it go when I partly shifted the previous spring, mostly because he was glad I was finally starting to shift and also because it had been only a partial shift seen by one person. Also, the punishment was tough stuff—exile, for as long as my dad decreed, to his location of choice. Corralled by his dragonsmoke, which is invisible but burns if crossed by a *Pyr* without permission.

That would be the exiled dragon.

As I snacked—and it snowed—and I thought about it, I was pretty sure I was in the clear on this incident, too. Neither Suzanne nor Meagan had seen me enter the bathroom. Neither of them had seen me before I shifted shape, so technically they'd seen me only in dragon form. Even if they suspected that there was a dragon shifter among them, they didn't know that Zoë Sorensson had become that dragon.

I could have believed all of that, if Meagan hadn't given me that look.

Had she really guessed the truth? I wasn't sure.

I was confident that I could argue the technicalities with my dad. I halfway believed I could win. I was pretty sure he wouldn't exile me for another comparatively small transgression. And I wasn't afraid of Suzanne or what she might tell her friends.

I was most worried about Meagan.

The standard solution for inadvertently revealing oneself as a dragon shape shifter is to beguile the human in question. But it seemed like a complete betrayal of my friendship with Meagan to beguile her. I didn't want to do it unless it was absolutely necessary.

I also wasn't sure it would work.

Because I knew Meagan and I knew that look. If she was convinced she'd seen a dragon, a whole pack of beguiling *Pyr* wouldn't persuade her otherwise.

I guessed she wouldn't tell the principal what she'd seen. After all, the school administration might think she was delusional. No, she'd come up with some story about Suzanne falling, and let Suzanne be the one to sound delusional.

And in the meantime, having shifted in defense of a human made me feel much more optimistic about the chances of convincing my mom to let me go to the concert. There's just something about becoming a dragon that makes me feel invincible.

Omnipotent.

In charge of my universe.

It is the good stuff.

Chapter 2

I should have guessed that my High Queen of the Universe moment couldn't last. I got all the way to the door to our loft before I sensed trouble.

Big trouble.

As soon as I unlocked the door and walked into the apartment, I got slammed with glacial temps. The next ice age had begun.

The mood between my parents in recent months had made home feel as cozy as a meat locker at times, but the tension between them hadn't escalated—until now. I had no idea what they'd been fighting about and didn't really want to know. Now I stopped on the threshold, scared to take a breath, much less step inside.

Would it be smarter to make a dash for my room?

Or should I just bail and come home again in an hour?

My mom came raging out of the master bedroom with a suitcase before I could decide. The suitcase wasn't what initially surprised me—not even the way it was only half-closed, with clothes hanging out the edges.

It was her tears. My mother was *crying*. Not pretty crying, either, like the kind you see in movies. Nope, she was gulping and grimacing, and the tears were running down her face and dripping off her chin.

She froze when she saw me, like she'd been caught in the act of doing something horrible, and stared at me.

A suitcase? How could that be good?

My dad emerged from the kitchen and stood behind her, looking shaken. "Eileen," he said quietly, but she ignored him.

I might not have the Wyvern's powers of foresight (yet), but I had a pretty good idea of what was about to happen.

And it sucked.

It sucked so badly that I couldn't really believe it.

My parents couldn't be splitting up.

Could they?

But I knew the truth as soon as I thought it, knew it with that absolute certainty that makes me think maybe I do have a bit of Wyvern stuff going on. It made me want to puke and at the same time turned me numb. It made me want to cry or scream—or just freeze this moment in time and make it stop. My mom watched me, then bit her lip.

"I'm sorry, Zoë," she whispered. She caught me in a tight and abrupt hug. I thought she might break my ribs, but I didn't dare pull away. My father watched with narrowed eyes but didn't move.

"I'm not abandoning you." My mom's voice was thick when she spoke and I could feel her shaking. "But I have to leave for a bit, Zoë. I'm sorry. I have to go away and catch my breath and try to remember why I love your father so very much."

Sometimes being right completely sucks.

Life as I knew it was ending—and I couldn't fix it, even though I was a dragon shifter. Those particular superpowers didn't come with the *Pyr* package.

My mom pulled back and caught my face in her hands, smiling at me before she kissed the tip of my nose. She used to do that when I was a kid. I had the most enormous lump in my throat and couldn't make a sound.

"You could come with me," she said, hope in her tone. "You could come with me and forget all this dragon stuff."

I looked at my dad, but he seemed to have been turned to stone. Just his eyes glittered. Was *that* what had set them off? For years my mom had been cool with our dragon-shifting abilities.

Or was it *my* shifting abilities that were the problem?

Why else would she ask me to forget the dragon stuff?

I spoke with care, feeling like I was on thin ice. "How can I forget what I am?"

My mom closed her eyes and took a deep breath. "Goddess, you even sound like him." Then she wiped her tears and picked up her suitcase, purposeful once again. "Well, that's that, then," she said with a finality that was terrifying.

Terrifying enough that I had to say something. I wanted some reassurance that she'd be back and so I said the first thing that came to mind. "Will you be back by my birthday?"

She looked at me, a thousand shadows in her eyes, and I was afraid of her answer. "I don't know." Before I could freak that my mom was leaving for good and my dad was just standing back, watching her go, my mom dug into the pocket of her sweater. "Just in case, Rafferty asked me to give you this for your birthday."

"Rafferty!" It's not often that my dad is surprised, but I could see that he was shocked. And really, it would have made more sense for his oldest friend to have entrusted him with a gift for me. Rafferty is another of the *Pyr*. He and my dad have been pals for centuries.

My mom's tone was challenging as she turned to glare at my dad. "Maybe Rafferty didn't think you'd let it go."

My dad frowned. My mom turned her back on him again, put down her suitcase, then held out a small fabric bag. I took it from her, not knowing what else to do.

There was something heavy inside it.

Something round.

"You might as well open it now," my mom said, shrugging into her coat and slamming things into her purse.

My dad exuded disapproval at that, because he's pretty big on his integrity. What could Rafferty have sent that might have tempted my dad to keep it? I opened the ties, and dumped the contents into my hand.

It was a ring.

No, it was *the* ring. My dad evidently saw it because he caught his breath sharply. No wonder.

For as long as I can remember, Rafferty has worn this ring. It's black and white, like black glass and white glass swirled together. It's not just an ordinary ring, though; it changes to fit his finger or his talon. It shifts with him, always the perfect size. I love it and he knows it, but I was astounded that he would let it go.

Ever. To anyone. It's part of Rafferty.

In fact, I felt like I had a piece of him in my hand. Did he really intend to *give* it to me? Forever?

He'd loaned it to me the previous spring in our battle against the Mages, and something weird had happened. I'd been able to call on the previous Wyvern and had gotten a clue from her to help save the *Pyr.* Afterward, the ring had looked the same as always, and every time I'd asked Rafferty or my dad about it, neither of them would answer.

So what had changed? Why was Rafferty giving me the ring now? Did he know anything about the party invitation, and how I thought the Mages were up to something?

If he disagreed with my dad about the threat posed by the Mages—and the power of the treaty—it would make sense that he'd asked my mom to give me the ring.

Unfortunately, there was no note. I would have bet everything that Rafferty wouldn't answer any question I sent.

No, he'd play that "figure it out" game that my dad also loves, the one that drives me bananas.

I was going to ask anyway. Just because.

I looked at my mom.

"He just said to make sure you got it. That's all I know." She hefted her bag.

"Eileen," my dad said, his tone low, "don't go."

"I can't stay and watch. Not anymore."

"But . . ."

She pivoted then, as ferocious as any dragon. "But *nothing*, Erik. Listen—I've stood by and watched you choose the *Pyr* over your marriage, time and time again. I've recognized that this was your role and your responsibility." My mom lifted her chin and glared at him. My dad even flinched a bit, which is saying something. "But I can't stand by and let you choose the *Pyr* over the welfare of your own daughter."

This was about *me*.

How could my new powers ruin everything?

"You're pushing her too hard," my mom continued. "You can't let her just be a kid, or come to things in her own time."

"But—" My dad did try to argue his side, but my mom cut him off. She was a lot more angry than he was.

"But *nothing*. How many nights did you take her out late to practice flying and shifting? How much time does she have left to spend with her friends? Human friends? Have you even noticed that Meagan isn't here very often anymore? That girl used to practically live here."

"Mom, that's something else. . . ."

"Is it?" My mom glared at me and I couldn't argue the point. It was about my dragon powers in a way, because I couldn't tell Meagan about them.

"But I want to learn about my powers," I argued.

"Of course you do. But it shouldn't be the *only* thing you do." My mom turned back to my dad. "I can't take it anymore. And if this is the only way to show you that I'm serious, then I'm going to do it, no matter how much it hurts. I'll live without you, if I have to." My mom sighed and tears shimmered in her eyes again. She ran her finger down my cheek. "I'll call you. Every day. I promise."

I nodded, my own tears blurring my vision. My mom was leaving.

"Where are you going?" my dad asked, low and hot.

My mom paused in the corridor outside our loft, but didn't look back. She spoke very softly and looked at her boots. "You told me once that you could find me anywhere, anytime, that if I was afraid, you'd come to me before I could even scream." She glanced over her shoulder and I saw her swallow. "Is that still true, Erik?"

My dad cleared his throat. He shoved a hand through his hair and looked as if he'd like to argue in his own defense.

If he could just think of what to say.

My mom didn't wait for him to find the words. "Fine." She spun and marched out the door. I heard her on her messenger as she strode down the corridor, calling a cab.

The loft seemed to echo with her absence, and she wasn't even out of the building yet. I felt cold and uncertain, and pretty sure I was going to be sick.

The worst possible scenario was really happening.

My parents were splitting up.

As if that wasn't bad enough, it was all because of me. I shut the door when my dad didn't move and leaned back against it, staring at him. I didn't know this script. I didn't want to know it.

He stared at the floor.

"Where will she go?" I asked. Saying something had to be better than bursting into tears.

"Her sister's, maybe. I don't know." My dad fixed me with a look. "Don't imagine for one minute that I won't find out." He raised a finger and shook it at me. "Don't imagine for one second that I don't love your mother with all my heart and soul."

That declaration came a bit too late, to my thinking.

"Really? You're the only one who could have made her stay, but you didn't even try," I said, hearing my own anger. "Maybe she's right. Maybe you don't give a shit."

I shouldn't have said it, but once I had, I didn't regret the words, not one bit. Our gazes locked for a moment and the air seemed to crackle between us. I saw my dad's nostrils flare.

"I felt you shift today," he said tightly. "Were there humans present?"

"They didn't really see . . ."

"Grounded!" he bellowed, jabbing his finger through the air at me. My dad almost never shouts, but he was roaring now. "You are grounded for breaking the Covenant!"

"You didn't even let me explain!"

"Nothing you can say can exonerate you." He pointed at me and his hand was shaking. "This time, you *will* be punished. The rules also apply to you. I made a mistake in being lenient last time." He turned to walk away but I shouted after him.

"You can't exile me, not without a hearing!"

My dad spun and his eyes flashed. "Can't I?" He murmured something low and deep, something even I didn't quite hear. I didn't realize right away what he was doing, not until the hair prickled on the back of my neck.

Then I knew. He was changing the permissions on his dragonsmoke.

Our home is encircled by my father's dragonsmoke, which is

both a territory mark and a protective barrier. Humans cross it easily, but a dragon can cross the dragonsmoke of another dragon only with explicit permission.

Exiled dragons were surrounded and trapped by my dad's dragonsmoke.

Guess who was getting locked in.

I pivoted, hauled open the door to the corridor, but his dragonsmoke shimmered before me like a wall of glass. I plunged my hand into it, not really believing that he would barricade me in the apartment.

The touch burned.

I pulled back with lightning speed.

I swore, whirled to face him, and slammed the door. I don't think I've ever been so furious in my life. We glared at each other, both livid, both shimmering blue around our perimeters, hovering on the cusp of change. The air crackled between us.

We'd never come this close to an actual dragon battle before, but I recognized that my dad wasn't in the mood to back down. My hand wasn't really hurt, but I'd felt the singe of the dragonsmoke and knew that if I tried to cross it, I'd be fried alive.

"Fine." I marched to my room, slamming the door so hard that two drawings fell off my bulletin board.

I dropped all my stuff and threw myself across the bed, letting myself cry. My mom was gone! My dad didn't care.

Would she ever come back?

I felt sick that she might not. When would I see her again?

I turned Rafferty's ring in my hands, not daring to put it on. I didn't even know all of its powers, but I knew better than to mess with it.

I wasn't, after all, having the luckiest day of my life.

"*Zoë?*" Even in old-speak, I could hear the wariness in my dad's tone.

"*I have homework,*" I snarled back in kind. "*Leave me alone.*"

And he did.

No doubt about it, this was going to be the worst birthday ever.

THERE ARE GOOD THINGS THAT have changed since my dragon powers turned up last spring. And there are some seriously less than great things, too. To call my transformation a mixed blessing would be an understatement.

I keep track of my dragon observations, primarily because of one exchange I'd had with Jared this past summer. I'd sent him a message when I couldn't stand it any longer, offering to take him for a dragon flight in exchange for his lending me his copy of the only known book on the *Pyr*.

He'd written back immediately, which had made me crazy with hope. At least until I'd read the message:

> You already owe me a ride, dragon girl. If you need a *Pyr* manual, why don't you write your own?

And that had been it.

Two sentences sum total from him since April.

He hadn't replied to any other messages. There'd been, um, a few from me.

I tried not to find this too depressing.

On the other hand, in May he had released a new song on his band's site called "Snow Princess," which I dared to imagine was about me. It was haunting and evocative and romantic as could be.

I've only listened to it twelve hundred and sixty-two times, according to the last displayed count on my messenger. It's a bit compulsive about tracking those kinds of things. Me, I would have just said I'd listened to it a lot.

Mixed messages seemed to be Jared's specialty. Leave it to me to fall for a guy who is mysterious and keeps his distance. I seem to specialize in long shots.

It *was* Jared's style to push me and to dare me. It was also his tendency to be right about dragon stuff. Not to belabor the point, but he has read the book, which gives him an edge over me.

And the fact is that I'm the only female dragon shifter, known among us *Pyr* as the Wyvern. Theoretically, this should give me a bonus pack of powers—but there being only one Wyvern at a time was seriously hampering my ability to even find out what those powers were supposed to be. The past Wyvern hadn't exactly left her diary to me.

But Jared was right in that sooner or later I'm going to die—sooner if the Mages get their way—because we dragons are just long-lived, not immortal. If all worked as it should, there would be another Wyvern born then. And she wouldn't have any more of a clue than I did as to how the whole Wyvern role and responsibility worked. I could do a service to the future of my kind by creating a guidebook.

I'd started documenting what I did know, compiling lists on my messenger. Before that message from Jared, I'd already begun a number of digital illustrations, inspired by boot camp, and I had a lot of lists on the go as well. Now I had a big honking file, called . . .

Ready?

On Becoming the Wyvern.

Not too snappy, but it got the job done.

Here's an excerpt for your entertainment:

GOOD THINGS ABOUT DEVELOPING DRAGON SHIFTER POWERS

1. I can shift shape. I have the dragon shift completely nailed. I've also mastered the shift to the salamander form said to be unique to the Wyvern.
2. I can spontaneously manifest in other locations, if my blood sugar is high enough and there are no serious

distractions. This gives me another item of success on the list of things I know the Wyvern can do. It's progress.

3. I can fly. This rocks. Totally. It's the only physical feat I've ever wanted to do, and so—no surprise—it's the one that's got me working out. All dragons can do it, not just the Wyvern, but that doesn't make flying any less amazing.
4. I've developed an interest in astronomy. It stands to reason that since my Wyvern powers were set in motion by a total solar eclipse I should learn more. I didn't expect to find it so fascinating. It is a bizarre twist of fate (and a shock to Mr. MacPherson, our science teacher) that I'm becoming a bit of a science enthusiast. Go ahead—ask me about astral dust.
5. As a result of #3, I am no longer a complete write-off in gym. I still can't catch a projectile or aim one at anything with accuracy, but I'm less likely to trip over my own feet when I run. So, I'm not quite such a liability on, say, a baseball team. Volleyball and basketball are still disaster areas, but again, it's progress.
6. As a result of my breach of the Covenant last spring when I flashed some dragon goodness at Suzanne, the über-bitch has not come near me since April. Complete bonus.
7. As a result of #1, the dragons I draw are better. I can check dragon anatomy with a mirror if there's room to shift. My dragons are more fierce and more lifelike, very much in demand as notebook embellishments at school. It's strange to be popular in any way for any reason, but I'm getting over it. Kind of.
8. I have breasts. They're small, too small to bounce even, but at least there's some dimensionality there—and some justification for lingerie.

Again, I'll take even incremental progress if it's all that's on the menu.

THINGS THAT COMPLETELY SUCK ABOUT DRAGON SHIFTER POWERS

1. The Covenant means that I can't tell humans about dragon business. This includes Meagan. This means I end up having to lie to her to protect the privacy of the dragon shifters.
2. My mom is right about lies—they're like cockroaches; there's no such thing as just one. The domino effect is alive and well in my life of lies, and I hate it. Because Meagan would still be my best friend if I didn't have to lie to her all the time.
3. The one human guy I know who knows the truth about my shifting talent is apparently no longer speaking to me. Or has forgotten about me. Or something equally ego-bolstering. I can't ask Meagan for advice on Jared because I can't tell her the whole story, because of #1.
4. I still have no real clue about how to fully develop my Wyvern powers, or even what they all are. There is no manual or other record. It's completely unfair that my friend Isabelle, who is practically family, was the last Wyvern in a past life, but doesn't remember any of it. This is really annoying. No. It bites.
5. The only possible reference book—less than ideal because it's so damn enigmatic, but at least it's *something*—is in the possession of Mr. Elusive, referenced in #3 above.
6. There was another solar eclipse on October 2, but nothing seems to have changed. I expected it to have *some* impact on my powers.

7. The next total solar eclipse happens August 12, 2026. Almost two years! With the Mages hunting shifters, I might be dead by then.

So, if nothing else, the next Wyvern would have some reference materials, courtesy of *moi*.

I CAME OUT OF MY room later, but only because I was starving. My dad was in the kitchen, measuring out pasta. There was butter and Parmesan on the table and a green salad. He didn't turn around when I arrived, just added another serving of pasta. The water boiled and he dumped it in, stirring. The timing was perfect, as if he'd anticipated my arrival.

But then, he does have the gift of foresight.

"I have had two firestorms," he said quietly.

I blinked in astonishment. He was confiding in me about his relationship with my mom. This was a first.

Then I blinked again at what he'd said. The firestorm is the mark of a dragon shifter meeting his destined mate and the opportunity for that dragon to conceive an heir. It's a once-in-a-lifetime—even a long lifetime—opportunity. "I thought we only get one."

"That's what we're told, but I had two."

Before I could ask about the other woman in his life, he continued. "They were both with your mother, although the first was in a previous life for her."

I waited. I didn't dare say anything in case my dad stopped the story.

He stirred the pasta, staring into the steam. "I thought that I was lucky to have a second chance, but your mother is right. There are things I have not done differently."

He fell silent for longer this time, so I prompted him. "How so?"

"I have not found a way to live more fully in the human world, as well as in our own. I have also failed to find the balance in raising children, between too much control and not enough."

Children. My eyes widened at that. "Children? As in more than me?"

He nodded. "There was a son."

"I have a brother?" I was stunned that no one had ever mentioned this. My brother would be a dragon, which meant he would have lived for centuries and I could hit him up for advice . . .

"You *had* a brother. Sigmund is dead." My father sighed. "But not before he turned *Slayer* and wrote a book documenting the ways to destroy the *Pyr*."

My mouth went dry. A *Slayer*? *Slayers* were extinct now, but they'd existed when I was born. *Slayers* were *Pyr* gone bad. They were selfish and evil and . . .

My brother became one? It's always a choice. Why would he choose to go bad?

What else didn't I know?

Wait—if my brother had written a book, I could guess which one. I named the book that Jared had, the only book on our kind that was known to exist. "*The Habits and Habitats of Dragons: A Compleat Guide for Slayers*, by Sigmund Guthrie."

My father nodded again, sadly.

There was another one of those huge silences, just the ticking of the timer filling the kitchen.

I had to know. "What happened to Sigmund?"

"He died, during my second firestorm with your mother." My dad paused again. "I used to see him sometimes, walking among the dead." The timer rang and he moved to drain the pasta. Relieved to have an excuse to abandon the subject, maybe.

My dad is not big on confidences and confessions. I could see how hard it was for him to tell me this much, and I appreciated that he was trying.

Although it sure wouldn't have hurt for him to have told me this sooner. Didn't I have a right to know?

He was just bringing the plates to the table when my messenger rang. Of course, I had it on me—it's like another part of me. My link to the universe.

It was my mom, calling from the airport to say that she was going to my aunt's place in England and giving me her schedule. She didn't ask about my dad, and he didn't ask to talk to her.

She sounded awful, as if she was still crying. I know my dad strained to hear her side of our phone conversation, his hunger for the sound of her voice more than clear in his expression. He tried to hide it from me but failed.

We ate in silence after she hung up, until I suddenly put down my fork. I couldn't stand it anymore.

I was going to take a page from Jared's rule book and push a little. I was, after all, a dragon girl.

"I was going to ask Mom tonight whether I could go to a concert on Saturday."

He didn't glance up. "Don't forget you're grounded."

"You could hear me out."

He flicked me a look. A wary look. "And what concert is this?"

On the upside, he was giving me a chance. On the downside, he was using "and" questions. With my mom, "and" questions are a bad sign. She asks them when she's already made up her mind to say no—"and" questions show that we're just going through the motions of making her look unbiased before she does say no.

I decided to hope that my dad didn't play the same way. "Jared's band is playing downtown. You remember Jared."

"And where is this?"

"At a co-op place downtown that doesn't serve booze . . ."

"No."

Come to think of it, a few more "and" questions to argue my case might have been good.

I stared at my dad in dismay. His face was set, which meant his mind was made up. I tried again. "But you've met Jared. I thought you thought he was okay. He helped us beat the Mages—"

He interrupted me with a fierce look. "And how old is he?"

"I don't know. Twenty. Twenty-one maybe." Independent, exciting, rebellious, hot, and a great kisser. I knew these would not be attributes of Jared's that would change my dad's mind. "Donovan trusts him," I said, throwing out the name of one of my dad's *Pyr* pals.

"But you are not even sixteen. No."

I was outraged. If Jared didn't think I was a little girl, why did my dad have to? "What difference does that make?"

My dad put down his fork so he could really glare at me. "Five years' disparity at your age makes all the difference in the world."

"I don't think—"

"But I do. And I say that you will not go to this concert."

"I think Mom would have let me—"

"She's not here. And you weren't grounded before she left. She would have declined you now, and I forbid you to go."

Forbid me? How medieval was that? "It's just a concert, and you know that he's a spellsinger. It's because of Jared and his abilities that the Mages' spells were broken last April! He helped to save you all—"

My dad interrupted me flatly. "Zoë, a young man of twenty-one has a vastly different agenda than a sixteen-year-old girl. You are idealistic. You are thinking of love and romance. Jared is thinking of *now*, he is thinking of sex, and he almost certainly does not have your welfare at the forefront of his thoughts, whether he is a spellsinger or not." He picked up his fork and resumed eating.

I stumbled to my feet. "How can you say that about him? You make him sound like a predator. You don't even know him!"

"I remember being that age," my dad said grimly. "And Jared's troublemaking reputation does precede him."

"This is so unfair. He said that no one trusted him, but I thought Donovan would have defended him to you."

"I assure you that if you were Donovan's daughter, you would also be forbidden from attending this concert."

"You're not being fair. . . ."

He looked at me. "And how many times have you had contact with Jared since last April? How many messages has he sent you?"

"One."

"And I will guess that it was in reply to one from you."

I blushed, but my dad kept talking.

"And what effort has he made to see you while he's in town for this concert? Has he invited you? Has he contacted you?"

"No." I folded my arms across my chest. "But he's playing at a club where I could go. It's like an invitation—"

"But it is not one. If he wanted to see you, he would have ensured that he did. He could have come here and met your parents and asked you to go with him. His failure to do any of those things tells me all I need to know about a romantic future with this young man."

"So, it wouldn't hurt for me to go and find out for sure."

He gave me a cold look. There was a lot of dragon in that look. I should have flinched, but I looked right back. He spoke very softly. "I guarantee you that if you go, Jared will recall that you are attractive and he will try to make the most of the opportunity you present. Now sit down and finish your dinner."

I would not.

"What if he's my destiny?"

"Is that what you truly believe?"

I fidgeted. "I can't see the future just yet."

"I can."

"You could be wrong."

"Then we shall address the matter at that point in time."

We? No way!

I noticed the blue shimmer that surrounded us and realized that my father and I were both on the cusp of change, facing off in the kitchen, a situation that could go up in flames. That made twice in almost as many hours.

And I didn't care.

"Is the firestorm a lie?" I demanded. "Is that why you've had two of them and screwed them both up? I thought a firestorm was supposed to be about destiny and forever! Because if it's a lie, then you should tell us all now, all us young dragons. You should give us the facts, not the fantasy. You should give us the chance to not fuck up our lives by trying to make your stories come true."

He stared at me. I stared back. I'd never talked to my dad like that, let alone used the f-bomb in his presence.

I felt my face turn red.

But I didn't look away.

Then I spun and took my plate to the sink, still a goody girl deep in my heart. It was a bit late to make an effort to stay out of trouble, but there you go. I dumped the pasta in the trash and rinsed the plate, my hands shaking all the while.

My dad was still staring at me.

The way a predator eyes lunch.

He was mad, but holding back.

Well, that made two of us. How could he not stop my mom from leaving? How could he think such crappy things about Jared? How could he ground me and lock me in with dragonsmoke without hearing my side of the story? I retreated to my room, knowing that he was the most unfair person on the planet.

I heard him toss his pasta after mine, right before I slammed my door.

But he didn't come after me, or make an appeal in old-speak.

Maybe he didn't care about either me or my mom.

I HAD HIDDEN MY NEW ring in a secret corner of my desk drawer, where I stash all the best stuff. It was beside the red rune stone that Granny had given me in the spring, with a little gap between them.

Just so you're straight on this, I don't actually have a living grandmother. Never have. Granny is this old woman I dream about sometimes. And last spring, she threw this round, flat rock at me. I'm not sure what it's for, but it seems like it must be important. It has a rune carved on one side, one that means "beginnings," so maybe that's why she gave it to me then.

Like I said, details on the Wyvern deal are sketchy.

For some reason, I thought the stone and the ring shouldn't touch each other and I decided to go with my gut on that. I dug the ring out twice that evening and turned it in the light, wondering why Rafferty had sent it to me.

And yes, worrying about the ring being a portent of pending Mage hostility.

Then I worried about my mom, and about my parents maybe never getting it together, about my never getting to see Jared again, and just generally fretted about the entire foundation of my universe.

Which seemed to suddenly be on pretty shaky ground.

I did send Rafferty a message, asking him about the ring.

There certainly wasn't an instant reply.

Or any reply.

Receipt acknowledged. That's it. It had been delivered.

I tried to work on an illustration I had started of two of my dragon friends. I was trying to depict Garrett fixing one of Liam's scales with his dragonfire, but I screwed it up and had to revert to the previously saved version. The only good thing was that I was working digitally.

I really wanted to call Meagan, even though I couldn't tell her all of what was bothering me. I pulled out my messenger, fingered it for a minute, then took a chance.

You there?

She answered immediately. But then, she always did her homework with her messenger on the desk beside her.

Z! You won't believe what happened today!

I smiled, reassured by her quick reply, then typed my own.

Neither will you. My mom walked out.
Maybe for good.

My messenger rang instantly on its voice setting. It was Meagan.

Like I said, she's the best friend in the world.

I GAVE HER THE SQUEAKY-CLEAN Covenant-approved version of what had happened—because I knew that my dad would be able to hear anything I said to Meagan, even if I whispered, thanks to that super-keen *Pyr* hearing. (And I could hear him breathing dragonsmoke, weaving it more thickly around the apartment. He was going to be a hard-ass about the Covenant this time, my rotten luck.) Basically, I told Meagan that I'd come home to find my mom walking out the door, that they'd been fighting, and that I wasn't sure when she'd be back.

All true.

Just not all of the truth.

We speculated on possibilities for a while, whether they would reconcile, but then I couldn't stand it any longer.

"You said something happened today," I asked, keeping my tone level. I knew what had happened in the bathroom, but I wasn't supposed to know. I was cool.

Until she answered me.

"It did!" Meagan said with excitement. "You'll never believe this, but you know those dragon shifter guys we see on television sometimes?"

"Yeah?" I sat up, a bit worried.

"One of them goes to our school!" Meagan crowed, unaware that my mouth had fallen open. "And he defended me against Suzanne. *Me!*" Her voice dropped to an excited whisper. "Who do you think it is? Peter Morris? Mike Gallagher? You know, it could be Tony Amario. I've always thought he was a bit mysterious."

It was good that she was on a roll. I couldn't think of a thing to say, but Meagan had plenty of guesses as to who the previously unsuspected *Pyr* student might be.

She didn't know—or hadn't realized—that there could be a girl dragon in her vicinity.

At least not so far.

You might have thought that that was plenty of action for one day in the life of a Wyvern, but one more thing happened that day.

When I fell asleep, Granny came back.

With a friend.

Chapter 3

I woke up in the middle of the night, shivering in my bed. I rolled over to pull up the covers and saw snow in my room.

But only when I looked with my left eye. When I opened only my right eye, my bedroom looked perfectly normal. If I closed that eye and looked just with the left again, I was out on the tundra, the walls of my room dissolved, a big tree right where the door should be.

I knew the eye game well. I'd learned to play it when my Wyvern powers first appeared. That had been the first time I'd dreamed of Granny, when she'd given me the rune stone. She'd also showed me how the eye game worked. It was kind of reassuring to have it make a second appearance—I'd been a bit disappointed by its absence all summer long.

Even better, Granny herself was back. I felt like waving hello. She still looked like Mrs. Claus, and she was still knitting with silent efficiency. Just like before, she could have been knitting a snowdrift.

But this time, she had company.

There was another woman beside her—at least, I think it was a woman. She was wearing a cape, with a hood, one that wrapped her completely in silvery gray. Her hood was filled with shadows, as if she didn't even have a head, but I could see her eyes gleaming in the darkness. She had a weird-looking gizmo in her hands, like a top that she constantly kept spinning. She moved so quickly that her hands were just a blur. I watched her, fascinated by the rhythm and eventually realized that she was making thread.

Like knitting wool. Yes! There was a loose stream of white over her shoulder, soft as a cloud, and she was feeding it into the spinning top, pulling it into long, twisted thread.

That must be a drop spindle. I'd heard my mom talk about them before and was pretty sure she even had one.

And sure enough, the spun wool that came from the bottom of the top, all sleek and slender and tight, seemed to be feeding the knitting that Granny was doing.

Would the sheep turn up next? I wondered.

"I am Urd," said the new arrival, startling me with her words. Granny had never spoken to me. She'd just chucked a rune stone at my head. I wasn't expecting audio. "You already know my sister, Verdandi."

I opened my mouth, intending to ask questions, but Urd suddenly held up one finger. It was creepy, that finger, like a skeleton's finger. I was kind of glad to not be seeing her face just then.

I did as I was told and kept silent.

"'Verdandi' means 'what is.' 'Urd' means 'what was.'" Then she pointed that finger at the ground, down to the root of the tree where there was a dark hole. I'd peered into the hole before. It was like a well, a dark hole that stretched down farther than I could see, with a shimmer of water's reflection at the bottom.

It gave me the heebie-jeebies, that well. Granny knit faster, as if she were troubled, and her gaze was locked on me. Her lips were tight with concern, the way my mom's get when she's fighting against her urge to argue with my dad.

Hmm. Guess she'd gotten over that.

Urd put down her spindle and did a little sleight of hand, reaching into the air and closing her fist on something that wasn't there. I blinked and then she opened her palm to show me what she held.

Rafferty's ring.

No, *my* ring.

"Hey!" I leapt from my bed to grab the ring from her. She waited until I almost had it, then closed her fist and flung the ring down the well.

I fell to the ground beside the well, too slow to snatch the ring out of the air. I could see it glinting as it fell, a red glow emanating from it. Then it splashed into that water way down at the bottom.

And disappeared.

I caught a whiff of shadows and rot. Whatever was down there, it could stay put as far as I was concerned. The ring, I was ready to concede, was lost. Even in a dream, I didn't see any reason to dive into a pit that I wouldn't be able to escape.

But Urd had other ideas. She moved fast. When I would have stood up again, I found her bony hand was on my shoulder. She was strong, stronger than anyone would expect, and she shoved me toward the well. I stumbled, because she caught me by surprise.

I fought and struggled, but Urd pushed me steadily closer. I twisted to fight her grip. She had fingers of steel, and she was winning.

No, she had fingers of bone. Skeleton hands.

I panicked when I saw that. I thrashed. I caught her hood with one hand and pulled, desperate for a grip on anything.

I heard it tear and looked up when I heard her laugh.

Holy frick! Her head was a bare skull.

One with eyes that burned like twin flames. She opened her mouth to laugh at me, and it looked like she had a snake for a tongue. She released me and I fell over my own feet in my hurry to get away from that face.

But she tripped me.

And I fell into the darkness of the well.

Down and down and down. Urd's laughter echoed all around me as I fell. There was an inky shimmer, like black water, but it was a long way down.

This was not good.

I WOKE UP, my heart hammering and my fingers knotted in the sheets. There was sweat running down my back.

There was no snow.

There was no tree and there was no dark well.

There was no sign of Granny, or her nasty sister.

But that black envelope from Trevor was perched on the carpet beside my stack of books. I was sure I hadn't left it there. I had the irrational thought that it was spying on me—although with Mages, that might not be very irrational at all.

I wasn't entirely sure of everything they could do. And the one guy who did know more had declined to fill me in.

Never mind that recent events meant it was unlikely I'd be able to hit Jared up for advice, live and in person, at his concert. Looked like I'd be solving my Mage-related issues myself, thanks.

I leapt from the bed, snatched up the envelope, and ripped it to shreds. Then I flung it out the window, watching the pieces flutter toward the pavement far below. That stupid dragonsmoke singed my fingers when my hand passed through it just for a second. There was an unwelcome reminder that my dad meant business.

Only when the pieces had all disappeared from sight and nothing else had happened did I shut the window and lock it securely. I rummaged in the drawer with the secret corner in a panic. To my relief, the ring was right where I'd hidden it.

My ring.

I locked my hand around it, still freaked, then opened my hand to look at it. Had it changed?

It had. It seemed to glitter a little in the light, as if the white part was full of snow crystals and the black part was full of stars.

What kind of magic did this ring possess, anyhow?

How could I find out?

I shuddered at the prospect and got into bed, sitting with my back against the wall and my knees pulled up to my chest. I had the ring trapped in my right fist, my left hand locked around the right. There was no way I was going to sleep again soon, not with Urd lurking in dreamland, on the lookout for me.

I checked with both eyes, but my room looked normal even with the eye game. I sat vigil, armed only with a ring, unconvinced of my safety. I had a feeling that Granny and her weird sister could change things on me without notice.

I could have called my dad. He might even have believed me. But I wasn't exactly feeling confident about his inclination to defend me or even see my point of view.

Call it a learned response.

The thing about being scared crapless by strange old women in the night is that it helps put things in perspective. There had to be something I could do to improve the odds of my not having a completely miserable birthday.

There had to be a plan I could make.

I like riddles and I had a great big clue, right in my hand.

Who would know about the ring? I wasn't going to ask my dad because I knew what he'd say. "Figure it out." Thanks very much. Rafferty had already proved to be unhelpful.

Then the answer hit me.

Of course. I could ask Isabelle.

Rafferty's adopted daughter.

Who was attending college right in Chicago.

Perfect.

THE NEXT MORNING MY DAD was standing in the kitchen, waiting for me. This was unusual enough to make me wary.

Especially after what I'd said to him the night before.

I had a definite sense that I would be called on the carpet for challenging him.

Was he going to escort me through his dragonsmoke? Or did he intend to leave me holed up here for the duration? Or would my exile be elsewhere? I both wanted to know and dreaded hearing his decision.

That there was a small black satchel at his feet just added to my uncertainty. It was bigger than his briefcase or laptop bag. He had his leather jacket on and his boots, and looked ready to walk out the door.

Was he leaving, too?

As much as I wanted to be an adult right this minute, this change was happening a bit fast—and in entirely the wrong way.

Maybe I should be careful what I wished for.

"You'll need to pack a bag," he said curtly. His British accent was stronger than usual, which was never good. "You'll be staying at Meagan's. Her mother knows that you're grounded, although there will, of course, be no dragonsmoke barrier there."

I opened the fridge, as if there were no urgency. I wasn't in a real hurry to make anything easy for him. I was sure he was going to tell me that he had to make a business trip to secure a pyrotechnics contract in another city. That's what he does—big pyrotechnics displays timed to music. It is cool, but I resented his ability to carry on as if nothing had happened, as if my mom's departure meant nothing at all. I was prepared to argue that I was nearly sixteen and could take care of myself. It seemed that someone should have asked me before making plans for my immediate future.

Wasn't this the same thing he'd done with my mom? Just decided and let her deal with the consequences?

Bottom line—if getting rid of me would be convenient to his career, I wasn't inclined to be convenient.

I considered a tub of yogurt, as if it held all the world's secrets. "For how long?"

"I don't know." He exuded impatience.

I put the plain yogurt back and picked up a flavored yogurt instead. Hmm. Peach. "I didn't hear you call anybody."

"Meagan's mother and I e-mailed last night."

"Why do I have to go anywhere? I thought this loft would be my prison."

My dad fixed a look on me, one that was so intent I shivered. I braced myself for a reckoning.

But he surprised me.

"Because I am going to follow your mother, and try my utmost to change her mind about remaining in this partnership." I had a moment to be shocked and delighted before he continued. "You cannot stay here alone because you are a minor. That is the law."

"Human law." I had to say it.

"Human law." His lips tightened at the concession. "Which in this case and in the very short term trumps *Pyr* law. Don't imagine I'll forget your transgression."

Right. Mr. Responsibility was back. Maybe he'd never left. Did he really care about my mom? Or did he just feel responsible for pursuing her? "How long will you be gone?"

He winced. "However long it takes." He glanced at his watch. "You have five minutes. I have a flight to catch."

A commercial carrier? What about Dragon Air? "You're not flying yourself?"

His eyes, if anything, glittered more coldly. "Your mother wishes to live like a normal human. Therefore, I will arrive to plead my case like a normal human. I have made arrangements for your care like a normal human. I suspect these are but the first of many concessions I will make in the near future."

I had the urge to tell him he should have made concessions sooner, but I bit back that piece of advice. It should have been good enough for me that he was going after her.

Funny, but it wasn't. I wanted him to show more emotion for once, to be visibly upset. Maybe to cry. Instead, it felt as if he was going to collect a forgotten umbrella from the Lost and Found.

"Four minutes," he said, biting off the words.

I was halfway out of the kitchen when I remembered who I was talking to. My dad. The dragon who hid his emotions—and his vulnerabilities—better than any six poker faces put together.

I turned back to watch him rinse his coffee mug. His expression was grim and as I looked more closely, I saw an unfamiliar tension in him. He was trying to hide his reaction and unable to do so. That meant he was really upset. I wondered whether he'd slept at all. And he had nearly lost it the night before. I guessed that he blamed himself even more than I blamed him.

In a strange way, that made me feel better.

"Do you think you can convince her?" I asked quietly.

I didn't miss his grimace, even though it was quickly gone. "I am not sure." It was maybe the first time I'd ever heard him speak without conviction. That made my stomach queasy. "But I guarantee you that I will do my best to persuade her."

"I think you can be pretty persuasive."

He smiled then, a humorless expression that lasted less than a heartbeat. "And I think your mother is a woman who knows her own mind." He frowned and spoke softly. "I shall try, Zoë. It's the only thing that I can promise."

When he looked up, there was a shadow in his eyes, a doubt

I never thought I'd glimpse in my dad. I'd always believed he was in charge of the whole universe, that he could do anything or achieve anything. He could do a lot, even more than most dads.

But he wasn't sure he could convince my mom to stay with him.

And that was ripping his guts out, doing more damage than the most ferocious dragon attack.

I crossed the room and gave him an impulsive hug, shocked by how tightly he hugged me back. We stood there for a long moment, clutching each other and I heard his breath catch.

My invincible dad was scared crapless.

He really did care.

"I'll be ready in five," I said to him when I pulled back, realizing belatedly that I sounded a lot like my mom when she has a To Do list. "Could you pack me a couple of granola bars and an apple? I'll eat on the way."

My inclination to play as part of the team was cut short, but quick. My dad drummed his fingers on the counter as I was leaving the room. I had a fleeting sense that he was going to say something I wouldn't like.

And he did.

"You should also be aware that I have decided to modify the Covenant in your case, given the circumstances."

I froze on the threshold of the kitchen to look back. "What?"

He gave me one of those glittering looks. "You are forbidden to shift to dragon form without prior approval from me."

I looked away in a futile effort to control my temper. The very idea that anyone could know when they would need to shift, in advance, in time to ask permission, was so stupid that only a parent could have come up with it.

This was about his lack of confidence in my abilities.

Or some need for control.

And I chafed at the restriction. "I can't shift without your permission?" I asked, making him say it again.

"No." He glared at me. "And I'm not giving it."

It was pretty easy to guess that the other older *Pyr* would back the choice of my dad, who is their leader, after all. "But you're leaving. What about self-defense?"

"You'll have no cause to defend yourself."

I flung out my hands. "What about the Mages and their plan to eliminate shifters?"

"We have a treaty with them. It's resolved." He ground out the words, convinced of the power of diplomacy. His eyes narrowed. "Did you not shift yesterday, in front of Meagan?"

"Well, yeah, but Suzanne had punched her—"

"But you could not have dealt with this threat in human form?"

I was at a loss there. I could have, but it wouldn't have been nearly as cool.

"You have shown that your judgment is not sound. We will discuss this more upon my return. Until then, you will not shift."

"But—"

"I do not want to exile my own daughter, but I will do it if you insist on my making an example of you."

"What if we're attacked?"

"You will not be. Two minutes."

I didn't share his confidence at all, but he was unshakable. His decision was completely unfair and unreasonable—but there is no *Pyr* court of appeals. I know I must have looked mutinous when I stared at him, but he stared right back.

Dragon-stared.

"One minute," he reminded me curtly.

One more time I retreated and slammed the door of my room.

I hurled clothes into a backpack, mad enough that there must have been steam coming out of my ears. This wasn't about me, or even about the Covenant. This was all about my dad keeping up appearances for his *Pyr* buddies. Maybe it was about my brother turning *Slayer*. Either way, it had nothing to do with me being safe.

That was when I knew what I would do. I wouldn't shift. I'd follow my dad's stupid rule to show that I was trustworthy.

But I would also prove him wrong, about one thing at least.

And Isabelle would help me.

MEAGAN'S MOM MET US AT school and stored my bag in their car. She tried to offer a bit of sensitive encouragement to my dad, but he was brusque with her. I took this as a sign of his own doubts and felt kind of bad for him.

"*You can do it, Dad*," I murmured in old-speak after he turned away, and saw him jerk in response. Then he shot me a vivid glance, got in the car and was gone.

I shoved my hands into my pockets and found the ring. I felt superstitious about putting it on without knowing everything it could do, and trusted my instinct. I wasn't going to leave it anywhere, either, though. I would just keep it close, and touch it sometimes.

"I'm sorry about your mom." Meagan bumped her shoulder against mine, the way we used to. "It's good he's going after her."

"Yeah." I sighed. "I'm glad about that."

"Fingers crossed," Meagan said and flashed me a smile. Her smile really did flash—she had a mouthful of metal. "Hey, you know, we could try one of my mom's visioning sessions after school and see if we can help your dad. We could get my mom to help—"

"I have to go somewhere after school," I said, thinking about the weight of the ring in my pocket. I'd have to persuade Mrs. Jameson to let me meet Isabelle somehow.

"That's okay. We'll go take care of that first, then do the visioning session. After dinner, if we have to." Meagan was trying to accommodate me, which said a lot either about how nice she is or about how long we've been pals. "Where do you have to go?"

She obviously thought I had a dentist's appointment or something. I felt my gut knot, because there was no avoiding what I had to say. I couldn't exactly ask Isabelle about the ring with Meagan present. It was pure dragon biz. "Um . . . I have to visit someone. Alone."

I just wanted to stop her before she planned everything, but I handled it badly. She tensed and I knew I'd hurt her feelings.

Again.

"I see." Her tone said it all. "And I suppose that if you're still staying with us on Halloween, you'll go to Trevor's party alone, too?"

"I told you I'm not going to his party—"

"Don't lie to me, Zoë!" Meagan snapped. "It's bad enough that you won't tell me things."

"But I swear I *can't* tell you. . . ."

"No, you *won't* tell me." She grabbed the door and hauled it open. "I suppose it's better to find out who your real friends are."

It would have been great if I'd thought of the perfect reply, but instead I just stood there with my mouth hanging open.

And you know what happened next.

"Meagan!" Jessica called and waved from down the hall. "Did you solve the bonus questions from math?"

Meagan grinned. "Even better! I have the coolest thing to tell you. You'll never guess what I saw yesterday."

And they were gone, speculating on the identity of the dragon kid in our school, leaving me behind—me, who could have told them the real story, IF it hadn't been for the stupid Covenant. Even if there was a marginal chance of my not getting exiled, it depended upon my playing by my dad's rules in the short term. Just the scorch of that dragonsmoke had been enough to convince me that he was serious about reinforcing the rules.

Even on me.

Derek appeared in my peripheral vision when I was opening my locker.

"Fight?" he asked. I didn't have to ask what he meant. I knew he must have been watching our exchange.

"Kind of." I shrugged, as if it would blow over. "How was the game?"

"Central won." He didn't sound surprised.

I wasn't either.

We ran out of conversation at that point. I got my books for the morning classes, sure that he'd leave.

He didn't.

He cleared his throat. For the first time I'd ever noticed, Derek looked uncomfortable. He almost shuffled his feet. That made me curious as to what he wanted to say. "So, they say you draw."

Now I was the one watching him intently. "Some. Yeah."

Those eyes were icy blue, his gaze fixed on me. "Dragons."

I swallowed, feeling like I was under a microscope. "Usually." I felt myself blushing. "Call it a weakness."

"I don't." I wasn't sure what he meant by that, but he was digging in his bag. He offered a new notebook to me, as if he thought I'd refuse to take it. "Draw me one?"

Kids asked me to do this all the time, to embellish one of their notebooks with a dragon. For some reason, Derek's request felt different, maybe just because he was different.

Intense. That was the word for him.

Like the weight of the world was hanging on my decision.

Or maybe I was making too much of it.

I tried to shake off my sense of foreboding. "Sure," I said, as if it was no big deal.

It wasn't.

At least it shouldn't have been.

"Gotta get in line early," he said, to my surprise. "Haven't you heard?" He was studying me again. "Everyone's talking about the dragon who spooked Suzanne." He jerked his head toward the bathroom, scene of the crime, which was closed off.

"Oh, I did hear something," I said, trying to sound disinterested.

"I thought you'd be all over that story, since it stars a dragon."

I blushed. Again. "I like them better in fiction."

"Really?" He couldn't have sounded more skeptical.

I changed the subject. "So, any preferences? Flying? Perching?"

"Kicking butt." He spoke with resolve. "I want to see a dragon kicking some bully's ass."

My mouth went dry. I had those prickles on the back of my neck again.

There couldn't be any way that Derek knew my secret.

Could there?

He looked one more time into my eyes, hard, as if he was trying to tell me something. I couldn't think what it might be. I couldn't think of a thing to say.

Not one thing.

Derek smiled a little, that secret smile he seemed to keep especially for me, then turned and walked away. I stared after him, wondering.

Was Derek intense because he *liked* me? It was an astonishing possibility. I'd never had a guy like me at school before. In fact, I had so far shown a talent for liking guys who didn't like me back. Or ran hot and cold about liking me back.

But Derek seemed to be interested. And he kept coming to talk to me. I didn't think it was just about a dragon drawing. He also didn't run hot and cold. He was consistent. I got my books out for class, pondering the possibilities. Just because it was strange and unusual for a guy to like me didn't mean it was impossible.

Right?

DEREK WAS RIGHT ABOUT ONE thing—the school was buzzing with the story and speculation was running wild. Some people thought the whole thing was a hoax, a story made up by Suzanne and spread by her friends to make her look special. But many people shared Meagan's conviction that one of the guys at school must be a dragon shifter. Who was the dragon hidden among us? People really wanted to know—and in the absence of any real information, they were prepared to make something up that sounded plausible.

It would have been funny if I hadn't been so terrified of being found out.

Suzanne was absent. I'd been right—Meagan had told the principal that she didn't see anything, just Suzanne freaking out. Apparently, Suzanne had talked a lot about dragons attacking her and the principal had concluded that she was tripping on something. Her parents had refused to let her have a blood test or to have her seen by a doctor, so she'd been suspended for the day.

Her groupies seemed a bit shaken by their idol's tumble from grace, and I overheard Trish defending Suzanne a couple of times. She even talked about identifying the dragon kid and "taking him down," which was pretty funny.

I wanted to see her try.

I just kept my head down—even if I found Derek watching me at every turn. You'd think I could have gotten control of my crazy blushing, but no luck. I spent the day as red as a lobster, hugging my secret close and avoiding conversation.

In other words, like usual, but more red.

On the upside, Meagan was Ms. Popularity, everyone wanting to hear the story from her side. That she deviated from her official version, telling Jessica and others about the dragon, just made her a bigger hit. Trish and Anna were watching Meagan from a distance—like circling piranhas—but apparently didn't dare get close to her.

Or maybe they were waiting for the Queen Bee to make a plan.

In math class, Trish was busy on her messenger, probably researching the *Pyr* for Suzanne. Everyone around me had dragon fever, and everyone was on the dragon's side. And that was when I realized three things:

1. I could instantly and immediately become the most popular girl in school, if I just revealed my secret. I could feel the tide of support for the dragon.

   I could become cool overnight.

   This was such a novel concept that it threw me a bit, enough that it took me until the end of class to remember my dad's last instruction.

   No shifting without authorization.
2. That made me wonder whether my dad, with his gift of foresight, had glimpsed the temptation in my future.

   Who wouldn't want to be cool? Who wouldn't want to be popular?

   All I'd have to do is shift shape in front of witnesses.

   And finally:
3. Courtesy of all the drama in my life, I'd completely forgotten about the English essay I had to hand in right after lunch. "The Depiction of Weather as a Character in *Jane Eyre*, *Rebecca*, and *Persuasion*." Crap. Crappity crap crap. I hadn't even finished reading the last book and time was a-wasting.

So much for lunch with Meagan and Jessica.

I SPENT LUNCH IN THE library, madly reading and scribbling, barely managing to pull together an essay that was somewhat coherent in time.

On the way to English class, I joined the group of people gathered outside the closed bathroom that had been the scene of the crime. I had a peek around the temporary barrier—easy since there were worker dudes who had moved it aside in their assessment of the damage—and smiled to myself at the diameter of the peeling scorch mark on the ceiling.

"They're trying to say that she was smoking something," Stacey said, with a roll of her eyes.

"It'd be a helluva toke to burn that much," Mike replied.

"I think we would have smelled it before it wrecked the ceiling," Tanya added, and they all laughed.

When I got to English class, Derek was already there, watching me from his fave seat at the back. I stumbled right on cue. He didn't miss one bit of it and I was glad to take my seat and turn my back to him.

The day couldn't end soon enough.

Gym was my last class and predictably painful, even with Suzanne absent. Volleyball. Ugh. Whenever I hit the ball—which was infrequent—it went straight into the net.

Eventually, the last bell rang. Meagan was ignoring me, probably because I hadn't showed at lunch.

I was late already, so I just headed out, reasoning that I'd patch things up with her later. I'd also have to think of a story to tell Mrs. Jameson. Maybe a dentist appointment. I'd sent Isabelle a message and she'd agreed to meet me at a coffee shop at four. I'd met her at the same place a couple of other times. I had to take the bus and the L to get there, but I was used to that.

I like meeting up with Isabelle. In a way, she's everything I want to be. In another, she's *been* everything I want to be. It's odd, hanging with someone who had your job before but doesn't remember doing it.

Last spring, I discovered that she's the previous Wyvern reincarnated. This would be incredibly useful, if she remembered all of the Wyvern goodness she once must have known and could thus help me get a grip on my slippery new powers.

Of course, it doesn't work that way. Nothing about this Wyvern gig is easy. She doesn't remember anything about a past life and is pretty much taking my word on the whole reincarnation thing.

Why am I so sure of who Isabelle was? Granny showed me. One thing I have learned is that what goes down in my dreams, especially when Granny is on the scene, proves to be real. Every time.

Maybe that's a Wyvern trick.

Memory or not, there was no telling what Isabelle had inadvertently learned about the ring while growing up in Rafferty's house. I still had hopes for more information.

Usually Isabelle's in England—where Rafferty and his partner, Melissa, live—taking courses on tarot cards and auras while being effortlessly gorgeous. She's older than me, but doesn't get snotty about it. This year, Isabelle had decided to enroll in some exchange program and study in Chicago. I'm pretty sure she did this to be close to Nick and I had to wonder how well that was working.

I got on the bus, reminding myself that my mom never minded if I went downtown to meet Isabelle before dinner. (Well, if I wasn't grounded. Details.) I felt as if I was (sort of) following house rules, even in the absence of parents and home.

For whatever that was worth.

In fact, the likelihood of having either again, or having things return to any kind of normalcy, seemed pretty low. I was afraid my dad had decided to compromise too late for it to matter.

Which made me wonder why I even cared about house rules.

And helped me to rationalize what I intended to do.

Sure, I'd never asked my mom about the concert and my dad had said I couldn't go, but they'd both left town. I was the only one in Chicago who knew I wasn't supposed to go. Even if Meagan's mom knew I was supposed to be grounded, it didn't seem as if she was too hot about enforcing it. Maybe she thought it unimportant compared to my parents' splitting up. Maybe she was giving me a break.

I'd run with it, either way.

If I could get to Jared's concert, prove that I was right about him, and maybe get a peek at the book or even learn the Mages' revised plan, that would justify defying my dad. Right? It might also score me at least one item from my birthday wish list.

I wasn't going to be irresponsible, though, or get myself into an unsafe situation. I'm not stupid. The co-op where Jared's band was going to play was in a crummy neighborhood and not the place to be alone at night. I needed someone to go with me—a partner in crime, as it were.

Which brought me to Isabelle.

ISABELLE WAS ALREADY SIPPING A big foamy coffee when I arrived. She was perched at a table for two by the window and if I didn't like her so much, I could have been green with envy that she could look so good and make it seem so easy.

Make no mistake—Isabelle is *gorgeous.* Even though I know it, I'm astounded every time I see her again.

The weather had turned crummy. It was windy and starting to snow, the kind of snow that falls in big flakes and then melts on contact with anything. I was wet and chilled after my walk from the L. I shivered and kept my fave shawl wrapped around my neck like a big cowl when I sat down.

They were playing hokey Halloween music, those novelty

tunes which just about made me barf. There were jack-o'-lantern posters on the walls and everything in the place was black and orange. They had posters up for a pumpkin spice coffee special and the staff were dressed up—one wore a witch hat and a green wig, while the other wore a zombie costume.

Isabelle was wearing a thick burgundy sweater with a wide cowl neck that showed her throat. She has that flawless skin that British girls tend to have, all creamy silk. I doubt she's ever had a zit. She's feminine and mysterious, and confident too. Like I said, Isabelle's everything I want to be. Her chestnut hair is loose and wavy over her shoulders—no bad-hair days for her. With her jeans tucked into her high boots and her pale pink lip gloss, she looked like a lingerie model.

Or every guy's winter fantasy.

That she has a scrumptious British accent would have sealed the deal for pretty much anyone. Most of the guys in the coffee shop were checking her out, probably imagining that I was her baby sister.

The plain one.

Isabelle had also bought a big foamy drink for me, which she pushed toward me. I'm not much for coffee, but was cold enough to drink it. I thanked her and wrapped my hands around the warm cup, realizing as I raised it to my lips that it was actually hot chocolate.

Yummy. I smiled at her in appreciation.

"Heard from Jared?" she asked, right when I was taking a sip.

I choked.

Figuratively and literally.

Chapter 4

Trust Isabelle to cut right to the chase. Here was my opening, if sooner than expected. "He has a concert here on Saturday, at this club. . . ."

"I know. Knightshade." She watched me carefully, and she knew I had ducked her question. "Did you message him?"

"Once. Last summer."

She looked a bit annoyed. "Didn't he answer you? Didn't he get in touch about this weekend?"

"Yes and no." I put down the cup. "He sent me a short answer last summer."

"Blowing you off," Isabelle muttered into her coffee. "Guys!"

"I think he's busy." I tried not to think about Jared being amused by high school girls who send him messages just because they've kissed him once. "And, you know, that's fine."

Isabelle's eyes gleamed. "Is it?"

"The thing is, I need to talk to him about that book on the *Pyr* he has. I need to look at it again. Reference, you know."

Isabelle started to smile. "Uh-huh," she said and I blushed.

"So I wondered whether you would take me to the concert Saturday."

It wasn't smooth, but maybe it would get the job done.

I probably looked as hopeful as a puppy.

Isabelle's smile widened. "Just to talk about the book, of course."

I blushed even more. "Look, I'm trying to not be pathetic about it. You could help."

"Try harder," Isabelle said teasingly.

I had to be red enough to glow in the dark. She reached across the table and squeezed my hand. "I wish he'd gotten in touch with you, Zoë. I thought you two had some magic."

"Me, too."

Isabelle sighed. She looked out into the falling snow. "Why is it that guys just don't get it?"

I was surprised by her despondency. "How's Nick?"

Isabelle grimaced. "Oh, he tells me he has a girlfriend."

"You."

Isabelle shook her head. "Teresa, I think is her name." She widened her eyes slightly and sipped her coffee.

I was appalled. "No way! You two are made for each other."

"Nick seems to think that love, romance, and sex are all the same thing." She shook her head and looked unhappy. I couldn't help hearing my dad's warning about Jared. He couldn't be right about guys, could he?

Isabelle sighed again. "I think maybe he's just not ready."

Nick is hot and fun and the life of the party, the jock everyone wants to be—or be with. I could see him having tons of friends and going to lots of parties.

But a girlfriend who wasn't Isabelle?

The idea bummed me out even more than the reality of my parents' trashed relationship.

I took a big swig of hot chocolate and it burned all the way down. "Maybe he'll appreciate you more after he's been with someone else."

"Maybe." Isabelle didn't look as if she believed that. She pulled out her tarot cards and began to shuffle them absently.

I love her tarot cards. They're huge, each card more than twice the size of a normal playing card. And the illustrations are beautiful. Isabelle seems to always pull a card that has meaning for the situation at hand, and I love watching her do what she does.

Maybe because she always tries to explain it to me.

Maybe because it fascinates and mystifies me. How could pieces of cardboard—even ones with great illustrations—give a glimpse of what the future will be? If there's a portal or a dimension or a sense that allows a person to peer into the future, shouldn't I be aware of it? The Wyvern is supposed to be able to see past, present, and future simultaneously, but I had no such prophetic abilities.

Maybe I was hoping that it was contagious.

Because Isabelle certainly had that power.

Or maybe it was in the cards themselves.

She glanced up at me without drawing a card and smiled. "So, what else is new, other than the fact that guys are jerks? Maybe that's not even new."

It was likely to be the best intro I'd get.

"Well, I wanted to talk to you about this ring." I dug it out of my pocket, then placed it on the table between us. Isabelle caught her breath at the sight of it. "My mom said Rafferty sent it to me for my birthday. I'm wondering why he would give it to me."

Isabelle eyed the ring but didn't touch it.

"He loaned it to you last spring."

"Well, yeah."

"And something happened."

I nodded. "It turned into the ghosts of Sophie and Nikolas."

"The last Wyvern and her lover."

"And they helped me defeat the Mages, as well as get Rafferty and me free of their spell trap."

"And then?"

"They spun back into the ring." I picked it up, turned it in the light. It didn't have any of that starlight inside it anymore. Strange. "Like Aladdin's lamp, but more portable."

"Do you get more than three wishes?"

"I don't know." We both looked at the ring. It appeared to be just a piece of glass, reflecting the twinkle lights hung in the windows. It was hard to believe at this moment that it had any power at all.

"Maybe Rafferty thinks you awakened something in it," Isabelle said. "Like now it's rightfully yours."

"Then he would have just given it to me in the spring, I think." I shook my head. "I think it's something else. I thought you might know."

Isabelle shook her head. "You could ask him."

"I did."

"Let me guess—he told you to work it out for yourself."

I nodded agreement. "He didn't answer at all."

Isabelle smiled. "Maybe he doesn't even know the answer."

She studied me for a long moment, then took a deep breath. "Let's see what the cards can tell us." She shuffled the deck of tarot cards as I watched. She drew a card and snapped it flat on the table beside the ring.

The Falling Tower.

I don't know much about the meanings of the cards, but this picture—of a castle being struck by lightning and tumbling to pieces—seemed somewhat less than optimistic.

IF I WAS WARY, Isabelle was spooked.

Her hand shook as she set the rest of the tarot deck down on the table. She stared unblinkingly at the card, which wasn't a particularly encouraging sign either. I waited, thinking that maybe she was meditating on it or something. With Isabelle, you can never be sure.

Finally I couldn't stand it anymore. "So, what does it mean?"

"Maybe Rafferty thinks he won't need the ring much longer," she said, her voice uneven. "Not in this life."

Now *I* was horrified. I hadn't even thought of it as a legacy. "Wait a minute. You can't mean that he's sick."

Isabelle folded her arms around herself and sat back. "He's not exactly young, even for a *Pyr*."

And Rafferty had had his firestorm, which is supposed to start the aging process in dragon dudes.

He couldn't be dying, though. "No, I don't believe it. It has to mean something else." I didn't want to think about a world without Rafferty.

Isabelle visibly braced herself to pick up the cards again. "Have you noticed that I always draw from the higher arcana when we're together?"

"Should I know what you're talking about?"

Isabelle turned the deck over and spread the cards across the table. "There are seventy-four cards in the tarot deck. Four suits of thirteen, similar to regular playing cards, which are called the lower arcana. In addition, there are twenty-two allegorical cards, called the higher arcana."

"You sound like a professor."

"Fortune-telling Through the Ages: Tools and Techniques is one of the courses I'm taking this semester." Isabelle leaned forward. "The thing is that the higher arcana are powerful cards. They usually turn up when a message is important. Like a warning, or a huge life change. But every single time I draw a card in your presence, it's a higher-arcana card."

I shivered despite myself. "So . . . ?"

"So the cards are responding to your energy."

I leaned forward, intrigued. Could I learn to use the cards? Was this where I would discover the Wyvern's traditional ability to predict the future? "What does this one mean?"

Isabelle grimaced. "Big changes. Dramatic and violent ones. Like electrical storms."

"Or ideas?" I suggested. "A bolt out of the blue?"

She considered that. "Maybe. More likely someone gets hit by lightning. Destruction."

Nice.

"You think Rafferty is ensuring that the ring has a new custodian?"

"Because he senses danger to himself." Isabelle finished my sentence so neatly that I knew she'd been thinking exactly the same thing.

Great. I'd just given Isabelle something to worry about.

She took a gulp of coffee, then shoved the card back into the deck, shuffling it with practiced ease. Then she offered me the deck. "Go ahead. Try it."

I hesitated. "Don't you believe they're your cards and attuned to your energy, and that anyone else touching them messes that up?" I remembered her saying as much before, whenever people had asked to touch the cards.

"They're already responding to you. Let's see how much."

I took them with some reluctance. The deck was heavier than I'd expected and the cards were so big that they were hard to handle. "What do I do?"

"Shuffle them. Think of a question. Then when it feels right, pick a card, and turn it up on the table."

Call me weak, but I thought about Jared. I wondered how a

guy could kiss a girl like that and then just forget that she existed. I thought about him insisting he couldn't give me the book because he wasn't going to risk losing the interest of a dragon girl. I wondered whether there was any chance I might see him this weekend—either to get the book or to get another kiss—and I yearned.

Then I chose a card and put it on the table with care.

The Hermit.

I was starting to think I didn't need a manual to understand these cards.

"IT'S RIGHT SIDE UP," Isabelle said.

"What does that mean?"

"You consider the orientation from the reader's perspective. Right side up means the card has its usual meaning. If it's reversed, or upside down, then the meaning is the opposite."

"So, the flip side would be the Party Girl."

Isabelle smiled fleetingly. "Something like that. The Hermit means a quest for information and knowledge. It indicates you going on a journey in search of the truth."

"Alone," I added, as this seemed to be key.

"Usually alone." Isabelle shrugged. "Although anyone can be alone in a crowd, too."

"Lost in their own world." I couldn't argue that the card had nailed my current status. I was certainly flying solo, whether I was seeking knowledge or not. Maybe it meant that I should put this moment of isolation to work, use it as an opportunity to investigate . . . what, exactly?

Isabelle glanced at her watch, then picked up her cards. She tapped them on the table so the stack was neat, then slipped them into a silk bag with a drawstring. She tucked them into her purse with care. "So, what's the deal with the concert?"

It was a typical Isabelle change of subject, a rough transition that made sense to her but left me a bit dizzy. "I want to go. I was going to ask my mom, but she's gone."

"Gone?"

I gave her the condensed version of events Chez Sorensson, but she didn't look either surprised or concerned. I decided to take that as a sign of confidence in a happy ending. "And the thing is that his band is playing at this club that isn't licensed. It's right here in town and it won't be a problem for minors to attend. And the concert's on Saturday night." I sat back and voiced my secret thought. "I think he's daring me to show up."

Isabelle considered this. "He does like to push you."

A Wyvern should be bold. That's what he'd said to me.

"I don't want to be a fangirl. I just want to know." I saved all the stuff my dad had said about young men just wanting sex, given that the generalization seemed to apply to Nick.

"Don't we all?" Isabelle murmured. "All right, we have to go. How else will we know if the cards are really attuned to your energy?" It was a typical Isabelle rationalization, in that it wasn't particularly rational at all. That made it hard to argue with her.

She pulled out a notepad. Isabelle and her paper books. She's a real throwback. "Give me the address and phone number of Meagan's house," she said. "I'll pick you up there."

"Really?"

"Happy birthday. Early."

I was simultaneously elated and terrified. I wasn't sure I could stand it if Jared turned me down, right to my face.

On the other hand, I wouldn't be able to live with myself if I let this opportunity slip away.

I told her the address, then confided one other potential obstacle. "I don't know if Meagan's mom will let me go to a concert." I told her the bit about my being grounded and why.

Isabelle tapped her pen on her notepad. "You could beguile her."

"Right! You're the one that says beguiling shouldn't be used for personal gain."

"Don't be ridiculous. This is about kismet and destiny, and following your quest in becoming the Wyvern. This is about self-determination! It's not selfish at all to ensure that you embrace your fate."

Only Isabelle can talk like that and not sound insane.

"Still. I'm not going to beguile Meagan's mom. It would be taking advantage."

Isabelle shrugged. "Suit yourself. We'll find another way. I'll pick you up at seven."

"But what about Meagan?"

"Meagan can come, too. My treat."

Wow. Maybe there *was* a magic genie in the ring. I thanked Isabelle, gave her a hug, then shoved the ring back into my pocket. I finished my chocolate on the way back to Meagan's place, unable to deny that the world was looking better.

Because I was going to see Jared this weekend.

It was sad to be so easily affected by the prospect of just seeing a guy, but I refused to think of myself as pathetic.

At least in this particular instance.

I was a dragon girl, on a mission.

A bold Wyvern.

One thing was for sure—I desperately needed a sexy bra before Saturday night.

STAYING AT SOMEONE ELSE'S PLACE is a bit odd. I wasn't sure whether I could just walk into Meagan's town house or not. I was living there, technically, but only for the short term—or so I hoped. Uncertain, I went with the conservative choice.

I rang the bell.

"Done with your real friends?" Meagan asked when she opened the door. I knew she wasn't being mean. She was hurt, because I had hurt her, and it was coming out of her pores. I wished I knew how to fix it.

I tried.

"I had to go see Isabelle." I chattered as we went to her room and felt her relax as I explained. "I think I've told you about her. She's like a cousin, but not exactly. Her dad and my dad are old friends."

Older friends than any human could have guessed. I was thinking that my dad and Rafferty had been hanging out for four or five hundred years, give or take.

Meagan's eyes flickered with interest. "The Isabelle in England?"

"That's her, but she's studying here for a year. Some kind of cultural transfer program."

"What's she studying?"

"I'm not sure." I realized that I wasn't. "She wanted me to meet her for a hot chocolate today, so I did. I thought maybe something was wrong. She sounded a bit upset."

Meagan immediately looked concerned. "That's why you wanted to meet her alone. Is she lonely, being so far away from home?"

This was the Meagan I knew best. Thoughtful and sensitive.

Was this why she'd befriended Jessica? Because Jessica had been alone, and maybe a bit lonely? That made me feel less jealous of how well they had hit it off.

"Maybe. She seemed glad to see me." I glanced at her. "I would have asked you but I wasn't sure what was up. Besides, I thought you'd be busy with Jessica."

Meagan blushed.

Lightning, interestingly, did not strike me dead.

Even though I'd lied to Meagan again. She could *not* have come to meet Isabelle, since we'd been talking about dragon business.

It was unnatural for me to get away with bad behavior. Even marginally naughty behavior.

Unless . . .

Was I moving into another upgrade zone for my Wyvern powers? Had the eclipse earlier this month had some effect after all? It seemed to be bringing me a decent string of luck—Meagan seemed willing to be my friend again and Isabelle was going to take us to Jared's concert.

"You didn't have lunch with us today," Meagan pointed out.

"No. I had to do the English homework I'd forgotten."

It was true, but Meagan wasn't buying it.

"Why don't you like Jessica?" she asked as if I was just making an excuse. "You hardly know her."

I shrugged. "She hasn't made much effort to get to know me, either. And it just feels like she's hiding something."

"Well, she is." Meagan smiled at my surprise. "Jessica's not her real name. She just hates her name."

I was intrigued. "Which is?"

"Josephina Maria." Meagan frowned. "Her parents came from Argentina. She's an only child and they're superambitious for her. They moved here for her and left everybody they knew. Her dad's a doctor, but he's driving a taxi because he has to get recertified to practice here. They really, really want her to get into an Ivy League college."

"Oh." No pressure on Jessica, then. I felt a twinge of sympathy for her.

Meagan gave me a look. "I thought you might have a lot in common with her. Your parents push you pretty hard."

I had to think about that. Maybe there was more to Jessica than met the eye. "Okay, I was wrong. Maybe we should have lunch together Monday. I'll get my homework done this time. Really."

"My mom won't let you forget it."

"Wait. I have a better idea. Maybe we should all go shopping together."

Meagan smiled, obviously happy with the idea; then her face fell. "Jessica's parents won't let her. She has to study all day every Saturday."

I did like the idea of being just with Meagan. "Will you shop with me?"

"Absolutely. Let's go to those vintage shops you like." We planned a bit; then Meagan gave me a nudge. "I'd like to meet Isabelle sometime, too. Doesn't she read tarot cards?"

"She does. She had them today."

She bit her lip and sighed.

I seized the moment. "She wants to go to this concert tomorrow night. This guy we know is in a band and they have a gig downtown."

"What guy?"

"He's a cousin of Nick's. . . ."

"The son of your parents' friends in Minneapolis," Meagan concluded, nodding as she remembered. "The one you got stuck hanging out with during spring break."

I felt a twinge of conscience then. I'd lied to Meagan in the spring about Nick being so hot, just so she wouldn't feel bad.

"Isabelle said you could come, too, but that we need to ask your parents."

"To a concert?" Meagan's face lit. "My dad will be good with that." I remembered a bit late that Meagan's dad is a concert pianist. That's why she takes piano classes. "Would your mom have let you go?"

In the absence of information, I went with optimism. If no one else was going to insist on my being grounded, I wasn't going to argue. "Sure. She likes Isabelle and is always saying how responsible she is." I smiled. "It's my birthday present from Isabelle."

"Then we'll ask." Meagan looked so determined that I had a feeling her parents had no chance. "And, hey, we have to figure out who the dragon guy is. Jessica thinks it's Derek."

"Derek?"

Meagan laughed at my reaction. "Don't you think he's kind of mysterious? He could have a secret like that. Jessica thinks his eyes are creepy."

"They are a really light blue. . . ."

"I knew you'd noticed!" She started to sing. "*Derek and Zoë, sitting in a tree . . .*"

"What are you talking about?"

"Oh, come on. He watches you as much as you watch Trevor. If you weren't always looking for Trevor, you would have noticed." Meagan made a kissing sound and I swatted her playfully.

"It's not Trevor who interests me."

"Who then? You're blushing like crazy."

"You'll see. Tomorrow night." And that was all I'd tell her.

Until I knew how Jared would respond to seeing me there.

MEAGAN'S MOM DID REMEMBER THAT I was supposed to be grounded and was all for saying no to the concert plan. Meagan's dad argued in favor of musical education and was ready to let us go. Meagan insisted that it wasn't fair to punish me for my parents' having problems. I tried to just eat my dinner and look like a good girl while Meagan's parents discussed it.

So, my dad had said I was grounded but not why. Of course, it would have been a breach of the Covenant to explain the details.

I had to like that the Covenant cut both ways.

As a complete bonus, my mom did call me on Saturday morning, just like she'd promised. She didn't have a whole lot to say, except that she was staying at my aunt's and checking that I had the number. She didn't mention my dad and neither did I. It was a short call, but made me feel less like everything was falling apart.

The Falling Tower. Hmm.

Meagan's parents let us go shopping on Saturday, which I took as a good sign. They were still waffling about the concert at dinner on Saturday night. I got the impression that they liked to debate issues endlessly, but didn't intervene.

I just hoped.

In the end, it was Isabelle who made the sale. She turned up looking even more perfect than usual. Her hair was pulled back into a ponytail and she wore a teal tweed jacket with her jeans. She was wearing glasses, even though I'd never seen her with glasses before.

Meagan's parents were sold with one look. How could it be bad for us to accompany such a respectable young adult anywhere?

The sucker punch was Isabelle's apparent delight that Meagan's mom is a visioning counselor. Isabelle launched into this discussion of a lab experiment in one of her university courses, which was investigating the ability of people to psychically create their own realities.

Meagan's mom was completely entranced.

Who says that only dragons can beguile humans? Some humans do pretty well at enchanting each other.

We were out the door and running for the bus in record time.

Heading toward Jared.

My stomach turned somersaults all the way. What if he didn't talk to me? What if he *did* talk to me? What if he kissed me again? I didn't know what to expect and just couldn't stand it.

"What kind of concert is it?" Meagan huffed after we'd piled onto the bus. "Classical? Chamber music?"

Isabelle laughed as she shoved her glasses into her purse. She pulled out a little case and balanced it on her lap, popping in her contacts as the bus rocked down the street. Meagan watched with awe, even though her own glasses were fogged. Isabelle shook out her hair, doing that model thing again. Meagan's eyes went round. "A rock concert, of course."

"You didn't tell my parents that."

Isabelle smiled. "I know. Sometimes we fairy godmothers have to manage information."

Meagan looked between the two of us in confusion. "What do you mean?"

Isabelle leaned close to whisper. "Zoë has a crush on this guy who sings in the band. They're playing a concert in town tonight, so I decided to take her."

"So we can be pathetic needy fangirls," I added.

"An early birthday present," Isabelle said. She nudged Meagan. "And I thought she should bring a friend."

Meagan glanced my way.

"And only my best friend would do," I added.

"Moral support," Isabelle concluded.

Meagan teared up and had to clean her glasses. I hugged her and we had a warm fuzzy moment. It's so easy to get along when you don't have to lie to your friends.

Then Meagan snapped her fingers. "Wait a minute. Is this the guy whose music you're always listening to on your messenger?" She gasped and grabbed my arm when I nodded. "The guy who *kissed* you on spring break? Is *that* the guy you're crazy for?"

I blushed from head to toe, which they both enjoyed far more than I did.

"Now I know why you had to get that new bra," Meagan teased, and my face got even hotter.

"And that purple shirt," Isabelle added. "Where'd you get a shirt that cool?"

"I think you gave it to me," I admitted and she laughed.

She leaned against Meagan. "I have such good taste, don't I?"

"It looks great on Zoë," Meagan agreed. "Makes her look both slim and curvy."

"He won't be able to resist her," Isabelle said.

I was so mortified that I wanted to sink into the bus floor. Given the slush and muck on it, that was saying something.

They laughed together at me, enjoying my discomfort, and then Meagan demanded that I do her eyeliner for her. She likes the way I do mine. More importantly, she can't apply eye makeup with her glasses on, and can't see to apply it without them. She took off her glasses and I took advantage of a red light. Two flicks of the wrist and it was perfect.

"You should get contacts," Isabelle said. "You have such great eyes."

"And a mouthful of steel." Meagan did her shark smile.

"Gives the rest of us a chance," I said and she smiled for real.

She put her glasses back on, then borrowed Isabelle's mirror to check out the eyeliner. "I am so getting contacts as soon as my braces come off. I don't care what my mom says. I'll figure out a way to buy them myself." She then demanded an earbud to listen to Jared's music. "What's your favorite song?"

" 'Snow Goddess.' Here." I gave her one and put the other in my ear. I did not present my theory that this song was about me, even though it had appeared for download on the band's site only after Jared and I had met—and we had met in an unseasonable snowstorm.

Kind of like the one that was starting now.

Hmm.

More importantly, Meagan and I were both listening to the same song at the same time as the bus rocked toward downtown.

Like we were best friends again.

It was sweet.

KNIGHTSHADE, THE CLUB, looked smaller than I'd expected. In fact, it looked kind of like a restaurant, but with dark drapes over the windows and lots of people standing outside.

There was a steady thud of bass carrying through the open door past the bouncer, and there was a line forming along the sidewalk. I think the city's entire allocation of black leather, shiny zippers, and facial studs had been claimed by the people who were already waiting there.

Never mind the tattoos. The bouncer was wearing only a tight black T-shirt despite the weather, the better to show off his muscles and the seriously fabulous koi tattoo that wound down his left arm. One look and I had a major case of tattoo lust.

My fascination with tattoos had started the previous spring when, yes, I'd seen the end of one on the back of Jared's left hand. It had protruded from the cuff of his leather jacket, although I hadn't actually seen all of it.

I'd seen the tip of a newt's nose and one little webbed foot.

I liked it a lot. And I'd done a ton of research since—easier than it would be for most people, because the partner of one of the *Pyr* is a tattoo artist. I'd nearly driven Rox crazy with my questions about tattoos and tattoo art, about design constraints and hygiene and everything else tattoo-related. I was sure that one of my own dragons would make a perfect tattoo.

His head would come over my left shoulder, eyes looking front, one wing spreading across my shoulder blades, the other down my arm, and his tail twirling around my upper arm to the elbow.

This was the one I wanted for my birthday.

Rox had endorsed the design—and she should know, being a fab tattoo artist herself—but she refused to put it on my skin. Being sixteen meant needing parental approval, and my mom wasn't giving it. Rox knew my mom, so there was no way around it. I didn't have the balls to go to another tattoo artist, because I *had* done my research.

But I had the drawing safely saved on my messenger, ready for the day I could have it transferred to my skin.

Like Meagan and her contacts, I was going to find a way to make it happen.

Somehow.

The bouncer was huge and he was casting a fierce eye over the line. He looked inclined to be picky. I was pretty sure he wouldn't let Meagan and me in, we being minors and all, despite there being no alcohol in the place. He would turn us away just because we wouldn't look good enough for the crowd he was building to suit himself.

But Isabelle turned a bright smile on him and he visibly melted. That was before she opened her mouth and her accent turned him to a puddle of acquiescence. Then she stretched up and whispered in the guy's ear. I thought he would fall to his knees in delight.

Maybe swoon.

"Wow," Meagan murmured and pushed up her glasses. I could almost sense her taking notes.

"I so want to be Isabelle when I grow up," I said under my breath.

"Absolutely," Meagan agreed.

Isabelle turned then, smiled and beckoned to us. The bouncer unclipped the red velvet rope that held the line at bay and gestured us in. Those in the line—most of whom were older, better-dressed, more stylish, and better-looking than me—watched hungrily.

"How'd you do that?" I whispered to Isabelle.

"I said we knew the band. It's true."

Both of us were crowding behind Isabelle, trying to look cool and blowing it. "We know Jared," I pointed out.

Isabelle laughed. "I've read the album notes, and done a little research. Fairy godmothers need to do their prep. We'll meet the others now."

It was dark and smoky inside. Everything was painted either black or deep purple, except the floor, which was black-and-white checkerboard. There was no furniture, just people standing in clusters.

Jared had chosen this place so I could come to hear him play—or to see him. Either way. I shivered with anticipation.

Isabelle scanned the dark interior, then pointed to the back, where the kitchen should have been. Instead there was a stage and a glittering curtain. "Backstage would be there."

She headed off at a purposeful clip, cutting her way through the crowd easily. Meagan followed, mimicking her new idol. I considered the irony of my having worried about Jared being my dragon stalker, particularly when I appeared to be stalking him, then pushed that thought out of my mind.

I'd keep our conversation focused and friendly. I needed a reference guide, and he had the closest thing to one.

This was about the book.

After all, if he'd wanted to see me before this, he would have made it happen. My dad and Isabelle were right about that. Jared was a get-stuff-done kind of a guy.

I decided to try for cool, elusive, and mysterious. I'd never manage indifferent, but this was a step in the right direction. Besides, mysterious seemed like the right attitude for a Wyvern, and I knew he was a dragon fan.

That plan went right out the proverbial window as soon as I saw him. He was wearing jeans and a T-shirt so tight that it could have been painted on. Every muscle was delineated, and he had a bunch of them. He was bent over his guitar, listening as he tuned it, completely lost in his task. He looked tons older than me, than all the guys at school, and I heard my dad's words all over again.

Like a warning.

One that I had no interest in heeding.

It's impossible to be cool, elusive, or even mysterious when your heart is racing. Just so you know.

"Wow," Meagan murmured. "Forget Derek."

And I had to agree.

I could see the entire tattoo on Jared's left forearm, too. It was a good one. Rox would have admired it.

It was a newt or a salamander, head on the back of his wrist and tail wound around his arm right above the elbow. It was looking up, as if surprised at its newty business. It had a red forked tongue that stretched down to his middle finger, which I knew hadn't been part of it before. The newt seemed to move as he plucked the strings of the guitar, as if it were possessed of a life beyond ink and skin.

Was it a Wyvern salamander? I dared to hope.

I had just enough time to realize I had no smooth intro before Jared suddenly glanced up. His eyes lit—those eyes are greener than any deity should allow—and he smiled at me.

My heart stopped.

Then galloped.

I was a goner, and we were still twenty feet apart.

Chapter 5

Jared's gaze flicked to Meagan and back to me, and I sensed that he was choosing his words. "Zoë! Awesome. And Isabelle, too."

Isabelle stepped toward him, perky as only she can be, and gave him kisses on each cheek.

"So Euro," Meagan sighed, her desire to be Isabelle visibly doubling again.

I could relate to that.

I wasn't entirely sure what to do, and couldn't bring myself to do the cheek kiss as casually as Isabelle. I stuck out my hand. "Hi."

Jared took my hand, tugging me closer to kiss my cheek. "Glad you're here, dragon girl," he murmured when his lips were right against my ear. His words were so quiet that only I could have heard them and they gave me palpitations.

"This is my friend Meagan," I said and she blushed.

"Nice to meet you," Jared said with an easy smile.

I was a mess. He still had my hand and I was still standing close to him. I could hear his pulse, courtesy of my sharp hearing, and it had accelerated.

Like he was glad to see me.

And mine was doing that spooky dragon thing of matching its pace to his. Believe me when I tell you that's a dizzying sensation. I managed to stand there, blushing like crazy, but clever conversation was completely out of the current range of my abilities.

Fortunately, Meagan was not impaired in that regard.

"I've h-h-heard some of your band's music," she said. "Do you write your own s-s-songs?"

Jared indicated a tall woman with orange hair and yellow leather pants. "Angie usually writes the ones she sings and I write the ones I do. A couple of our songs are collaborations between us."

Meagan nodded and bit her lip, thinking. "So, you're the one who l-l-likes minor keys so much."

Jared looked at her then, really looked at her. I knew he was surprised. "Yeah. They're kind of ethereal." He smiled that crooked smile, the one that drove me crazy, and his gaze flicked to me. He winked and the bottom fell out of my world for a moment. I held on to his hand a bit more tightly. "I like a bit of mystery, maybe a dreamy quality."

I said nothing, trying to maintain my mysterious air.

Actually, I was trying to find some equilibrium again. Just being in Jared's vicinity made it difficult to remember to breathe.

Meagan nodded with excitement, then pushed her glasses up her nose. "I like the way you transitioned from the minor key for the chorus in 'Snow Goddess.'" She wasn't stammering anymore, and I liked that Jared made her feel comfortable.

They talked about music and keys and timing for a couple of minutes, the two of them clearly finding some common ground.

It might as well have been Greek to me. I had no idea what they were talking about. I just liked the song.

Isabelle, meanwhile, went to talk to the drummer, a tall skinny guy with dreadlocks who had been openly checking her out.

"Sorry!" Meagan said abruptly, glancing at me and blushing again. "It's just really interesting to talk to someone about the structure of music."

"You don't have to apologize," I said and bumped her arm. She smiled again. "Meagan plays piano," I told Jared, then glanced at her. "But I didn't know you were so into composition."

"It's math. I love math." She smiled sunnily, then elbowed me in a very unsubtle way. "Hey, I'm going to talk to Isabelle and the drummer."

"Rick," Jared said.

"He has those new syntho drums, doesn't he?" Meagan's eyes were shining and she was nearly salivating at the prospect of checking out new gadgets.

Jared nodded. "And the traditional percussion, too. He says the syntho drums don't replicate all of the sounds."

"Oh, but they should," Meagan said, frowning as she pushed her glasses up again. "The sine waves were perfectly matched by the engineers behind the project. It was a really interesting initiative and—" She glanced between us, flushed and smiled again, then excused herself.

"She's nice," Jared said, watching Meagan.

"My best friend."

"Cute," he said, surprising me. I thought I was the only one who saw beyond Meagan's glasses and braces. He winked at me, appreciation in his gaze as he glanced over me.

Okay, I was having heart failure again.

I tried to look mysterious and was pretty sure I failed. Instead, I watched Meagan.

It was better than losing myself in the green of Jared's eyes.

Rick seemed a bit condescending when Meagan first spoke to him, as if he was entertaining a fangirl, but within seconds, Meagan's technical questions brought out his enthusiasm. He started to show her the syntho drums and tapped out a couple of beats so she could compare the sound. She was riveted.

"They'll be buddies before the night is through," Jared said with a smile. "Unless Rick talks her ear off about the specs."

"Meagan will love it."

He slanted a long look at me, one that was simmering hot and ten thousand shades of green. His voice dropped low, to that pitch that makes me shiver. "I missed you, dragon girl."

My knees went weak right on cue. I couldn't even look at him.

And maybe because I wasn't looking at him, I thought more clearly. If he'd missed me, then why hadn't I heard from him? His words simultaneously made me feel special and fed my own doubts.

"Funny I never heard from you, then," I said, trying to keep my tone light.

It didn't work. I sounded desperate.

He gave me a steady look, like a warning. "I don't answer to anyone."

That didn't sound promising. I pulled my hand out of his and folded my arms across my chest, needing to keep a bit of distance until I had things straight. "You left before we could talk last spring."

"Places to go," he said, turning his attention to his guitar as if he didn't care that I'd pulled my hand away. He was doing it again, leading me on, then becoming evasive.

Because I'd expected some contact from him?

Well, that wasn't unreasonable, was it? My frustration grew—because I knew I hadn't expected much, because I wanted him to be everything wonderful I believed him to be, and because I really really really didn't want my dad to be right.

I needed to know for sure, no matter how much reality bit. "And you blew me off when I sent you that message in the summer."

"No, I told you the truth."

This wasn't going at all as I'd hoped. I'd secretly dreamed of a happy reunion—or at least another kiss. Right now, his guitar seemed to be more interesting than me.

I hugged myself a little tighter. "I owe you a ride. I thought that was what you wanted." Great. Now I sounded hurt.

Well, I was, but still.

Maybe that was why he didn't answer me, just kept tuning the guitar.

Okay, I'm not stupid. "Have a good show," I said and started to turn away.

Jared froze in the act of plucking a chord, then laid his hand flat across the strings. I glanced back at him, ever (pathetically) hopeful. He put the guitar down, then looked up at me, the intensity of his expression taking my breath away "Okay. Here's the deal. I have had it explained to me by a certain individual that I need to stay in my place." He arched a brow, inviting me to figure out what he meant.

"What place?"

"Away. From you."

"Who?"

His gaze flickered and I knew. There was only one person whose advice he took.

"Donovan," I guessed and Jared frowned. Donovan was Nick's dad, Jared's uncle, and the *Pyr* who had sold Jared that vintage Ducati motorcycle. "But why?"

"Well, he has a good point." Jared folded his arms across his chest but leaned closer to me. Our arms brushed against each other as his gaze bored into mine. My mouth went dry and my heart did a cartwheel or two. My doubts faded big-time. "You're not on the same timeline as I am, Zoë."

It was disgusting that he would make the same argument as my dad.

"A couple of years doesn't make that much difference," I protested. "I mean, it's a lot now, but eventually . . ."

"And that's just the thing." His voice dropped impossibly lower, so I was feeling it as much as I was hearing it. "You're going to live for centuries, Zoë, maybe even more than that. It's part of the dragon plan. Me, I'm in for maybe eighty years."

"But . . ."

He reached out and touched my cheek with one fingertip. I quivered, the touch of his finger making me feel hot and unsettled. "The thing is, it doesn't matter how fascinated I am by you or how good I think it could be between us. I've read the book." He slid that fingertip down to my chin. My knees were dissolving. I could barely listen to what he was saying, especially with my heart pounding so loud. "You're going to have a firestorm with some guy, and it's going to be your duty to your kind to follow the heat of that firestorm."

I parted my lips, but he touched his fingertip to them. Oh. Was there ever a better way to silence anyone? I could feel the callus on one side from him playing guitar. He watched his finger's progress, his gaze heating exactly the way my blood did.

I wanted to protest. I wanted to argue with him, to defend the cause of true love and the power of choice, but I sensed that he was right.

Because the firestorms I'd witnessed had been overwhelmingly powerful forces, a tide of heat and desire that shorted the mental circuits of a *Pyr.* The firestorm heated to greater intensity the longer it was denied, and never sputtered until it was satisfied. None of the dragon dudes I knew had managed to step away, even if they had been dead set against satisfying the firestorm.

I didn't know what I could say that wouldn't be untrue or at best unreasonably optimistic. My chest was tight.

There was no air left in that club.

We stood there, his gaze boring into mine and my heart leaping all over my chest, and then he looked away, his expression grim. And when he did, something changed. The connection between us was severed, cut as cleanly as if it had never been. Or a door was closed. His interest in me was nonexistent.

I think he practically forgot I was standing there.

I felt forty-five thousand kinds of stupid. Even if I really wanted to have something with Jared, that wasn't enough to ensure that he wanted something with me.

If he had really been interested, he would have contacted me. He wouldn't have been able to *not* contact me. He wouldn't have been able to leave me standing here, wanting something—anything—from him.

Maybe it was time I stopped liking guys who didn't like me.

"Too bad I wasted a birthday present," I said, turning away. There was no reason to prolong my humiliation. "See you around."

"Your birthday? When's that?" he asked, to my surprise.

I glanced back, wary. "Soon." I sighed. "I only wanted three things."

His eyes glinted. "What else?"

That he'd guessed seeing him was one was mortifying, but I answered him anyway. "A grudge match with Kohana."

"Forget it." His protective determination made me smile. I was the dragon, after all.

And what difference did it make to him anyway?

"What else?" he demanded.

"A tattoo."

His surprise was clear. "No way."

"A dragon, here." I gestured to my left shoulder, my tone nearly daring him to question me. "On my back and upper arm. Watching out for me."

"Got an artist in mind?"

"Me. I drew it. I love it."

He watched me carefully. "But . . . ?"

"My mom says no ink before I'm legal."

He smiled, as if he had a secret, and turned back to his guitar. You can believe I wanted to know what he was thinking. You can believe I knew he wouldn't share.

I'd had enough. I turned away again. "Have a good show," I said, but my heart wasn't in it. I felt the weight of his gaze on my back, and my feet dragged. I like to think Jared might have called me back—once a relentless optimist, always one—but Angie in the tight pants clapped her hands abruptly.

"Let's get it together, people!" she said as she strode past. "We need to put some money in the jar."

Jared tugged the guitar strap over his shoulders. He looked even more like a renegade with that electric guitar slung low over his hips than he did riding his Ducati. He saw me looking and after a long moment, he blew me a kiss. My heart leapt, which just made me feel even more stupid.

Then he was gone, striding to the stage.

I needed some air.

THE FIRST CHORDS OF "Snow Goddess" rang out as I got to the door of the club. It was an anthem, a love song, a call to fight for justice and love. It made my blood simmer and my heart thump.

Just like Jared did. With the touch of one fingertip, he'd left me jangled, my lips burning. I wondered whether he was confusing me on purpose.

How could he blow me off, then play that song? He could read people's thoughts. He knew what I was thinking. He knew what I wanted.

And he'd deliberately done the opposite.

I made the mistake of glancing toward the stage. Then I

couldn't take my eyes off him as he played and sang. He was really enjoying himself, totally into it, and I understood that making music was what he'd been born to do. I listened to him, savoring how his voice seemed to resonate in the deepest part of my heart. I felt the power of his song enthrall the audience.

It certainly enchanted me.

I'd seen Mage spells before and I'd known that the Mages had wanted to recruit Jared once upon a time. I'd assumed it was because of some raw talent he had, and on this night I saw that it was true.

I shoved my hands into my pockets and found the ring. I pulled it out, saw that it was twinkling again, and on impulse, shoved it onto my finger. It was mine now. Why shouldn't I wear it? To tell the truth, I wasn't in the mood to think about repercussions from anything.

Suddenly, the scene before me changed. I could see the vibrations of Jared's songs spiral into the air. They weren't orange and binding like Mage spells. They weren't yellow bolts of lightning like the weapons Kohana and the Thunderbirds threw.

They were spirals, bouncing and frolicking through the air. Plus there were little explosions in between the dancing spirals, like sunbursts. They were all different colors of light, as joyous as a rainbow. They reminded me of confetti and streamers, the kind that people throw from the deck of a ship in old movies as the ship pulls out from the dock.

As the spell light emanated from Jared's throat and his guitar, it was cast over the crowd. It infected the mood in the club. Instead of being pressed together to listen, or just marking the beat, people started to dance. The pulse of the music slipped into our veins and took us all to the same rocking place. Most people weren't drunk. We were just lost in the joy of the music.

It was wonderful.

I wondered whether that was how he mixed me up and turned

me inside out. I wondered whether he was casting a spell on me. I couldn't see that any of his spells targeted me, though. They were dancing around the crowd, cajoling people into dancing along. The crowd swayed, a few people sang, and the mood became festive.

Because of Jared's spell.

At that point I remembered I'd intended to ask him about the book.

A bit late.

Had he steered the conversation deliberately, setting me off balance so I didn't ask for the book? I didn't want to think about it, but once I had the thought, it stuck. Was Jared manipulating me?

I needed to think, and do it away from Jared's spell. I told Meagan I'd be back, and waited for her nod. I strode across the club, shoved the door open, and stepped into the night.

The thing was, I had a hard time believing that anything anybody said to Jared would stop him from doing whatever he wanted to do. He said he didn't answer to anybody. Even Donovan couldn't have that power over him. Donovan's argument was just a convenient excuse for blowing me off.

But why? What else didn't I know?

IN THE END, I can only blame my complete fixation on the problem of Jared for the fact that I missed the obvious. I should have been paying attention. I should have been using the keen *Pyr* senses I'd been born with instead of trying to figure out Jared Madison.

That's how Kohana surprised me. I wasn't looking for trouble, and so it—or he—found me.

Maybe he even guessed that I would be under Jared's spell.

Maybe he was counting on it.

I was surprised when I stepped outside the club. The cold air was bracing, but I'd expected that. What I hadn't anticipated was that there would be no one on the street.

I mean, not one living soul.

It was really cold, the sky inky black and the windows on every side dark. The only motion was a fistful of dry leaves blowing down the gutter. The pulse of music behind me sounded as if it was coming from another world.

It had been snowing when we arrived, but there was no snow now. Where had it gone?

I looked harder. I could have stepped into a cemetery, or a dead zone, which made no sense. It wasn't that late, and although the club wasn't in a fabulous area of town, there had been some other businesses in the vicinity.

Now every shop window was boarded up. Not as if businesses were closed for the night—as if they were closed for the duration.

Abandoned.

But we'd been in the club for only an hour.

The hair stood up on the back of my neck. What was going on? I looked down at my hand and guessed.

I tugged the ring off and the street looked as I had expected it to. Quiet, but not deserted. Pretty much as it had been when we'd arrived. Snow falling thickly all around. I couldn't see the spells from Jared, but I could hear the music.

I shoved the ring over my knuckle again. Instantly, the desolate scene appeared.

This was way better than the eye game.

But it must be happening for a reason.

I was reassured to see the happy confetti of sound generated by Jared traveling out into the night. It was brilliant against the shadows.

But I also noticed now that orange spears of light were emerging. I recognized them as Mage binding spells. They were spilling out of sewers and manholes, from basement windows and vents, spreading into the night like a net. There were zillions of them, more with every passing second, and I had the sense that they were breeding. They trussed up the confetti spells and tossed them into the gutter. They would imprison anyone trapped within them. I'd watched them do that in the spring.

But now they were coming for me.

Suddenly, a raven cried far overhead. At least I thought it was a raven until I saw Kohana leap from the roof of the building across the street and spread his arms wide. I knew it couldn't be anyone else but him. My *Pyr* sense of smell gave me that clue.

He shifted shape in midair, becoming a dark Thunderbird. I'd seen him in this form before and I knew he was fast. He gave a cry as he targeted me, his claws outspread and his eyes gleaming.

"I knew you would come to him," Kohana cried. "I knew when I heard his music that you'd be here."

It wasn't a crazy assumption. Kohana had seen us together at boot camp.

I pivoted and tugged on the door of the club, but it had locked.

I looked up and saw Kohana closing in fast. He didn't want to chat. I pulled at the door again in desperation, then pounded on it. The music ensured that no one heard me.

I was tempted to defy my dad's edict, but he'd know I shifted and then he'd know where I was, and then there would be hell to pay on a number of levels. Exile wasn't a tempting possibility for my future. There was nowhere to run and nowhere to hide, so I made a quick decision.

I closed my eyes, summoned every scrap of Wyvern within me, and wished with all my heart to be someplace else.

Someplace safe.

I was immediately engulfed in the blue shimmer I knew so well, its light skimming over my skin like an electrical tide. I closed my eyes tightly against its brilliance just as I heard Kohana shout.

He didn't sound happy, which I took as a good sign.

IT WAS DARK. Fuzzy. A bit stuffy.

I could hear the music, but it was muffled. I was hyperventilating but not shredded.

I'd take good news as it came.

I smelled a chocolate bar and felt a lipstick under one foot. The scent of a familiar perfume gave me an idea of where I was, but it wasn't until I felt the case for her contacts that I knew my precise location.

In Isabelle's purse.

Which meant that I'd changed to salamander form en route.

This spontaneous manifestation stuff still had a whiff of the random about it. When I forgot to concentrate or was tired, odd things happened. I mostly went where I wanted and became what I wanted to be, but every once in a while, stuff happened.

Like ending up in salamander form in Isabelle's purse.

Really, if I was going to be in salamander form anywhere, I would have voted for being in Jared's pocket. Although, given that he was onstage and being watched by several hundred people, that probably wouldn't have been very discreet.

"Where did Zoë go?" Isabelle shouted at Meagan.

"She said she'd be back in a minute. I thought she'd gone to the bathroom."

Isabelle swore with an earthiness that made me blink. It does sound better with her accent, but I recognized that she was worried about me.

Which meant I had to get out of her purse, and do it without freaking anybody out.

There was really only one place to go.

I gnawed on her chocolate bar, which was a British Mars bar. They are so much better than anything we get here that I can hardly believe it. I took a beat to deeply appreciate Isabelle's tendency to carry such things, then summoned the shimmer again.

It was both easier and harder the second time. The shimmer tends to be more biddable the more I call it, but the shift does kick my butt. Which is a long way of saying that I manifested off balance in human form, then fell into a whole bunch of gear backstage and created an avalanche.

It must have made quite a noise, because when I opened my eyes, Rick and Angie were glaring at me and the music had stopped. Behind the band, I could see members of the audience who'd followed them. Jared winked and offered me his hand, and I was glad to accept his help. Isabelle was behind them, looking both exasperated and relieved. Meagan was swiveling her head between the club and the backstage area, clearly trying to calculate how I had managed to get backstage without her seeing me.

"Do us a favor, Jared," Angie said, her tone impatient. "Keep your girls away from the gear. The insurance doesn't cover whatever they break."

"I'll take care of it," Jared said, his hand tightening over mine for a second. It felt good to have someone know that I wasn't just being a pain, that I hadn't had a lot of choice. And how sad was it that this teeny bit of attention from him fed my relentless optimism all over again?

The thing was that once again, I had the fleeting—and tempting—sense that Jared and I could make a good team.

Then I was on my feet and Jared gave my fingers a last squeeze, then was gone.

As if he barely knew me.

Business as usual. This was a guy who could seriously deal in mixed messages. I wasn't sure what to think and I was starting to believe he wanted it that way.

"I hope she's worth it," Angie muttered as they walked back to the stage. "We'd better do another short set, to keep the crowd happy."

Isabelle took one look at me and saw a whole lot more than

I probably should have let her see. "Let's head home," she said, all bustling responsibility. "It's getting a bit late and I don't want Meagan's mom to be worried."

She looked pretty concerned herself, her gaze lingering on me, but I was too bagged to care. When the three of us stepped out into the night, the street looked just as it should, and there was no sign of Kohana. I couldn't see those Mage spells coming out of the sewer grates, either, not even with my ring on.

They must have spun the spells to coincide with Jared's music. Were there Mages in the crowd all night? Were they using him? I wanted to go back and talk to him, maybe find out what he knew—relentless optimism is tough to beat down—but Isabelle hooked her hand through my arm and tugged me toward the L.

I did, though, have time to confirm that the door didn't even lock behind us. Weird. Why had it been locked when I was alone outside? Had that been because of a spell? Spun by who? Jared? The Mages? Or Kohana?

Isabelle frowned at me. Her eyes narrowed and then she reached into her purse. She was visibly surprised that the Mars bar had been opened and part of it eaten.

It wasn't as if she had mice in her purse.

Just an uninvited salamander once in a while.

I smiled, shrugged, and saw her understand.

She slipped her other hand through the crook of Meagan's arm. "So, what did you think?" she asked brightly, handing the chocolate bar surreptitiously to me as she set off for the main street at a brisk pace. The snow was up to our ankles and Meagan kicked some happily as we walked down the street.

Meagan was excited. She talked about the music and the band and Jared, and more about musical composition again, giving me plenty of time to make the chocolate disappear. No chance of her noticing that I was off my game. I practically inhaled the chocolate bar, throwing it back as fast as a hungry dog.

It was exactly what I needed to feel human again.

Even if I did glance back as we turned the corner, seeking the silhouette of a guy or a bird on a roof.

I didn't see Kohana.

But that didn't mean he wasn't there.

Chapter 6

What is it about Mages? I had to wonder about the pervasiveness of their spells. I had them on the brain after the events of the evening, but the weird thing was that Meagan did, too.

Was it a coincidence that she talked about Trevor Wilson?

Or was something more sinister at work?

I was crashed on the twin bed in her room and the lights were out. It was late and we should have been asleep, but Meagan was still wound up after the concert. I was fine with her chatting, just kind of dozing as she talked about the music and the band and the syntho drums and, wow, that Jared.

I pretty much agreed with the wow part.

I kept thinking about the protective flash of his eyes when I'd told him about wanting a grudge match with Kohana and the wild roller-coaster feeling of our hearts matching their pace. Never mind Kohana's assertion that he knew I'd be with Jared.

Was Jared trying to protect me by staying away from me?

You know I liked that idea.

A lot.

When Meagan took a deep breath, I suspected she was going to say something I wouldn't like, but she still surprised me. "I'll bet Trevor knows Jared's music."

"What?" I was wide-awake at the mention of the apprentice Mage's name. "Why would you think that?"

"Because he's so into music. Haven't you seen how he plays the sax? He closes his eyes and moves with the music. Just like Jared with his guitar. Trevor told me he's always in trouble in marching band for losing his place in line."

I rolled over to look at her. Even in the shadows, I could see her eyes shining. In fact, she was nearly radiating. "He told you that? When?"

"Well, he's failing trig again. I'm still tutoring him." She acted as if it was no big deal, but now she was blushing. Then she grimaced. "I really don't understand why he doesn't see the link between music and math. I've been studying it a lot, because I thought it might help him."

Meagan—good, sweet, generous Meagan—was trying to help a guy who was part of a team bent on world domination. And I couldn't think of any good way to warn her away from him. "Doesn't sound like he appreciates your help," I said, keeping my tone neutral.

She sighed. "No. He invited you to his party, not me."

"I'm not going."

"He asked you out last spring, too. Is it really true that nothing happened?"

"Nothing happened. I didn't go." I took a breath. "I'm not going on Halloween, either."

"You don't have to do that for me."

"I don't like him."

"Really?" She rolled over to face me. "He's so hot, Zoë. And so talented. He's not like the other guys whose parents have tons of money. You can tell by the way he plays the sax. He's *sensitive*."

I did not snort.

"How can you not like him? Is it because of Jared?"

"No. I didn't like him before. Maybe because he was dating Suzanne." I looked at her. "I mean, that says something, don't you think?"

"Lots of guys just see that she's pretty."

"On the outside."

She mused on that. "But she's probably different to Trevor."

"Maybe I don't like him because he's not very nice to you."

"What do you mean?"

"He should have asked you to his party, especially if you're tutoring him that much."

There was a beat of silence and I could see her blinking at the ceiling. When she spoke, her voice was very soft. "Do you think he thinks I'm just useful?"

"I think he's just not a very nice person," I said, my tone fierce. "You deserve better."

She turned to study me, probably noticing my tone. "You really don't like him, do you? All he did was ask you to his party."

That wasn't all Trevor had done, but I couldn't tell her the truth. That was getting old fast. "I can't explain it," I said, which was pretty much true. "He just gives me the creeps."

"Huh." Meagan turned her back again. I could practically hear her thinking. "You usually have really good instincts about people. I'd like to just know what he's thinking, though."

"I'm not sure my instincts are good about Jared," I admitted. I could do it only because it was dark and I was tired and we were alone.

"He is so hot, though," Meagan said with a sigh. A moment later she sighed again. "Guys are so hard to understand."

I almost laughed—our thoughts were so similar. "I know *exactly* what you mean."

I heard her fall asleep then, and listened to the sound of her breathing for a while. I could hear the snow falling outside, and was thinking about the similarities to the previous spring. Even though I was exhausted, I didn't really want to fall asleep.

I had a feeling Urd was waiting for me in dreamland.

I kept the ring on my finger, just in case.

URD APPARENTLY HAD OTHER SOCIAL obligations. She was a no-show.

I slept hard and dreamlessly. When I woke up, I could hear Meagan doing her piano practice. I smelled fresh coffee and heard her parents discussing the news in the kitchen. Nobody seemed to expect to see me soon, so I pulled out my messenger and did my tabulation of issues outstanding and associated clues.

I needed to figure out, in no particular order:

1. Why had Kohana attacked me this time?
2. How could I change his plan, whatever it was?
3. What was the Mages' scheme for Halloween?
4. What should—or could—I do about Jared?

Each and every item on this list was a pressing concern. Cumulatively, they were almost paralyzing.

I wasn't even sure where to begin.

The simple fact was that I needed backup. When you need support with dragon details, there's only one group of confidants who will do—other dragons.

As disappointed as Isabelle was with Nick, he was still my buddy. He was a hundred and seventy pounds of almost pure testosterone, and I could count on him.

I took my file *On Becoming the Wyvern* and sent it to Nick, along with a note that it should be opened if I died.

Kind of a last will and testament.

Or an insurance plan.

Then I sent it to Liam and to Garrett, along with the same message.

All three replied instantly, in characteristic fashion, their responses making my messenger chime three times in rapid succession.

Garrett, who had an affinity with fire, replied with quick heat:

WTF?

Nick, who had a connection to the earth, needed the facts:

What's going on, Z? What's happened?

And Liam, whose affinity was with water, showed his usual empathy:

Z! R U OK?

I loved these guys. I realized that all over again when I read their messages. In fact, it made me tear up a bit. They were the real dragons at my back. And I hadn't been keeping them in the loop, the way I should have done. So I typed a message and copied all of them:

We need to talk. Kohana showed up
last night and wanted to fight.

They understood the urgency of the situation immediately. We agreed to do a joint call in half an hour. Then Nick replied:

You've got to set it up, Z. Since you're the only one with the flash new messenger.

I smiled. It still bugged him that I'd won the big prize at boot camp in April, but I wasn't above rubbing it in. I typed back:

You're right. It'll probably take me half an hour to persuade it to link to your antiques.

Not true. It would link almost instantly, but I could just about hear them groan simultaneously.

I had time to dress, eat, and conjure an excuse.

I needed a walk, I decided. Meagan's folks would be good with that on a Sunday morning, and it would be the perfect way to score a little privacy.

THERE WAS A PARK OPPOSITE the Jamesons' town house, a pretty little park that everyone seemed to just walk past and admire. Ideal for my purposes. I swept a bench clear of snow with my gloved hand and had the guys connected in no time.

"First, tell us exactly what happened," Nick said.

I did. I didn't leave out one thing—not the invitation, not my mom and dad, not the incident with Suzanne, not my dad's reaction, not the attack by Kohana.

Oh, I did leave out the fact that Isabelle was disappointed that Nick had a girlfriend. I was saving that for later, when I could talk to Nick privately.

There was a beat of silence when I was done and then they all talked at once.

"What about this Halloween party?" Nick said. "Sounds like a trap to me."

"I'm not going."

"Why do you think Trevor invited you?" Garrett asked. "What could they have planned?"

"You really shouldn't have revealed yourself at school," Liam chided then. "Now that your dad has forbidden you to shift, you're not going to be able to protect yourself. What if you hadn't been able to get away last night?"

"At least I'm not exiled."

"Yet," Liam added.

"We need to know more about Kohana to understand *his* plan," Nick said.

"No, we need to know more about Mages and their plan," Garrett argued. "Then we'll be able to guess his, and we can make a plan ourselves."

I love a good riddle and I like solving these kinds of problems. So I took charge of making the list. On my messenger, I could do that as well as talk to them. "All right. We've got a bunch of questions here and not a lot of time. Let's divide it up, then talk after we each track down a chunk."

"Good plan," Nick said.

"We need to find out about the other shifters. Kohana said that there were only four kinds left, and that the Mages meant to eliminate all of us."

"Your dad made a treaty with the Mages," Liam said.

"But they'll never stand by it," Nick said. "Zoë's right in that." We'd been through our skepticism before.

"The thing is that we have to be careful not to be the ones to breach the terms of the treaty first," Liam said. There was some discussion, and Liam agreed to hunt down the exact text of the treaty.

"It's fair to assume that Kohana intends to betray the *Pyr* into being next," Garrett said with heat. "Why else would he go after Zoë?"

"But why would he play on their side?" Nick asked.

"He thought before that the Mages would cut the Thunderbirds some slack in exchange for turning in another kind of shifter," I said. "Maybe they've even promised to do that."

"But they won't keep that promise, either," Nick said.

I love how linear Nick is. It's right-and-wrong, either-or, black-or-white for him on every issue. He's a total straight arrow.

"You're right," Garrett agreed. "But the key to figuring out a way around that lies in understanding the Thunderbirds. What's their objective?"

"Survival?" Nick suggested.

"What else?" I asked.

"Maybe we're just the Mages' next target and that put us on the Thunderbirds' map," Liam said.

"No," I said. "I think it's about that treaty Kohana mentioned last time, the one he said we *Pyr* broke centuries ago. He thinks we're lower than pond scum."

"But what was the deal?" Nick asked. "How'd we break it?"

"And can we fix it?" Liam asked.

We didn't know.

"We only have Kohana's word that there ever was a big fight between our species and a deal," I noted. "But he keeps saying the *Unktehila* are oathbreakers who forget our own history."

"It's not much of a recommendation," Nick conceded. "If he's right."

"We can't exactly fix it if we don't know what the problem was," Liam said.

"I'm on it," Garrett said. "My mom has an amazing collection of New Age references at the bookstore. I'll have to sift through a lot of garbage, but I might be able to find something useful."

"Good. Thanks." I consulted my list. "Keep an eye out for these other shifters, too. We know there's us and there's the Thunderbirds. Kohana had said that the other two kinds were wolves and jaguars."

"We need better info about them, too," Garrett said. "Find out where they live, who their leaders are, whether they've already been fighting Mages."

"And we need to contact them," I added. "Maybe the way to beat the Mages is to work together."

"Kohana isn't giving that idea much support," Garrett noted.

"Well, we've got to find Kohana," Nick said. "Before he finds Zoë again. I'll see if I can sniff him out—or more of his kind."

"And I'm coming to Chicago," Liam said. "It won't take me long to find the treaty terms, and you can't be alone right now, Zoë. You might need someone able to shift to guard your back."

The guys agreed heartily on that, and I was relieved that Liam was coming. "What will you tell your parents?"

"I'll think of something," Liam said, which said something about his determination. He's an even worse liar than me. "Maybe I'll just tell them the truth."

I smiled at that.

"You don't think the Mages prompted Eileen and Erik's fight, do you?" Garrett asked. "I mean, we know that they can turn people's thoughts in different directions."

"And it would be a good way to ensure that Zoë is undefended." Liam sounded thoughtful.

We fell silent for a moment, and I knew I wasn't the only one worried about it.

Then Garrett sighed. "Okay, I've got to say it, Zoë, even though you're not going to like it."

"Go ahead." I didn't know what to expect.

"What about Jared? I know you like him, but the Mages did try to sign him up, didn't they?"

My heart clenched. "He declined, though. He told me."

"Do you really think the Mages take no for an answer that easily?" Garrett asked quietly. "I'm not saying he's lying to you, but I am wondering how anyone gets away from those guys."

There was a slither of uneasiness between us. I was pretty sure we were all remembering how Adrian's spell the previous spring had made us act against our own will.

"I trust him!" My protest sounded a bit shrill, even to myself.

"Maybe I'm wrong, but if we're checking out the angles, I think that's one to consider." Garrett tried to be conciliatory. "Maybe you can get the story from him, since he's in town."

"Don't get all prickly, Zoë," Nick said.

"No, your concern is fair. I see that. I'll go talk to him." My heart skipped and leapt at just the prospect of seeing Jared again.

How sad was that?

"Maybe someone should go there with you," Liam said. "Wait for me to get there before you go after him. Just in case."

"You've got to take care of yourself, Zoë," Garrett said. "You're our Wyvern."

"And we've got to work together, like we did last time," Nick said. "Let's all get to Chicago as soon as we can."

"Careful what you tell your parents," I said. "My dad is sure I'm wrong about the Mages. My only chance of avoiding exile is to prove that we're right."

"Without shifting," Liam said and I could practically see them all roll their eyes.

"If they don't trust the Wyvern, then we don't need to confide in them," Nick said. "Let's prove Zoë right and then tell them the deal."

Truth be told, I was relieved at their plan. Besides, I might be able to talk some sense into Nick about this girlfriend thing once he was here. My messenger chimed and I saw that I'd missed a call from my mom, but that it was receiving a message from her. I liked that she was doing what she'd promised. I would read it as soon as we were done.

"Do you think you can get the book from Jared?" Liam asked. "That might tell us something about Mages and other shifters."

I was skeptical that it would, doubly skeptical that he'd let it go. "I'll try, but he's told me that he's not giving it up."

"There has to be someplace else we can get some answers," Nick said. "I don't like waiting on chance."

That was when I knew. The answer was in the dark, at the bottom of the well. Urd might not be a looker, but she'd pushed me down there for my own good.

Just the way her sister, Verdandi, had given me the rune stone last spring, knowing I would need it.

For something.

Trusting them and my dreams was key.

I knew what I had to do. I didn't like it, but I knew there was no other choice.

I needed to go back into that dream and go down the well.

By choice.

It was a Wyvern thing.

MEAGAN WAS FINISHING HER PIANO practice when I got back to the town house. We hung out as I read the message from my mom. My mom was doing all right, or at least she wanted me to believe as much. She still hadn't mentioned my dad.

Meagan and I tried to decide if that was important to the ultimate resolution, but we were interrupted when she got a call on her messenger. I grimaced as she crowed to Jessica about completing her math homework first. She told her about the concert in glowing terms, and I couldn't help but notice how easily they talked.

Like I wasn't even there.

Then Meagan chatted to Jessica about potential *Pyr* candidates among the guys at school. Apparently they agreed about Derek having a dark secret—it was in his eyes. I never saw anything much in his eyes, but no one was asking me.

I went to the fridge, feeling a bit forgotten.

"Your mom called," Meagan's mom said as she came into the kitchen with a magazine. She pulled out a stool and sat down.

"My mom called you?" I nearly hit my head on the freezer door, I straightened so fast.

"She wanted to make sure you were staying out of trouble."

I smiled, mentally adjusting my halo. "Pretty much."

Meagan's mom smiled. "That's what I told her, that there was nothing to worry about."

She started to read her magazine again and I was turning away, but then I stopped. "Mrs. Jameson?"

"Mm-hmm?"

"How did she sound?"

Meagan's mom glanced up. "What do you mean?"

I shrugged. "You know. Happy? Sad?"

Wildly in love?

Ready to return home?

In the act of filing for divorce?

I didn't say any of those things, but Meagan's mom smiled a little, as if she'd heard them. "She sounded"—she flipped a page of the magazine absently, as if searching for the right word, then smiled at me—"cautiously optimistic."

I decided to take that as progress.

"Good. Thanks."

Meagan was walking through the intricacies of a math proof with Jessica. I figured I'd better do some of my own homework. I drained my juice, rinsed the glass, then headed for Meagan's room to get the backpack I'd left there.

"I'll do a visioning for your mother tonight, Zoë," Meagan's mom called after me. "Just a gesture of goodwill."

I stopped, then glanced back. My mom rolls her eyes whenever Meagan or her mom talks about her mom being a vision counselor. I wasn't so sure. I'd been a bit spooked that Kohana had shown up the first time after Meagan had done a visioning session for me in the spring, and I wasn't quite so skeptical anymore. Who knew what Mrs. Jameson could conjure up? "That's very nice of you. Thanks."

Her lips tightened, as if she'd heard my uncertainty and was a bit offended by it. "You know, Zoë, the future doesn't have to happen by accident or by chance. And the thing is, if a woman can't imagine a future with a man, then nothing he says or does can persuade her to be with him. She needs to be able to *see* that future in order for it to be a possibility at all."

I stared at her for a long moment, then swallowed. "That makes sense." I headed to Meagan's room, my thoughts churning.

Mrs. Jameson had given me an idea.

Sending visions was supposed to be part of the Wyvern's arsenal. I'd forgotten that, maybe because I hadn't shown much promise in that department just yet. But somehow I had to send a vision to my mom before it was too late.

If it wasn't already too late.

First things first—a visit to Urd.

I CRASHED EARLY, unable to concentrate on my homework. Meagan had hers done already and was easy to convince about going to bed early. She'd been power-yawning all day after our late night out.

Her parents, I'm sure, thought we were being responsible.

I was jumpy as I settled into bed, terrified of what I might see. Was Urd Death in disguise? The skull head certainly wasn't a reassuring detail. Did that mean I would die if I went back down that well? Could I even get there from Meagan's room? What would happen when I hit the bottom of the well?

It was hard to imagine that it would be anything good.

We said our good nights and I heard Meagan fall asleep almost right away. I could smell her toothpaste—she used a lot, making sure her teeth were superclean around her braces—and fabric softener from the sheets.

I took a deep breath, hoped for the best, and closed my eyes.

I'M NOT SURE HOW MUCH time had passed before I shivered. I reached for an extra blanket instinctively, then knew.

I opened my left eye to find snow drifting over the bed.

Holy frick.

It was happening again.

This dream could recur forty million times and it would still freak me out each and every time.

I rolled over, terrified. Granny was knitting snowdrifts busily, her sister motionless beside her. Like an angel of death. Not much of an angel, really. A skeleton of death.

With a drop spindle that whirled and whirled, spinning yarn.

I tried to keep calm and walk through the dream exactly the same way as I had before. Urd silenced me with a finger; she introduced herself and her sister; she conjured my ring out of the air.

I shouted and lunged for her, just as I had before.

She threw the ring down the well and we struggled. I knew when the fabric would tear and I would see her face, but still the sight shocked me. Then she flung me down the well, just as she had the last time, and I was falling to the eerie echo of her laughter.

So far, so good. (Relatively speaking.)

I swallowed and braced myself for a disgusting and painful landing.

But no. The air changed. There was suddenly a powerful updraft, one that didn't stink. It slowed my descent, as if I was a feather. I landed on my feet, as easily as that.

And the inky water that had pooled at the bottom of the well? It was a black mirror of ice. I stood on it, astonished, and saw the white orb of Urd's face reflected in it from far above.

Like a moon shining down the well.

Until she smiled and I saw the green flick of her snake-tongue.

I jerked and looked up, way up, but she moved away. I heard something metal clang into place, like a manhole cover, just as I was plunged into complete darkness.

The prospect of finding my ring seemed a bit slim.

The mirror of ice cracked beneath my feet then and I felt cold water lap against my bare feet. Which way should I run? Where would it be safe? Could I run without falling through the ice?

Just then, just when I thought things couldn't get worse, I heard the sound of a match being struck.

I spun to face the flickering light. A guy held the match aloft while it sputtered, the light touching his face. He looked like one of my mom's grad students, a little bit scruffy, maybe thirty years old. Sandy hair. The kind of person you'd walk right past without a second look.

He smiled and waved with his other hand. "Hey, sis," he said and then he swore as the match sputtered. I saw the glowing tip as he tossed the match in the water and heard it sizzle on impact.

Sis?

Holy shit. Urd had tossed me into the land of the dead.

SIGMUND LIT ANOTHER MATCH, but this time, he used it to light a candle. "You're going to want to get off that ice," he said. "No telling how deep the well water is, and there's nobody who can save you if you go under."

"Right." I could see that the ground was dry near him. Approaching my dead brother who had turned *Slayer* wasn't an appealing option for my longevity, but I didn't have a lot of choices.

And I was already in the realm of the dead.

I had nothing left to lose.

I slid across the ice and it cracked behind me in long, jagged lines, revealing a fathomless darkness. The well seemed to be stone, the walls uneven and gray. The space was about fifteen feet across. Round. So, Sigmund was standing on a kind of lip at one side, maybe one formed naturally.

"Some well," I said when I was safely on dry ground. "Big."

Or maybe we were really small.

You can't be too sure when you're dreaming.

"High volume in certain seasons," Sigmund said. "It's fed by all sorts of strange rivers." He gave me a look. "You seriously don't want to know."

He didn't look dead. Not really. A bit faded around the edges. Less vital than real live people. But if you didn't look twice, you might not notice it. "You're Sigmund, right? My brother from my dad's first firestorm."

"*Our* father." He stuck out his hand. "Sigmund Guthrie."

I shook his hand. He didn't feel dead, either. At least his hand didn't feel the way I expected dead people's hands to feel. His skin felt kind of papery, not, you know, like rotten meat. "Zoë Sorensson. How come you have a different last name?"

"Long story. How's this for the short version? When I was born, I was Sigmund Sorensson."

Ah, a name change. I would guess because my dad—*our* dad—had ticked him off. It wasn't much of a stretch for my imagination, given my recent interactions with that dragon. I folded my arms across my chest. There was no wind here, but it was still cold. Damp. "So, is this the land of the dead? I'd think it would be more crowded."

Sigmund smiled. "Technically, it's not, but you can get there from here."

"Excuse me?"

"The well is fed by several rivers, like I said, so when the tide is right, it's like an ancient sewer system down here. You can get from here to there, if you really want to go, but I have to tell you, there's not much to recommend it in the way of sights. Lousy company, too. Morose." He seemed to find this funny.

"Good to know. Thanks." I looked around, reminded myself that I had very little to lose. "So, does anyone ever get out of here?"

"Sure. The sisters send down the bucket every day. They have to water the tree, you know. Just hop in and they'll haul you up."

I was skeptical that Urd would do me any kind of favor like that, but I couldn't see the point in arguing.

"You came down here without knowing you could get back out?" I nodded and he whistled. "Braver than you look."

"Actually, I didn't have a lot of choice. I was chucked in the well." I remembered something else. "You didn't happen to see a ring fall down here, did you?"

"This one?" He held up the ring, smiling at my obvious relief. I reached for it, but he tossed it in the air, keeping it out of my grasp. I was terrified that he'd drop it and it would fall into that black water.

"Hey, give it to me!"

"Why should I?"

"Because it's mine!"

"Go ahead and make me."

I snatched and he moved it away once again. Then he laughed, his eyes twinkling. "Guess that's what brothers and sisters are supposed to do, isn't it? Had to try it out, just once." He offered me the ring.

I smiled and reached for it again. "Did you like being an only child?"

"No." He did his sleight of hand with the ring just before I could snag it and I was annoyed. Just like a little sister is supposed to be. "You?"

"No, but I'm starting to see its appeal."

He laughed easily. I kind of liked him.

"Catch," Sigmund said and tossed the ring toward me. It was an easy toss, but I stretched too far. (Told you about me and projectiles.) I grabbed the ring out of the air; then my foot slipped off the lip of the stone. Sigmund grabbed me and pulled me back, his hand firm around my elbow.

I leaned against the stone wall, my heart pounding, the ring clutched in my hand. "Thanks." I shoved the ring onto my finger.

The view didn't change. Interesting.

"No problem. Big brothers are supposed to look out for their sisters." He grinned wickedly. "As well as pester them and stuff frogs into their beds. Sorry. I've got to cram everything in together. We've got a lot of time to make up."

I laughed at that. "I can't even make fun of your girlfriends. Not without knowing them a little."

"Oh, that's too bad." He waggled his eyebrows in mock dismay, making me laugh again.

We were close together then and I saw that he was a bit taller than me. He didn't look that much like me, yet I could see some similarity around the eyes. I wondered how much else we had in common.

I had to ask. "Did you really turn *Slayer*?"

"Yup." He slanted me a glance. "Take it from me: bad choice."

"But why?"

Sigmund exhaled slowly. "Let's just say it was part of the whole name change and teenage rebellion thing."

I seriously felt that I had a lot in common with my brother then. We stood in silence for a moment, and I wondered whether he was waiting for me to ask the questions. I did. "Did you really write that book?"

He grimaced. "Yes. Bad choice. There was only ever a single copy of it, but it made plenty of trouble just the same."

I turned to look straight at him. "One copy? Are you sure?"

"Well, yes. I created it, page by page, bound it myself." He shrugged. "A work of art, from my own hands. Not that I'm being cocky or anything, but it was good work. Lasted over a century, too."

"Someone could have copied it."

He shook his head. "I had it for years in my possession. Locked away securely. No one could have copied it without my knowing. When I couldn't keep close watch on it, I ensured that it went to Sara's aunt's bookstore."

"Garrett's mom, Sara?"

He nodded.

"Someone could have copied it there."

"No. The Mages put a glamour on it so no one could see it who shouldn't." He winced. "They were involved by then, unfortunately."

"And who did see it? Someone must have, ultimately."

"It was Erik, of course. *Dad.*" Sigmund smiled. "It's his foresight that gives him an edge. And maybe the connection to me. He might have smelled my scent on it." He shrugged. "Either way, he spotted it. He handed it to Sara and then she saw it, too. She kept it locked up for years after that." He shrugged. "Until it was stolen."

Stolen.

That was the copy of the book I knew about, the one that had been lost from Sara's shop. Although no one had ever said "stolen" in my presence, just "lost." And I hadn't known that bit about the glamour.

Either way, there was a puzzle here. "But there must be two copies."

"Why?"

"Because my friend Jared has a copy and he found it before Sara's was stolen."

"Found?" Sigmund's eyes danced with mischief. "Maybe

someone's lying to you, little sister." Before I could argue with that, he pursed his lips and blew out the candle.

I reached for him in the darkness, but my hand closed on empty air. "Sigmund? *Sigmund!*" My own cry echoed in the well, but there was no other sound.

He was gone. I was abandoned in the dark in silence.

Except there was the sound of metal scraping, followed by the faint creak of a chain. I looked up to see a bucket swinging as it was lowered down the well and the white orb of a grinning skull face above it.

At least Sigmund had told me how to get out.

Although I wasn't that hot to see Urd up close and personal again, given the choice, I'd take the bucket lift. It had to be better than trying to find my way through an ancient sewer system in the dark—much less waiting for the tides to be right.

Because now I really had to find Jared and ask him some questions. Maybe just one question. Was he lying to me about the book? I really didn't want to believe it, but whatever he told me about the book would help me decide what to do about him.

With him.

Remembering that he could read my thoughts but I couldn't read his did exactly nothing to build my confidence.

I grabbed the bucket when it swung by, climbing up to the handle as it sloshed into the dark water. Sure enough, it was steadily hauled upward, the chain creaking as Urd's face became more clear overhead. I held on tight and hoped for the best.

It seemed a long shot.

And about halfway up the well, the entire scene disappeared.

I was almost afraid to look.

But I opened my eyes to find myself back in Meagan's room. No matter which eye I used, everything looked normal.

And it was three fifteen.

I fell back on the pillows, planning my strategy. As I stretched out, my foot touched something cold and wet. Yuck! I flung back the covers, struggling to keep from screaming.

And a leopard frog hopped out of my bed to the floor. I swear it winked at me before it hopped under Meagan's bed. I fell to the floor and peered after it, but I saw only dust bunnies on the hardwood there.

The frog was gone.

As if it had never been.

Brothers.

Chapter 7

Monday morning seemed to be filled with complications. I knew I needed to ask Jared about the book, as well as about the Mages, but Liam had wanted me to wait for him to arrive in Chicago before I did anything. When was he going to get here? We weren't that close to Ohio. I'd checked the site for Jared's band and saw that they had a gig in Des Moines Tuesday night.

So I didn't have much time. They might even be gone already.

I wasn't inclined to wait on Liam but was a bit nervous about acting alone. Had Kohana followed me to Jared on Saturday night? Or had he followed the sound of Jared's spellsinging? Would Kohana still be there, waiting on me to show? I decided he must have better things to do. Jared probably wouldn't be spellsinging when I found him this time, so there'd be no music to draw Kohana's attention, wherever he was.

My mom called when Meagan and I were walking to school.

Another short and sweet call—she sounded more cheerful, which could have meant anything—and I filled Meagan in on the details afterward. The call reminded me of my plan to send my mom a vision—somehow—and try to turn the tide.

No pressure.

I had so much on my mind that I wasn't exactly a source of sparkling conversation.

As usual, Jessica was waiting at the school doors. She and Meagan called to each other and hugged like long-lost sisters, then scurried off to compare notes on homework and guys with secrets.

Derek was, as usual, loitering against the lockers, watching me and being ignored by everyone else. I hadn't finished his drawing, so I just smiled and pulled out my messenger again, needing to do something other than talk to him. I was self-conscious, given Meagan's theory about him having a crush on me, and thinking that I really had crap judgment when it came to guys.

Proof of that was that I sent Jared a message, trying not to look desperate while I waited for his reply. On the upside, it came quickly. On the downside, he blew me off.

Again.

I don't know why I was surprised. He said he couldn't meet me later. He and the other band members were packing up their gear to head out after lunch.

Then I realized that Jared was assuming that I would be in school until close to four.

I had a sudden uncharacteristic urge to cut class.

IN THE END, I didn't have to skip. English was canceled at the last minute because Miss Ross got sick abruptly—the school nurse was muttering about flu, but Fiona was already spreading rumors that Miss Ross might be pregnant. Nice—and we were given a free period. I had lunch right after English on Mondays, which left just enough time to get downtown and back. If I was lucky. (It also, yet again, foiled my plan to get on Meagan's good side and have lunch with Jessica. Given the choice, I thought seeing Jared was more important. You probably saw that coming.) I fled the school like a bat out of hell and raced to the bus stop.

There was a bus idling there. I was sorely tempted to spontaneously manifest downtown—thereby saving lots of time and two bus fares—but it was broad daylight.

And I could hear someone loping along behind me.

"Hey!" Derek bellowed when the bus driver put the bus in gear. He was so loud that I nearly stumbled.

But the bus driver must have heard him. He stopped the bus and opened the door.

I halted, panting by the door, and glanced back.

Derek was catching his breath, too, and his eyes were gleaming. He gestured for me to go first and I did.

I wasn't enormously surprised when he dropped into a seat near mine. "Going downtown?" I asked.

He nodded once, then averted his gaze.

That was okay. I didn't feel like talking, either. It was snowing again, just light flurries that swirled around the bus. There were half a dozen riders on the bus, mostly older people. I fiddled with my ring as we rode.

I couldn't help stealing glances at Derek. He *was* kind of cute. It was true that he wasn't in Jared's league, but apparently Jared was out of mine.

I didn't mind how serious Derek was. I liked that he was tall. I liked that he was focused. I had the sense that he would do whatever he said he would do, that he'd be totally straight with everyone and would not—just for example—mess with someone's mind for inexplicable reasons or personal entertainment. Derek would be in or out, with you or against you.

Like Nick. The first guy I'd liked who hadn't liked me.

I was thinking I needed to review my romantic strategies.

That gave me something to do on the bus.

I liked Derek's eyes, too. That pale blue was really something.

Derek got on the L with me, too, but didn't sit beside me. I found myself intrigued by him and his silence, maybe because he offered a different puzzle, one that wasn't so key to my survival. An idle mind game. I could do with a few more of those.

Derek nodded once at me when he got off the L, two stops before my intended destination, and I felt curiously relieved.

He hadn't been following me, then.

Maybe Meagan was wrong.

The street outside the club was busier than it had been at night and even though I kept myself on guard, I felt pretty safe. I couldn't sense any other *Pyr* and didn't catch one glimpse of Kohana.

Everything seemed perfectly normal.

Which worked for me.

There was music emanating from the club. Loud music. And it was a bit erratic, as if the band was rehearsing. I had to pound on the door to get anyone to answer and then Rick hauled the door open.

His annoyance changed quickly to a grin. "Hey, Jared. Last chance!" He disappeared into the darkness of the interior, leaving the door standing open.

Jared was wearing a dark T-shirt and jeans, and my gaze fell to that salamander tattoo. He smiled when he noticed me looking, then gave me a stern look. His eyes kept twinkling. He leaned in the doorway, looking like trouble. "You're not skipping school, are you, dragon girl?" He pretended to be horrified. "I thought you were one to follow the rules."

"Maybe you're a bad influence."

He laughed, then studied me. "Seriously."

"We got a free period, and I have lunch right after. I'm taking advantage of the opportunity."

"To get into trouble?" His eyes glinted, as if he had definite ideas of what kind of trouble I could get into.

I had to look away.

"I need to ask you a couple of questions." It shouldn't have surprised me that his good mood vanished. He looked wary, but didn't say anything. I took a deep breath. "I want to know about the Mages."

Jared evaded my gaze. "I'm not sure there's much I can tell you." His tone was neutral.

Too neutral.

I chose to trust my instincts and pushed him.

That had been his advice, after all.

"I *need* to know about them. Self-defense."

Jared scuffed his boot and gazed down at it, considering something. Calculating. What didn't he want to tell me? Garrett's suspicions swirled into my thoughts and took hold.

"And the book," I added. "I need to know the truth about the book."

He glanced up in surprise. "What about it?"

"How you got it. *When* you got it."

Jared looked at me hard then and I could see that he wasn't really surprised by my question. He also didn't look inclined to tell me more. He was studying me closely.

I remembered that he could read my thoughts, a little bit too late to hide them. I saw his lips tighten and remembered that I had no secrets from him.

Although he could have plenty from me. I disliked the fact that I was even thinking about the advantage of building firewalls between us—never mind that the only way I would be able to check on my own success in doing so would be by seeing him again.

Which seemed unlikely at best.

Jared turned away when I thought that, and made to close the door. "You don't trust me."

I put my hand on the door to stop it. "I do trust you. I'm just wondering whether that's very smart."

"I told you. . . ."

"I'm not asking for you to check in with me all the time, like I've got you on some kind of leash," I said, interrupting him. "I'm starting to think that counting on you is a long shot. I'd just like to know how long the odds are."

"Against what?"

"Against *anything*." I'd said more than I'd meant to say, but it was done, lying between us like a roadblock.

Jared took a breath and pursed his lips. "So, you're just like everyone else after all," he said softly. "I thought dragons were extra perceptive. I thought a dragon girl would see the truth."

"Not fair," I said, my anger rising. "Why does trusting you mean that I can't ask you any questions? Why can't I ask you where you got the book, since everyone is telling me that there's only one? I'm not saying that you're lying to me. I'm saying that people have questions and I can't defend you without some answers. I'm saying I want to trust you, but you have to give me *something* to base that trust on."

"You're all shimmery." His gaze danced over me.

"Well, what do you expect?" I flung out my hands. "I saw the Mage spells Saturday night, and they were feeding off your music. Your songs were helping them build their power. I want to know why."

"You saw what?" he said, his face pale.

There was no doubt that I'd shocked him.

But I was still angry. "I told you. You know what I want to know. You can tell me or not. It's not like you owe me anything, as you've made clear."

I turned to walk away. I hated arguing with him. I hated that he was hiding things from me. And I hated that his decision to do that was destroying my trust in him.

Did everything I believed in have to turn out to be a lie?

All in the same week?

I GOT ONLY ABOUT FIFTY feet before Jared fell into step beside me. He was still shrugging into his black leather biker jacket, but he threw me an irreverent look. "Probably would have attracted too much attention if I'd asked you to keep me warm," he murmured, a mischievous glint in his eyes.

"Don't go there. Not now." I was angry, but I couldn't keep myself from blushing, which only seemed to amuse him.

"Okay, I'll answer three questions," he said, indicating the alley that ran behind the club.

"Why only three?"

His smile flashed. "Careful, dragon girl, that's one." He sobered and grabbed my hand. "Come this way."

Like an idiot, I couldn't say no or hold my ground or even stop my stupid heart from galloping. I should have been frightened by the power this guy had over me—but in this moment, it irritated me. "Have I told you lately that you can be really annoying?"

Jared laughed. "Trust me, Zoë, I don't have an exclusive on that." My heart stopped and raced at that. He seldom called me by my name. That he did made me hope that something would change.

That he was going to make a concession, just for me.

He tugged me toward the alley then, his grip so warm and strong on my fingers that I couldn't say a thing. He led me around the back of the building that housed the club.

He pulled down the ladder on a rickety metal fire escape. I halfway thought it would break as soon as it had any weight on it. He locked his fingers together to give me a boost. I swung onto the bottom rung, glad I'd been working out as hard this summer as I had. The metal ladder shook but held.

After I started to climb, Jared jumped and caught the bottom rung with his hands, swinging up behind me. It got colder as we ascended, the snow swirling all around us.

Eventually we were on a broad, flat roof. There was a water tower in the middle and nothing else.

But snow and sky and distant buildings.

I took a steadying breath. The building was maybe six stories high, a good distance away from the cluster of tall office buildings and taller than its immediate neighbors. The wind off the lake was chilly and I could see that the water was choppy. The snowstorm would get worse soon.

I turned to face Jared, only to find that he had been watching me. "I don't think we'll be overheard here," he said, zipping up his leather jacket against the wind. His hair was being tossed around. "Go for it." He held up his thumb, demanding my first question.

I decided to start small. "Why did the Mages' spells come out of the sewer grates on Saturday night?"

"When?" If nothing else, I had his complete attention.

"During the concert." I was ready to have a nice calm conversation, but the tone was already turning.

Jared frowned. "You couldn't have seen that from inside the club. The windows are blacked out."

"Well, no. It was when I left."

Jared leaned closer, his eyes snapping. "What?"

"I went outside. Alone."

"Why did you do that? Why would you leave alone?"

"Why *wouldn't* I do it? You weren't exactly being friendly. I had to think."

"Outside, alone, in a crappy part of town." His disgust was clear.

"Not quite alone. Kohana attacked me."

"What?" He stared at me, obviously unhappy with what I was telling him. Then he shoved one hand through his hair. "Holy shit, Zoë, that was stupid. You could have been killed."

His concern might have been gratifying if he hadn't been so sure that I'd lose a fight. "Thank you very much."

"I've seen you fight."

"Not lately." I folded my arms across my chest and glared at him. Our gazes locked and held, a definite sizzle in the air between us. "I refuse to be a damsel in distress."

He almost smiled, then shook his head. "You shouldn't have gone outside alone."

"And you shouldn't have been singing spells. Isn't that what drew the Mages closer? Weren't they using your music as fuel for their spells?"

He eyed me, wary again. "I'm not sure. What exactly did you see?"

"I can see spells. They're like beams of light. I saw the ones that you and your band were making and I saw Mage spells coming out of the sewer grates and manhole covers and basement windows. As if they were responding to the sound of your songs. They were wrapping around them."

"Absorbing them and feeding on the energy." Jared paced, his agitation clear. "You probably think I was making them stronger on purpose."

I blinked. That possibility had never occurred to me.

He saw that, too. I knew it because some of the tension slid out of his shoulders.

"Why did they try to recruit you, anyway?"

He winced. "And the implied question would be how did I decline the privilege."

"You said you took a pass on their offer."

"But you only have my word on that, don't you?" He spun to face me. "And what exactly is that worth, Zoë?"

"I'm trying to trust you."

"But should you?" His tone was challenging. I didn't like it. "Isn't it the point of a Mage spell to make someone believe something that isn't true? Maybe I've enchanted you, to persuade you to trust me against your own instincts. Maybe I'm deliberately drawing you into danger. Isn't that what you think?"

"No. It's what some of the guys think, but I trust you. That's why I'm asking questions. You need to tell me what's really going on."

His smile was more of a grimace. "What if I told you that I got the book by stealing it from Sara's shop? That ripping off the book was my initiation test from the Mages, the challenge they gave me to prove myself?" He stepped closer and raised one finger, holding my gaze with defiance. "What if I told you that I realized then that their plan was to recruit me, both because of my innate talent and because of my connection with the *Pyr*?"

"Because Donovan is your uncle?"

He nodded once and his voice softened. "What if I told you that they wanted me to be the bait to snare and destroy you?"

I held my ground, fighting to hold on to my instinctive trust of him. In reality, everything was spinning around me, spinning like a maelstrom of falling snow. Jared had stolen the book? Jared had been courted by the Mages to trap me?

I took a deep breath. "Then I would know why you declined."

"How do you know that, Zoë?" he demanded with heat. "How can you be sure?"

"You helped me. Last spring. You broke Adrian's spell and helped us save the older *Pyr*—"

He interrupted me. "That could have been a trick to gain your confidence," he argued, his voice rough.

"Or it could have been the truth."

He stared at me then, and I held his gaze, letting him look into my thoughts. Because the truth was that I did trust him, and

I knew in my gut that if the details seemed to condemn him, it was just because I didn't have all of the facts.

I wanted to believe in him.

I wanted him to be everything that I believed him to be.

And maybe if I believed in Jared the way no one else did, maybe if I trusted him the way no one else did, maybe that could help him be the person I thought he could be.

The guy I yearned for.

I stared right back, unblinking, and I let him look.

FINALLY JARED SIGHED AND CLOSED his eyes, relief rippling through him. "I knew you were different," he murmured.

I'd thought he might touch me, but he turned away. He walked the perimeter of the roof. He scanned the sky, thinking, his fingertips drumming on his leg.

I gave him time to decide.

It seemed like I'd passed the test, after all.

"Okay, here's the deal." Jared spoke quickly when he came back to face me. "Mages work with an inherent ability. Only a few people are born with the particular kind of musical talent that the Mages can twist to their own use. You can't learn spellsinging. You either enchant with your song or your music or you don't. They sense those people, or maybe they hear their amateur spells. Either way, they target them and try to recruit them. More Mages mean more power."

"Because volume is part of the power?"

"Sure. If I can make your sternum vibrate with my spellsong, it's going to be a lot harder for you to ignore both me and it."

So, it was similar to beguiling.

"But not all musicians are spellsingers."

Jared shook his head. "No. Not even close. I know a lot of musicians and I've asked a lot of questions. Most of them don't know anything about Mages or spellsinging."

"But some . . ."

"Do." He finished my sentence and held my gaze. "Those are the ones who lie when asked about it. Those are the ones who might be Mages already. I just keep my distance from them." He shoved a hand through his hair. "You're sure their spells were absorbing mine?"

"Gobbling them up."

"And getting brighter afterward?"

I thought about it, then nodded. "Yeah. They were feeding on your strength."

"And what did you feel?"

"A pull. Like being tugged toward a vortex."

"Which was?"

"Underground."

"Fuck." He marched to the other side of the roof, almost vibrating with tension. He shoved his fists into his pockets and stared at the lake, the wind lifting his hair. I'd never seen him so troubled.

I followed him and put a hand on his shoulder. "Tell me."

"Don't you see, dragon girl?" He spoke through his teeth, then turned to face me. "I always wondered why they took no for an answer. I always wondered why they just let me walk away. I just figured they didn't want me very badly." He shrugged. "I mean, nobody else ever did. Why should Mages be different?"

I slid my hand down his sleeve, but he shrugged off its weight.

"But they didn't let me go," he said, almost snarling the words. "They let me think I was getting away, but they're still using me to get to you."

"You don't know that. . . ."

"Yes, I do. Every time you're close to me, they show up. Now when I sing, they're stealing my energy to make themselves stronger." He swallowed. "To give themselves the power to destroy you. The plan is carrying on, and I'm complicit, even though I didn't know it."

"No . . ." But I was thinking of what Kohana had said.

He pivoted, maybe sensing that I'd stiffened. "What?" His gaze searched mine when I didn't immediately answer.

"Kohana said that when he heard your song, he knew I'd be in the vicinity. That's how he found me."

Jared winced, swore and turned away. "They're doing it, even without my cooperation," he murmured and my heart felt like a lead weight in my chest.

There was silence between us. I heard a bird cry. I felt the wind grow more harsh. I heard a dog growl on the street below. I felt the cold of winter chill me right to my marrow.

I reached out and touched his sleeve, knowing he needed something from me, acting on impulse. When he glanced my way, I couldn't look away from the vibrant green of his eyes, from his need.

"*I trust you.*" I filled my mind with that thought, letting him see my conviction. I felt him shake a little; then he touched my cheek with his fingertip again. I felt him come closer and closed my eyes, not wanting him to read my thoughts at this moment.

Maybe he had to see my eyes. I wasn't sure, but he always looked deeply into my eyes before he understood my thoughts.

I couldn't bear for him to see that I needed so much right now.

I was surprised when he touched me. His hands landed on my shoulders, his fingers curling around them. I felt his breath and then his lips brushed mine. That barest touch filled me with yearning and made me shiver. My heart was thundering, doing that crazy thing of matching its beat to his. Our noses were almost touching, his hands framing my face and I didn't want to step away from him.

Ever.

"I'm not going to let them win," he said with quiet force. I opened my eyes to meet the conviction in his gaze. "I'm not going to be a part of that."

"What can you do?"

"Only one thing—leave." He smiled, but it was bitter. "They're not going to follow me to you. Not again, dragon girl."

"But . . ."

"So long as there are Mages hunting you, I won't risk it."

As much as I hated his conclusion, I feared he was right.

But I couldn't let him go just yet.

I leaned against his chest, touched my lips to his pulse at his throat. He kissed my forehead and pushed his fingers into my hair. "I'm sorry, Zoë. You trusted me and you shouldn't have. Turns out everybody else knew better."

I had a lump in my throat the size of Illinois.

He tipped my chin up and studied me for a long moment, then forced a smile. "Be good, dragon girl," he said, then turned and strode away without looking back. There was defeat in the line of his shoulders and a good chunk of it in my heart. The snow danced around him, white against black, and then he disappeared over the lip of the roof.

He still didn't look back.

And I was alone, the snow falling thickly around me.

I DON'T KNOW LONG I'D been standing there when I heard a van start. An old one. I heard doors slamming and heavy things being moved. Rick's and Angie's voices carried from the alley behind the club as they packed up, and I strained my ears for the sound of Jared's voice.

No luck.

I guess he wasn't taking any chances on inadvertently loosing a spell or two in my vicinity.

The van drove off, its tires leaving grooves in the snow on the street. I moved to the lip of the roof to watch, certain that he was driving out of my life.

Instead I saw a lone figure in black, one bag slung over his shoulder, standing at the curb, watching the van as it traveled down the road.

His band was leaving, without him.

Then he turned and started to walk in the opposite direction.

Alone.

As if he needed to think.

As if this wasn't any easier for him than it was for me.

I watched him go, wishing it could be different. I felt cheated, as if something I'd never really possessed—never mind had time to appreciate—had been stolen. But I was the Wyvern. If the future was going to be different, I was going to have to be the one to change it.

First up would be thwarting the Mages' plan. They considered me and my kind to be prey.

Well, that just meant that I was going to have to turn the tables on them. Treaty or truce would never be good enough. We would have to eliminate the Mages, one by one, in order to live safely again.

If I could lead the *Pyr* to victory, I could see Jared again. It was a heck of an incentive.

Even if I had no clue how to manage the deed.

Before I could think further than that, everything went to hell.

THE BIRD'S SECOND CRY STARTLED me. It was closer, closer than it had been.

And I realized a bit late that I recognized that cry. I'd guessed wrong: Kohana had been waiting on me. Heart pounding, I spun to look for him.

He was swooping down toward me, talons extended. His eyes blazed yellow, a sure sign that this was no ordinary bird. He was larger than most birds, too. He held a brilliant yellow thunderbolt in one claw.

I'd seen his arsenal before. Those thunderbolts exploded on contact, burning everything in proximity. Like lightning strikes.

Here was my chance to finish him forever.

Screw my dad's new rule, the Covenant, and the risk of exile.

I roared and called to the power deep within me. The change rolled through me with breathless speed and I leapt into the air at the same time.

I felt my wings beat, lifting me higher. I saw the fire I exhaled at Kohana.

I saw his surprise, and I took advantage of it. I lunged toward him, struck him hard, and knocked him toward the earth. He was still fast and still slippery, but I was much, much stronger than I had been.

Plus I was mad. He'd lied to me. He'd targeted me. He'd tried to eliminate my friends. He'd allied with the Mages in an attempt to save his own kind, but he was stupid to trust them.

And he was part of the reason I was losing Jared.

I decked him and the rhythm of his flight faltered. I was right behind him, breathing fire on his tail, as he retreated. He spiraled into the snow-filled sky, but I snatched at him when he slowed to turn and pulled a fistful of ebony feathers out of his skin.

He screamed, but I let them fall, wanting more.

I snatched him and tightened my claws around him as he struggled. I had to be three times his size. He squirmed and fought, but I didn't let him go. My talons were long and white and sharp, and they drew blood where they pricked him. He fought against me and I squeezed, remembering his deception.

And the price we had nearly paid.

"You lied to me," I charged.

"No better than you deserve, *Unktehila*." He sneered. "Oathbreaker."

I held him captive. "Tell me more about this supposed treaty."

"Don't you know your own history?" he demanded.

"Maybe you're making it up."

"The Mages demanded a shifter." Kohana writhed in my grip. "It was me or you."

"So you would turn us in to save the Thunderbirds?"

"My first loyalty is to my own."

"Right!" Now I scoffed. "Only a moron would believe anything the Mages promised."

His eyes shone. "No one says they know all of the truth."

"Where do I find the wolf and jaguar shifters, if they really exist?"

"Open your eyes, *Unktehila*." He was mocking once again, and I tightened my grip.

Before I could ask more, pain flashed in his eyes and I was stupid enough to ease my grip just as he struggled violently. He wiggled free and I snatched after him. He danced beyond my reach, laughing, then spun and flung one of his thunderbolts. I winced and ducked, but was surprised to realize that he hadn't aimed it at me.

He laughed and flew away with astonishing speed. I followed the trajectory of the thunderbolt and my heart stopped cold.

Jared's hands were fisted in his pockets and his head was down as he continued to march away.

And Kohana's thunderbolt was headed straight at him.

I knew Jared couldn't see it, that even if he turned, he wouldn't be able to perceive it until it exploded against his skin.

It would kill him.

No! I forgot Kohana and his mocking laughter, pivoted, and dove toward Jared. I wasn't at all sure I could get to him in time, but I had to try. I flew harder than I ever had, pushing myself beyond what I knew I could do.

I drew alongside the thunderbolt maybe two hundred feet above Jared. I couldn't stop it. I couldn't reach him in time to push him aside. So, I did the only thing possible.

I threw myself into the thunderbolt's path.

I closed my eyes against the bright yellow flash of light and bared my teeth at the burning pain. I felt it shoot through me like a jolt of electricity, and I felt myself shifting forms involuntarily.

A sign of distress in dragon physiology.

Usually impending death.

I had time to realize I was falling, to know that I had zero regrets, and then everything went black.

Say good night, Zoë.

IT WAS THE NAUSEA THAT woke me up.

My stomach was roiling and I hurt in places I hadn't even known I had. My back was blazing with pain, and I could feel concrete beneath my chin. The snow was freezing cold where it landed on me, but in a way, it felt good against my burning skin.

I opened my eyes. My hand was white and webbed, so I knew I had unconsciously shifted into salamander form.

I had a definite sense that I wasn't alone and looked around without moving. The street was completely deserted, doors closed and windows black.

But there was a wolf, sitting right in front of me.

Watching me.

The wolf was shaggy, his fur a thousand shades of gray and silver. His eyes were icy blue, shining with a disconcerting intelligence. He didn't blink. Major teeth, which made me wonder whether newts made a nice light snack.

Did I look tasty? Like a bite or two of barbecue?

In self-defense, I closed my eyes, summoned my will, and shifted to human form again. Then I was sitting with my back against the brick wall, my hands braced on either side of me. Ow ow ow.

The wolf didn't move, or even blink.

Was it possible to think of a wolf being unsurprised?

I glanced around and didn't recognize the street at all. How far was I from the club? There was no sign of Jared or of Kohana. How long had I been out? I winced and stretched. And how badly damaged was my back?

Suddenly there was a shimmer of pale blue light, which spooked me into getting up. I knew that light and shouldn't have been surprised when the wolf disappeared.

A heartbeat later Derek was squatting before me. Eyes the same shade of pale blue. Same intent stare. Same scent.

I belatedly did a little bit of math.

Open your eyes, Unktehila.

Okay, I felt stupid.

"You okay?" he asked. I realized that his voice was always low and deep, rough like a growl.

Duh.

"More or less." I moved my fingers and toes, scanned myself. My back hurt like hell, but I couldn't exactly see it. "You followed me."

He nodded, glanced away, looked back to hold my gaze again.

"Why?"

"I thought you might need help." He shrugged. "I was right."

"But you got off two stops before me."

"You were suspicious. Worried. I didn't want to throw your game."

"How'd you know all that?"

He touched the side of his nose.

Right. Wolves had keen senses of smell, too.

"I couldn't smell that you were a shifter."

He smiled. "You probably can't smell emotion, either, or sense the future before it happens."

"Can you?"

He nodded, but before I could get jealous, he shrugged.

"I have a feeling when something big is going to go down, but I only see about two minutes ahead of the moment." He stared at me again and I realized that was the longest sentence I'd ever heard him utter. "Sometimes it's too late to matter."

"I wouldn't have expected anyone to stop the thunderbolt," I said.

"You did." He stood then, and brushed off his jeans. "And that guy? He has no idea of what you did for him." He spat into the snow, his disdain clear. When he looked at me again, his eyes seemed colder.

I froze at his words. "What do you mean?"

"He had his earbuds on. He didn't hear anything. He didn't turn around until I'd scooped you up."

"You what?"

"Someone could have stepped on you. You had to get out of there. The guy might have been curious, but I growled and he backed off."

Jared didn't know I'd followed him. He didn't know I'd taken that hit for him. I was disappointed by that bit of news.

"Where did he go?"

Derek shrugged. "Who cares?"

"Maybe I do."

"Maybe you shouldn't." His eyes flashed. "He *left* you."

"There's a situation. He's doing his best. . . ."

Derek waved off my explanation, fixing me with a steady look. "Don't you know that dogs see in black and white?" Then he looked down the street, his eyes narrowed. "Who's going to tend your back?"

"No one."

He shook his head. "Wrong. You need help. It's bad."

It did hurt. And he had seen it. For a moment I couldn't think of anyone who I could let see the wound, but then it came to me.

Isabelle. "I know someone at the college."

He arched a brow. "Science labs?"

I smiled. "Arts student."

He pointed. "We can catch the L over there."

I had no chance to ask if he was going to keep me company. Apparently I now had a guard wolf.

It wasn't such a bad thing. Derek set a good pace, striding effortlessly down the street as I tried to keep up. He scanned our surroundings constantly, his gaze sliding from side to side, and I could see him inhaling with care.

Taking the scent of everything.

I was a bit short of breath, so it took me a minute to ask what I wanted to know. "Couldn't you follow his scent?"

He turned to face me, his expression chilling me. There was a challenge in those pale eyes. "Couldn't you?"

I could, but I wouldn't. "But you knew I'd been with him."

"And he left. Problem solved."

Problem? "Why don't you like Jared? You don't even know him."

Derek shrugged. "He's human. He's half-Mage. Neither is a great credential in my world."

"He turned down the Mages. . . ."

"Technicality." Black and white, just like he'd said earlier. Derek held the door to the station for me, and met my gaze once more. "And he led you straight into a trap."

"He didn't do it on purpose!"

His gaze slid away. "I'm just glad I was there to help."

We rode the L in silence, as if we were complete strangers.

But Derek was never more than half a dozen steps away. Guarding me. Truth be told, I appreciated it. I wasn't at my best, and it was nice to have someone to rely upon.

Then I had a troubling thought. Was Derek, like Kohana, going to betray me to the Mages to save his own kind?

He inhaled sharply and glared at me across the car. I guessed that he'd caught a whiff of my suspicion. "Mages are liars," he said with low heat. "Only idiots trust liars."

With that, he turned to stare out the window again.

The real question was whether I could trust a wolf.

I CALLED ISABELLE FROM THE train and she agreed to meet me at her dorm room. Derek disappeared once we stepped onto the campus, but I knew he wasn't far away. I could smell wolf, even though I couldn't see him.

Isabelle was outraged and appalled by the story of the attack, but she also had some ointment for burns. I figured she would have packed it instinctively, having grown up in a *Pyr* household, and I was glad to have been right. It was some herbal stuff, cool and soothing, and I felt better within minutes.

I also scored another chocolate bar. I didn't care if she gave it to me out of pity. It was delicious.

She gave me strict instructions not to get the injury wet, and insisted I come back the next day for another lathering since I couldn't reach the spot. I promised to do so, and headed back to the L.

There was no sign of Derek. The train pulled in and I picked a seat. I wondered whether he'd abandoned me.

But he stepped into the car just before the doors closed, and sat down facing the other direction.

Ever vigilant.

We got back to school in time for the last class of the day, arriving separately.

And you know, it didn't break my heart to have missed gym.

Chapter 8

I came out of a particularly excruciating history class—excruciating mainly because my back hurt and my thoughts were spinning and I got called on four times to answer questions I hadn't even heard, based on a reading I hadn't even done—to find Liam leaning against my locker, watching the other students go by.

I was really glad to see him.

The girls were all checking him out and he seemed to be amused by their reactions. Every time I see Liam, he's taller and broader. His hair has darkened to an auburn that makes it unreasonable to call him "Carrots" anymore.

I still do.

I remember him having a face full of freckles and orange hair, and that counts.

"Carrots! How'd you find my locker?"

He inhaled pointedly and I understood. We dragons don't just smell the presence of our kind. With time and familiarity, we can recognize the scents of those dragons we know.

Apparently, though, we had nothing on wolf shifters.

"Gotta take that gym bag home," I joked and gave him a hug.

He watched me intently, even though he leaned casually against the lockers. "You okay?"

"*Spooked*," I answered him in old-speak. "*I went to see Jared today*."

His eyes glittered and I knew he was going to chew me out. Before he could do that or I could explain, someone cleared her throat.

"Um, excuse me, p-p-please."

The locker Liam was leaning against was Meagan's.

She was beet red when he apologized and moved out of the way, so flustered that I was afraid the stutters would overtake the words. "Meagan, this is Liam. Liam, my best friend, Meagan."

"Nice to meet you." Liam gave her a smile as wide and honest as a thousand acres of prairie. Meagan blinked. Her mouth opened and closed. She reached for her lock and dropped all of her books.

I squatted down beside her to help pick them up.

She flicked me a resentful look, as if I'd been holding out on her. "How come you suddenly know all these hot guys?" she whispered.

I blushed because I knew Liam would hear whatever we said. "Liam's not hot," I said, as if he was my kid brother. "I grew up with him."

"Where? When? I grew up with you!"

"He's the son of a friend of my dad's."

Meagan glanced up, then looked at me again, then nodded. "Okay." She straightened up, with her books piled against her chest, and smiled at Liam. "Nice to m-m-meet you, too. Do you live in Chicago?"

Liam was all easy charm. "No. Ohio. We have a dairy farm."

His manner reassured Meagan a bit. "Are you visiting for long?"

"No, I just came to hang out with Zoë since her folks are away." He nudged me. "Hey, Zoë, maybe we should go see that movie you were talking about."

A movie. The last thing I wanted to do was go to a movie. I was sore enough that I wanted to go to bed.

And maybe never leave it again.

"*You can bring me up to speed,*" Liam said, in old-speak. It was as much a threat as a promise.

"That's a great idea," I said out loud. "Way better than homework."

He turned to Meagan, flashing that easy smile. "You want to come, too, Meagan?"

I think she nearly had a heart attack.

For once, even math homework didn't have much appeal for Meagan. She shoved all her books in her backpack, blushed when Liam insisted on carrying it for her, and came to the movie with us.

I don't even know what it was about. I spent the whole ninety minutes briefing Liam in old-speak. And getting shit in old-speak for taking unnecessary chances. I felt better just talking about the encounter with Kohana, and we decided that he would walk us back to Meagan's, then keep watch over the Jamesons' town house.

I really like the idea of a dragon on the roof, on guard. We were going to breathe some dragonsmoke together later, mostly because it was a relaxation exercise.

We left the movie theater to find the snow a foot deep in the streets.

I wondered what had happened to Derek. Was he in the vicinity, but just out of sight? Or had he done all he was going to do?

I did like the idea that he might not be smelling trouble in my immediate future and so could leave me to my own resources.

Maybe I'd been wrong to be suspicious of his motives.

Maybe I'd offended him. I felt guilty about that, as well as a bit flustered. Had I made sure Derek was cured of liking me? Had he liked me just because he had a plan like Kohana's? Or did he like me just because I was a shifter and we had something in common?

All the possibilities made my head spin.

Plus I probably should have talked to him about our making an alliance with the wolf shifters. Did they really call themselves werewolves?

It made my palms sweat just thinking about hunting Derek down the next day and asking him questions. Maybe he would smell my intent and make the first move.

I could hope.

"It's so weird," Meagan said. "This theater isn't anywhere near the L, but all I could hear was rumbling trains throughout the movie."

"Me, too," I said, deliberately avoiding Liam's gaze. One look and I knew I'd laugh. "They ought to do something about that."

I heard his snort of laughter, and then he was making snowballs. He shoved one down the back of my jacket and the fight was on.

"YOU ARE SUCH A LIAR," Meagan said, hours later when we were crashed in her room and I thought she was asleep.

"What?" I nearly sat straight up in bed.

She threw a pillow at me. "You are such a liar. You said Liam isn't hot."

I closed my eyes in relief. "Is he? I don't know. I've known him too long, maybe."

Meagan made a snort of skepticism. "I don't care how long

you've known him—you'd have to be blind to not see he's hot." Then she laughed again. "Maybe you're the one who needs glasses, Zoë. Want to borrow mine?"

We laughed together and I had a minute to think that everything was back to usual.

She rolled over to face me and I had a heartbeat to brace myself against whatever she was going to say. "Hey, I meant to tell you. Jessica found this site today, about the *Pyr*."

My throat got tight. "The what?"

Oh, I am such a lousy liar.

"The dragon guys! I told you there has to be one at our school."

"Oh, right."

"Why aren't you interested in this? You draw dragons all the time."

"I dunno. Maybe they make more sense to me as fiction."

Right. Liar, liar, pants on fire.

"As if," Meagan scoffed. "Real is ten zillion times better."

I didn't say anything to that.

"So, listen, this site says that the *Pyr* have these powers."

I looked around the room, wishing I knew where this was going. "What kind of powers?"

"One's called beguiling. They kind of hypnotize people by creating flames in their eyes. People stare at the flames and the dragon guy makes suggestions and they end up agreeing. How cool is that?"

The only possible solution was to sound skeptical. I tried. "Flames in their eyes? Really?"

"I think it would be awesome to see that dragon guy again. I wouldn't mind at all if he beguiled me."

"I think it sounds silly." My tone was cranky and gruff, sour enough to spoil Meagan's mood.

Smooth move, Zoë. Lie to her and piss her off. That's the way to treat a friend.

I heard Meagan typing in the darkness once she stopped talking to me, so I tugged out my messenger as well. Garrett had sent a message that he'd found some information and would call me in the morning to tell me about it. Nick was outraged that Kohana had attacked me. Both of them were very, very quiet about Jared.

"Huh," Meagan said suddenly. "Jessica thinks you were holding out on me, too."

"What?" That surprised me.

"She says you must have been trying to keep Liam to yourself."

I'd had enough of Jessica. "No way. Liam is just this guy I grew up with—"

"Zoë," Meagan said, interrupting me firmly. "I'm not fooled. Whether Jessica's right about this or not, you've been lying to me since spring break."

Caught. If I could have thought of a good comeback, I would have argued my own side. As it was, I was totally out of my daily allotment of lies. I just shut up.

Meagan sniffed with displeasure after a moment—sounding a lot like my mom—then rolled over so her back was toward me. She wasn't asleep. I could still see the glow of her messenger and hear the sound of her typing.

I knew who she was messaging.

Jessica. Jessica. It was always about Jessica. Jessica was right and I was wrong, and there was nothing I could say to change that.

Why did Jessica give me the creeps? I'd assumed I was just jealous of the attention Meagan was giving her. But maybe it was something else.

Or maybe thinking it was something else was a pathetic cover for jealousy.

There was only one way to find out more.

I told myself that I might like Jessica better if I just talked to her for once. It sounded like something my mom would say. I wasn't convinced, but I'd give it a try.

Because, you know, I didn't have anything else to do.

WE WERE BACK TO OUR awkward pattern again the next morning, much to my regret. Meagan and I walked to school in comparative silence. Actually, we kind of trudged along. It was painful, especially when I thought of how easy it used to be between us.

And I couldn't think of a good way to fix it.

Just how much trouble was I already in for shifting to fight Kohana? It was easier to dismiss the prospect of exile when I was angry and acting in the heat of the moment. Walking along with Meagan, I could only remember the burn of dragonsmoke on my hand and shiver. I'd gotten injured, too. There was negative reinforcement.

How was I going to negotiate a treaty with the wolves? I hadn't any clue how to go about it.

It was galling to admit that my dad might know something.

Jessica waved from the doorway to the school. Waiting, as usual.

"What about those trig problems?" she asked, all aglow with the thrill of solving them.

"The third one was tricky," Meagan said. "Because of the wording."

"Right. You had to look for the arctangent."

"You guys want to sit together at lunch?" I asked.

They both looked at me as if I'd just dropped in from Mars.

"On Tuesdays, we go to the library instead," Jessica informed me. "C'mon, Meagan."

"Didn't know the library was off-limits," I said. "I'll keep that in mind."

I hauled open the door to the school. Meagan hesitated for a minute, but then she stayed with Jessica.

So I knew where I stood.

I opened my locker a bit more savagely than was strictly necessary and threw my books in. I heard a step beside me and glanced up, surprised to find Trevor there.

Smiling.

Like a starving man checking out lunch.

I smiled back.

Like lunch that bites all the way down.

He was as neatly turned out as ever. I swear someone ironed his jeans. He was pretty good-looking, if a bit stiff. As I surveyed him, I had to admit what an oddity he was. He could have been a jock, but he was a music fiend. He could have been a geek, but there was the way he played the sax.

But that was Mage stuff. He was enchanting everyone who listened.

His parents were totally loaded, which didn't hurt. He had this vintage MG in British racing green that he drove to school every day and they lived in one of those huge houses on Riverside Drive.

If he hadn't squealed into the parking lot with that car every day, I don't think someone like Suzanne would even have noticed him. Much.

Someone like Meagan would, though. If anything, Trevor seemed a bit too squeaky-clean to me to be real.

But then, I knew his secret.

And he knew mine.

Maybe he played it squeaky-clean because he really was sneaky. Maybe it was an act. And only the music—or the spell he cast with it—was real.

I had a vague sense of Derek's presence, somewhere in the hall. I liked knowing he was looking out for me.

"Get my invitation?" Trevor asked.

"Yes, thanks. What a surprise." I rummaged in my locker for my sketchbook and pencil box. Tuesday morning was the bright spot of my life—art class.

"You didn't get back to me about it."

"I didn't see an RSVP on it."

He smiled. "Just wanted to have an idea of numbers."

I shut my locker. "Sorry I can't make it."

"Busy?"

I shrugged and smiled. "Just one of those things. But thanks anyway."

To my dismay, he fell into step beside me. "Maybe you could just stop by for a while."

"I don't think so." I tried to be polite. "Maybe another time." After hell froze over and the planets dropped out of their orbits, the sun splashed down in the Pacific Ocean, etc.

He chuckled and I glanced up to find that his smile had broadened. "Or maybe I just have to find a way to change your mind."

Before I could ask, Trevor winked and turned away, leaving me looking after him. I felt threatened, that was for sure, although I couldn't imagine what he might do.

I didn't want to imagine what he might do.

I caught movement from the corner of my eye and saw Derek's back as he strode down the hall in the opposite direction. Meagan was standing back by the door with Jessica, her gaze locked on me. She looked hurt. I might have said something to her, but before I could think of what that might be, she pivoted and headed to class with Jessica.

Perfect. I could just guess what Jessica was telling her. That I was keeping Liam to myself while I did Trevor on the side.

A perfect start to another perfect day.

I HEADED FOR ART CLASS, glum. That had to be a first.

"You okay?" Derek asked. I jumped, shocked to find him behind me. I hadn't heard him coming at all. In fact, I'd thought he was going the other way.

"Sure. Thanks. How about you?"

His gaze searched mine, as if he wasn't going to take my word on it. "You're angry." I watched his nostrils flare. "Hurt."

I had to cede to a sense of smell that sharp. I smiled. "You have any human friends?"

His lips twisted and he glanced down the hall, as if scanning for likely candidates. Knowing he wouldn't find one. Resigned to it. "It's impossible." His gaze slid back to mine. "Better to run solo, or stick with those who understand."

He put a slight emphasis on this last word, and held my gaze for an unblinking moment. I couldn't read his expression. He was just watchful. Intent.

Okay, so he liked me because we were both shifters.

He almost smiled when I thought that and I knew I'd nailed it in one.

Now or never.

"I want to talk to you. . . ." I started to say, but he straightened and stepped back.

"Call for you," he said, right before my messenger chimed.

I looked between it and him, and must have looked surprised.

He smiled. "Told you."

"Two minutes' warning."

He shrugged. "Sometimes three." Then he sauntered away.

Oh, I wanted some of that. It wasn't much foresight, but it was more than I had. As Wyvern, I was supposed to have buckets of foresight, but thus far I had none.

Zero.

Nada.

And if ever there had been a moment when I'd have liked a peek at the future, this was it.

I answered my messenger and it was Garrett. I asked him to hang on for a second.

"That must be useful," I called after Derek.

"Good or bad, it just is." He shrugged. "Like Jessica."

Well, that was fair enough. I watched him head off to class. He moved with an athletic grace, his steady, long stride looking effortless even as he covered a lot of distance. I had the sense he could walk like that for days. He kept to the side of the corridor, evading the gaze and the notice of most of the students.

Like a moving shadow.

Or a wolf in the night. Solitary and purposeful.

I gave myself a shake and remembered Garrett. "Hey, sorry."

"Got a date?" he teased and I smiled. We weren't on video, though, so he didn't know it.

"I'll tell you in a minute. What did you find?"

"There's a book in my mom's store about Native American legends and stories. You know how your mom always says that myths and stories have their roots in a truth?"

"Right."

"Well, here's one that you'll find interesting. There are legends in many Native American tribes about Thunderbirds. They're supposed to be strong and fast, supernatural birds. The idea is that they cause storms by the beating of their wings, they can throw thunderbolts, and they cause lightning by the flash of their eyes. In some tribes, they control rainfall. The Lakota call them *Wakiya*."

"Okay." I started to walk to class, remembering that Kohana had called himself that. The description certainly was consistent with his powers.

Garrett continued, excitement in his voice. "But here's the thing—in some Pacific Northwest tribes, Thunderbirds are believed to be shape shifters. They open their beaks and pull them back like a hood, then shed their feathers like a coat. They married humans ages ago, so there are families who pass this ability through the generations."

"Like us." I stopped in the hall, focused on Garrett's voice.

"Just like us." I could hear that Garrett had one more morsel to share. "In fact, the Sioux tell a story that the Thunderbirds fought and defeated a race of reptiles centuries ago. Guess what the reptiles were called?"

"*Unktehila.*"

"Bingo. We must have made a treaty based on territory—they said we were defeated because we retreated to our own turf."

"Europe," I said. "And we forgot the deal over time because so many of us were killed."

"And ultimately we came back to North America," Garrett concluded. "That's Kohana's beef with the *Pyr*."

"And why he calls us oathbreakers."

So, the Thunderbirds were allying with the Mages to enforce the terms of an old treaty, intending to drive us *Pyr* out of North America and off the map if necessary. And the Mages found that useful. I guessed that Kohana and other Thunderbirds had a trick up their sleeves for the Mages, and wondered what it was.

Did Mages have a weakness?

How could I persuade Kohana and the Thunderbirds to fight *with* us, instead of against us?

"It says these families tend to live on the northern end of Vancouver Island," Garrett concluded. "That they stick to themselves and are very secretive."

"Sounds like the Covenant to me."

"Sure does. Maybe we have more in common than any of us realize."

That gave me an idea. "Can you have another look in your mom's books?"

"I think I've been through everything, Zoë. . . ." Garrett started to argue.

"I need you to look for something different." I dropped my voice to a whisper. "Werewolves." If I was going to negotiate a treaty with Derek and his kind, more knowledge would be better.

Garrett didn't say anything for a minute. Then he spoke softly. "You found one."

"Right under my nose." The bell rang. "I've got to go."

"I'll look," Garrett said.

"Good. Thanks. Later." And I ran.

ART CLASS WAS A RELIEF, although I wasn't exactly as focused as usual. My still life in charcoal was less than my best effort and it showed. Mr. Hughes wasn't fooled. He didn't say anything, but his lips tightened before he returned to his desk.

He made a bunch of notes and I tried not to be so egotistical as to assume that they must be about me.

I was thinking about everything BUT school, it seemed.

Math class was next and right before lunch. I slid through the back door of the classroom and took my usual seat at the rear. I wished I could be invisible in this class, as I was falling behind on the work. I pulled out the homework that I hadn't completed and hoped we wouldn't have to turn it in. Meagan and Jessica were sitting together at the front, whispering. They never got in trouble for that—after all, they were the class stars.

"Bitch," Suzanne said, dumping her books one desk over from me. She always sat beside Trish in math class. I tried to avoid attracting their attention, as a rule.

"Bitch yourself," Trish said, making a joke, but Suzanne didn't laugh.

She threw herself into her chair instead. Her ponytail was less than perfect, a few loose tendrils hanging from one side, and her eyes were red. She folded her arms across her chest and glared at the front of the class.

Trish looked around, then leaned closer to her sidekick. I didn't even have to strain my hearing to eavesdrop. "Who?" she whispered, just as Mrs. Dawson strode into the room.

"Jessica." Suzanne said her name in a low hiss of fury. "Didn't you hear? Trevor just dumped me for that slut."

I was shocked. Suzanne and Trevor had been going out forever. More or less.

This made no sense. What was really going on?

"Get out," Trish said, outraged on Suzanne's behalf.

Suzanne grimaced. "That's pretty much what he said." And she settled in to look daggers at Jessica.

Was it love?

Or did it have something to do with me? I had a bad feeling then, remembering Trevor's threat. But if he thought that his dating Jessica would change my mind about attending his party, he had another think coming. They were welcome to each other.

I recalled Derek's comment about Jessica and wondered whether he knew anything else about her. Maybe he just didn't like her either. I had to finish that drawing for him—it would give me the perfect reason to start a conversation with him.

"Take out your homework assignment, please," Mrs. Dawson said. "I'll be marking them today instead of giving a pop quiz. Put your name on the top right corner to ensure that you get credit. Meagan, would you collect everyone's homework, please?"

It figured that it'd be collected on the one day I didn't get it done. I winced and wished my luck would change.

"*YOU DIDN'T EVEN FINISH* your math homework last night, did you?" Meagan asked when I got to my locker after science class. I knew she'd noticed. Big clue: my hand-in sheet was almost completely blank.

Meagan was already packing books for her lunch break in the library. Looked like lunch was going to last through Friday.

"No." It seemed best to stick with simple answers. After all, I couldn't exactly tell her what had interfered with my concentration.

"You're going to need tutoring if you don't watch out."

Being tutored by Meagan along with Trevor didn't exactly sound like a dream come true to me.

Did Meagan know about Jessica and Trevor already?

Should I warn her, or let Jessica do her own dirty work?

An evil part of me thought that this might be what ended Jessica and Meagan's new friendship, given how much Meagan liked Trevor.

I should have guessed I'd be totally wrong about that.

Or at least anticipated that a math whiz like Jessica would have planned for every eventuality.

"Are you ready, Meagan?" Jessica asked. I fought to hide my dislike. Even the sound of her voice grated on me, although I didn't know why.

"Almost. I just need one more book." Meagan was rummaging in her locker.

I glanced up, thinking I might try to make nice, but instead my mouth fell open in surprise. Trevor was with Jessica, his arm slung around her shoulders. She was smiling, as if she had a good joke to tell, holding one finger to her lips as she watched Meagan. This was not going to be a happy surprise. Trevor smiled, looking even more predatory than he had earlier.

What was he up to?

"Hi," I said, and dumped all my books in my locker. I needed to get away from school, even for just an hour. I grabbed Derek's notebook and my fave pencil set, shoving them into my backpack.

"Got your costume ready for Saturday?" Trevor asked and Meagan hit her head on the metal shelf in her locker. She straightened up and pushed her glasses up her nose, blinking at him in astonishment.

"You know Trevor, don't you?" Jessica said to Meagan. "He said you tutored him."

Meagan began to blush, red heat rising up her throat, and I felt bad for her. I knew that Jessica was living her fantasy. "Sure," she said, sounding squeaky. She looked at his arm and Jessica's smile and swallowed. "I didn't know you did."

"We met at the math lab, the one you missed." Jessica smiled and I wondered whether she knew she was twisting the knife in the wound. Meagan had missed that lab to go to the movie with Liam and me. Jessica smiled up at Trevor. "He couldn't figure out his homework and we just hit it off."

"Thank goodness for Jessica," Trevor said. "I aced my test this morning. First time ever."

They beamed at each other, the perfect smitten couple, and I ached for Meagan. I reached out to touch her shoulder, aware that Trevor was watching my gesture.

His eyes shone in a way that gave me the creeps.

"Oh, by the way, Meagan," Trevor said, smiling broadly. "Jessica wanted me to invite you to my Halloween party Saturday night. It's late notice, but I hope you can come."

His gaze flicked to me, triumphant.

Okay, so he had invited Meagan. I still didn't see how this would compel me to attend. Our gazes locked for a second. Why did he think this would change my mind?

Meagan meanwhile glanced up at the prospect, her expression ecstatic. "Thanks." She smiled and took a step away from me. "That would be fun. Thanks!"

"I thought we could all study together at lunch today," Jessica said. She nudged Trevor. "He still needs help with math. Maybe between the two of us, we can whip his skills into shape for midterms."

"Okay. Sure. That sounds great." Meagan zipped up her backpack and almost tripped over her feet in her haste to follow them.

The way Trevor smirked at me, glancing back over his shoulder, didn't make me feel any better.

I sensed someone else watching and glanced around. Derek was leaning in the far corner of the hallway, arms folded across his chest. Before I could say anything, he headed for the exit, slipped out the door, and was gone.

"*Want to grab a tofu burger?*" Liam asked in old-speak. I couldn't see him but he must be in the vicinity. He'd been bragging in the summer about getting better with casting his old-speak over a larger area.

I smiled and leaned my forehead against my locker in relief. Trust Liam to know that I needed a friend.

And some fuel.

That having lunch with a dragon shifter would be a return to routine said a great deal about my life.

"*MAYBE BEING A WILDCARD MAKES* you a magnet for shifters," Liam said, speaking around a mouthful of his second super burger special. "Isn't that what Kohana called you last spring?" I nodded. "Because if there are four kinds of shifters left, two have found you already. Maybe the third one isn't far behind."

"Jaguars," I said. "The last kind was supposed to be jaguars, according to Kohana." I'd cut my tofu burger in half and still hadn't finished the first half. I was too busy trying to find a solution to our problems to eat.

"It might be true. Lions are big cats, and Adrian became a lion when he shifted on the lake. Maybe the Mages have been taking cat shifters out in smaller groups."

"Or maybe Kohana lied."

Liam was already checking out the second half of my burger. "These things aren't very filling, are they? I could eat a dozen of them."

"What if some of the cat shifters have been eliminated, but not all?" I suggested. "Lions but not jaguars?"

Liam shrugged. "It could happen. Maybe there are other kinds left, too."

"Just not lions."

Liam grimaced. "Or maybe Kohana just lied. Maybe all the cat shifters are already gone and it's just us and the wolves." He was watching that last half of my tofu burger as if it was the source of the universe's secrets.

"You want this?"

"You're not hungry?"

I shook my head, then watched the rest of my lunch disappear. "How do we fight back against the Mages even if we do make an alliance?"

"Maybe we could find another spellsinger," Liam suggested.

"Yeah, but we could end up recruiting someone who would just betray us."

Liam dropped his gaze and ate, clearly not wanting to say anything about Jared.

My messenger chimed and I tugged it out. "It's Garrett," I said to Liam, then answered. I knew Liam would be able to hear Garrett even across the table, with his *Pyr* hearing.

"I've found something weird," Garrett said. "This book just jumped off the shelves at the bookstore, like it was looking for me."

"Okay, that's weird."

Liam rolled his eyes in agreement with that but otherwise kept eating.

"No," Garrett insisted. "The weird thing is that it's not in the inventory. My mom says she's never seen it before, and she knows every book in the place."

The hair stood up on the back of my neck. With another used-bookstore owner, I'd have my doubts, but Sara was incredibly organized. I leaned over the table, making sure Liam didn't miss a syllable. The restaurant was a bit busy. "Okay, I'll bite. What is it?"

"It's in Latin. I had to use a translator utility to even figure out the title. It's called *The Treatise of the Shadowmakers.* I think it's a book of spells."

"What kind of spells?" Liam asked.

"Well, the last section of the book is called 'Metamorphosis.'"

Liam and I looked at each other. "It could be a Mage book," I suggested.

Garrett sighed. "Is it really their book? Or was it planted, to trick us? Like a diversion. I'm skeptical, especially the way it turned up."

"We have to read it," I said.

"First I have to scan the whole thing and run it through that Latin utility," Garrett said. "Then we have to figure out what it actually means. Even what I've looked at so far isn't exactly crystal clear. You okay there for a couple of days? It'll be easier for me to do the grunt work here."

"Liam's here," I said.

"Nick's coming," Liam added.

"And it seems that I have a wolf at my back."

"You never told me about that," Garrett said and I told him then.

"Seems like too big of a coincidence for Derek to just happen to be at your school," Garrett said when I was done. Liam nodded agreement.

"I know. I'm going to ask him. Crap!" I remembered the drawing I needed to do and dug in my bag, hastily clearing the table. "He asked me to do a drawing for him. I figured I'd ask him some questions when I give it to him." I set to work as Liam claimed my messenger and gave Garrett the play-by-play.

"Let's ask Isabelle if she knows anything," Garrett suggested.

I nodded. "We'll wait for Nick." We could throw them together, force them to spend some time with each other. Then Nick would have to see the truth. It could be a subtle but effective strategy.

"Sounds like a plan," Liam said.

"I'd better get to it," Garrett said. "It's a long book."

"Nice messenger," Liam said, teasing me when the call was over. "Sure you need it?"

"Of course I do!" He made me jump for it, laughing that he could so easily hold it out of my reach.

When I'd snagged it again, Liam gathered up our trash and gave me a look. "Don't you have class?"

I did, and I was late. I grabbed my stuff and ran.

I SLID INTO ENGLISH CLASS a good ten minutes late. My hopes of passing under the radar were completely trashed within seconds.

Because I was handed a summons to the guidance counselor's office and dismissed.

Seemed I was ten minutes late for an appointment I hadn't even known I had.

I've never been much for guidance counselors. They mean well and all, but there's not very much I can talk to them about. What are my life plans? Becoming the prophetess of the dragon shifters. How do I intend to earn a living? No worries—over centuries, any wage can add up, plus my dad is pretty good about sharing from his hoard. Do I want to have a family, and if so, do I intend to keep working? Well, yes, I'll breed when I have a firestorm and continue to be a Wyvern on the side.

It all sounds a bit delusional, doesn't it? And I have no plans to be locked away forever because I believe myself to be a dragon shape shifter. No goals to be like Jack Nicholson in *One Flew Over the Cuckoo's Nest*, getting my brain zapped at regular intervals.

Because the truth is that even though the *Pyr* have been revealed, and even though most humans are aware that there are dragon shape shifters in the world, no one imagines for one second that they know one or could meet one live.

Except Meagan, and that's new.

And my own fault.

So I mutter and murmur and the good people in the counselor's office write concerned little notes to the effect that I am devoid of ambition. That couldn't be further from the truth, but I have to let it go.

My parents think it's funny, which doesn't exactly make the guidance counselor happy.

On this particular day, I was less than thrilled with the meddling. I had things to do, and information to ferret out, and plans to make. How was I going to find Derek if I didn't follow him out of English class?

The prospect of another pointless hour spent with earnest, caring counselors was enough to make me want to let loose and incinerate the offices. Just for the sake of expediency. Then they'd have to believe me.

Of course, some fool might shoot me in the heat of the moment (ha), so I thought it better to keep my cool (ha ha).

My assigned counselor is Muriel O'Reilly. She's way too young to have a name like Muriel, but there you go. She's organized and her office is all soothing yellow and she smiles far too much.

Muriel smiled when I knocked on her office door.

"Hello, Ms. O'Reilly. I got a slip to come down."

"Hello, Zoë. Please call me Muriel." Muriel always wants to be called Muriel. (If my name was Muriel, I'd want to be called Bob.)

It is good, though, to have some constants in the world.

She gestured to the hot seat in her office and got up to shut the door behind me. Okay, so this was serious business.

I sat and waited for the bomb.

She sat back down behind her desk, folded her hands together, and regarded me with solemn compassion. "So, what seems to be the problem, Zoë?"

I do like that Muriel cuts to the chase.

Unfortunately, I wasn't clear on which particular problem was the issue in this place at this time.

Feigning ignorance is a good tool.

"What problem?"

Muriel opened the file. "You've been missing classes, and disappeared for the better part of the afternoon yesterday. Apparently, you haven't been completing your homework assignments and your grades are slipping. You were inattentive in art class, which is very uncharacteristic." She closed the folder and studied me, exuding earnest care. "This might be little cause for concern in another student, but we like to know our students individually. You've always been a good student, Zoë, and have no record of missing classes. Is there a problem?"

"No," I lied. "Everything's fine."

"Problems with other girls?"

"No." I tried a smile.

"Boys?"

"No." Mages, Thunderbirds, werewolves, and rebel rockers, but that was different.

"There's no need to be defensive. I'm here to help you." Muriel smiled. "To be your friend."

I smiled back. It was a better choice than laughing out loud. "There's no problem," I insisted. "I'll try to do better. In fact, I'm missing English class right now. Can I go?"

Muriel frowned. "Zoë, I had hoped that you and I could resolve this."

"Nothing to resolve," I said, trying to look enthused. "I'll just go back to English class. . . ." I stood up.

Muriel didn't. "I don't want to call your parents about this. I know that your mother in particular dislikes whenever there are academic issues."

"My mom's away," I said before I thought it through.

Muriel checked my file. "Away?"

"She, um, well, she left. And my dad went after her, to talk."

Muriel completely failed to hide her astonishment. She began to take notes at lightning speed. "Then who is staying with you? You don't have siblings and you are a minor. . . ."

"My dad arranged for me to stay with Meagan and the Jamesons while he's gone. So, it's all taken care of." I smiled.

Muriel put down her pen and sighed. She fixed me with a look of such concern that I almost squirmed. "I'm very sorry to hear about your parents and their marital difficulties, Zoë. Would you like to attend our course for students whose families are being damaged by divorce?"

I grabbed my bag. "No, I'm good, thanks. I don't think my family's going to be damaged by divorce." I smiled. "My dad, he can be pretty persuasive, and I'm sure . . ."

But I wasn't sure.

And Muriel knew it.

I really didn't want to think about it.

I ran out of words and we stared at each other for a moment. Then I slung my bag onto my shoulder. For once, the earnest compassion got to me. I felt my tears rising, but I blinked them away.

"Maybe later," she said softly. "Thank you for telling me about this, Zoë. If you don't mind, I'd like to chat with Mrs. Jameson about our concerns."

"Sure. Whatever. English!" And I was gone.

Muriel meant well, but she didn't know the half of it.

And I wasn't going to be the one to tell her. The Covenant, you know.

Which just meant I was going to have to cram in some extra schoolwork to avoid suspicion.

In my spare time.

Such as it was.

No pressure.

Chapter 9

There was no way I was going back to English class. I wasn't interested in hearing about the weather as a character or in learning what I hadn't thought about including in my essay. I certainly didn't want to see that grade.

Instead I went to the library and did what I do best. I worked on that drawing for Derek and thought about what I needed to ask him.

It was shaping up to be a pretty good drawing. The dragon filled the cover of his book. It was rearing back, its tail coiled behind and beneath it, its wings stretching off the edges of the page. It had a fearsome number of teeth and was breathing fire, its claws raised to strike and its eyes flashing.

I'd sketched the pose in pencil, and now was filling it in with marker. First the outline in black, then all the detail of the scales. This dragon had a bit of an Asian look to it, so I'd put the traditional pearl in one claw. On impulse, I drew continents on the pearl, making it into the planet Earth. Kind of an inside *Pyr* joke, seeing as how we're supposed to be the defenders of Earth. This dragon was kicking butt in defense of his hoard. I did some Asian clouds behind him, the kind you see in tattoos.

I was trying to decide whether I should go with color or leave it a black line drawing when I felt someone beside me.

Derek.

Of course.

"Cool," he said and sat down beside me.

I knew he was watching me, but didn't look up. "Color or just like this?" It was his book—he could decide.

He leaned closer, his elbow pressing against mine. I could feel how warm he was, smell his skin. It was an awful lot like the moment I'd had in that other library with Jared in the spring—complete with the librarian watching us like a hawk.

I even felt something fluttery in my stomach. Not as strong as it was with Jared, but it was there.

Awareness.

And just the way I did when I was with Jared, I forgot whatever I was going to say next.

Derek glanced up at me then, those pale blue eyes seeming to pierce right through me. "What color would it be?"

I couldn't quite catch my breath. "Whatever you want."

The corner of his mouth lifted a little, not quite a smile. "What do you want? It's your drawing."

I looked away from his intensity, studying the drawing. "I guess I'd make him shades of purple, with some charcoal. It would contrast with the orange flames."

"Him?"

I looked at him again. "Sure. All dragons are guys."

"What about dragon shifters?"

"Most of them are guys."

"But not all." Derek reached for the drawing, turning it to examine it more closely. "I want you to color it like a girl dragon." And he pushed it back at me, a dare in his eyes.

"Which is?" I wasn't sure whether he'd seen me as a dragon or just as a salamander.

"White." He spoke with conviction and I knew he'd seen. "A thousand shades of white, from mist to snow to starlight."

It was strangely poetic for Derek the gruff. I looked at him, and was surprised to see the back of his neck turn red.

As if he were embarrassed.

Huh.

I leaned forward, bracing myself on my elbows and whispered. "Is there a reason you came to this school this year?"

His gaze flicked at me, then away, then back. "You."

Now I was blushing, but I didn't look away. "Why?"

He eyed the librarian, then pulled another notebook from his backpack. He wrote, then turned the page toward me.

There is a prophecy among my kind, that when the stars stand still in the sky, all shifters will be hunted. The only way to survive will be to form a larger pack, one that includes other kinds of shifters. The key to that union's success is our accepting the dragon unique to her kind as our pack leader. I came to make that union.

He spun the book and pushed it toward me, staring across the library while I read what he'd written: *I came to make that union.*

Those words left me uncertain, self-conscious, jittery. My Wyvern sense made me feel that his interest was about more than a treaty negotiation. How exactly did wolves seal their alliances?

The way he watched me made me pretty sure I could guess the answer and it left me flustered.

"Why you?" I asked quietly.

He smiled a little. "Not everyone believes in prophecies."

So, there was doubt among the werewolves, but Derek believed. Whether he'd been assigned to be an emissary or had chosen the role, he was here to make the union work. And I could guess that a big part of that would be my proving myself worthy of being pack leader.

From what I knew about wolves, males took precedence, particularly males in their prime.

No wonder there was skepticism in the pack about me, a young girl dragon.

I took a breath, then tapped the first sentence, the part about stars standing still. Derek tugged out his messenger, typed in a search term, then offered it to me.

It was a site about the Great Lunar Standstill. A Great Lunar Standstill, it turned out, was a momentous astrological event.

And we were in the middle of one.

I skimmed the details and learned:

1. A Great Lunar Standstill occurs roughly every nineteen years.
2. There's a theory that ancient peoples were totally into tracking Great Lunar Standstills and that monuments like the Standing Stones of Callanish were built to showcase Great Lunar Standstills. Astrologers warn to expect great upheavals, transformation, and change during such events.

There was a bunch more, but it made my eyes glaze over, even with my newfound love of astronomy. When I finished reading, the notebook with Derek's handwritten message was gone, presumably tucked back into his bag. I gave him his messenger and our fingers brushed. I was pretty sure it wasn't an accident. I swallowed, and he watched me closely, his eyes gleaming pale.

"So, how do we make this happen? How do we convince . . ."

Derek shook his head and frowned to silence me, flicking another look at the librarian. Then he leaned close, his gaze fixed on me. "You lead. You triumph. You win them over. And until they believe, I'll defend you." His lips set. "Count on it."

Okay, I had to prove myself worthy of leading a pack of wolves.

No pressure.

"Dragon's done," I said, pushing his notebook toward him.

Derek pushed it back. "You didn't sign it."

"I never do."

"You should start. You have to claim ownership of what you do."

"Mark territory, you mean," I said, thinking of wolves.

He smiled then, really smiled. It illuminated his face, making him look a lot less secretive. More approachable.

He nodded.

I signed.

"Thanks, Zoë," he said quietly. "I mean what I said."

I didn't doubt that for a minute. I watched as he tucked the notebook into the bag from the store, then inserted it in his pack with care.

"Aren't you going to use it?"

He gave me a hot look. "It's too special for that."

And then he was gone, leaving me with lots to think about.

MEAGAN AND I WERE WALKING home from school, and I was still thinking about Derek. If it was up to me to figure out how to lead an attack on the Mages, I needed to have a foolproof plan. I didn't want to put my friends in unnecessary danger.

Actually, Liam and Meagan were walking together, talking, and I was trailing behind. Liam had turned up at our lockers and was talking to Meagan about movies. They had dissenting opinions about the latest hot boy star. Predictably, Meagan was cutting the star a lot of slack and Liam wasn't.

Unpredictably, disagreeing with Liam was having a miraculous effect on Meagan's stutter. She was so busy mustering her arguments that she forgot to be nervous.

I liked that a lot. I had visions of us becoming close again, now that Jessica was busy with Trevor.

Maybe the apprentice Mage had done me a favor.

As if.

Nick suddenly pulled up beside us in his little electric-blue compact car. "Hey, Zoë!" he shouted, as if surprised to see me. I knew Liam had probably told him where we were, or he homed in on our respective scents. "How are you?"

"What are you doing here?" I cried, as if surprised as well. (Maybe we overdid it a bit.) He parked the car and climbed out, all long-limbed and athletic. I felt Meagan's mouth fall open once more.

"Hey, Liam." Nick smiled at Meagan. "Hi, I'm Nick."

She blinked, pushed up her glasses, and looked between the guys and me.

"I've known Nick forever," I said.

"I'll bet he's the s-s-son of a friend of your father's," Meagan guessed.

"How'd she know that?" Nick asked.

"Meagan's brilliant," I said. "Everyone knows it."

"Nice to meet you." Nick shook her hand. "Any friend of Zoë's is a friend of mine." He was a bit too cheerful, if you ask me, but Meagan blushed scarlet at his attention.

"My dad needs hotter friends," Meagan muttered under her breath and I tried not to laugh. Liam looked away to hide his smile. Nick was fighting his own smile, his eyes dancing.

"What are you doing here?" I asked again.

He looked embarrassed. "I thought I'd come down to see Isabelle."

"You know Isabelle, too?" Meagan asked. Nick nodded.

This was my opportunity to give him a hard time. "What does your girlfriend think of that?" Nick looked mortified. "He dumped Isabelle," I told Meagan and she regarded Nick with horror.

"Maybe he needs glasses," Liam said, teasing.

Nick turned red. He looked away. He shuffled his feet. "Teresa and I are just kind of seeing each other, sometimes. It's no big deal. It's just, you know, just . . ."

"Sex," Liam supplied. He managed to look innocent while he did it, too.

Nick glared at him.

Meagan choked, outraged on behalf of her idol.

That was when I guessed who else Donovan had been advising.

His son, Nick.

Nick turned to Meagan. "I figured I'd come and talk to Isabelle, try to straighten things out. Maybe we can just be friends."

"I don't know why you'd want to date anyone other than Isabelle," Meagan said and Nick blushed even redder.

The thing was, I didn't think he knew either.

I DIDN'T HAVE A TON of spare time in the evenings for the rest of the week. As much as I would have liked to hang out with Liam and Nick, Meagan's mom had other ideas. She was taking her custodianship of me really seriously so I was guessing that Muriel had called. I got parked at the dining room table to do my homework under surveillance, every night from six thirty to ten.

And she took my messenger until I was done.

Meagan, of course, was finished with everything by eight. She stayed with me and read, and was helpful when I needed it.

In our respective beds at night, we argued about Trevor and Jessica. Meagan thought it was a sign of Trevor's sensitivity that he had seen the finer qualities of Jessica, even though she wasn't flashy like Suzanne. She refused to condemn Jessica for getting the bonus prize that she had wanted herself.

Maybe she thought that one day, if Jessica and Trevor didn't work out, Trevor would notice her. She certainly accepted every invitation from Jessica to include her in their plans.

I had deep dark feelings about all of this, but I couldn't say much without sounding like more of a bitch than Suzanne.

After that topic was exhausted every night, we argued about her Halloween costume. Meagan was determined to be Mozart, even though that was the least likely costume to get her noticed by any guy alive. She thought it would make Trevor aware of the interest in music they had in common. I thought she should go with something more sexy. Meagan was sure she was right, though, and had a long silver wig, a brocade jacket from a vintage store, breeches, and buckled shoes. And a conductor's wand.

Her glasses at least didn't look out of place. And who knew—maybe she and some other hot guy with musical skill would hit it off.

Maybe there was a guy like Trevor out there for her who wasn't an evil apprentice Mage.

I had to hope.

I had no costume, as I was determined I wasn't going anywhere.

Despite Meagan's entreaties.

Her messenger wasn't chiming very often, a sure sign that Jessica had found something more interesting to do. I was angry that she was treating Meagan so shabbily, but I wasn't sure what I could do about it. Meagan kept cutting her new friend slack, which made me even more mad. The guys kept me posted on their investigative progress, which was fairly minimal.

I had the definite impression that they were having more fun than me.

Derek was circling, not approaching unless I beckoned to him. All I needed was a foolproof plan to save the world.

Sadly, I hadn't refined that one yet.

I got one stern message from my dad, informing me that we would talk when he got home. I knew what he wanted to talk about, and that message made me hope he'd stay in England for a while.

Maybe for good. A "talk" with a pissed-off dragon is never a good time.

I heard from my mom every morning. She never said anything about the incident with the counselor, but someone must have told her something because she was more intent on asking questions. I'd put my nickel on Mrs. Jameson. It was good to hear my mom's voice, even though I couldn't read one thing in her tone and she wouldn't talk about my dad.

In bed, when Meagan was asleep, I tried to send visions to the *Pyr*, with no idea whether I was successful or not. The guys never mentioned having any dreams or receiving anything from me, but it was better than dozing off and meeting Urd.

By Friday, I was beat. I took one look at my English homework that night and thought I'd put my head down on the table and sleep.

Dostoyevsky. What joy was this. I'd be in a coma before I finished the first chapter.

Meagan finished early yet again, probably to starred reviews, and went to the piano to do her practice. She had her classes on Saturday morning for that, and I dared to imagine that I might have some free time.

She worked a scale, warming up. The Jamesons had a grand piano in their living room. In fact, it filled the living room with its glossy blackness. An imposing instrument. The sheer size of it made Meagan look petite and her hands seem small.

It was pretty much the only thing in the living room. This

made a kind of sense for the piano to reign supreme, as Meagan's dad was a concert pianist himself—she came by that talent honestly. And the piano got a lot of use. They'd had an enthusiastic discussion on Sunday morning about keys and timing and all the stuff she'd pulled out of Rick about the syntho drums.

I sighed and cracked open my required reading. It was even more boring than expected. I read the first page five times, Meagan's aria tickling at the edge of my thoughts. The music was pretty. And it made me concentrate better, as if Meagan was sending me her scholarly vibes.

I read four pages before I made the connection.

Then I pulled my new ring out of my pocket and pushed it onto my finger.

The living and dining rooms were filled with dancing beams of light. They were joyous, not like the confetti that Jared had sung but more like ripples and waves of light. They reminded me of mirrored streamers, and they swirled around the room like a joyous whirlwind. They were all shades of red and purple and blue.

Meagan glanced up at me and smiled, playing a little trill with her right hand. She looked so happy and at ease. I understood then that her destiny wasn't with brainiacs and math geniuses.

It was with musicians.

Because the ribbons of light told me that Meagan was a spellsinger.

Crap.

I was suddenly very afraid that the Mages knew it, too. This put a whole new spin on things.

Was Meagan their real target, instead of me?

What could I do? I'd never manage to persuade her not to go to Trevor's Halloween party, not without explaining everything to her. I was in enough trouble with my dad that I didn't want to rush into breaking the Covenant again. I couldn't even beguile her, because she knew the deal and would realize just who—and what—I was.

I had to admire that Trevor had accomplished his goal. He had ensured that I would be at his party. Despite my reservations, I had to go to protect Meagan.

From whatever the Mages were planning.

OF COURSE, Liam and Nick didn't see it that way.

We had an argument in old-speak Friday night. I was in Meagan's room and supposedly drawing, but they were a big distraction. They would have gone on and on, but I finally just ended it.

Meagan had already gotten up to look out the window. "So weird that there's thunder in a snowstorm," she said.

She turned to look at me, and I shrugged.

"Maybe it's an airplane flying low," I suggested and she looked out the window again. I wouldn't have put it past her to figure it out, though—Meagan is smart and she was already looking for *Pyr,* armed with data about us. She had that Einstein look, which was trouble.

I had to end the old-speak.

And that meant inflicting a decision on the guys.

"I've got the ring," I said, interrupting Nick. *"It cut the spells before and it'll do it again. We won't be trapped."*

"It's too risky," Liam argued, ready to go at it again.

"It's more risky for Meagan if we're not there."

"I vote we stay away," Nick said. *"You have no idea what they're planning."*

"But we have to defend our Wyvern," Liam said.

"Suit yourselves either way," I said, knowing exactly how they'd take that challenge. *"I'm going. Maybe it'll be my chance to persuade the wolves to join us."*

They mumbled and grumbled a bit, but agreed that we'd all go. We set a time to meet and the old-speak fell silent.

I wondered when Derek would turn up but wasn't sure how to find out. School was over for the weekend and I didn't know where he lived.

Would he just sense it?

How sharp was his sense of smell?

Could I find him with mine?

I watched Meagan at the window until she turned away. "Either way, the thunder seems to have stopped," she said, getting back into bed.

"Maybe I'll come to the party after all," I said as casually as I could manage it.

Her face lit. "Really?"

"I need a costume, though."

"Why don't you come to my piano lesson tomorrow, and then we'll go shopping from there?"

"Great idea," I agreed, knowing it would give me the perfect cover to guard her.

And maybe I could find Derek.

I SHOULD HAVE KNOWN THE harmony between Meagan and me couldn't last.

We were in my fave vintage shop, One More Time. Normally, I could spend everything I had within moments of crossing the threshold, but on this day, I just couldn't focus. I hadn't found anything for my costume, because that particular concern didn't have my attention. Compared to everything else that was going on, shopping for the perfect Halloween costume seemed ridiculously frivolous.

I'm not good at keeping up appearances.

Mostly I was trying to figure out how to warn Meagan without breaking the Covenant again.

So, I was fingering this crimson feather boa, trying to imagine something really simple that wouldn't look (quite) like I didn't care, when Meagan got a call.

From the look on her face, I knew it was Jessica.

"Sure," she said. "That's great. Seven's no problem. See you then." She ended the call and flashed me the stainless smile. Her eyes were sparkling in a way that didn't make me feel good. "Guess what? I'm going to get a ride in Trevor's MG!"

I dropped the boa. "What?"

"Trevor and Jessica are picking me up. They have to come early, because he wants to be home before everyone arrives." She hummed a bit, poking at things as she practically skipped through the store. "Isn't it nice of them to think of me?"

"No!" I was right behind her, close enough to see how startled she was by my reply. "I mean, why don't you just get a ride with me and the guys, like we planned? I thought you wanted to see Liam again." I tried to not sound panicky. "Nick is coming at eight. That'll give you more time to get ready."

"Oh, but I want to ride in Trevor's car. It's so cool."

"But Jessica is dating him. Won't you feel out of place?"

"I don't think so." Meagan pivoted to face me over a rack of kerchiefs. "After all, she's being really nice about it. She knows how much I like him, and she's not trying to be mean."

"How can you tell? Sounds to me like she's rubbing your nose in it."

"No, you're wrong." Meagan was emphatic. "You just don't know her like I do."

There wasn't much I could say to that. I was freaking, though, at what might happen to Meagan before I got to the party. I had zero data about the Mages' plans but I do have an active imagination. I didn't want her to be alone with Trevor—or Trevor and Jessica—for a whole hour. I flicked through the kerchiefs and seized a purple one, not really seeing it. "Let's go."

Meagan was skeptical. "That's your costume?"

"And this." I plucked a white plastic cowboy hat from a shelf. There was a plastic gun beside it in a cheap toy holster, lucky for me. "This too." Jeans, boots, a skinny shirt, and I'd be ready for the shoot-out at the OK Corral.

"I think you could try harder," Meagan said.

"I think Jessica could be nicer to you." I went to the cash register, wondering what I could do to change her mind.

Short of telling her the whole truth.

"We had a long talk about it. It's not her fault. She likes him, too." Meagan leaned against the counter beside me, checking out the bangles. They had a couple of sweet Bakelite ones, but I barely saw them. "She said when she tutored him, it just felt like magic between them." Meagan turned a smile on me. "Isn't it romantic?"

I couldn't believe it.

"So, explain this to me. You're Jessica's friend and so you want her to be happy."

"Right."

"I'm your friend, so I want you to be happy."

"Okay."

"Why doesn't Jessica have this concern, if she's your friend?"

Meagan's eyes flashed. "You're still jealous of her."

"I think you deserve better friends!"

"Oh, like ones who don't confide in me?"

So, we were back to that. Meagan left the shop and I ran after her, jamming my acquisitions into my backpack. The hat had to go on my head. Nice bonus to look like an idiot while I was trying to be persuasive. "Meagan, we need to talk about this."

She stopped in the street so abruptly that I nearly ran into her. "Go ahead," she said, a daring glint in her eyes. "Tell me what happened last spring."

I was tempted.

I was *really* tempted.

But my back was hurting like hell after taking that thunderbolt and I could still recall the sting of the dragonsmoke on my hand. If I told everything to Meagan, when she wasn't specifically in danger, it'd be exile city for me.

I dropped my gaze.

Meagan sniffed and walked away. I trailed behind her feeling like ninety-seven thousand kinds of loser.

It wasn't an easy choice.

It also wasn't one I didn't question over and over again for the rest of the day.

In fact, I sent my dad a message, asking for permission to break the Covenant because I feared Meagan was in danger. I didn't say what danger, because I knew he wouldn't believe anything I said about the Mages, and I also didn't want him reminding Mrs. Jameson that I shouldn't be allowed to go to a Halloween party at all.

This did undermine my argument.

The lack of those details was probably why he immediately declined my request.

But then, providing those details wouldn't have done me any favors, either.

I was getting tired of no-win situations.

Meagan and I returned to her house in silence. I mostly was thinking about how nice it would be to catch a break once in a while.

Before the party would have been good.

THE DOORBELL RANG PROMPTLY AT seven and Meagan practically flew to the door in her excitement. I was right behind her.

She'd made a change from her Mozart idea, maybe because I'd finally gotten through to her. She was dressed as Rapunzel, an idea of her mother's, with long hair made of yellow yarn coiled around one arm. She and her mom had argued about her glasses ruining the costume and the immediate necessity of contacts, but Meagan had lost.

We were both sure who was at the door, but we were both wrong.

It was Derek.

Dressed as he usually was for school.

"Hey," he said, nodded at both of us and shoved his hands in his pockets. He looked uncomfortable.

I was ridiculously glad to see him and it probably showed. Meagan was looking between us (Einstein all the way) and started to smile when Derek didn't say anything more. I didn't say anything either, because everything I wanted to tell him couldn't be shared in front of Meagan.

"You two probably have lots to talk about," Meagan said, flashing a smile. "I'll just go back inside."

Before she could do that, we heard the roar of a car engine. The MG peeled around the corner, going way too fast, and squealed to a halt in front of the house. The top was up, but Jessica was waving out the window and calling Meagan's name.

Trevor honked the horn.

I wanted to shout, but Derek gave me a look and shook his head. I decided to trust his view of the future.

Meagan scooped up her miles of yarn hair, and ran to the sidewalk. Jessica got out of the front seat and they hugged. My eyes nearly fell out of my head. Jessica was wearing a superhero costume, all formfitting spandex that could have been painted on. She was far more curvy than I'd ever imagined. She turned so I could see her face and my mouth fell open in shock. She had ditched her baseball cap. And she did have one whopper of a secret—she was so gorgeous that she could have been a pinup girl.

Was this Trevor's influence?

Then Meagan piled into the backseat and all my fears returned with force.

"Hey, Zoë!" Trevor shouted. "If you're ready, why don't you come, too?"

"No," Derek said, fast and low.

"Not quite ready, thanks," I shouted. "I'll see you later."

I heard Meagan say something to Jessica about me and Derek and hoped wolves didn't have as sharp hearing as dragons do. Jessica giggled and Trevor squealed the tires as he pulled away.

"You're sure?" I asked Derek.

He inhaled deeply. "There's nothing good ahead, but it's still brewing. I don't think anything bad will happen before you get to the party."

"But she's a spellsinger and doesn't know it."

He looked at me in shock. I realized I'd never surprised him before. "So that's it."

"What?"

"A scent I didn't know." He nodded and I watched him add that information to his knowledge. "Okay. That makes sense."

"Are you still sure she's okay?"

Derek shot me a look. There was just a glimmer of doubt in his eyes, and only for a second, but I saw it.

"The guys are coming soon to pick me up. I'll be okay."

He stepped back then. "See you there," he murmured and disappeared into the shadows. I saw the blue shimmer of light only because I was watching closely.

I had to watch even more closely to see the silhouette of a wolf slipping through the darkness, heading toward Riverside Drive.

Almost a whole hour to wait.

It was going to kill me.

ALMOST EXACTLY AN HOUR LATER, Nick parked down the street from Trevor's house.

We could hear the music clearly, even a block away. There was the sound of laughter as well, and, courtesy of my ring, I could see those Mage spells spinning in the air over the house. A spiral of orange Mage spell light surrounded the house, as if it stood at the center of a vortex.

Or a hurricane.

"I'll bet his parents are gone," Nick said. "It sounds like a good party."

"That's because they're spellcasting already, just as we thought."

"Shit," said Liam.

"Look, just so you know, there's something different about this spell," I said. "It's not a net, like last time, that's closing around the perimeter. It's more like a vortex. It seems to be drawing in, kind of the way water goes down a drain."

"Shit again," Liam said, eyeing the house. "I don't like that they're learning new tricks."

"Or maybe trying out different ones," I said.

"I think it sounds like a great party," Nick said and reached for the door handle. "We might have fun."

I grabbed his arm in sudden understanding. "You're *supposed* to think it sounds like a great party. You're supposed to want to go in. It's a lure."

"The spell's already working on you," Liam said. I wasn't the only one remembering that Nick had been susceptible to Adrian's spell in April.

"A trap," Nick said with a nod, his gaze locked on the house. I could almost feel him fighting the spell.

Liam leaned forward, his tone urgent. "Remember that they can make you think whatever they want. That's what they did before, Nick. We've got to listen to Zoë."

"Right," Nick said, but he couldn't seem to look away from the house.

This was not good. And we hadn't even entered the house yet.

"Maybe you should wait for us," I suggested. "Hang with the car in case we need to make a quick getaway."

"Are you kidding?" His confident grin flashed. "I'm not going to miss a great party."

Liam and I exchanged a look as Nick got out of the car with purpose.

"I'll stick with him," Liam said. "You have other things to worry about."

"Right."

We looked funny gathering on the sidewalk in our costumes. Nick was dressed as a football player, his shoulder pads so huge that I had barely fit in the car beside him. Liam had made a Viking costume for himself out of some furry fabric. He had a blond wig and fake beard, an axe and big mukluks. I was a gunslinger.

I reached for Nick, but he was already striding toward the house, his cleats tapping on the sidewalk. Liam swore and went after him.

Just what I needed—someone else to guard.

The orange spell net swirled with greater speed as I watched. The sight made me dizzy, a carousel of throbbing light that almost obscured the house. I thought I might puke. I took off the ring and shoved it into my pocket, unable to deal with the eye candy and think straight at the same time. I had let Meagan go in there, with a bunch of Mages and who knew what else.

They knew that she was a spellsinger, and one way or another, they intended to recruit her.

They'd have to get past me first.

A SHADOW SEPARATED ITSELF FROM the landscaping as I marched down the sidewalk. I glanced sideways to find a wolf loping beside me, his head down and his ears folded back.

"Derek?" I asked and the wolf glanced me a look that was filled with disdain.

Right. Who else could it have been? He didn't have to talk for me to understand what he meant.

"Liam, Nick, this is Derek." It was a bit strange to be making introductions to a wolf, but the situation demanded it. Derek regarded them steadily, as if assessing their power.

"You told us about him," Liam said.

"Hey, Derek," Nick said and reached to scratch his ears.

Derek backed away, lifting his lip to display a large sharp fang.

"He's a wolf, not a poodle," I said and thought his eyes glinted with humor.

"Right," Nick said. "Glad to have you with us either way."

"In which form are you going in?" I asked Derek.

Again, I got the unblinking stare.

"Going with the element of surprise. Okay." I considered our costumes and made a choice. "You'd better stay with Liam, since you two look as if you might belong together."

"You can help me remind Nick to not listen," Liam said to Derek.

"No leash?" Nick teased and got a growl from Derek for that.

"Wolves don't wear leashes and collars," Liam said. "They need their autonomy."

Derek matched his pace to Liam then, and I knew they'd get along just fine.

"Well, you'd better tell them he's your dog and just looks like a wolf," Nick said and Liam nodded.

"I'll beguile to get him in, if I have to," Liam said. "We're going to need him."

Jessica seemed to be waiting just inside the house for us. She watched us come closer, that coy smile playing over her lips. She checked out Nick and her smile broadened.

He grinned right back at her. "Who's that? The cute girl with Meagan?"

Before I could answer, Jessica looked straight at me. I could see the glint of her eyes in the darkness as they narrowed.

Then she bared her teeth and hissed at me.

I put on the ring again and nearly fell over in shock. When I looked at her with my enhanced vision, it was clear that she was a jaguar, tawny, spotted, and powerful. With the same long-lashed amber eyes as she had in human form.

Shifter type number four, present and accounted for.

Open your eyes, Unktehila.

How could I have missed this? I felt more stupid than I ever had in my life—which was saying something. Derek had even warned me. There *were* jaguar shifters and evidently at least one of them went to our school.

Was that why Trevor was dating her?

What else hadn't I noticed?

Meanwhile, Jessica's tail lashed the way a cat's does when it's playing with a mouse. I saw her dig her claws into Meagan's shoulder.

And push her deeper into Trevor's house.

Was she helping the Mages?

Then she beckoned to Nick.

He moved at light speed, apparently forgetting all about us.

"Wait!" I cried, but he was already heading up the steps. He disappeared into the house, surrounded immediately by the golden spell light of the Mages. He was laughing, making friends with his usual easy charm, shaking hands with Jessica.

"What's wrong?" Liam said, but I just ran for the door.

Derek snarled and bounded after me. There was no time to consider our options or make a better plan. Nick and Meagan were in there already, so we had to follow.

I couldn't help thinking that this was exactly what the Mages had hoped would happen. And we hadn't been able to do anything about it.

"ZOË!" TREVOR CRIED AT THE door as if I were the homecoming queen. I wondered just how drunk he would need to be to actually be so glad to see me. Obviously he was just gleeful that his plan was coming together so well.

The music poured into the street, pulsing with energy. The orange spell light was so bright that I had to keep my eyes narrowed. I didn't dare take off the ring, though. I needed all the information I could get.

Of course, I would never let Trevor know what I could see. Dumb ol' dragon, that was me.

"I can only stop in for a few minutes," I said with a smile. "We're just on our way to a party at the college."

Trevor's eyes glittered. "No problem. Come on in." His gaze fell on Derek and I wondered how much he knew. "Is your dog trained?" he asked Liam.

"Absolutely," Liam said. He buried his fingers in the scruff of Derek's neck, as if they were old allies. "I can count on him anywhere."

Trevor looked from one to the other for a moment, then smiled as he stepped back. I guessed that if he knew what—if not who—Derek was, then he hadn't counted on his presence tonight. That smile, though, made me wonder. Was he glad to have more hunted shifters present?

I was afraid that we weren't just contributing to the success of the Mage plan for the evening, but unwittingly improving upon it.

We had to lift our collective game.

I recognized a bunch of people from school, although the costumes made it tricky. Cleopatra was there, a caveman, a Martian, at least four vampires, Julius Caesar, the president, Cinderella (she was wearing one clear shoe, which was the clue), an Amazon tribesman with a bone through his nose, Dorothy in her gingham dress and ruby slippers, a zombie, and a mummy with bandages unraveling all over the carpet.

Worse, the room was thick with Mages. Thanks to my ring, I could see them, their forms flickering. They slipped from form to form in rapid succession, their edges blurring with the transformations. I'm not sure whether they do it on purpose, or whether I was seeing their truth. Either way, the cycling between forms—minotaur, unicorn, snake, eagle, centaur, griffin, etc., etc., etc.—was a shocking display of all the shape-shifter species they'd eliminated. As before, it blew me away to see how many kinds of shifters there had once been. I wondered whether every kind of creature had once had a partner species: one kind shifted and one kind didn't. The Mages were cleaning up the shifter varieties, leaving just the unshifters.

And themselves, with all shifting powers.

The sight was a telling reminder of their plans for us.

The orange spell light wound all around them, a glowing ribbon that bound everyone more closely together. When I could stand to look at it, I could see its path—it led straight to the basement. I could hear people laughing down there and I truly didn't want to go down those stairs. I took off the ring for a moment to give myself a break from the visuals, and shoved it into my pocket.

There was also a lot of smoke in the house. Pot, incense, and cigarettes. The combination was overwhelming. I saw a couple of bottles of Jim Beam making the rounds and some huge jugs of cheap wine. There was a lot of giggling and a good number of fondling couples. Someone pinched my butt as I moved through the crowd, looking for Meagan.

There was no sign of her, which worried me.

How could she have already disappeared?

I headed toward the kitchen, as if looking for a drink. Artificial stimulus was the last thing I needed. Meagan was there, much to my relief. She was standing against the counter, looking a bit lost. She was explaining her costume to someone, with enough exasperation that I knew it wasn't the first time she'd been asked.

Jessica was beside her, in her superhero costume.

Standing guard, was my first impression.

Claws sharp.

Anyone else I knew would have been self-conscious—okay, except maybe Suzanne—but Jessica was working that costume. Guys were clustered around her, salivating. It seemed that the bookworm had shed her chrysalis, thanks to Trevor's attention.

Just like a twisted fairy tale.

Suzanne sulked by the fridge. I almost hadn't recognized her, because of her dark wig. She was yet another vampire, a line of blood painted down her chin, with plastic fangs and tons of eyeliner. She looked fit to kill when Trevor charged into the kitchen and flung his arm around Jessica. Jessica purred and ran one long-nailed finger down his chest and then they kissed with enthusiasm. The guys hooted and Jessica smiled as she nestled against his side.

As content as a cat in the sun.

She was in her element, no doubt about that.

"Bitch," Suzanne muttered and tossed back half of her glass of tomato juice. I was surprised by the wit of that, and wondered whether I'd underestimated her. I'd bet it had a little bonus in it—her eyes already looked glassy.

Then she looked at me and her eyes narrowed. "Freak. Don't think I don't get it, Sorensson."

"I don't know what you're talking about."

Suzanne laughed without humor. She pointed a finger at me. "No one calls me crazy. Understand?"

"I never called you crazy."

"But other people did, and it was because of you. I might not have proof of what I saw, but you can count on me getting it." She sipped her juice with satisfaction, malice shining in her eyes. "Then we'll see who the real loser is."

It said something that I had bigger problems than Suzanne feeling vindictive. I smiled and made some innocuous comment about her being drunk early, then ignored her.

Meagan glanced at me and smiled. Her eyes lit at the sight of Liam. Derek was right at my knees, Liam behind, and Nick ahead of me, and it felt good to be among friends.

I accepted a Coke that I didn't want and gave it a careful sniff before I sipped it. It seemed to be okay, but I didn't plan to drink it anyway. I leaned against the counter near the back door, as if totally at ease, and pushed my ring onto my finger again.

The vivid orange spell slapped me in the retina. It was brighter than any I'd ever seen, swirling and spinning with a manic energy. It spiraled down the stairs to the basement in an accelerating tunnel of power. I could feel its allure and see its effect upon even the humans who were present.

Liam went over to talk to Meagan. She was obviously relieved to find someone she knew—never mind that he was a hot guy—and they started to dissect (again) the movie we'd seen together the other night.

Derek growled a little and I knew he was displeased that we weren't sticking together. He went to Liam, though, and sat in front of him. His pale gaze was restless, and he snarled at anyone who touched him.

Nick bumped my shoulder with his, then took a swig of his beer. "*Down there?*" he asked in old-speak. I knew he couldn't see the spell, so I looked at him in surprise. He grinned crookedly. "*I really* really *want to go down there.*"

So, he was feeling the effects. He knew it, but his thoughts were still muddled. I nodded agreement, not wanting to say anything aloud or in old-speak. I saw the spell swirling around Nick with greater intensity. Had he drawn it closer because of his old-speak? I remembered that the Mages could hear old-speak and I quietly freaked.

I had no chance to warn Nick because he moved away from me, the orange light surrounding him with its glow. He gravitated toward the basement stairs. I exchanged a look with Liam and saw Derek's eyes narrow. I pretended to sip my Coke, as if everything was peachy, although I had a feeling everything was sliding into the crapper.

Good thing I was faking because Adrian walked into the kitchen just then.

If I'd been drinking for real, I would have choked.

Chapter 10

Adrian was the Mage who had pretended to be a dragon the previous spring and had cast a spell at boot camp that had turned the guys against me. Adrian had disappeared in the ensuing battle and we figured he'd been recalled to Mage headquarters—wherever that was. Since then, there'd been no sign of him.

I'd known that I hadn't seen the last of him.

But now I pretended not to know it was him.

Because he was in disguise. Beneath his construction worker costume—complete with hard hat, lunch box, and MEN AT WORK sign—he was wearing a glamour that made him look sixteen, short and blond. He watched me with care as he entered the room, but I pretended to be interested in my drink.

Like I hadn't even noticed him.

My ring showed me the truth. Adrian flickered between forms on the periphery of my vision, his presence enough to make me queasy. I caught a glimpse of the human disguise he'd worn at boot camp—the easygoing college pal, the helpful guy with dark hair and dark eyes—as he shifted between forms. I had no idea whether the college pal was his real form or not, but it seemed to be one he liked. It made frequent appearances in his playlist.

Did Mages don glamours to fake out non-Mages? I wondered. The answer was not lurking at the bottom of my Coke. Suzanne sidled over to him and made a joke about his costume. She could see only his glamour.

Uh-huh. Even with the glamour, he wasn't exactly the hottest guy at the party. He smiled back at her and that was good enough for Suzanne. Maybe she *was* drunk. They sidled up close to each other, even though he kept checking me out.

Had he been planning to hit on me? I never thought I'd feel any gratitude toward Suzanne, but in that moment, she might just have been my favorite person in the universe for saving me some trouble.

The spell spun more wildly in Adrian's proximity, another golden thread weaving into its gilded spiral. It was moving faster and getting brighter all around us. Sparks danced from the Mages in attendance.

I felt the hair rise on the back of my neck as the clock struck nine. A visible frisson of energy crackled through the house. The party quickly got louder. The temperature rose. The beat of the music became more insistent.

Nick got even closer to the basement stairs.

Shit.

The spell targeted him, swirling around his head like a swarm of fireflies. I could see him fighting it.

And I knew that he was losing.

"Hey, Nick," Liam said. "Come tell Meagan about your car."

Nick shuddered from head to toe, then grinned. It was a shaky grin, far from his usual smile, but I was proud of him for trying. I was thinking we should snatch Meagan and bail.

But then the Mages would just regroup. I wanted to know what they were up to.

"Great idea," Nick said. He visibly gritted his teeth to head toward them, defying the allure of the spell. I could see that his temples were dark with sweat, but he moved toward Meagan.

Just when I thought we were out of the proverbial woods, Trevor laughed. "Hey, I've got a great idea! Let's jam!"

"Excellent," Jessica said. "I'm ready to sing."

They headed for the stairs, arms wrapped around each other.

"Meagan plays piano, you know," Jessica said to Trevor.

"Really?" He smiled at Meagan and she blushed, right on cue. "That's great. I have an electronic keyboard, but I'm not good at it. Will you come jam with us?"

Meagan's face lit up.

There was no way she'd refuse.

And there was no way she could play in a houseful of Mages without them realizing that she was a spellsinger.

I saw from Trevor's expression that he, at least, knew what she could do.

"Hey, but I wanted to talk to you," I said to Meagan. I had no excuse, not even something feeble.

"We can do that later," she said predictably, and followed Trevor. "Do you have your sax here?"

"Not the one I play at school. My dad bought me an amazing antique one. You should hear the sound of it."

"I can't wait."

Liam went after Meagan, his expression concerned. "I've never heard you play," he said to her and she smiled at him.

Derek snarled and went after Liam.

Nick looked at me, swallowed, and followed Liam.

Shit. The worst-case scenario was happening and there was nothing I could do about it.

I followed them all, my guts churning with dread.

"I love jazz," Suzanne purred at Adrian.

"Me, too." I saw Adrian smile, then heard him on the stairs behind me. If I'd hesitated, I'm sure he would have pushed me.

Shit shit shit. Without knowing what was going to happen, I couldn't make a plan of what to do to stop it. I heard the door at the top of the stairs slam and click behind us. I pivoted in surprise and Adrian smiled.

"Nothing like a little privacy," he said and Suzanne giggled.

Trevor played a trio of notes on his sax below us, warming up. I leapt down the last steps in time to see Meagan familiarizing herself with the controls of the keyboard.

She played a score, the same one she always used to warm up, and I could see that she loosed a shower of spellsinger lights. Trevor smiled encouragement. Adrian practically rubbed his hands together with glee. Jessica smiled to herself and other Mages drew closer, easing toward Meagan from the perimeter of the room.

My mouth went dry

Then I saw the spell lock shut, trapping us in a maelstrom of orange light.

This was so not good.

I PRETENDED TO BE OBLIVIOUS to the spell and its power, even though anyone with a speck of perception would have noticed that my heart was pounding in terror. No one could have heard my pulse, though, because they started to play.

And it was loud. I couldn't believe the amount of equipment down there. It would have made any member of Jared's band salivate, and showed a remarkable investment. I guessed then that Trevor's parents were Mages, too. I knew I'd never again look on anyone with any musical talent without wondering about their spellsinging abilities.

The ring was the only thing that let me see whether they were making spells. The color and behavior of the musical spells was the only clue as to whether the musician in question had joined the Mage team or not.

There were syntho drums and electric guitars, two bass guitars, the keyboard, a trombone, a trumpet, and Trevor's sax. There were amps like crazy, the collective sound making the beams of the house reverberate in time.

They were all warming up, creating a cacophony. The swirl of spell light was dizzying, contributing to the whole in a crazy swirl of gold. I couldn't discern any pattern or rhythm to it—it seemed that the spells spun more wildly because they were confined. To make the visual feast even worse, the Mages who played were flickering between forms as they did so. It was as if they weren't even real.

Nick stood on one side of me and swore under his breath. Liam was on my other side, his fingers buried in the scruff of Derek's fur. Derek had his ears folded back, as if offended by the sound.

Or its volume.

I wished I knew what he could see coming in the next two minutes.

"Wow," Liam said, obviously well aware that the Mages would hear us.

"And then some," Nick agreed, squaring his shoulders. They both looked at me.

"Wait for it," I said softly and then I smiled. Adrian was hovering near me, watching. I was determined to keep surprise on my side. "I'm sure they'll sound great once they warm up."

Trevor held up one hand and they fell silent. "Let's start with something classic," he said. "Everyone know 'Begin the Beguine'?" One of the Mages on guitar played a riff, Meagan joined in on the first bar, and they hit it.

They did sound good.

Or maybe their collective spell was persuasive like that. The spell light created a cohesion then, spinning like a spiral in a thousand shades of yellow and gold. I was reminded of hot caramel spirals drizzled over desserts. When they cooled they were hard, brittle and sparkly, perfect swirls of sweetness.

That's what the Mage spell started to look like. Meagan's spellsinging bounced around within the confines of the Mage spell as she played on, oblivious to what they were doing. Her music was blue and purple, in marked contrast to the Mage colors.

But confined by their spell.

Caged.

And their spell targeted hers, and sucked hers dry.

I fought the urge to shiver.

That was nothing compared to when Jessica began to sing. I was shocked. I'd never heard her sing. She had a gorgeous voice. Molten and rich and deep. Far more sophisticated than I would have expected from a teenage math whiz.

And she sang scat. She sang nonsense, ad-libbing a tune that riffed on the music. I didn't know what it was called then, but Meagan told me later. I thought, actually, that it was pretty cool that she could do that on the fly.

Jessica, it appeared, had bunches of secrets.

Her scat singing sent out an array of little bubbles, all different sizes and shaded from copper to burgundy. Trevor leaned in close beside her, getting into the music. She matched rhythm with him, the two of them jamming so perfectly it was obvious that they'd done it before. Meagan's fingers faltered as she watched with awe. The other band members kept the beat, letting Trevor and Jessica improvise with each other.

The temperature in the basement rose even further. It got hot, like the air was simmering. Pulsing. There was something exciting about the beat, a driving rhythm that made me keenly aware of my own skin. Someone turned on a strobe, which was timed perfectly to the beat. I looked at the way that light cut through the spell light, and swallowed in dread.

The Mage spell looked sharp. Like golden knives in the darkness.

And it was moving.

No, it was closing, a trap tightening on its prey.

But to my astonishment, its target was Jessica.

JESSICA SANG, her head tipped back and her eyes closed. She was lost in the music, unaware of the danger she was in. The strobe light flashed. The spell closed in around her like a gilded cage.

Should I warn her?

Or was that what they expected me to do?

Trevor finished their improv and played a little flourish on his sax, bridging back to the chorus. Meagan was watching, her fingers still as she looked around.

I knew she sensed that something was wrong.

Because Jessica opened her eyes then. She almost smiled, and I saw her take a breath, as if she was going to join in on the chorus.

But the Mage spell snapped right around her. She was enclosed in a net of golden light, light that buzzed all around her. She visibly panicked that she was trapped, and began to struggle, but to no avail. Her shadow stretched across the floor, surprisingly dark.

Derek snarled and would have taken a step forward, but Liam held him back with a touch and he reluctantly sat down. His ears were up and his fur was bristling.

Was she really in danger, or was this a trick? I couldn't tell.

The Mages sang louder.

And they stepped closer, forming a circle around Jessica. She thrashed in the golden mesh, but it continued to tighten. The next moment she was struggling on the floor, more like a fish in a net than a girl. I assumed everyone else would think she was having some kind of convulsion. The Mages barricaded her from the others, blocking their view. I was surprised that no one tried to move closer, but then I noticed that all the other kids were staring, unblinking. They weren't moving at all. Not even breathing. It was as if they'd been frozen in time. Or struck to stone.

Enchanted.

There was a shimmer of blue and Jessica shifted, becoming a golden jaguar right before everyone's eyes.

It looked like an involuntary shift and I knew what that meant. She *was* in real trouble.

Adrian bent toward her and she hissed, then slashed at him with her claws. He laughed as the mesh kept her contained.

And then he took a bite out of her shadow.

She screamed, and it was the yowl of a great cat.

The Mages swarmed her, clustering closer as each bit at her shadow. I was horrified to see that the attack was diminishing her strength. It was even more creepy that all the kids who weren't shifters or apprentice Mages were completely frozen. Only Meagan was still moving, and I had to guess that was because of her spellsinging abilities.

Even though they were undeveloped.

"You can't do this!" Nick shouted.

"You're hurting her!" Meagan screamed and threw a tambourine at them. It bounced off the back of the Mage closest to her, who turned to face her. I could see the darkness of Jessica's shadow running down their chins, like chocolate sauce.

"Stop!" Liam roared. He bounded forward and shifted shape in midleap. He shimmered that pale blue, then became a massive dragon. Liam in dragon form is the vivid green of malachite, his scales and talons tipped with silver. He ripped open the back of a Mage with his talons before the guy even saw him coming.

"That's it," Nick said. "We're in." He shifted shape as well and defended his buddy's back as the Mages turned on Liam. Nick was so bright in color that it was like looking into the sun. He breathed a stream of fire and about ten Mage costumes went up in flames.

Derek let out a howl and jumped into the fray. I saw him bite the ass of a Mage, and am pretty sure he ripped out a chunk of flesh. He immediately went for another chomp.

A couple of Mages screamed. The music faltered as dragons trashed the place. The Mages lost their rhythm under attack. Some turned to fight dragons and the wolf directly. Others flickered through their forms in agitation. Still others continued to consume Jessica, gobbling bites of shadow and looking over their shoulders as if fearing they'd be interrupted at their feast. She was shifting from human to jaguar and back again, moaning. I knew that wasn't good, but I had to choose my priorities.

I went for Meagan.

Trevor appeared beside her when I was halfway across the floor. I shifted shape, livid that he would try to get between me and my friend.

There was no choice.

I was already in deep with my dad.

Meagan gasped in shock when I became a white dragon, spitting sparks in every direction, but Trevor smiled.

"Don't worry, Meagan. I'll defend you." He spoke in that low, soothing tone, the same one Adrian had used on the guys at boot camp. Meagan touched his shoulder, looking at him with a kind of adoration.

Shit.

I spun the ring on my talon, wishing with all my heart for the help of the last Wyvern, who had appeared once before when I was in serious trouble.

Nothing happened. The ring didn't illuminate. There was no red pulse and no answer from wherever it was that the former Wyvern currently resided.

The guys were thrashing Mages on every side, but that didn't change the fact that we were trapped. It was up to me to get all of us out through the barrier of the Mage spell.

And I had to do it alone.

No pressure.

FIRST THINGS FIRST.

I leapt toward Meagan and Trevor, talons bared. Trevor immediately sent up a barrage of spells, singing with low power. They were weak enough—few enough, new enough—that I shredded through their web and managed to scatter some of them. I exhaled a torrent of dragonfire before he could reinforce them. The spell light blackened and fell dead on the carpet, turning to ash underfoot.

Trevor paled and backed away. There was nothing between us and he was too freaked to make more spells.

I didn't intend to give him a chance to recover.

I headed right after him, breathing fire all the way. He stumbled over some wires and bumped into Meagan, who looked less impressed with him than she had.

I felt a presence behind me, smelled that it was Adrian but pretended to be oblivious. I leapt closer to Trevor as if closing in on my kill, felt Adrian raise his hands, then bailed pronto.

I manifested as a salamander on Meagan's shoulder, counting on her fascination with reptiles and knowledge of the *Pyr* to keep her from screaming. She did jump a bit.

"Wyvern?" she whispered, doing the math right on cue.

It's a bonus to have a genius friend.

"Just stick with me, and I'll get you out of here," I said.

She barely nodded, her gaze fixed on Adrian.

He was looking around, his eyes narrowed with suspicion. He started to kick over equipment, looking for me, and Trevor joined the effort. There were still half a dozen Mages singing, and I could have done without the sound.

Plus less volume and/or less music could only help our cause. If nothing else, the spell wouldn't be fed so easily. "Can you unplug the amps?" I asked Meagan.

She nodded again, then eased toward the wall. I hadn't even noticed the fuse box there—Meagan was going for the big kill.

I had to like that.

Trevor and Adrian were still looking for me. They started to argue about who had fucked up.

Time for another surprise.

"Here I go," I said to Meagan, just so she wouldn't be too startled.

She touched my back, encouraging me. I gathered my strength and disappeared, then spontaneously manifested again, right between Adrian and Trevor, a huge white dragon where there was no space for one.

"Looking for me?" I asked as I grabbed them each by the back of the neck. I slammed their heads together as hard as I could.

When I'm in dragon form, that's pretty hard.

They both went down, out cold. A trickle of blood ran from Adrian's nose, which worked for me.

At the same moment, Meagan hit the master switch and the basement went dark. The amps were silenced and even though a few Mages were still singing, I could see by the way the swirl of light dimmed that the spell had taken a hit.

I could see Jessica's limp form on the floor, her shadow in tatters and her body motionless, the golden swirl of spell light illuminating her. In an ideal universe, I would be able to save her, too, but I wasn't even sure it was possible. I had to protect my own kind first.

Just for the record, I wasn't positive that was possible, either.

Time was of the essence.

I shifted back to human form, grabbed Meagan's hand, and raced for the stairs. She should never have been involved in the battle between the shifters—I had to get her out of there. The basement was lit by flame and the occasional spurt of dragonfire. Liam swung his tail to clear a path for us, and Nick decked a couple of Mages. When they were staggering, he ignited their costumes with dragonfire, then laughed as they jumped around, trying to extinguish the flames. Derek stood guard at the bottom of the stairs, his pale eyes filled with menace and his teeth showing. A Mage dared to reach for him, but he snapped, nearly taking off the guy's fingers.

Meagan hesitated at that, but I tugged her toward him. "He's with us," I said and she came with me, even though I knew she wasn't convinced. In a flash of blue, Liam and Nick returned to their human forms, taking up positions behind Meagan.

To her credit, her eyes widened but she didn't say anything.

There was still the problem of the spell that kept us locked in the basement, though, and I wasn't sure how we were going to get through it. It seemed to be congealing at the top of the stairs, like a cork in a bottle. It wove into itself at frantic speed, creating another golden mesh barrier. I had no doubt that it would fold around us if we got close enough—or touched it—just as the other spell had enmeshed Jessica.

There were no windows in the basement—probably by design—and no other way out. We were on the stairs, Meagan and me and Liam and Nick, with Derek snarling at our rear.

I had to use everything I had.

I shifted shape, taking dragon form with a vengeance.

I tried to cut the spell with my talon, just as I had the previous spring.

No luck. My nail bounced off it, not even making a scratch.

That was when the Mages started to sing again.

Their chorus would have made the hair stand up on the back of my neck in human form. As it was, my scales prickled. I glanced back to find them standing at the bottom of the stairs, arranged like a chorus. They were bruised and battered and looked pissed off.

They were singing with passion.

Fortifying the spell.

I was pretty sure they had a taste for more shadows.

"Now what?" Meagan asked in a tiny voice, but I didn't have an answer.

I SHOULD HAVE GUESSED WHAT was happening when I saw the flames that were already burning in the basement begin to flicker in unison.

They moved together, like candles directed by the same wind.

But there was no wind in the basement.

And there was no wind anywhere that could make them burn brighter simultaneously. There was no wind on the planet that could coax all flames to get bigger at once. The flames grew. The fire became more yellow and more hot, gradually turning to huge white flames.

I wondered for an instant whether this was the Mages' work, but I couldn't believe they'd be that interested in ensuring their own incineration. The way they themselves started to look around with alarm supported that conclusion. There was perspiration on more than one face and terror in more than one expression.

Then who? Or what?

I gasped in sudden understanding. Who else had an affinity with fire? Who else could make the element of fire do his bidding? Help had arrived.

"Garrett!" Nick shouted.

"Who?" Meagan asked, just as a massive garnet and gold

dragon ripped the basement door off its hinges and flung it aside. He took out part of the ceiling too. Godzilla come to take our side. I heard Meagan gasp and might have gasped myself.

Garrett was magnificent.

The Mages' song faltered big-time.

The firelight danced off the golden scales of his chest, lovingly caressing the metallic strength of each one. The Mage spell began to wink out, the mesh thinning as Garrett worked his power. I heard the Mages gather their strength behind me, and I knew we had to take advantage of the spell's weakness before they rebuilt it. I slashed my talon at the spell, and a bit of it broke beneath my touch. Whether it was because of my ring or because it would have shattered anyway was irrelevant.

I shoved Meagan through the gap. Garrett caught her against his chest and continued to roar. The hole wasn't big enough for us to go out in dragon form. But I wanted the strength of my dragon to get us out of there.

The guys were still in human form, still right behind me. I reached back, grabbed Liam and shoved him through the gap. He barely fit, but I was glad to see him safely on the kitchen floor.

When I reached back again, Nick was ready to argue with me. "You go next," he protested, but I snarled at him and flung him through the space.

"Point taken," he said when he landed in a sprawl beside Liam.

The Mages' song broke out with sudden intensity and I saw the gap getting smaller. These spell lines were different. They looked like wire or rebar, and even though Garrett kept trying, he didn't seem able to weaken their spell again.

It really sucked that they were fast learners.

Or maybe they just knew more about the rules than we did.

"Quick!" I said to Derek. He bounded up the stairs toward the hole. It was closing fast, spiraling in with force. There wouldn't be time for both of us to get through.

"Zoë!" Nick and Liam shouted, probably sensing that there was a problem. They raced back to the top of the stairs and reached for me.

But as Derek dashed past me, I shifted shape to my salamander form. I fell on his back and hung on as well as I was able to in his long silver fur.

Just so you know—salamanders don't have a particularly good grip. It's those soft toes.

Derek jumped through the closing hole in the nick of time, yelping when the spell light singed his back paw. Then the spell clanged shut behind us.

It sounded like a big brass gong.

One that would have sealed our collective fate.

But we were all in the kitchen, surrounded by vamps and tramps and costumed kids from school. They were still enchanted, just like the ones in the basement, staring into space like zombies. Frozen in time.

"Let's get the hell out of here," Garrett said. He made it to the bay window in the kitchen in one step, Meagan in his grip, and kicked out the glass. He soared into the sky and I was glad to see her finally safe.

Derek jumped through the broken window behind him. I shouted as I started to slip. I was seriously in need of some sugar and didn't think I could shift again.

"There!" Nick said, pointing to me.

Liam snatched me out of the wolf's fur just before I fell to the ground, then shifted in midstride himself. He ascended into the night with a mighty beat of his wings, Nick in dragon form right behind him. The three *Pyr* flew in formation, ascending ever higher, and I watched Derek trot into the protective shadows.

"What about the other kids?" I asked, as the golden Mage spell fell into chunks and extinguished itself. I heard shouting then, the enchantment over the other kids evidently failing. To my relief, some kids came out of the house and started to yell for help.

The guys hovered and we watched until the fire trucks were arriving at Trevor's house. It took only moments. Pretty much everyone had spilled out on the lawn and they were chattering with excitement as the firemen turned their big hoses on the house. The hiss of flames being extinguished was louder than it should have been.

Once everything looked to have ended well, I shivered, exhausted and feeling vulnerable. There had been evil in that basement and only after we were safely away did I realize how close a call we'd had. My grip on consciousness was slipping and I decided not to fight it.

There'd been enough fighting already.

"*Where to?*" Garrett asked in old-speak. "*We have to talk.*"

"*Isabelle,*" I managed to whisper.

And then the world went black.

I AWAKENED IN HUMAN FORM, crashed on the bed in Isabelle's dorm room. Liam and Nick were sitting on the floor, Meagan was spinning in Isabelle's desk chair, and Garrett was leaning against the door, with his arms folded across his chest.

There was definitely some tension in the air. I noticed that Isabelle was ignoring Nick and Nick was checking his messenger with unnecessary concentration. The back of his neck was red. Liam was glancing between the two of them expectantly.

Garrett rolled his eyes and seemed impatient.

Meagan was stealing glances at Garrett and was a flustered shade of pink. I had a feeling she wasn't going to be dreaming about Trevor anymore.

"Eat this," Isabelle said as soon as my eyes opened, handing me a chocolate-coated granola bar.

Meagan smiled at me, which was an encouraging sign. "So I

guess this is what you weren't supposed to tell me." There was laughter in her tone.

I smiled. "Pretty much."

She slanted a glance at Garrett and her blush deepened. "Another one of your dad's friends' sons?"

I nodded, too busy chewing to say much more. I swallowed. "I'm sorry. We're not supposed to reveal ourselves in both forms to any humans."

"But you defended me from Suzanne."

"And I'm already in big trouble for that." I grimaced. "I'm sorry. I wanted to tell you." We looked at each other and maybe we would have hugged if we'd been alone. Then I did the introductions. "Meagan, Garrett. Garrett, Meagan."

Garrett smiled and shook Meagan's hand, his fingers almost engulfing hers. He'd bulked up even more over the summer. Meagan visibly swallowed, then gave me a look. She dropped her voice to a whisper and leaned toward me. "Can my dad be friends with your dad?"

I grinned, knowing I had to warn her. "They can hear you. We have sharper senses than humans."

She blushed even more crimson then. Garrett smiled a little but pretended not to notice.

I took the last bite of the granola bar, feeling my body respond quickly to the food.

Predictably, Meagan was making all the connections while I was recovering. "And that's why Suzanne calls you a freak?"

I nodded.

She grinned at me. "I knew you were lying when you said you didn't believe in the *Pyr*. I just didn't guess this was why." She glanced around the room, obviously awed that she now knew not just one but four dragon shifters.

Her gaze lingered on Garrett a little bit longer.

"You would have figured it out."

Meagan pushed up her glasses and considered me. "So, now that I know some, do I get to know the rest? Or do I only get half of the story?"

"*We can't,*" Nick said in old-speak.

"*We have to,*" I argued in kind. "*She's got innate spellsinging talent.*"

"*And I bet we need her help,*" Liam added.

Garrett inhaled sharply and spoke for the rest, his tone authoritative. "*Tell her.*"

Meagan glanced around herself. "Old-speak," she said. "I read about old-speak on that Web site. That's what it was when I thought I heard thunder, wasn't it?"

I smiled and nodded. "See? Another day or so and you would have had it all."

"They can talk to each other at a really low frequency," Isabelle said. "We humans hear it as thunder."

"Then you're not a dragon either?"

"Just raised by one." Isabelle offered the others some of her chocolate stash. Meagan took one.

She looked around. "What were you saying to each other just now?"

Isabelle smiled. "Something they don't want us to hear, probably."

"We were deciding whether to tell you the whole deal," Liam said to Meagan.

"Zoë says yes, and we agree," Garrett added and Meagan blushed again.

"Because you have a power that Mages can use. They're trying to recruit you," I said. "You have to know it all."

Meagan's eyes widened.

Isabelle cleared her throat, maybe giving Meagan a minute to absorb that. "Even though I've had the rundown of events, I don't understand how Garrett broke the spell."

"Or why you couldn't," Liam said to me.

"Or why you were even here," Nick said to Garrett.

"I figured out the book and came to tell you about it," Garrett said. "Zoë wasn't at home or at Meagan's place, so I followed your scents and realized pretty quickly that you were in trouble."

"Lucky for us," Liam said. "What about the spell?" he asked me.

"The ring didn't work this time. And my nail didn't cut the spell mesh the way it did before."

"Shit," Nick said. "Do you think they've changed their spell?"

"Time to tell us what you found in that book," I said to Garrett and he nodded.

"It's strange and you're not going to like it much." Garrett pulled out his messenger and tapped up the file. "I should probably share the scanned file with someone for safekeeping. I don't want them to guess that we have it, though."

"Send it to my desktop," Isabelle said. "I'm not *Pyr* and they're less likely to target me."

I wasn't sure of that and I could see that Garrett had his doubts as well. "Send it to Meagan, too," I suggested and she gave him her messenger address, stammering a little.

I liked that he pretended not to notice.

He sent the file and Meagan started to read it on her messenger even as he talked about it.

"Like I told you earlier, the original is really old. It looks handwritten and the book has ancient binding. I hid it in my mom's bookstore, because we might need it again."

"It was in Latin?" Liam asked, pulling up the file on Isabelle's desktop. She had a big screen and we all looked at the text. It made no sense to me.

Garrett nodded. "Once I scanned the pages and digitized the text, I ran it through a utility that translated it to English. It was pretty slow and there are breaks where letters weren't legible."

"And probably other places where it's just enigmatic," Meagan said.

"Right," Garrett agreed. "The text seems to be a handbook or guide for apprentice Mages."

"Lots of music theory," Meagan said, nodding as she scanned through it. She paused and frowned. "They find minor keys particularly powerful."

I remembered what she'd said about Jared's music and sat up to contribute what I knew. "The humans who can become Mages have an innate musical talent. They call those people spellsingers. Their musical gift allows them to evoke a strong emotional response from other humans, in essence to enchant with their song or their music. If they never met a Mage, they would just be good performers with this gift."

"But the Mages pervert this natural inclination and use it to gain power over other people," Garrett said. "And more is better. So they specifically listen for people with this talent and try to recruit them."

"Apprentice Mages, like Trevor," Liam said.

"And Adrian," I said.

"Whatever happened to him?' Nick asked.

"He was there tonight, wearing a glamour. Didn't you see that blond kid dressed as a construction worker?"

The guys were shocked. "*That* was Adrian?" Liam asked.

"Live and in person."

"So, there are Mages and apprentice Mages," Meagan said, returning to the story. "But what's the point?"

Garrett gestured to the displayed text. "The point is to bring back the master Mages. The master Mages pushed their powers to the limit and lost their physical forms. So the plan is to build a big enough group of Mages to create enough spellpower to make it possible for the master Mages to manifest again."

I nodded. "So they get power for their spells by eliminating shifters and assuming our forms—"

"Which the master Mages can then utilize," Garrett added.

"—plus recruiting spellsingers to increase the power of their spells."

"But what about Jessica?" Meagan asked. "What were they doing to her tonight?"

"I'm not exactly sure." Garrett looked grim. "But the master Mages are called ShadowEaters."

Chapter 11

There was an outbreak of questions at that, but Garrett answered one from Meagan first.

"How?" she asked when there was a lull.

He smiled at her, and I wondered whether something was starting between them.

"The book lays out a development plan for apprentice Mages. It starts with the question of identifying spellsingers, then has lessons on building spellsinging power, and the casting of spells for deliberate results. There's a lot of talk about shadows and darkness and death that doesn't make a lot of sense to me."

"Might be a code," Meagan said. "That was a common way to hide arcane knowledge in books. Zoë and I can probably crack it."

"I never thought of that," Garrett said. "That'd be great."

"If we have time," Nick said.

"The first section ends with something called the Invocation of Midnight. It seems to be a ceremony that allows the Mages to become ShadowEaters. It's like a graduation ceremony, but there are lots of warnings about not doing it too soon."

"When's too soon?" Liam asked.

"I'll guess it's when you can't shift back to your human form," I said and Garrett nodded.

"That seems to be what happened to this last bunch. They did it too early, before there was enough spellsinging power for there to be a return trip."

"A successful ceremony requires the NightBlade." Meagan mused, scrolling through the text.

"What's that?" Liam looked from Meagan to Garrett.

"It doesn't say," Garrett answered. "At least not clearly. But you need it for the ceremony at the end of the next section, the Invocation of the Eclipse."

"Why?" Nick asked.

"Because in that one you make a sacrifice with the NightBlade."

We shuddered in unison.

"Is that what we saw?" I asked. "Is that what they were doing to Jessica?"

"I don't think so," Garrett said. "Or maybe it was just practice. Because the Invocation of the Eclipse has to happen on the night of a full moon."

Isabelle got up and checked her calendar. "That's not until November fifteenth, more than two weeks away."

The day before my birthday. Coincidence?

"But why Jessica?" Meagan asked. "What did she ever do to them?"

There was a beat of silence. "Did any of you see her shift forms?"

"She looked like a cat at the end," Liam said.

"A jaguar," I corrected. "They wanted her because she's a shifter."

"Wait a minute," Meagan said. "You lost me on the curve there."

"The Mages are targeting different kinds of shifters," I said. "The idea being that once they've eliminated all of us, they'll control our forms."

"And the ShadowEaters can use them," Meagan said with a nod.

"Last spring this Kohana guy, who is a Thunderbird shifter, told Zoë that there were only four kinds of shifters left," Liam said.

"Right before he lied to Zoë and tried to make it three," Nick said.

"Because he's helping the Mages, maybe hoping to get some amnesty for Thunderbirds," Garrett said.

"Thunderbirds, dragons." Meagan counted on her fingers, then looked around.

"Jaguars and wolves," Liam supplied.

"You had a wolf with you," she said to Liam. "Is he one?"

Liam nodded. "You know him from school."

She glanced at me.

"Derek," I said and her eyes widened.

"Is that why he likes you? Because he knows what you are?"

"He *likes* you?" Nick teased and I blushed right on cue.

"What about Jared?" Isabelle asked.

"I don't know," I said to Meagan, trying to ignore them. "But he did know what I am, right from the start."

"He seems to turn up at the right times," Liam said. "Should you trust him so much?"

"He says he can see several minutes into the future," I told them. "A very short range of foresight. And he can smell even things that we can't discern, like emotions."

"Wow," Nick said. "That's cool."

"It would be better if we knew more about his allegiances," Garrett said.

"He says he's like an emissary from the wolves," I said. "They have a prophecy that they have to make a union with other shifters and follow the dragon, but some aren't big on having a girl as pack leader."

"That's his story," Nick said. "How do we know it's true?"

Nobody knew the answer to that.

"So how come you're all at the same school?" Meagan asked.

Isabelle cleared her throat. "Maybe the Mages are targeting the new generation."

"And Jessica? What do you know about her and the jaguars?" Nick asked.

"Nothing. I had no idea that she was a jaguar shifter, not until last night," I admitted. "I think maybe Derek knew." I thought for a minute. "That might explain Trevor's interest in her."

"But what happened to her?" Meagan asked.

There was a beat of silence and then I said it. "I think she might be dead."

We fidgeted then, all of us uncomfortable with the prospect.

"But what if she isn't?" Meagan asked. "What if they're planning to do this big ceremony on the full moon and sacrifice her then? How can we find her? Could we save her?"

Garrett grimaced. "It could be like stepping into a trap."

"But Meagan's right—we can't just abandon her," Nick said.

"*If* she's still alive," Liam said. "We need to know for sure before we take that risk."

"Can you ask your cards?" I asked Isabelle.

ISABELLE SHUFFLED FOR A LONG time. I wasn't sure whether she was trying to focus or was avoiding the question. Then she handed the deck to Meagan. "You were closest to her. Will you shuffle?"

"Sure." I could tell that Meagan was thrilled.

"You need to focus on Jessica. Think about your question."

"Is she dead or alive?" Meagan said, nodding with resolve. She closed her eyes and shuffled the cards for a few minutes, then handed them back to Isabelle.

Isabelle cut the deck and turned up the card.

The Devil.

"What does that mean?" Garrett asked, leaning forward.

"Nothing good, I'll guess," Liam said.

"She's in hell?" Meagan asked.

Isabelle shook her head. "The Devil is a card that denotes slavery or entrapment. It can mean that someone is a slave to physical pleasure, for example, or that they're literally beholden to someone else. The person is trapped, either by choice or by circumstance."

"So, she's their captive, somewhere," I said.

"But why?" Nick asked. "What's the point?"

"Maybe she's bait," Garrett said. "Maybe they think that holding her will draw other shifters."

"Or the rest of the jaguars," Liam suggested.

Nick frowned. "I wonder whether Jessica is their equivalent of the Wyvern."

"Their wildcard," Isabelle said with a nod.

"Kohana told me last spring that there's a wildcard in every kind," I said. "One who can do more than most. And he implied that he and I are the wildcards in our respective kinds. If Derek is acting as an emissary, maybe that's how he got the job."

"Maybe you wildcards are the ones who have to make the treaty Derek talked about," Liam suggested.

I shivered again then, not wanting to experience whatever they had done—or were doing—to Jessica.

"That's it," Isabelle said with a nod. "They've cast a spell to draw you together so they can eliminate all the wildcards at once."

"Because if they eliminate the wildcards, there's no chance of that union happening," I said with excitement.

"Which means the Mages will win," Nick added.

"Which would also explain Jessica and Derek being at your school," Liam said.

"Kohana, too." Garrett said.

"So, are we going to help Jessica?" Meagan asked, looking around the group. We nodded as one, staring at the card.

"We have to," Liam said.

"We can't leave another shifter trapped like that," Nick said.

"But the real question," Garrett said, "is how we *can* help her."

No one had the answer to that.

WE AGREED THAT WE NEEDED to take some time to rest and keep thinking. Garrett and Nick escorted us back to Meagan's house and Liam remained behind to watch over Isabelle, just in case.

I probably wasn't the only one who noticed how Nick and Isabelle were pointedly ignoring each other, and that he didn't volunteer to defend her. I couldn't see the point in starting a discussion with him just yet, though, plus I knew that anything I said to him aloud or in old-speak would be overheard by Garrett. I knew the guys were too bagged to carry me, so I shifted to dragon form myself for the sake of expediency.

We didn't talk much. I just flew beside Nick over the city, noting how the guys stayed on either side of me. Protective. I liked that. Meagan was clearly thrilled to have another ride from Garrett and her eyes were shining when we set down in the park across from the house.

We agreed to meet back there first thing in the morning. The guys took off quickly, their scales looking gilded in the streetlights, and Meagan sighed.

Then she flicked me a look and smiled. She touched her ear, a question in her expression and I nodded agreement. She was right—they'd be able to hear anything she said. She fluttered her fingers against her heart and I grinned.

Sometimes words just get in the way.

"So, you're the dragon who defended me," she said as we walked through the snow to her house. "Twice."

"What are friends for?" I joked and she grinned at me.

"I liked the idea of it being a guy dragon."

"Well, what about Garrett? He defended you."

Meagan blushed as red as a beet and pulled out her messenger. I could see that she was scrolling through the text Garrett had shared. "We need to beat the Mages, but we have to crack the code on this mumbo jumbo to find out more."

"Two weeks to the full moon doesn't give us much time," I said. "Still, we have to try." I walked beside her for a minute, choosing my words. "Look, you have to be really careful."

"Me? Why?"

'Because you've got spellsinging abilities and the Mages know it. I'm afraid they're going to try to recruit you. . . ."

"Don't worry about me, Zoë."

"I am worried about you. They don't take no for an answer and you could get hurt."

She stopped with one hand on the door and looked at me. "How do you know that?"

"Because they tried to recruit Jared, and he tried to decline, but they've been using him anyway." I thought about his conviction—and Kohana's assertion—that they would use him to get to me, and I feared they'd do the same with Meagan.

"Then give me his number," she said easily. "I'll ask him for advice."

"But . . ."

"Zoë, I can take care of it. You've got to figure out how to make this union work, save the shifters and defeat the Mages."

Right.

"If I can convince them to follow me," I had to say. "And if I had a plan."

"But think about it. If your powers as Wyvern mean that you

could foil the Mages' plan single-handedly, that would be a good reason for the wolves to have a prophecy about following you."

She was right.

But how could I persuade the other shifters to work with us? Derek's wolves needed me to do some big wolf thing to prove I could be a good pack leader. Jessica had been captured by the Mages and we dragons hadn't managed to save her. And Kohana seemed determined to surrender any of us in order to defend the Thunderbirds. If I could bring him—the most reluctant ally—into the union, maybe the others would follow.

But how?

A little bit too late, I realized I'd lost a negotiating tool when I'd had it right in my claws.

I should never have relinquished the feathers I'd tugged out of Kohana's tail during our last fight. It's dangerous for a shifter to lose the cloak of his alternate form. We have to keep track of both to be able to shift between forms. We dragons have to keep track of both our clothes and our scales. It must be the same for Kohana—he'd need his clothes and his feathers. There are tons of stories about people stealing the seal skins of selkies or the pelts of werewolves and holding the shifter in thrall. Those stories are based in truth.

I'd had some of Kohana's feathers. That could have given me some power over him, or at least an edge for negotiation, but I hadn't thought of it at the time. It seemed unlikely that I'd be able to find those particular feathers again. I could only assume Kohana would have gathered them up if it could be done.

I wondered if I could get my hands on more.

And if so, could I use them to get him and the Thunderbirds on our side?

IT WAS LONG AFTER MEAGAN had run out of superlatives to describe Garrett's dragon form—never mind his human one—and I was still staring at the ceiling of her room. I could hear the slow rhythm of her breathing, the quiet impact of snowflakes outside, the resonant hiss of two dragons on the roof, breathing dragonsmoke.

I closed my eyes, and missed my dad—well, actually, I missed our night flights over the city. I didn't much miss getting chewed out or barricaded within a ring of dragonsmoke. We never talked much when we flew, except for his occasional tips on technique, uttered in old-speak. And even as frustrated as I was with him, a night flight would have been good. I was restless.

Fortunately, there were other dragons in my proximity.

And I had just about nothing left to lose in terms of my dad's approval. He was already livid with me—or would be, once he figured out the full range of my disobedience. At this point, I had to save the day, somehow, in order to survive the reckoning that was coming.

Even then, the odds against me were long.

Right now, I needed the ego boost of being a dragon.

I slipped out of bed and pulled on my jeans and sweater. I crept out of Meagan's bedroom without disturbing her. The dead bolt on the front door made a slight snick when I unlocked it and I froze in the foyer, certain that I'd be caught, but no one stirred.

I could hear Meagan and both of her parents breathing at the slow rate of sleep.

Once outside the door, I raced around the house to the dark shadows of the back garden. I bounded into the air and shifted shape, loving the power of my body. I soared to the roof easily, and Garrett smiled at the sight of me.

"Wondered how long it would take you," he said in old-speak.

"Anyone want to fly with me?"

They exchanged glances and then Nick straightened. He spread his golden wings wide, stretching. *"I'm up for it."*

"I'll stay here," Garrett said.

I leapt off the roof, hearing the swoosh of Nick's wings behind me. I beat my wings hard, racing him a little, heading straight for the stratosphere. It felt so good that any repercussions of the parental variety would be worth it. The falling snow swirled around us, as if we were dancing with it. I saw the gleam of golden scales to my right as Nick came up beside me.

He grinned as he soared past. "You're not that fast."

"Faster than you think!" I pushed harder and caught up to him. "Losing your edge, Nick?"

"Not yet." He hooted and flew even faster.

"You just don't want to lose to a girl!" I taunted, sailing past him one more time.

He laughed and came raging up behind me. He caught my tail to hold me back, and I spun around to cuff him playfully. We wrestled, rolling through the air, our scales shining like jewels in the night.

Once upon a time, physical intimacy like this with Nick would have stopped my heart cold. Now he was like a big brother—another one—just a guy I could tease and harass and whose company I could enjoy. We cavorted through the air, each giving the other a talon as necessary to keep the game going.

I saw the glint of mischief in his eye just before he spiraled down into the city. He looked like a feathered golden spear, but one that turned corners with grace. I knew he was up to trouble, and was curious to see what he had in mind. I raced behind him, then laughed when I saw where he was going.

He buzzed the webcam of the local television station, flashing dragon teeth for the camera. Then he lifted his tail, like he was mooning it, even without pants. I laughed, wondering what anyone watching would make of that display.

I knew what the dads would make of it.

We spun together, showing off, then raced for the clouds, claw in claw. We pushed ourselves to go higher and faster, streaming through the night until we were panting for breath.

We landed on the top of the Sears Tower, beside the antennae, and surveyed the city in triumph.

"It's cool, isn't it?" Nick said with satisfaction.

I was still out of breath. "What is?"

"Being a dragon. Being powerful. Being able to breathe fire." He gestured with one claw at the twinkling city, dusted with snow. It didn't even look real from here. "Being able to fly."

His words reminded me of the ride that I owed Jared, the one I might never be able to deliver, and that flattened my mood. "Good and bad," I said.

He considered me, probably noticing my change of tone. "What's bad about it?"

"I still can't do everything I'm supposed to be able to do."

"But you can do a lot more than before." Nick shrugged with his usual confidence. "And we had enough ammo to finish those Mages tonight. Tell me that wasn't exciting."

"I don't think they're finished."

"So we live to fight another day." He grinned at me. "Our dads fought *Slayers* for centuries before they defeated them. Consider it part of the adventure. Imagine how good it will feel when we totally finish them." He bumped shoulders with me. "Come on, Zoë. What's really eating you? Is it that Jared isn't around? Where'd he go, anyway?"

I chose between reasons, because there was something I wanted to know. "Your dad warned him that I might not ultimately have a firestorm with him and so he bailed." Only half of the story, but Nick looked away, frowning. I knew I'd struck a nerve. "I'm thinking that it sucks that we don't get to choose who we fall in love with—or even if we do fall in love, we can't act on it until we know about the firestorm. The choice is made for us."

"Worked out all right for our parents."

"Aside from mine splitting up," I had to note. Nick eyed me and I saw his wariness. "I don't know. Maybe they will. Maybe they won't. The fact that they're thinking about it isn't much of an endorsement, though, is it?"

"They'll work it out," he insisted. "They did before. They love each other, don't they? Isn't that what counts?"

I thought of the things my mom had said about my dad always choosing the *Pyr* over her and I wasn't sure that love was enough.

"But what if the firestorm doesn't work out?" I asked.

"What?" Nick was incredulous. "It has to. That's the way it works."

It was my turn to stare at the city. I didn't think it was that simple. I heaved a sigh. "What if the old plan for us doesn't work anymore?"

Nick swallowed and spoke with force. "You make it work."

"How so?"

"You make more *Pyr*. You do what you can. You try to do what's right." He said this last word with even more emphasis and glared stubbornly over the city. It was all black and white to him.

I had to say it. "Do you really think you're doing the right thing by staying away from Isabelle?"

Nick avoided my gaze. "I might be." He turned to look at me before I could argue. "The firestorm is right," he said with force and I wondered who he was trying to convince. "And I will follow it. I won't make promises I might not be able to keep."

"But she thinks that you're meant to be together."

Nick looked down. He tapped his nails on the lip of the roof, thinking. "I hope she's right," he admitted so quietly that I had to strain to hear him.

Then he looked at me, his gaze tormented. "But what if she's wrong? What if we're just attracted to each other? What if it's just sex?"

I didn't know what to say to that.

Nick's voice dropped low. "If my firestorm is with someone else, I have a duty to my kind. We all do. And I'll have a duty to my son, whenever I have one."

"Your dad reminded you of this."

Nick looked away. "It would be easy to be with Isabelle, Zoë, but in the end, it might be wrong. It would hurt her more if I had to turn away from her later."

"So you're turning away now."

He dropped his head. "Sometimes you're crazy enough about someone to protect them even from yourself." And this time, when he met my gaze, his was clear with conviction.

I felt better for having Nick explain himself to me. He wasn't being a jerk, like Isabelle thought. He was being thoughtful. Considerate.

"They say patience is a virtue," I said, smiling at him. "But I think waiting bites."

Nick laughed and made a mock bite in my direction. I snapped back at him, and we leapt into the air simultaneously. We swung our tails and played at fighting again. Then Nick pointed back down to our neighborhood. "Race you to the roof!"

"Last one there is *Slayer* bait!" I retorted, using an old taunt from our childhood. We flung ourselves through the sky.

Nick was ahead of me, all golden strength.

"Look! It's Isabelle!" I cried and he halted to look.

"Where?"

"Not here, fool." I raced past him, laughing as he roared behind me. He caught my tail and spun me around. We fell onto the roof of the town house in a tangle of talons and scales, laughing all the while.

I shoved a fistful of snow into his face. He breathed fire at me in mock fury and I swung around to swat him. He caught my wing and we wrestled on the roof. I couldn't get a good hit in because we were laughing too hard.

"Nice quiet return," Garrett noted. *"I bet no one will notice."*

"Anything happen while we were gone?" Nick asked, brushing himself off and taking a serious tone.

Garrett shrugged. *"Just that."*

I realized suddenly that there were a lot of cats meowing. They were making that yowl that tomcats make at night, but it sounded like there were a lot more of them than was typical. I hadn't even noticed any tomcats around Meagan's house before.

"There must be hundreds of them," Garrett said. I looked at him in surprise. *"It started about an hour ago. And keeps getting louder."*

We stood up and looked as the cries became steadily louder. I could see the silhouettes of dozens of cats in the street. Maybe hundreds. They were all different colors—soot gray with white socks, black with white tuxedo bibs, ginger and tortoiseshell and whiter than snow. They walked with the delicate precision of cats, silent but purposeful. They clung to the shadows, as if they didn't want to be seen, but the gleam of their eyes gave them away.

Like gemstones shining in the dark.

They also were moving in the same direction, as if they gravitated toward some unknown destination. I wondered—were they all shifters? Or were cats in general drawn to a cat shifter's distress? What were they going to do? Where were they going?

"They're gathering," Nick said.

But why?

Then I noticed that something else had changed. I could see the orange swirl of Mage spell, bright again, winding out of the sewer grates with greater potency than before.

They were up to something, spinning their web and making it stronger. Were they feeding on Jessica's strength? What was the deal with the cats? Were they drawn to Jessica's distress? Or were they leading the way for us? Was she still alive, then?

I saw a black cat hesitate on the lip of a sewer opening. It looked around, then stared straight at me. It held my gaze for a long moment, then turned and slipped through the grate, as sinuous as a snake.

Gone as surely as if it had never been.

I felt a shadow pass over me, and it chilled me to the bone.

"*What is it?*" Nick asked and I told them what I could see.

No one liked that news.

Garrett looked grim. "*We should sleep while we can.*"

I wondered, though, whether I would ever sleep again, with my thoughts spinning so fast.

Like a Mage spell.

I watched the orange light, tugging down into the world beneath the city. I thought about the cats, maybe answering some summons we couldn't discern.

That was when I knew exactly what we had to do next. We had to go down into the sewers, just like those cats, and confront the Mages in their den.

Wherever it turned out to be.

I DIDN'T TELL THE OTHERS my plan until the morning, when we all met up in the park. I'd spent the night trying to think of alternatives, but hadn't come up with a single one.

Predictably, there was dissent. The guys weren't big on risk, especially with so many unknown variables. Meagan was instantly ready to go and help her buddy.

We decided to vote.

Meagan voted first, in favor of the quest, then spent time busily researching the Chicago underground on her messenger. She was so proud of herself for finding maps that I didn't have the heart to tell her that we wouldn't need them.

I'd just follow the spell light.

Nick was sure the light I'd seen was a lure to draw us into a trap. Garrett pointed out that we weren't sure of Jessica's motives. Had she been targeted by the Mages and trapped? Or was she complicit with them, like Kohana? Liam wondered whether Jessica's capture was just an illusion, meant to draw us closer. Meagan was insulted by that idea, but before they could argue, Isabelle drew another card.

She'd been quietly shuffling the whole time. She brushed aside the snow on the park bench, then snapped the card onto the painted wood.

The Chariot.

"Always the court cards when Zoë is around," she murmured with a smile. We waited expectantly. "The Chariot indicates a conflict being resolved. Someone intervening in a situation."

"Like a rescue?" Liam said and Isabelle nodded.

"It has a military sense, like a planned campaign being executed."

"Successfully?" Garrett asked.

Isabelle nodded again. "It indicates preparation and planning, so check your plan and coordinate it. But yes, the card is right side up, which means triumph."

"Upside down for Zoë," Derek said softly.

I jumped to find him behind me, in his quiet human form. The guys looked startled—they hadn't heard him approach, either.

But he was right. Isabelle could have placed it on the other side of the bench, but she'd put it between us. I stared at the card as the guys reviewed events of the night before and planned their assault.

Was I crazy to let that detail bother me? What did the card mean when it was reversed? Failure? A temporary victory? Either possibility spooked me.

But it didn't much matter. The guys were on board. Derek and Meagan and Isabelle were in. We didn't have to tally the vote to know that we were going underground.

It had been my idea in the first place, so I couldn't bail.

OUR THINKING WAS THAT THE Mages would be tired after their festivities of the night before. They'd be expecting us to take time to regroup. We would strike early and fast, before we were anticipated, and maybe have surprise on our side.

It was all a rationalization, but we convinced each other of its merit. Meagan located access points to the underground on her map and we tried them in succession. The first manhole we tested was locked down or stuck. The second was on a street that bustled with traffic, probably because it was close to a big church.

The third was on a quiet side street. It also seemed to be locked, but Nick was impatient. He shifted shape quickly and hauled it open in his dragon form. Garrett went first into the hole, Meagan right behind him. Liam and Isabelle followed, then Derek, then me. Nick shifted back to his human form while we were slipping into the wet darkness, then pulled the manhole cover over the opening again.

Sealing us in darkness.

There was a ladder fixed to the side of the shaft and we descended in silence. Every sound echoed and was magnified, and we seemed to understand as one the need for quiet.

I could hear water running.

I could smell sewage—although I didn't need *Pyr* powers of perception for that.

And, thanks to my new ring, I could see the dizzy orange swirl of Mage spell light. It emanated clearly from one direction. It danced in spirals, tugging deeper into the system. I pointed and the others followed me, letting me lead the way.

The guys arrayed themselves behind me, Isabelle between

Garrett and Liam, Meagan between Liam and Nick. There was a faint shimmer around the guys, as they were agitated enough to be on the cusp of change.

It said something for my state of mind that the sudden brilliant shimmer of light blue to my right reassured me. It reassured me even more when a silver-gray wolf matched my stride, his pale eyes shining with wariness. I buried my fingers in the silken fur at Derek's neck and felt the tension in him.

It was the kind of place where a person could do with a pet predator.

Chapter 12

I don't know how long we walked, never mind how far. The spell light was swirling ahead of me, leading me on a golden path that seemed to take us deeper and deeper into the underground. There was water in the bottom of the tunnel, but we walked to the left and the right of it, keeping our feet mostly dry.

It got colder. It got darker beyond the spell light. It was impossible to guess the amount of time that had passed. There were boarded-up passageways and blocked tunnels, but the spell cut a steady course through the darkness.

Like a thousand threads, twining together into a thicker rope.

Or a spiderweb, drawing its victims into a place of no return.

It was strange because I had this sense of dread, yet at the same time, the radiant spell had a soothing effect. Maybe it lulled me into complacency. It was pretty. It had a pleasant glow. It made me feel serene and outside of any tension.

Maybe the spiderweb analogy was a good one. Don't spiders drug their victims so they struggle less?

Either way, we drifted along the path that was laid for us, lulled into believing that we'd made our choice and now had to follow it to the end.

There wasn't a lot of conversation.

We weren't alone either. Derek kept looking over his shoulder and snarling into the shadows behind us. I finally looked back to see, and realized that not only did the spell light dim noticeably right behind us—like it was gathering us close—but there was a procession of cats heading in the same direction.

The cats from the street. They walked a little higher up the sides of the tunnel to keep their feet dry. They trailed behind us, as if trying to avoid the full power of the spell light. They also seemed to be enchanted by it. I saw one sitting in a side tunnel, batting at a swirl of gold as if it were a butterfly.

Then the cat rubbed against it, its expression euphoric.

A moment later it joined the procession.

What was going on with these cats? Were they another variety of cat shifter? Were they drawn to the plight of a jaguar shifter? I know cats tend to be mysterious, but this was extraordinary.

Another cat mewled at Isabelle from a side tunnel. He was a big handsome cat with presence to spare, sitting like a statue. He looked almost leonine, with a mane of long fur framing his face, his coat striped in coal black and gold. He had a white bib and white socks, and golden eyes. He purred with loud approval when Isabelle scooped him up into her arms.

"He must weigh thirty pounds," she said with surprise, hefting him higher.

"Then leave him behind," Nick suggested in an undertone. "You don't need the extra responsibility." I saw that he was nervous, too, his gaze darting back and forth. Even though he couldn't see the spells, he must be feeling their effect.

And trying to fight them.

Isabelle's eyes flashed and she hugged the cat more tightly. "Not a chance. That's not what I do." She and Nick glared at each other for a charged moment, and then Nick turned away.

"We've got to make sure we keep Zoë's back," Nick said to Garrett. "Not like the last time."

Garrett nodded, strain in his features. "It gets to you, doesn't it?"

"What's it like for you guys?" I asked.

"Like an earworm, a song you can't get out of your mind," Garrett said. "A pulsing, insistent one."

"A violent one," Nick agreed, wiping sweat from his brow. "Feeding doubt."

"Just don't give it anything to root in," Liam said. "Remember that we're a team and we're not going to split ranks."

"*Pyr* forever," Garrett said grimly and the guys nodded as one.

"*One for all and all for one*," I teased in old-speak, but they didn't smile.

They just crowded a little closer.

I saw Isabelle's expression soften as she watched Nick, but I had bigger responsibilities at the moment than fixing their relationship.

"What do you see it doing, anyway?" Nick asked me.

"Getting brighter. We're arriving somewhere."

"Can't get there soon enough," Garrett said. "This pulsing in my head is going to drive me crazy."

"That's the point," Liam said. "Fight it!"

"So we'll be all worn-out by the time we really need to fight," Nick muttered. "Fucking brilliant strategy."

Meagan hummed something that sounded familiar.

"Mozart's Eine Kleine Nachtmusik," Isabelle said.

"Also known as Serenade no. 13 in G Major," Meagan answered and continued to hum. I'm not sure whether it kept spells at bay or not, but we all tried to join in. It's a memorable piece of music, though not easy to hum.

We walked a bit faster.

The cat settled against Isabelle, his gaze flicking between Derek and me, that luxuriant tail lashing at the air. I must have looked at him too long, because he bared his teeth to hiss at me.

Fine. I wasn't in the mood to make friends anyway.

The tunnels were getting bigger in diameter. I couldn't even sense how high this one stretched overhead. It had to be four or five times my height. The concrete radiated a chill that went right through my bones.

The swirling spell light was getting brighter.

Just when I thought I couldn't stand the tension much longer, we turned a corner and the tunnel widened even more. Daylight was visible far ahead, as if the tunnel dumped out. There was a frenzy of Mage spell light crisscrossing that opening, almost blinding me with its intensity.

"Uh-oh," I said and Derek snarled.

"Let's get out of here!" Nick said. The guys pushed past me and ran for the opening. They couldn't see the spell light.

It was a lure, one that would trap them!

"Look out!" I shouted and raced after them. Derek galloped beside me. Even the cats hurried.

"No!" I shouted. "Stop! It's a trap! There's a spell over the opening, like a net!"

They ignored me. The girls did, too.

I ran faster, and kept shouting.

Suddenly Derek halted and turned back. He growled. I saw the hair stand up on the back of his shoulders, and his ears flattened against his head. He was staring back the way we had come. I looked back and strained my ears.

Water. I could hear water.

A *lot* of water.

The others heard it, too.

That made them stop and glance back. Once they looked away from the opening and that network of spell light, they seemed to recover themselves and comprehend what I had said.

"Zoë?" Nick said, his voice strained. "What do we do?"

There was a splash as a wall of water collided with that last corner. It frothed and the wave of it swelled; then it gushed toward us like an ocean wave.

No—like a tsunami.

It filled at least a third of the tunnel's height and it was headed straight for us.

"Fuck!" Nick shouted.

"Holy shit!" Garrett cried and grabbed for Meagan. "Link hands!"

We grabbed hands as we ran away from the water. At least we'd keep track of each other in the deluge.

"Wait. We'll be washed right into the spell trap!" I shouted. "Like fish in a net."

"That can't be good," Liam muttered. The cat arched his back and lashed his tail, spitting. Isabelle held him more tightly.

"What do we do, Zoë?" Garrett demanded. "Drown or get trapped by Mages?"

There were no good choices and the water was surging closer. I had the scruff of Derek's neck in one hand and Meagan's hand clutched in my other. There was a cat winding around her ankles, a soot-colored one with white socks, and she snatched it up. She held it tightly against her chest, her eyes wide with fear.

But there was one thing we *could* do.

"Shift!" I shouted to the guys and let the shimmer rock through my body.

In a heartbeat, I was in dragon form and took flight in the tunnel. I snatched up both Derek and Meagan as I went, lifting them above the sudden flood. Meagan's fingers dug into me in panic, the water lapping at her feet. The herd of cats howled and yelped as they were washed away in the torrent.

The guys had followed my lead immediately and shifted, the pale blue light of the change illuminating the tunnel. Garrett had snatched up Isabelle. Liam hovered in the middle, watching the water with concentration. It churned beneath us, racing for the opening, murky and dark.

Fortunately, the tunnel was big enough for us to hover above the water.

So far.

Nick reached over and took Meagan from me. "Why didn't we think of that right away?" he asked with irritation. "Why do they have to screw with our heads like this?"

"Because they can," Garrett said.

The water gurgled and sloshed around that corner and it was clear that there was more coming. "Time for Plan B," Nick said, looking at me. We flew a little higher, crowding against the top of the tunnel. I hit my wings on the concrete with every beat, but it was better than drowning.

Soon more water surged around that bend.

And it flowed faster.

We were either going to drown or be Mage bait.

I had to do something.

I turned the ring on my talon and whispered in old-speak. *"Help me, Sophie. Help us, please."*

My mouth went dry. Would Sophie help me again? Or was her assistance a onetime offer? We could use all the help we could get. If there were still a pair of ghostly genies trapped in the ring, they might know what to do.

I saw the ring pulse with red.

I felt it spin of its own accord. My heart skipped in anticipation and I dared to hope.

Then the light went out. The ring turned cold. It stopped turning on my talon.

Sophie had declined to respond.

Shit.

I looked at the raging water and heard the guys' panic. The water seemed to be moving even faster.

I caught my breath as another wave crashed around the corner, nearly filling the tunnel to the top. It headed straight for us. The guys crowded higher against the top of the tunnel.

And a black bird soared around the corner in the last sliver of space. He had blazing yellow eyes and carried a lightning bolt in each claw. He flew straight toward me, his purpose clear as he sped up.

This was the chance I'd been hoping for.

DEREK BARKED.

I roared with dragonfire, daring Kohana.

Kohana took the dare. He threw a lightning bolt at me and kept coming. I dodged it and it collided with the spell trap in a flurry of sparks. He screamed at me, the infuriated screech of a raven. He was close, almost close enough to snatch, when Derek suddenly lunged at him, teeth bared. The move ripped him free of my grasp, but his teeth closed on Kohana's wing.

Kohana lost the rhythm of his flight and dipped low with the weight of the wolf. He screamed again and glared at Derek, loosing a flash of heat lightning from his eyes.

I saw the jolt hit Derek and smelled burning fur. He lost his grip on Kohana with a whimper and splashed into the water that swirled beneath us. He was washed away in a heartbeat, swept into the spell trap before my very eyes.

Isabelle screamed. The water surged higher and engulfed our lower bodies. Meagan hummed even more loudly. The guys shouted in fear and anger.

But I snatched at Kohana with both front claws. I wanted his feathers. I wanted his shape-shifting coat. I wanted to have some power over him. Some feathers came free as he struggled, and I didn't drop them.

I wasn't going to let those feathers go. "Give me the whole coat," I muttered. "Then we can make a deal."

I felt him panic.

I braced myself for his reaction.

He took off like a shot for the wall of Mage spell, dragging me behind him.

"Zoë!" Garrett shouted. "No!"

I knew Kohana was trying to frighten me into letting go. I knew he was worried, which meant I was right about there being power in his feathers. That weakness *was* the same for all shifters. I held fast, even tightening my grip.

Just before we collided with the spell net, everything disappeared in a blinding flash of blue light.

I OPENED MY EYES CAUTIOUSLY when the wind stilled. I was in human form, with those black feathers in my right hand, sprawled across a huge red rock.

One with petroglyphs carved in it.

I recognized this rock. I'd visited it in the spring, when the elder *Pyr* had been trapped on it by Mage spells. It was somewhere in Minnesota.

How the hell did I get here?

A massive black bird crouched beside me to offer one wing tip. He looked a bit the worse for wear.

He also looked angry.

I remembered that the red rock was a sacred place for the

Thunderbirds. Kohana had told me that the earth's songs were strong there.

I wasn't taking any help from him.

I glanced pointedly at his wing, then got up by myself. Our gazes locked and held, as I brandished the feathers in front of him.

His eyes turned more vivid yellow, almost snapping with hostility. It was a reasonable approximation of the way I often felt about him. "Okay," Kohana said. "Let's make a deal."

I smiled. "Not yet. When you only get one wish, you've got to make it count."

He snatched at me with his claw, but I pivoted and called to the shimmer. I knew exactly where I wanted to be and it wasn't with a Thunderbird intent on sacrificing me to the Mages. I didn't think Kohana could travel through time and space like me, although I knew he could travel in dreams with ease.

This would be like a test. The shimmer consumed me, illuminated me, danced through my veins. I envisioned my destination, looked him in the eye one last time and smiled.

Then I was out of there.

"Zoë!" Kohana roared, but he didn't follow me.

Which meant he couldn't.

Either his own abilities or the feathers in my hand made sure of it.

I wasn't overly concerned with the technicalities.

I WAS SHAKING WHEN I opened my eyes again. I had hopes in terms of my destination, but like I said before, this spontaneous manifestation feat has a bit of unpredictability to it.

Then I breathed a sigh of relief. I knew the inside of this purse, even when it was soaking wet. I scored another chunk of Isabelle's chocolate stash—I had to love that she'd restocked—as I eavesdropped on the situation beyond the zipper of the bag.

"We must have been in the Deep Tunnel system," Meagan said and I heard her tapping on her messenger. "Stupid old thing. It never links right once it gets wet."

"What's that?" Isabelle asked and I knew she didn't mean the messenger. I could hear the purring of a cat really close. I guessed it was the one she'd picked up in the tunnel.

"The Deep Tunnel system was built to move floodwater and storm water out of the city," Meagan said. "Huge engineering project. The idea was to move the water quickly to reservoirs and old quarries, where it could be slowly released into the lake and river. There! It's working again."

"Do you have any idea where we are?" Isabelle shivered so violently that I even felt it in her purse.

"Well, there aren't that many options, and they're mostly all in the suburbs. Good! I got a satellite connection. And"—Meagan tapped busily—"our location. Ta-da!"

"Not too far to the subway," Isabelle mused and I guessed she was checking out a map. "Let's get moving before we freeze into icicles. Maybe we'll find the guys."

Oh, no. Meagan and Isabelle were alone? At that news, the bottom dropped out of my stomach.

"I don't think so," Meagan said.

The purse swung as Isabelle started to move. "What do you mean?"

"We didn't get away because we were brilliant," Meagan said. "We got away because we're human. They just didn't want us."

Isabelle caught her breath. "But they wanted Zoë and the guys."

"And probably Derek, too." Meagan sounded determined. "We have to figure out what we can do to help."

"We have to figure out how we can get dry before we get sick," Isabelle said and I could hear her teeth chattering. "It looks like we're off the edge of the world."

"No, we're not. Maybe there's a coffee shop or something once we get to the street."

"Coffee. Don't give me fantasies that might not have a chance of being fulfilled." Isabelle sighed. "One of those is enough."

Before she could get too depressed, I left the purse and appeared beside them in human form.

"Zoë!" Meagan shouted and caught me in a tight hug. The soot-colored cat, caught between us and just as wet as Meagan, was a bit less glad to see me. It meowed with outrage, then leapt out of Meagan's arms.

It shook itself, then glowered at us both.

"Zoë!" Isabelle echoed and hugged me from the other side. The big cat she'd picked up also jumped to freedom. The two cats sat elegantly on their haunches in the gravel. They looked disdainful for a moment, then began to groom their paws.

As if nothing had happened at all.

I wished they could tell us the deal with all those cats, but no luck.

It did look as if we'd fallen off the edge of the world. We were on the shore of a reservoir that must have been made from a quarry. A gravel "beach" stretched around its perimeter and the water was gray in the winter light. I could see the dark circle of a pipe on the other side of the lake, one that would spew into the pond.

"Is that where we were?" I asked and Meagan nodded. She wrapped her arms around herself, shivering. Both Isabelle and Meagan were soaking wet and it was snowing slightly.

There was no sign of the guys or Derek.

The rest of the herd of cats was gone, too.

"How'd you get away?" Meagan asked and I showed them the ebony feathers I'd torn out of Kohana's hide.

"He wanted to make a deal to get them back."

"I hope you said no." Isabelle scoffed. "He'd just lie to you again, take what he wanted, and betray you all over again."

"I know. That's why I'm here, with the feathers. I'll wait to make him an offer he can't refuse."

"Which is?" Isabelle asked.

"I'm not sure yet."

"Can't hurt to have something to negotiate with," Meagan said, "but I don't really understand why they're important."

"Any chance of a little dragonfire?" Isabelle asked me, shivering. "I'll tell Meagan about the feathers while we get dry."

"I'll trade you for the rest of that chocolate bar in your purse."

She blinked with surprise, then opened her bag, staring at the chocolate bar that had one end gnawed off.

I grinned. "I thought you'd brought it for me."

Isabelle laughed and handed me the rest of it. As usual, the sugar hit helped enormously. I flung out my arms, shifted, then treated them both to the full furnace while Isabelle talked. Even the cats came closer, evidently getting over their distrust of me for the sake of the heat. Once everyone was dry and we headed toward civilization, the cats trailed behind us.

But then, there wasn't a Mage spell to draw them in any specific direction anymore. The sky was devoid of orange spell light. We could have just happened to be walking beside a quarry reservoir as a blizzard began.

Did that mean the Mages were satisfied with what they had?

Or that they were just busy, doing to Liam and Garrett and Nick and Derek whatever they had done to Jessica? The idea made me sick.

What did they do to shifters? I wasn't entirely sure I wanted to know, but I guessed that was the key to saving the guys.

How could we find out?

"Does your having his feathers mean Kohana can't shift at all?" Meagan asked.

"I don't know. I only have some of them. If I had the full coat, that would be the case. Maybe his power is just compromised."

"Well, there's got to be something going in our favor," Isabelle said. "Let's get out of here. I need that coffee now."

WE FOUND ONE COFFEE SHOP that was open and huddled in a corner as we sipped hot beverages of choice. It was warm enough in there for the windows to steam up. I put Kohana's black feathers in the middle of the table, between us. There were three of them, each more than a foot long, and they gleamed with dark highlights.

I thought I'd had more than that, maybe because they were each so wide. The quills on each feather were as wide as the whole length of my hand, at least six inches across. It was hard to hold even three.

I was amused to see the two cats take up position immediately outside the window, as if they were standing sentinel over Meagan and Isabelle. They sat with their backs pressed against the glass, surveying the street and flicking their tails in the air.

Then they cleaned their paws some more.

We talked the situation through, backward and forward. I had a slew of notes on my messenger, so many that it was hard to make sense of them.

"Do you think the guys are okay?" Meagan asked for the hundredth time.

"What do you think they'll do to them?" Isabelle asked, clutching her second extra-large cup of coffee.

"I don't know," I admitted, tapping away on my messenger. Sophie wasn't answering me. The guys were captured. I could tell my dad and the older *Pyr*, using old-speak or more mundane methods, but I wasn't at all sure they'd believe me.

Or that they could solve the problem. They might just get trapped, like they had the last time. Or they might get all agitated about exile over the breach of the Covenant and my breaking my dad's new rule. I felt that it was up to me to fix this first.

I wished I had the stupid book on the *Pyr* that Jared had, even though it hadn't been enormously helpful any of the other times I'd had a peek in it. I also wished that I could have asked Jared for more insider Mage information.

No luck.

I wished we had cracked the code of that Mage book.

This was one big puzzle, one that I had to solve myself.

The truth was there was no such guarantee, but I refused to take the easy path and believe that everyone was out to get me, much less that we were all doomed.

Saving Derek would have to get me some points with the wolves. And I had to think that the jaguars would be similarly relieved to have Jessica safe.

A rescue mission, then.

Based on zero data. Where were the Mages holed up? In what state were their captives? How could they be freed? We needed information and I had no idea where to get it.

Meagan finished her cocoa. "What do we do, Zoë?"

I surveyed my checklists of Wyvern abilities assumed and yet to be conquered—okay, out of a certain level of desperation—and that was when I knew something I'd left off the list.

The previous spring, I'd navigated my way through my father's memories to find his location. I'd followed the conduit that led to him and walked in his memories.

I wondered whether I could do the same to Trevor and learn what that apprentice Mage knew. There wasn't a conduit to him like the coppery lines I saw to each of the *Pyr*, but maybe I could follow the spell light to Trevor and slip into his mind. If I found the right memory, I could discover where the NightBlade was and what they had planned for the captive shape shifters.

It would be risky, but it had to be quicker than breaking the Mage book's code.

And we didn't have a whole lot of time.

"WHAT CAN GO WRONG?" MEAGAN asked. We were holed up in Isabelle's room that Sunday afternoon, partly because it was snowing like crazy outside. By the time we'd come out of the coffee shop, the blizzard had gotten serious and the dorm was the closest haven. The storm had provided the perfect excuse to not go back to Meagan's place, although Meagan's mom had pinged her about six times since she'd told her where we would be.

Neither Isabelle nor Meagan liked my plan, but neither of them could think of a better one, either. The cats had come with us—I'm not sure we could have left them behind at this point—and sat on opposite ends of Isabelle's windowsill, staring into the flying snow.

Meagan studied me with concern. "How will we know if something does go wrong?"

"And what can we do to help if it does?" Isabelle asked.

"I don't know." I smiled at them, trying to soften my words. "I'm guessing you won't be able to tell, and you won't be able to do much, but I really don't know."

Isabelle grimaced. "Could you get stuck there?"

"I haven't gotten stuck yet."

"You haven't poked around in someone else's memories yet," Meagan noted.

"Actually, I have. I did it with my dad. Last spring, when they were in trouble. I visited his memories to find out where he and the other *Pyr* were."

"So you could save him," Meagan said. "I think he'd be more likely to cut you some slack than Trevor if he caught you in his mind. After all, you want to steal his memories."

She was right. Deciding to poke around in someone else's memories without authorization was a lot like breaking into their house.

Still, I couldn't see another way to find out more.

"Would you actually be stealing them?" Isabelle asked, suddenly thoughtful. "Or would you just share them? Kind of like breaking into an office and reading the files but leaving them there?"

It was an interesting idea. "I'm not sure," I admitted, feeling as if the whole thing was very elusive. "This Wyvern thing isn't very well documented."

"Well, it wouldn't be all bad if you made him forget something. If you could." Meagan considered me and shrugged. "Just throwing that out there."

"Maybe you could mess with his memory so he messed up whatever they plan to do to the guys," Isabelle suggested.

It sounded unlikely to me, but I was determined to remain positive. I was terrified enough as it was. "I'll see what I can do."

"What about us?" Isabelle asked.

I remembered Jared helping me before with this kind of deliberate dreaming, but he knew his powers as a spellsinger. Meagan was uninitiated and might inadvertently make trouble for me.

I smiled at them. "Just watch the door. Hum something in a major key."

"Something easier," Isabelle said.

Meagan frowned. "The Hallelujah chorus of Handel's *Messiah* is in D Major."

"Excellent," Isabelle said. "We sang that in choir at Christmas."

I left them to it. How did anyone pass undetected in another person's mind? I didn't know. I slid my ring onto my finger so I could see any spells coming. I held Kohana's feathers in one hand, just in case I had to negotiate anything. He'd turned up when I did dream stuff in the spring. Maybe this would be similar.

Meagan and Isabelle watched me but didn't say anything. I could almost taste their worry.

But there was nothing I could say to reassure them.

I closed my eyes and breathed deeply, trying to lull myself to sleep. My heart was thumping, though, a sure sign of my trepidation.

How would I find Trevor's memories?

How would I know when I got there?

What was I really looking for?

How would I know when I found it?

I pushed these questions around and around in my thoughts, heard my breathing slow and my pulse calm. I relaxed and entered the same meditative state we use for breathing dragonsmoke. I recalled how I had found my dad's memories by feeling for the other *Pyr.* I'd seen a network of sparkling copper lines then, and followed the right one to him. I'm not sure what told me which one, but I knew it when I saw it.

You have to believe I was hoping for a similar conviction this time. I did not want to end up in the wrong Mage's memories.

So, I thought about Mages and their spells. I thought about Trevor's MG and his parents' house and all that musical gear. I thought about how they must live and looked in my mind for the orange spell light.

I saw it flickering and pulsing almost immediately. I followed it cautiously, drifting behind it but not coming too close. It swirled out of the sky toward a neighborhood and I saw that it was leading me to Riverside Drive. The spell light spiraled toward Trevor's parents' house, where we had been the night before. Snow fell thickly all around, piling on the roof and the walkway. The house didn't look very damaged, much to my surprise, and I couldn't smell any sign of fire.

It was surrounded by golden light, though.

I guessed that the Mages could cast a kind of enchantment on humans, too. Maybe it was an illusion. Maybe what had happened to us had seemed like an illusion to everyone else. I'd have to find out later.

One spell thread was thicker and brighter, so on impulse, I chose to follow that one. As I got closer to the house, I heard a saxophone playing. The spell thread I was following resonated with the music of the sax, undulating through the air.

Like a summons.

I steeled myself for trouble, turning the ring on my finger. Then I latched on to the spell line, swung myself onto its rippling width, and slid down the line into the house.

It led into a bedroom. I had a glimpse of Trevor with his antique sax, his eyes closed as he played, and his hair mussed. Then I slid into the mouth of the sax, and through the instrument. I braced myself for biological information I didn't need, expecting to be dumped into his mouth.

Instead, I found myself in a forest.

One filled with the silence of falling snow.

I was surrounded by dead and blackened trees, a forest with no perimeter. It just went on and on and on, essentially the same in all directions.

Was this Trevor's memory? Or some other dimension?

How could I move through it without leaving any tracks?

I stood there, knee-deep in snow, and considered my options.

There didn't seem to be many.

MEMORIES ARE STRANGE PLACES TO visit. I guess everyone organizes his or her mind differently. I'm not even sure that people see their memories the same way that intruders like me do.

My dad's memories had been ruthlessly organized. Maybe he'd had time to get all that together, seeing as he's centuries old. It had appeared to me like a long corridor with a black stone floor and a white ceiling. There'd been no discernible light source—the ceiling just appeared luminescent.

Each wall had been lined with stainless-steel filing cabinets, one after the other after the other. I'd been pretty intimidated by this, until I'd noticed that each drawer was dated.

And they were in order.

I shouldn't have been surprised.

After that it had been easy. Find the right drawer, open it, be deluged by my dad's memory. Piece of cake.

To tell the truth, I'd expected something similar from Trevor's memory. The dead forest threw me off my game, making me wonder if I'd taken a wrong turn and ended up in Granny's snowy sphere instead. I had a good look at the tree closest to me, the one I could check out without making any more tracks.

Something glimmered at the base of it, halfway obscured by the snow. I brushed the snowflakes away carefully and saw that it was a gold plaque, screwed to the tree.

And engraved on the plaque were the words DECEMBER 2010.

A month's worth of memories? In this tree? How? I tipped my head back to look up at its bare branches, so dark against the gray sky.

My heart stopped cold. There was a large black bird sitting in the boughs overhead.

Watching me.

It had yellow eyes, that bird, which told me who it was.

"More to you than meets the eye," Kohana said, and it sounded like admiration in his voice.

"I said, no deal."

"And I'm making a gesture of goodwill."

"Right." I didn't believe it for one minute. If Kohana was here, then I was history.

Or soon would be.

I pivoted and would have run, but I didn't manage to take one step. Kohana swooped down and grasped me by the shoulders of my jacket. I squirmed, biting back my yell of protest, but he took flight.

"At least you can shut up when someone does you a favor," he muttered. "Scream and we'll both be finished."

"Why would you be helping me? To trick me into trusting you again?"

"Messing with Mages, especially if it doesn't look as if I'm the one responsible, is always a good thing as far as I'm concerned."

"You're just trying to get me killed."

"If you'd taken one step, you would have managed it yourself. They don't take kindly to intruders." He made a sound that could have been a laugh. "Maybe they know we're here even now."

They?

Kohana flew over the forest, which truly did look as if it extended to the horizon in every direction.

Did he really imagine I was going to trust him?

Before I could think of asking, he hovered over a tree.

"Do your salamander thing," he ordered.

Then he dropped me.

We weren't very high above the trees. There was a hole in the trunk of a tree, one that could be seen only from the top. As I fell straight toward it, I realized his intent. I shifted shape, even as the branches of the tree touched my feet.

I barely managed the change in time. I lost some skin sliding into the hole, had time to wince, and then Trevor's memory engulfed me.

Kohana had dumped me into the memory of the night Trevor had joined the Mages.

Chapter 13

We were somewhere out in the country. It was hard to tell exactly, because the air was so thick with Mage spells. The scene was almost lost in blindingly bright gold, a swirling network of spell light on every side. I could see individual spells of every shade of yellow and gold, tangling together to create an impenetrable mesh.

If I peered through the spell light, though, I could see a gathering of people, singing in a field. Well, a field with statues in it. Where were we? It was night, although the sky was clear and the moon was full. That moon cast its silvery light over the chorus of singers.

No, it wasn't exactly a field. It was a cemetery! A big one. But I could see the lights of streets and buildings beyond its dark perimeter. Gravestones glowed in the moonlight, more than a few showy memorials among them.

I saw a crusading knight carved of white stone, leaning on his shield as if he were watching the festivities.

The people who were singing—they must have been Mages—stood in concentric circles. Those in the two inner circles faced the center and the people in the last one faced outward. Sentries, maybe.

I hoped they wouldn't be able to see me.

I darted forward in salamander form, having a good bit of distance to cover but not wanting to risk a larger form. They'd probably notice a dragon.

On the other hand, I might not be discernible. I wasn't part of the memory, after all.

I stayed as a salamander, just in case. I did wish I might have been a darker color than white, as the moonlight had to be making me look like a silver flash. I paused to catch my breath at the base of a statue that had been enclosed in a glass box, presumably to protect it.

It depicted a little girl, holding a parasol and smiling slightly.

Did she wink at me?

Or was I just losing my mind?

I darted closer to the singers, keeping to the shadows. Most of the Mages had their eyes closed, which worked for me. I scooted past the outer circle, slipping between two participants, just as the chorus rose to a crescendo.

I saw the Mages on either side of me respond to the song, beginning to flicker between forms in that way that made me nauseous. I kept my head down and passed through the next circle, slipping between the ankles of another singer.

He started to stamp his foot right when I was between his feet, which made me race forward.

The occupants of the inner circle were seated, hands folded in their laps. They seemed to be kids and when I saw a younger version of Trevor, I guessed that they were apprentices. They had front-row seats for whatever the action was going to be.

There was a figure in the very center of the circle, bound with spell light just as Jessica had been. She wasn't moving. I switched between my alternate visions of the scene and discerned that she was still breathing.

And that she had a fishy tail.

A mermaid.

A shape shifter.

An older woman stood in the middle of the circle, beside the mermaid. She watched the moon as the song grew louder. Then she nodded and reached into her sleeves. I was sure they were flowing and empty, but she pulled a dark weapon from the folds of fabric.

The Mages gasped in appreciation.

The woman smiled.

The moonlight slipped over the weapon in a strange liquid way, making it look like it was coated in quicksilver.

I had a bad feeling about this.

"Behold the NightBlade," the woman sang as she held the blade high. The chorus echoed her words, singing them so that they reverberated. "Gift of the ShadowEaters. Carved of a meteorite. Possessed of the power to liberate shadows."

She waved the blade as she sang this. I assumed she was making symbols in the air, but I couldn't figure out what they were. The spell light was so vivid and the light emanating from the blade was blindingly bright.

"We invoke the ShadowEaters," she sang. "And invite them to our feast. Come, come among us, exalted ones. Come and partake of our offering."

The mermaid began to struggle, panicking maybe, shifting between human and half-fish form in agitation. The apprentices smiled, more than one leaning forward in anticipation.

The beat of the song changed and the words changed into a

language I didn't know. The spell light began to pulse with insistence. The woman bent, murmuring in that same language, repeating a sentence over and over again. She took that blade and cut closely around the mermaid's body.

The mermaid thrashed. The mermaid fought. The mermaid screamed.

Then she was completely still.

The woman straightened, holding a dark form in one hand, the blade in the other. The mermaid's shadow dripped over the woman's fingers, limp.

Liberated.

"Last of her kind," she roared. "An offering worthy of our exalted ones. Come, feast with us, O blessed ones."

And they did. Silver forms materialized between the Mages, seeming to emerge from thin air. Or shadows. They were indistinct forms, faintly human but difficult to discern. I felt as if I could see them better out of the corner of my eye.

But they were real. They had a strange, powerful presence. As soon as they arrived, I felt astonished.

And terrified. There was something enormous and dark about them, and the threat they posed wasn't just smoke and mirrors.

The Mages and apprentices stared in awe at the forms flitting between them, appearing and disappearing. Many of them forgot to sing. The woman with the knife exalted and laughed as they all spun gleefully around the shadow that she offered.

It got visibly smaller.

ShadowEaters.

And then, abruptly, they disappeared.

The woman was obviously disappointed, and I wondered what she had hoped for.

Then she raised her hands, still holding one piece of the mermaid's shadow in her hand. "And so we are blessed to share in the feast, to revel in the power, to know that the divine ones still show us their favor." She tore the shadow into pieces and handed it to the other Mages and apprentice Mages.

She consumed the piece of shadow she held with glee.

I looked around to see the other participants eating as well. Some nibbled, some devoured, and some threw it back with gusto while others savored the treat. There was no singing, just the frantic orange spin of spell light.

And the sound of chewing.

"And so we are driven to give flesh to those who have gone before," the woman cried. "And so we again will offer the shadow of the last of a shifter kind to the ShadowEaters, until they have consumed enough to walk among us once again."

This was the surge of power they would get by eliminating all shifters.

The woman raised her hands again. A shout rose from the Mages in the circle, the ones flickering between forms. Suddenly, in unison, they all shifted to the form of mer-people. I was surrounded by mermaids and mermen, by glittering glistening scales and luxuriant hair.

Laughing in their triumph.

Meanwhile, the mermaid whose shadow had been taken was dissolving. She turned into a fine mist, one that appeared to be a ghostly version of the mermaid in life.

The woman smiled coldly.

Then she deliberately blew on the mermaid. The form of the mermaid wavered, recovered, and then all of those gathered blew in its direction in unison.

The mermaid was dispersed.

Her body was completely gone.

I had just watched one more species of shifter pass into the realm of myth and fantasy.

That was when I knew for sure that I was going to puke.

THE GOOD NEWS WAS THAT I managed to spontaneously manifest back in Isabelle's dorm room.

The bad news was that I did puke, and on arrival.

It's not the most elegant way to make an entrance.

Fortunately, Isabelle thinks fast about all matters connected with spontaneous manifestation. She caught it all in the plastic wastebasket that was parked under her desk. She pushed me into her desk chair and I sat there with my feet braced against the floor and my head between my knees. The last thing I wanted that chair to do was spin.

"That bad?" Isabelle asked and I nodded. I couldn't shake the image of that mermaid being devoured and destroyed. I closed my eyes more tightly, as if that would make the sight go away.

Instead I saw a figure in a hooded cloak, its facial features hidden in the shadows of the cowl.

The last thing I needed was a visit from Urd and her laughing skull face. I opened my eyes and gulped down the glass of water that Meagan offered.

"You done?" Isabelle asked, holding up the wastebasket, and I nodded again. She left with that prize and I heard the water running in the bathroom.

"Chocolate?" Meagan asked, offering some of Isabelle's hoard. "Isabelle always gives you food."

I told you she was brilliant.

By the time Isabelle came back into the room, I'd pulled it together a bit.

"It helps with the change," I told Meagan. "My blood sugar seems to take a big hit." I wasn't sure my stomach was trustworthy, but the chocolate tasted good. I chewed slowly and willed my horror to subside. "Thanks."

Meagan gave me an expectant look. "So tell us."

"It's gross."

"We can take it," Isabelle said. Both cats turned, as if they, too, wanted to know.

I told them what I'd seen. I didn't leave out anything. When I was done, I wasn't any less upset than I'd been at the time.

Meagan grimaced. "That's what they're going to do to Jessica."

I stared at the wrapper of the chocolate bar, knowing she was right. "And they'll be one step closer to helping the ShadowEaters manifest," I said grimly.

"Two, if Derek is like the wolves' Wyvern," Isabelle said.

"Three if they get Zoë and the guys, too," Meagan concluded.

It wasn't the most upbeat possibility imaginable. "But we have to try to save them. We can't just stay away," I said and the other two nodded agreement.

"Did you recognize the woman who was leading them?" Isabelle asked.

I shook my head.

"Any of them?" she insisted.

I shook my head again. "Just Trevor."

Isabelle absently patted the striped cat, which had come to sit in her lap. "What about the memory forest?"

"Just a dead forest that went on forever."

The gray cat seemed to consider its options, then came to Meagan. I saw her wince as it kneaded her lap with its paws and knew it had its claws. It settled into a ball quickly, watching me as she scratched its ears.

"How many trees were there?" Meagan asked.

"I don't know. Thousands." I smiled. "I didn't count them."

Meagan didn't smile back. She chewed her lip and rubbed the cat. "If each month is a tree, how could Trevor's memory be such a big forest?"

She was right.

Kohana had said *they*.

She took my silence as skepticism. "Seriously. He's seventeen or so. That means he's lived seventeen times twelve months. Two hundred and four trees, give or take six or so. Were there more trees than that?"

"Lots more."

Isabelle looked between us. "So, either he's not what he seems to be—as old as he seems to be—or it's not just his memory."

"Well, he doesn't wear a glamour, like Adrian. I'd be able to see through that with the ring."

"There could be another way for them to disguise their identity," Isabelle said.

"But Trevor's an apprentice. It doesn't make sense that he'd know more tricks than Adrian."

Meagan stroked the cat's head, thinking. "If he is the age he appears to be, then what are all the other trees?" She glanced up at me. "Maybe they have a kind of hive memory. Shared real estate and shared memories."

"That's creepy." But it made sense.

"What else did you notice?" Isabelle asked.

"It was a full moon in the vision," I said.

"That's when the book says the ceremony has to be held," Meagan said.

"November fifteenth," Isabelle reminded us. "The night before your birthday."

Meagan drummed her fingers on the mattress and I wondered what she was thinking. "Could you tell where the ceremony was held?"

"They might not meet in the same place every time," I had to note. "It was a cemetery, though."

"That could help. Were there any distinctive gravestones?"

"A knight. Like a crusader. And a little girl in a glass box."

"We've got to be able to research that," Isabelle said. "Draw it for me and I'll see if I can find it online."

"It'd be better to find out where the guys are being held," I said. I was drawing as I spoke, Meagan watching over my shoulder. "And spring them early, if we can."

"Maybe we should each work on something different," Meagan said, her tone purposeful. "Isabelle can look for the gravestones. I'll take another run at breaking the code on that Mage book."

"What about me?"

Meagan grinned. "You'd better get your homework done so you don't get called into the counselor's office again. You don't have time to take the families-of-divorce course." Her messenger chimed and the gray cat leapt out of her lap in indignation.

Her dad.

Coming to pick us up.

THE STRANGE THING WASN'T THAT Jessica and Derek weren't at school on Monday.

The strange thing was that only Meagan and I noticed.

When Jessica wasn't at the front door, waiting for Meagan, we exchanged a look and headed for our lockers, not at all short of apprehension. Of course, we'd guessed she wouldn't be there, but it was that relentless optimism at work again.

The halls were filled with a golden orange glow that illuminated every corner.

"Can you see anything?" Meagan asked in an undertone.

I nodded. "What do you feel?"

"There's this awful music that's trying to slide into my head."

"Block it out as best you can. Hum something else."

She started to hum the Hallelujah chorus from Handel's *Messiah* again, gritting her teeth as she forced out every note. The light had to be a spell, one that acted like a glamour. One that made it seem as if Jessica and Derek had never even existed.

It had spread throughout the whole school, so we all had to walk through spell soup.

My messenger pinged. It was Isabelle. "Weird," she said when I answered the call. "I just called Sara, pretending to be looking for a textbook for one of my classes."

"Is Garrett there?" I asked, hope in my voice even though I was pretty sure I knew the answer. Meagan turned to watch me.

"No," Isabelle said. "Which is what I expected. What I didn't expect was that Sara isn't worried. In fact, it took her a minute to remember that Garrett *should* be there."

"Sara is not a crap mom."

"No, she's not." Isabelle paused, then whispered, "It was like she didn't even remember him for a minute."

That gave me a very bad feeling.

Meagan leaned closer to listen in as Isabelle continued. "Then she gave me some story about him staying at a friend's place, which didn't even sound plausible when she said it."

"So, their spells reach that far," Meagan mused.

"I'm going to call Delaney and Ginger to ask about Liam," Isabelle said. "Then Donovan and Alex. But I'm pretty sure all of the parents will have a similar story."

"And no one else even notices," I told her. "Being captured means you cease to exist." I shivered when I said that, thinking of that mermaid. I'd never felt so powerless in my life.

"Why do we remember, then?" Isabelle asked.

"Well, I'm a wildcard. Meagan is a spellsinger."

"And they want Isabelle to remember," Meagan said grimly.

I nodded. "Because it's not over." I looked at her. "Maybe they think you'll want to join the winning side."

"Not a chance." Meagan straightened and scanned the corridor, looking grim and purposeful. "There has to be something we can do."

"Maybe you can find out more," Isabelle said. "And I'll check on the guys. Talk to you at lunch."

"Right."

First, I had to confirm our impressions. Suzanne was striding toward us, her blond ponytail swinging. She would have walked right past us, as usual, but she looked to be in a much better mood than she had been the week before, so I dared to speak to her.

"Have you seen Jessica?" I asked her.

"Who?" She looked to be genuinely puzzled. Then she rolled her eyes as if I'd been putting her on. "Don't pretend you know people I don't, freak," she muttered, and tossed her ponytail.

"What about that fire Saturday night?" Meagan said.

Suzanne looked at her with disdain. "Just because some loser set his costume on fire with a cigarette didn't mean the fire department had to come." She tossed her hair again. "It was probably a neighbor, trying to get Trevor in trouble."

Meagan and I exchanged a glance. The entire basement had been an inferno when we'd escaped.

But then, the house had been fine when I'd invaded Trevor's memory on Sunday.

I was starting to think that Mage spells were even more powerful and spooky than I'd believed.

Meanwhile, Suzanne went straight to Trevor. He put his arm around her shoulders and she kissed him, acting as if they had never broken up. I had to assume that the other kids hadn't noticed anything on Saturday night. When they'd been frozen, maybe it had been like time stood still for them.

Meagan and I went to our lockers in silence. Trish's locker is on the other side of Meagan's. Usually she ignores both of us, and that remained consistent.

Meagan gave me a questioning look and I nodded.

"Hi, Trish," she said brightly. "Didn't Suzanne and Trevor break up last week?"

Trish looked at her in surprise.

"Are you kidding?" she asked, with all the disdain she reserved for Meagan. Actually, she saved a good chunk of it for me, too. "They'll never break up. Their love is *forever*." Trish sneered. "Not that he'd notice you, even if they did."

Trish marched off to join Suzanne and Trevor.

Was Trevor smirking at us?

"This is so weird," Meagan murmured to me.

"Just play along. We'll talk about it after school."

She nodded and tightened her lips. Then she hummed a little more loudly.

"Hey, Meagan!" Trevor called and we both looked back to find him strolling behind us with Suzanne. "Great piano work Saturday night."

"I had no idea you could play like that," Suzanne added.

At least somebody remembered something.

Although I could have done without the Mages remembering Meagan's gift. I hovered close to her, not knowing what to expect from him. He looked as if he was really enjoying himself. His eyes were all sparkly. Jubilant. As if victory was within his grasp.

There was nothing to like about that.

"Um, th-th-thanks." Meagan pushed her glasses up her nose and clutched her books to her chest.

Trevor came to lean against Trish's locker. His smile was so friendly that I completely distrusted it. "You want to join our jazz improv group? We meet after class on Mondays and Thursdays, and we could use a piano player."

As if that was going to happen. I started to turn away, positive that Meagan would decline.

"Sure," she said and I spun back to stare at her in shock. She nodded firmly, her stutter completely banished. "That would be great."

Trevor's smile looked hungry to me. "See you there, then."

"Absolutely."

The first bell rang. Trevor and Suzanne turned away, talking quietly together as they headed to class. Meagan and I walked in the opposite direction. I had a major case of the creeps. "Are you nuts?" I whispered.

"Someone has to find out more," Meagan murmured. "I'm the most obvious choice, so I volunteered."

"No way. It's stupid."

She stopped and glared at me. "It's not stupid. It's brilliant. I'm going undercover."

"Don't you see? Their spell is getting to you, too, making you think things you wouldn't think otherwise."

"Bullshit. I know what I'm doing."

"But . . ."

"You're the one who said we should play along. How else are we going to find out where the others are? How else are we going to figure out how to save them?"

I shook my head. "It's too risky."

Meagan waved that aside. "If you want me to calculate the probability of success, I'll work it out for you."

"That's encouraging."

"But you have to know that if we do nothing, our chances of success are much lower."

"And you can tell me how much."

Meagan smiled.

I made one last appeal. "I'm good with risk. I just don't like you taking the risk." I sighed, because she wasn't persuaded. "I don't think this is a good idea at all. Let's think of something else."

"I don't think there's a better one." Meagan got that stubborn look, the one that told me she'd never change her mind. "I'm going in."

I'D ALWAYS THOUGHT THAT IF I could just break the Covenant and tell Meagan the truth about my abilities, we'd be best friends again like we used to be. I'd always thought there'd be nothing left to argue about and we could be a team.

But it wasn't working out that way. Instead, we were fighting all over again.

We argued more about her decision to join the improv jazz group over tofu burgers at my fave restaurant. It was a relief to escape the pervasive power of the golden Mage spell that was filling the corridors at school. I'd thought it might help us think more clearly.

It hadn't done one thing to change Meagan's mind.

"The problem really is that you don't trust me," she said.

"No, the problem really is that you don't know what you're up against."

"What are you afraid of?" she demanded.

"Other than everybody dying or disappearing?" I eyed her and she nodded. "Okay. Mage spells can change your thinking. They can make you believe things that you know aren't true. Only a more advanced spellsinger can defeat them."

"And I'm not trained yet." She nodded thoughtfully, surveying the restaurant. "Okay, that's fair. Give me Jared's number."

I sat back in shock. "I don't think he'll help."

Meagan smiled. "Want to make a bet on that?"

"He bailed on me. He left. . . ."

"Sure, but I'd be the one contacting him." Meagan made a flourish in the air with her fry. "And I'd be doing it to save you. Trust me—he'll help." She ate that fry with great satisfaction.

Was she right?

Couldn't hurt to try.

Would it be good enough?

Just pulling up his address made my pathetic heart go flippity-flop. I was even blushing when I forwarded it to Meagan. Derek was nice. Kinda cute. Maybe he was even safe—well, given that he was a wolf shifter—but Jared . . .

I had a feeling that no one was ever going to turn me inside out the way Jared did.

I just wasn't sure that was a good thing.

Meagan typed away, composing an entreaty to Jared. I desperately wanted to see it, but tried to be nonchalant. "You haven't eaten anything," she said without looking up.

"I'm not hungry."

"You'll need your strength to shift, if you have to." She pushed my tofu burger, still in its wrapping, toward me and sounded stern. "Eat."

"Promise me that you'll be careful."

She smiled. "This is going to be awesome. You'll see." She leaned closer. "All you have to do is trust me."

I couldn't say anything to that.

"Promise," Meagan insisted.

"Okay. I promise. But you have to ask me if you have any doubts. You can't take any more risks and . . ."

"Pinkie swear," she said, interrupting me. She held up her pinkie finger the way we used to promise things to each other in elementary school.

The sight made me smile. A little.

I pinkie swore. There was nothing more I could do.

I DIDN'T KNOW WHAT TO do with myself after school. As hard as I tried to persuade her, Meagan had insisted it would compromise her cover if I came to the jazz session. That drove me a bit nuts, as I was worried about what might happen to her. She was sure that nothing would happen in front of everyone. I reminded her that a lot had happened Saturday night in front of everyone, and she reminded me that almost everyone had been enchanted. I didn't see why that same spell couldn't be cast again.

We went round and round, each certain that she was right.

She was determined to do this and since I couldn't stop her, I played by her rules.

For now.

I did seriously consider the merit of spying on her in my salamander form, but I had promised to trust her. It was a bit early to bail on a pinkie swear.

I tried to be responsible and do my homework.

In the end, I was too restless to make much progress and it felt strange to go to her house without her.

So, I went to my house.

My rationale was that it was time to check on the place, pick up the mail, water the plants, etc., etc. The truth was that I wanted to be alone, and I wanted to be alone someplace familiar. Someplace safe. It's never a bad thing to slide inside the protective barrier of your dad's dragonsmoke.

I closed my eyes when I unlocked the door to our loft and felt the glittery caress of his dragonsmoke. It was piled high and thick around the perimeter of the apartment, woven all around it like a protective cocoon. Stepping through the chill of my dad's dragonsmoke—breathed slowly and deliberately to defend his territory from invaders—made me shiver.

Then it made me want to cry.

Because I could already feel that the barrier was degenerating. Dragonsmoke erodes over time, gradually dispersing. My father's barrier had been a fortress wall, but in his absence, it was thinning. Not enough for anything to be at risk, but I could feel the difference and that made me keenly aware of his absence.

And the reason for his absence.

Would my parents come back?

Together?

The loft felt lonely and empty. Cold. The decor has always been a bit austere, but on this day, it felt impersonal. Vacant.

I locked the door behind myself and went through all the rooms, checking the locks on the windows. There was a smell in the kitchen and I realized that no one had remembered to take the trash out on that last day. Clearly, icky trash hadn't been at the forefront of my mom's thoughts when she'd walked out. It was out of character, though, because she always had a departure checklist. This time, she'd been too upset to follow it.

Or too determined to leave to care.

I did the dutiful thing. I took out the trash and emptied the dishwasher, cleaning up the kitchen in the hope that she would come back and wouldn't be disgusted when she did so. I got proactive with the contents of the fridge, too. I sorted the mail, leaving it on appropriate desks, as if everything would return to routine just because I wanted it to. And then I ran out of jobs to do.

That was when it occurred to me to visit my dad's hoard.

A dragon's hoard is a personal treasury of items of both monetary and emotional value—deeply personal and vigorously defended. I think sometimes that the secrets are more valuable than the gold.

My dad's hoard was housed in a windowless room with only one entry. It was located roughly in the middle of the loft—by design, not accident—nestled between the kitchen and the walk-in closet adjacent to the master bathroom. The master bath wrapped around the other side of the room that held the hoard, and if you hadn't been thinking about space, you might not have realized that an entire room was secreted there. You had to slide the clothes down one bar in the closet to even see the door, which was painted the same color as the closet walls. The hoard door was locked, too.

That was enough to keep human intruders away. My dad also had defenses against dragons. His dragonsmoke was almost impenetrable around the door of the hoard—when I pushed his shirts aside, I could see its frosty glitter. Unlike the dragonsmoke that surrounded the loft itself, this barrier permitted no one to cross other than my dad.

I had never been invited into his hoard. I had seen specific items that had been removed for me to view them elsewhere in the loft. I'd always wanted to know what else was in there. I'd never had the opportunity to find out—though it hadn't been for lack of trying. The dragonsmoke barrier had kept me out, even in my dad's absence.

But now I could spontaneously manifest elsewhere.

I should be able to bypass the barrier.

My dad would never know that I had crossed his dragonsmoke barrier. He'd never feel it burn me for daring to go where I shouldn't. He'd never feel it break. I would simply go around it.

I would prove that he couldn't exile me in the traditional way.

And I would finally know what else was in his hoard.

If that wasn't incentive, I didn't know what was.

Chapter 14

It was ridiculously easy. One minute I was standing in the closet, gathering my nerve. The next, the whole world was sparkling with blue light.

I opened my eyes to find myself in a darkened room. I could smell that it was sealed against the world, and against the light that outlined a door I saw the glitter of dragonsmoke.

"Well-done," someone said.

My heart leapt and I spun in terror. There was a radiance on the far side of the hoard, one that illuminated very little. I took a cautious step closer, mustering the cusp of change.

"You're learning fast, Sis," Sigmund said, a smile in his voice. "I love that you don't mind breaking the rules."

My dad had said that he saw Sigmund sometimes in his visions, so I had to check. "You aren't going to tell on me, are you?" I moved closer to the ghost of my big brother. He was leaning over something, cradling it in his hands. I couldn't tell whether the faint light was coming from it or him.

"Erik probably knows." Sigmund shrugged. "All that foresight. Maybe he guessed that you would come in here. I did." He smiled at me. "Or at least I hoped you'd have the nerve to do it."

I looked around, my eyes having adjusted to the darkness. There were the expected piles of coins and jewelry and shiny trinkets. The gold gleamed warmly, even with such faint light, but I saw that there was a lot of silver, too. Buckets of gems. I bent and grabbed a fistful, letting them run between my fingers like dried beans.

"It's incredible," I said.

"Just like the stories say." Sigmund sounded bored. "Over centuries, you can collect a lot of stuff. Erik was always big on financial security."

I glanced up. "What was in your hoard?"

He smiled. "Books." His tone turned rapturous. "Books with leather bindings and embossed covers. Books filled with secrets, inscribed by hand or letterpress on vellum or parchment. Engravings and drawings and symbols and knowledge. Books. I loved them as I never loved anything else."

"What happened to your hoard?"

His lips thinned and he turned away. "I destroyed it." I saw him swallow. "I burned it all, so no one else could ever have it."

I wondered how many things had been written in those books that might have been helpful to me. "Anything about Wyverns in those books?"

His eyes gleamed in the darkness. "You'll never know now, will you?"

That made me mad. "You could have left it as a legacy. You could have helped me out a bit here."

Sigmund frowned and tapped his fingers for a minute. He wouldn't look at me. "What you want is over here, you know."

I wasn't sure whether he had told me that because he felt guilty, or whether it had been his plan in the first place. I went to his side. "How'd you get in here, anyway?"

He gave me a look filled with pity. "I'm dead. I can go wherever I want. Usually no one sees me, though."

"You always turn up when I'm in the dark, and nearly give me a heart attack."

"Always been fond of dark corners," he said. When he smiled, he looked so mischievous that it was hard to be grumpy at him. "And deep shadows." He wiggled his eyebrows, then pointed down to the shelf in front of him.

I couldn't figure out what it was at first. "It's broken," I guessed finally.

Sigmund picked up the bigger piece of stone and turned it for me. It was dark stone, really dark, and when he held the pieces, I could see that it had once been a polished sphere. But it was broken now, and the fact that the pieces were carefully preserved in my dad's hoard told me that it had been important.

Whatever it had been.

"The Dragon's Egg," Sigmund supplied. "It used to show the location of a firestorm." He spun one piece, but it was lopsided. "The story of how it was found is lost."

I would have bet that my brother knew how it was found, but he averted his gaze, a sure sign that he wasn't telling.

"What about the story of how it got broken? Is it in your book?" I asked.

He shook his head. "Happened after publication."

"But you know."

"Once upon a time, a *Slayer* captured both the Wyvern and the Dragon's Egg. The *Pyr* Nikolas was given the choice of saving just one."

I looked at the broken stone. "He chose the Wyvern."

Sigmund sobered. "He loved the Wyvern. He would have

done anything for her. But it is forbidden for any of our kind to be intimate with the Wyvern." He grimaced. "It's similar to the human edict against sleeping with one's sister." He arched a brow.

I ignored his expectant expression. "Why?"

"Maybe if you go back far enough, we dragons are truly all brethren."

"Is that why she died?"

Sigmund shook his head. "It's why she lost her powers." He snapped his fingers. "Presto! All gone."

"What?" She lost her powers because she had sex? *Once?* I was going to live for hundreds of years, but to keep my powers I'd have to be a virgin forever? "But I'm just *getting* my powers!"

"Then you'd better follow the rules, Sis."

"What rules? There's no rule book or guide."

Sigmund scoffed. "Don't play games. You know instinctively what most of them are." Then he looked pointedly around the room to the door.

That was a telling reminder. "Right. You couldn't have mentioned this need for me to follow the rules before I entered the forbidden territory of Dad's hoard."

He grinned and I figured he was teasing me. "So, did you break an important one? Guess you'll find out when you try to leave. Think your powers have gone away already?"

I folded my arms across my chest. "You are not helping."

"We could both be dead in here. How fun would that be?"

"Not helping."

"Of course, you might not waste away to nothing and die before Erik gets back. You might be alive." Sigmund winked. "Until he killed you."

"Hello, could we stay on topic, please?" I indicated the Dragon's Egg. He didn't have to know that he had me seriously worried.

He patted it. "Erik could also use this like a scrying glass, see the future before it happened."

Sigmund was too smug and I guessed he was hiding something from me. "Don't tell me you can see the future, too?"

"All the dead can." He smiled. "We just don't care anymore."

"Do you care about anything?"

Sigmund straightened and looked straight at me. "I wouldn't be here otherwise, kiddo. Think about it."

I did.

Then he beckoned to me, inviting questions.

I had lots. "What happened to Sophie?"

"You have the answer on your finger."

I looked down. I'd seen a white dragon and a black one come out of the ring the previous spring. I knew they were Sophie and Nikolas. Being trapped in a ring with your beloved didn't sound to me like an ideal fate.

I would have asked another question, but when I looked up again, Sigmund was gone, one piece of the Dragon's Egg rocking slightly from his touch.

Scrying, huh.

Maybe it was time to give that a try.

I STEPPED CLOSER TO THE chunks of the Dragon's Egg. It would have been bigger than a basketball when all one piece—now five pieces lay on velvet in my dad's hoard.

I picked up one—not the biggest, as it was half the orb—and turned it over so that the smooth outside was facing me. I could see the reflection of myself in it, distorted the same way a fish-eye lens would distort it.

I made a face at myself and my reflection made it back.

Much uglier, though.

Then I got serious. I stared into the surface of the stone. It was very black, so dark that it was easy to think that the surface wasn't hard. It made me think of looking into a deep shadow, one that goes to depths beyond expectation.

I looked more deeply. I thought about Wyverns past and my almost complete lack of data about their history. I thought about needing to solve riddles without having very many clues.

And it suddenly seemed as if the piece of the orb I held was full of stars. It could have been a chunk of night sky in my hands. I stared more deeply and one star brightened.

It shot across the piece of stone—or deep inside it—like a falling star.

It flashed.

Then all the stars that had been in the stone disappeared.

I didn't have time to be disappointed. A verse popped into my head. I heard the words as clearly as if someone had read it to me, but it was in my own voice.

As if I was reading a verse to myself, even though I'd never heard this one.

I put down the piece of stone, tugged out my messenger, and tapped in the verse before I forgot it.

Wyverns past of snowy white
Gather to initiate
The newest member of their kind;
Always with hope that this one unbinds
Past errors and misjudgments
That condemn each Wyvern to lament
That love can never touch her life
Without instead a sacrifice.
Each new Wyvern may hold the key
To change the Wyverns' destiny.

Then I read it again. Twice.

What did it mean?

Could I be the one holding the key?

Suddenly I realized that the doorbell was ringing.

The time to find out whether I'd lost my powers or not was right now. I held my breath and called to the shimmer that let me move through space. It didn't answer right away, as if it just wanted to make me sweat.

I did.

My mouth went dry.

The doorbell rang again.

I shouted in my mind for the shimmer, wishing with all my heart to be on the other side of the door to the hoard and the dragonsmoke barrier. I squeezed my eyes shut, hoped hard, and . . . presto.

It worked.

THE DOORBELL RANG A THIRD time as I fell into the closet, making a whole pile of my mom's shoes cascade to the floor.

I zipped out of my parents' suite and ran to the front door. There was a delivery guy already turning to leave.

"Oh, there is someone home," he said, then came back to the door.

"Sorry. I was, um, busy."

He eyed me, obviously tabulating possibilities, then decided it wasn't his business. Maybe I was mastering my dad's glare. "I've got a package for Zoë Sorensson."

"That's me." I saw the scribbled dates of failed deliveries noted on the label; then he turned for me to sign for the box. It had been sent overnight from Pennsylvania.

I don't even know anybody in Pennsylvania.

"I came twice last week. The ones that require a signature are a pain in the neck." He looked at my signature. "Have you got any identification? Can't be too careful."

I got my wallet and he had a look at my student card. Then he waved and shouldered his bag. "Have a good day," he said, heading for the elevator.

I shut the door and leaned against it, the package in my hands. It had no return address, really, just a post office box. It was flat and rectangular, not light but not heavy, either. I leaned closer and gave it a sniff. Then my eyes widened in surprise.

Jared.

I smelled *Jared*.

I ripped the box open then, making a mess of the kitchen one more time. I suppose I shouldn't have been surprised by its contents.

But I was. I stood there, staring at it in shock.

It was a book.

An old book I'd held in my hands a couple of times before.

The Habits and Habitats of Dragons: A Compleat Guide for Slayers, by Sigmund Guthrie.

There was no note, but really, the fact that Jared had sent me the book said it all. He didn't want me to contact him anymore. He didn't want to see me again.

He was bailing on this dragon girl.

Forever.

If you don't think that was the most depressing news I'd heard all day, you can think again. And if I was feeling a bit sorry for myself and my previously undiscovered talent for making everyone disappear from my life, at least there was no one to see it.

"Did you know?" I called to no one in particular.

I'm pretty sure I heard Sigmund chuckle in reply. But he didn't give me any more answers, and he didn't appear to advise me.

Brothers.

Well, I had the only reference book in existence on the *Pyr*. Might as well use it.

I MEANT TO START READING my brother's book from page one, but when I opened the cover, the book fell open to a later page.

There was a bookmark.

With a note.

And it was from Jared.

YES!

It wasn't a long note or an especially romantic one. It wasn't even signed. But I knew it was from him because it was short and to the point, as well as challenging. That was Jared all over.

Where's your beryl, dragon girl?

The bookmark was in the page with the appropriate entry.

> Beryl—a gem or token of power, typically given from one *Pyr* to another. In the ancient history of the *Pyr*, there are far more references to beryls and their use, although even then, the vast majority of *Pyr* would never have any personal experience of a beryl. Like so many rare items, a beryl is frequently believed to be a myth.
>
> According to *Pyr* lore, a beryl can seal an agreement. There is some implication that beryls carry power, although the references are vague as to how those powers are assumed by the recipient.
>
> The one common element in stories involving beryls is the strong association between beryls and Wyverns. There has been some speculation that there is only one beryl, which takes different shapes at different times under the command of the one Wyvern, and that this token is passed as a legacy from each Wyvern to her successor. As each Wyvern must die before her successor can

be conceived, it is unclear how this transaction might occur, or whether this tale—like so many others associated with the Wyvern—is simply fabrication.

I read it twice. Where *was* my beryl? I looked down at the ring on my hand, the one Rafferty had given to me.

Was it my beryl?

How was I supposed to shake any power from it?

There was a puzzle and I had to solve it.

Sooner would be better.

BY THURSDAY, I was convinced that this was going to be the worst two weeks of my life.

Unless things got infinitely more miserable on the Friday before my birthday.

I was worried sick about Meagan, because that goofy golden spell light was everywhere. It circled her like a flock of Day-Glo fireflies. I couldn't even look at her without feeling like freaking out.

We were arguing like crazy.

We were also making zero progress on finding where the others were being held captive.

And Trevor was loving it.

After Monday's session, Meagan had nothing but suspicions. Trevor had made just enough suggestive comments to lure her into coming back. And he had asked her to attend some ceremony on the night of the full moon with him.

She thought this was progress. I thought it was terrifying.

Meagan was confident that she could resist their spells and that she could get more information. I wished I shared her confidence. I had to believe that no matter how much—or how ferociously—she hummed, no matter how completely brilliant she was, the spell would eventually get to her.

I halfway thought it already had. She talked nonstop about Trevor and how amazing he was.

Would I be able to count on my best friend when everything went down? Or would she—against her will—be just drawing my kind into a final fatal trap?

I wasn't sleeping much, which was okay, because I wasn't hot to meet up with Urd and her skull face anytime soon. Take my word for it—the prospect of actual death makes it tougher to confront figurative and/or symbolic death in an unemotional way.

On Thursday when Meagan went to jazz practice with Trevor, I went back to her house feeling useless and futile and edgy. Homework was exactly what I wanted to do. Uh-huh. My messenger sounded just as I was settling in and I seized the excuse.

It was a message from my mom.

She said my dad would be home for my birthday. She didn't say more than that, but I understood the implication.

She wasn't coming back for it.

That was pretty much the last straw. Did I have to lose every single person I cared about? Jared had bailed on me, probably forever. The guys were trapped by Mages. Derek was trapped, too. My mom was staying in England.

If this kept up, my dad would have a fatal accident on the way home, Meagan would be sucked up and destroyed by the Mages, Isabelle would trek off to some ashram to find her inner fortune-teller, the other *Pyr* would be trashed by the Mages, Derek and Jessica would have their shadows eaten, and I would be completely alone.

I heard Meagan's mom come home and shout hello. I yelled back at her that I was studying, an activity that she adored. I knew she wouldn't interrupt me.

Except to maybe come and confiscate my messenger.

Then I remembered what she'd said about my mom needing

to be able to envision a future with my dad to even want to be with him.

I couldn't see the future, much less conjure up some illusion of it for my mom. I had no idea what happened in the dark corners of their relationship and really did not want to know.

But I wanted her to come home.

And that meant I needed her to want to be with him.

Maybe the answer was in the past. There must have been some reason why she loved him in the first place. There must have been something good. She'd known what he was right from the start, but that hadn't mattered seventeen years ago. Maybe I could find her memory, if she was with my dad.

I closed my eyes and put my hands flat on the desk. I looked for the coppery conduits that led to each of the living *Pyr* and I found the one that was my dad's. I checked every line I could see, but there weren't any that led to the guys. They were in some lost zone, where I couldn't reach them.

I went back to the line that led to my dad and followed it, hoping against hope that this strategy would work. I was startled to find myself in his thoughts, that room of stainless-steel drawers stretching into the distance behind me. It was like I wandered out of that room, to go look out the windows.

I was where he was.

I saw what he saw.

I recognized Trafalgar Square. I'd been to England enough times with my parents, to visit my aunt.

It was snowing in England, too.

More importantly, a woman in a black cape, a woman with long red-gold hair and a decisive stride, was walking away.

And my dad wasn't pursuing her. He just watched her go.

I sensed his bleak mood and felt his yearning. I knew he believed there was nothing more he could say. I understood that he was convinced that he had failed.

I took a chance and leapt from his thoughts to my mom. I wasn't sure it would work. It was an intuitive choice, a jump I made without thinking too much about it. I wasn't sure I could slip into her thoughts, but I sure was going to try.

I prayed.

I hoped.

I leapt.

And I found myself in a kitchen filled with happy, colorful clutter. There was a sealer jar of knitting needles and baskets of wool, the colors spilling to the floor. A pile of books toppled on the counter, several cracked open in front. A kettle was whistling, being ignored even though it was boiling.

One entire wall of the room was a bulletin board. I moved closer to look. It was covered in photographs, postcards, scribbled notes, letters, and greeting cards.

I saw the snapshot of a dark-haired baby nestled in a familiar afghan—the one that was still on the end of my bed—and smiled.

I'd found my mom's memory.

I poked around, stirring a few things that seemed evocative of when she'd met my dad, and then I hoped for the best.

And got the heck out of there before I learned too much.

MEAGAN WAS JUBILANT WHEN SHE got home from jazz.

She sat and bubbled and enthused, exuding confidence and Mage news.

I could only watch the sparkles in her eyes.

They were gold.

Mage light.

They were getting to her and she didn't even know it.

She'd been late getting home. She bounced in, that golden light having invaded her eyes and its lilt infecting her voice. Trevor had driven her home. Trevor had confided in her. The next Friday was going to be Trevor's initiation to the next level of Mage apprenticeship.

Trevor had kissed her.

This was not good.

And there were eight whole days until the ceremony. Two more jazz band practices. A seemingly infinite stretch of time for the Mage spells to wind into Meagan's thoughts and undermine everything.

We argued again, and she told me that I was wrong.

She was lost, or close enough to it.

It was time for me to make that deal with Kohana.

I DIDN'T WANT TO MEET Kohana in the dreaming, because I wasn't entirely sure what was possible there. Never mind that he was more adept with whatever was going on in that alternate reality.

Nope. I would meet him in plain old Chicago. I had his feathers and I knew he didn't like that. I had to believe that he was waiting for an opportunity to begin our discussion again.

I gave it to him.

I had three feathers. I needed to let him see that I had them, but I didn't want to lose my grip on them. On impulse, I shook out my ponytail, found some dark thread and bound one feather into the hair hanging on either side of my face. They flipped around a bit, catching the wind in a different way than my hair usually did.

He'd notice that.

He'd probably guess it was a lure, but I figured he'd take the bait.

The third feather I hid. Insurance. Even you don't need to know where it was.

Then I pulled on my leather coat and went walking, my hands shoved in my pockets and my hair blowing around.

I hadn't even gone a block before I felt his presence. His yellow gaze seemed to burn into my back. I kept walking, pretending I didn't know or didn't care that he was there.

By the second block he was following me, covertly. He darted from roof to roof, staying just out of sight, but I was aware of his hungry gaze.

I deliberately turned into the park, heading for the center where the trees would offer perches to Thunderbirds.

And he came, like a projectile out of the night.

"*YOU SAID YOU DIDN'T WANT* to make a deal," Kohana said by way of introduction. He was in a nearby tree, eyes glowing as he looked down at me. We were alone in the park, just the way I wanted it. I felt in control of the exchange—a rare enough thing with Kohana that it made me a bit dizzy.

"Maybe I changed my mind." I twirled one feather. "I'd like some information."

"In exchange?"

I nodded and brushed the snow off the bench there. I sat down, seemingly at ease, and waited.

He looked around. He hopped to another branch. He looked at me, then scanned the perimeter of the park. He clearly suspected a trick. I did my dragon thing and didn't move one muscle. I could have waited through eternity for him to make up his mind. I breathed long and slow and deep, watching him without blinking.

I knew what he would do.

Although I smiled when he did it.

He landed in front of me, a black bird as tall as I am. His eyes blazed vivid yellow, and he fidgeted with the thunderbolts in his claw. "An answer for a feather," he offered.

"Only real answers count," I said. "No games."

I sensed his impatience. He looked away, then back at me again. "No tricks."

I untied the one feather from my hair, then held it between us. "Why does being a wildcard make me Mage prey?"

He didn't like the question. "That's complicated."

"It's one question." I spun the feather. "Answer it or not." I'd snagged some matches from Meagan's mom's array of candles and now I pulled them out. I lit one, scratching it on the bottom of the box, and held the flame toward the black feather.

Kohana caught his breath, then spoke quickly. "A wildcard is a one-off, a rogue variant in a species. A wildcard has extra powers. There's only one in every kind at any time, or there might not be one at all."

He stopped and I held the flame closer to the feather again.

"All right. All right. There is a story that there will come a day when special children are born to each kind of shifter. These children will have powers previously unknown outside of legend and they will change the world. They can change it either way, for better or for worse, but the change will be irrevocable."

I threw the match into the snow and it hissed as the flame went out.

"Answer your question?"

"Not really." I lit another match.

"Those children are the wildcards. You're one and I'm one, and Jessica and that wolf guy."

"Derek."

"Whatever. Four species of shifters left, four wildcards to bring it all home—or screw it up, from the Mages' perspective." He shrugged, his eyes glinting. "You should be able to work out the rest."

I let the firelight dance over the quills of the feather, thinking. "What kind of extra powers?"

He frowned. "Depends on your kind. There's never been an *Unktehila* in the dreaming, for example."

I arched a brow at that.

"Never," he insisted. "*We* keep track of our history."

I had to wonder what other kinds of bonus powers I could get. And what they could be used for.

What were his extra powers?

I thought I might know. "You told me that we would need a spellsinger to fight the Mages. But you're fighting the Mages and you're alone. Where's your spellsinger?"

If ever a bird could smile, he did.

Then he lunged for me. He cast his thunderbolts in all directions, setting off explosions of light all around the bench. Then he snatched one feather out of my grasp and grabbed at the one still in my hair.

"Hey!"

"Don't break your terms, *Unktehila*."

"That's only one answer!" I shifted shape as quickly as I could, intending to fight him for custody of one feather, but he ripped hard.

"I count two!" he replied.

My hair tore and broke, right when I was in the middle of the blue shimmer of change. He had the feather—and a chunk of my hair.

Before I could seize his traitorous little butt, Kohana the Thunderbird was soaring into the cloudy sky.

I let him go.

For now.

Chapter 15

When in doubt, ask Isabelle and her cards.

It wasn't a brilliant plan, but it was the best one I had. I was going to send her a message but she sent me one first, asking me to come to her dorm room. When I got there, she had books all over the place. I assumed she was studying.

Books. Told you she was a throwback.

She insisted on checking the burn on my back again. She slathered on some more cream, even though she said it was nearly healed. I knew that—I could feel that it was better.

"Do you think the guys are okay?" she asked, her question echoing my own worries.

"I don't know. I don't like not knowing." I tugged my shirt back on. "Theoretically, they're just being held captive until the ceremony—"

"Bound by spells, maybe."

"—but I hate not being sure." I dropped onto her chair. "I'm not a fan of the fact that I don't know what to do to save them on that night either. On one hand, it seems to be ages away. On the other, I don't feel like we have nearly enough time to prepare." I pulled out my messenger. "I got this prophecy. Does it make any sense to you?"

Wyverns past of snowy white
Gather to initiate
The newest member of their kind;
Always with hope that this one unbinds
Past errors and misjudgments
That condemn each Wyvern to lament
That love can never touch her life
Without instead a sacrifice.
Each new Wyvern may hold the key
To change the Wyverns' destiny.

Isabelle made me read it twice. I was hoping, you know, that it might tweak some kind of Wyvern memory for her.

"So there's an initiation test for you, based on your making a sacrifice."

"I hate how vague this stuff is."

Isabelle smiled. "Well, maybe I can help. I found something last night. In fact, I can't believe I didn't look at this before." She handed me a couple of books, her excitement obvious. "See? There was a lunar eclipse last spring and then the solar eclipse two weeks later."

It had happened in April. "That's when we were at boot camp."

She went on for a few minutes about nodes of the moon and astrological signs, then must have seen that I was glazing over. "Point being that astrologically it was time for a new beginning."

She pointed her finger at me. "The cue for the new Wyvern to take center stage."

"And the Great Lunar Standstill Derek mentioned?"

"Just started. We'll be at the midpoint in January, and it will end in the spring." Isabelle tapped her messenger. "Right when there's another solar eclipse, at the end of March." She looked at me. "Three solar eclipses over a year, and a lunar standstill. What if Wyvern powers are linked to solar eclipses?"

It made a lot of sense. "And the initiation?"

"There's always a test before the new kid gets the keys to the kingdom. Do you know how to invoke the past Wyverns?"

"No."

"What you should sacrifice?"

I shook my head. There were too many questions and no answers. "Am I right in thinking that I have to solve this to save the guys and Jessica?"

Isabelle looked worried. Then she reached up and snagged her tarot deck. The cat watched from the windowsill with interest. "Pick a card before you go," she said, shoving the deck at me.

I picked and turned it over.

The Moon.

Right side up.

"Intuition and tides," Isabelle said with delight. "Mysteries of the feminine variety."

"A Wyvern card!" I said with excitement and we laughed together.

"I should give this deck to you. It responds so well to your presence."

"No, it's yours. I'll get another one."

"Take a copy of the translation on that book about the Mages," she suggested. "Maybe something will leap out at you if you let your intuition guide you."

Couldn't hurt. I loaded the file onto my messenger and turned to leave.

"Hey, wait!" Isabelle called when I was at the door. "Can you take the cat?"

"Excuse me?"

He regarded me with slitted eyes.

"I can't have a cat in the dorm."

"But he's been here."

She grimaced. "Well, now they know. They say he has to go, but I don't want to take him to the pound or toss him out."

"You have noticed that he hates me."

"Oh, don't be silly. He's just a big teddy bear." Isabelle crossed the room and scooped up the cat. When she carried him toward me, I saw him put out his claws. "You'll get along just fine."

"I don't think so," I said at the same time that Puss spat and slashed at me with one claw.

"Naughty, naughty," Isabelle chided him, kissing the back of his head. He began to purr as she talked to him, still keeping a wary eye on me. "You'll get used to each other. But you have to let me come and visit him."

I really didn't want the cat. "But . . ."

She held out the cat. "He can't stay here, Zoë. They're going to take him to the pound tonight if I don't find him a home. Please?"

The cat glared at me.

There were tears in Isabelle's eyes.

What could I say?

At least he'd retracted his claws.

I took the cat, stunned by the weight of him. I swear, he made himself heavier, just on principle. I don't think either one of us was particularly thrilled about the situation.

But neither one of us could say no to Isabelle, either.

"I forgot to tell you!" Isabelle said, leaning around the

doorframe of her room. It must be said that I looked back with some trepidation. She smiled. "I found the cemetery. It's called Graceland and it's at the north end of the city."

Bonus!

I LOOKED FOR MAGE SPELLS all the way back to the Jamesons', but there wasn't a single one to be seen. I didn't even see any cats. The city was quiet enough to completely creep me out.

I thought about going to that cemetery, just to check it out, but I didn't want to tip my hand. The Mages might be watching it already. Instead, I found a map of it online and tried to memorize the layout.

Then I made a list of the clues I had in matters Wyvern. I needed all the data I could get to ensure that we could save our friends.

Mrs. Jameson thought I was hot for my homework when I got back to their place, but I was doing some more research online. I hadn't forgotten that Urd had introduced herself and her sister to me—I just hadn't thought it was important.

Now I realized that Granny never gave me anything that wasn't important.

Even a clue.

The cat shot away from me as soon as he had the chance, leaping to a windowsill in the living room. The other cat, the one Meagan had picked up, sat on the piano and ignored us both.

Urd and Verdandi, it turned out, were two of the three Wyrd sisters who guard the well at the foot of Yggdrasil, the world tree. Urd spins, Verdandi weaves (or knits), and their third sister, Skuld, has the scissors to snip the thread. They're supposed to weave the fate of everyone.

Even better, just as Urd had told me, her name meant "what was." Verdandi meant "what is" and Skuld meant "what will be."

Past, present, and future.

The three realms that the Wyvern was supposed to be able to see simultaneously.

Three solar eclipses.

And a test of initiation that involved me fixing an error of the past.

I was starting to see a pattern. Urd, mistress of matters past, was in my dreams because my initiation test would be soon. I'd guess it would be concurrent with that eclipse.

And I had to nail it to save the others.

All I had to do was figure out what the Wyvern's error was, how to fix it, and how to invoke the Wyverns past in the first place. All while ensuring that my best friend wasn't sucked into the maw of the Mages, saving three of my dragon buddies, a wolf shifter, and a jaguar shifter, and getting my parents back together again.

No pressure.

ON SUNDAY AFTERNOON, Meagan was doing her piano practice while I worked on my endless homework at the dining room table. Truth be told, I wasn't making much progress.

Because the spell light coming out of her piano was gold.

Spiraling.

Making me shiver.

"I think you should stop going to those jazz practices," I said when she finished a piece and sorted through her sheet music for the next one to practice.

She gave me a look. "I don't agree. I'm finding out lots of stuff."

"Like what? Do you know where they are?"

Meagan shook her head and worked a scale with one hand. "Not yet. But I know they're okay."

The little trill of orange spell light that danced into the air made my tone more sharp than would have been ideal. "How okay is it to be captive?"

Meagan stopped and glared at me. "Don't you trust me? Don't you think I know what I'm doing?"

"I don't think you understand how dangerous they are. You're sitting here, spinning Mage spells. I can see them!"

"Well, of course I am." Her tone was dismissive. "I have to practice. Otherwise they'll know I'm a spy."

"Maybe they know it already. You and I have been friends forever."

"But I've had a crush on Trevor forever, too. He knows that—that's for sure."

"Look. I could beguile you. It might help you to defend yourself."

She gave me a scornful look. "I can defend myself without your help." She pounded out a dark melody with force. "And if you think I'm going to just stop trying to learn more when I could help Garrett, you really don't know anything about me."

I leaned on the piano, desperate to make her listen. "Meagan, I can see the spell light all around you. You're not just making it. You're attracting it."

She smiled with a confidence I didn't share. "All the better to fool them into trusting me." She held up her hand, her finger and thumb an increment apart. "I'm this close to learning the location of their hideaway."

"They're messing with you."

"You're not the only one who knows anything, Zoë." Her lips set. "Derek and Liam and Nick and Jessica and Garrett are okay. For now. Trevor promised me that."

Was it true? Did I dare to believe it?

Had Trevor lied to Meagan?

I watched the golden spell light dance around her head as she played, swirling like a swarm of fireflies, and I had to wonder.

Was it Meagan who was lying to me?

How far had she been tugged into the Mages' plan?

Was that why she wouldn't listen to me?

If so, how could I save her?

MY DAD CAME BACK ON Sunday afternoon.

I sensed his return even before he called Meagan's mom to say I should come home.

I packed up my stuff with mixed feelings. Had my mom come, too? I thought not. How could my dad have failed to change her mind? Didn't he care? Didn't he want her to come back? What was I going to say to him?

I was worried about leaving Meagan alone. I might have stayed a few days, choosing my friend over my dad. I lingered in the living room to say good-bye, but she ignored me. In fact, she seemed to be so busy with her piano practice that she didn't even care that I was leaving.

I trudged home, uncertain what to expect. On the way there, I sent Jared a message, asking—no, begging—for his help with Meagan.

I got a single line reply:

She knows what she's doing.

Perfect.

Whatever I had expected to find at home, it wasn't what I found. Mr. Super-Neat had dropped his bag in the middle of the floor and left it there. That was more characteristic of me. He sat on the couch, still wearing his jacket and boots, staring into space.

I'd never seen him look so despondent.

Defeated.

Lost.

I slammed the door behind myself, just to make sure he heard it, and he jumped a little. He forced a ghost of a smile to his lips. It faded so quickly that if I'd blinked, I would have missed it. "I'll go shopping tomorrow," he said, his voice flat. "Why don't you order pizza tonight?"

Would my real dad please stand up?

The cat had slipped through the door before I slammed it and now sauntered into the loft. He sniffed my dad's bags, then headed for the kitchen. I figured he must be hungry and gave him some water, as well as a bowl of the food Mrs. Jameson had given me. She'd bought it for Meagan's new cat—now named Mozart—and had given me a care package of it.

The cat didn't eat the food.

My dad didn't eat the pizza.

The cat took up a vantage point on the far side of the loft and watched my dad.

My dad stared into space.

I even loaded up an old movie that night, the one with Sean Connery providing the voice of the dragon. He hates that movie. Just hearing the title of it mentioned gets him all fired up (ha) and launches him into his Dragons 101 lecture.

On this night, he just stared at the screen, indifferent.

Which said it all.

I went to bed.

I'm not sure he noticed I'd left.

The cat trotted behind me with purpose, then leapt to my windowsill to stare at the night.

"You're going to need a name," I said to him and he gave me a look, as if I had no business choosing a name for his regal fabulousness.

His choice.

THE SHORT VERSION OF THE story is that Meagan and I argued big-time on Monday.

I said (again) that she should bail on jazz practice.

She declined.

I said that she shouldn't let Trevor drive her home.

She declined.

I insisted on being allowed to accompany her to jazz.

She declined, saying I would blow her cover.

I intended to do it anyway, but I got another note from Muriel the guidance counselor.

Yup, I was enrolled in the program for kids of families damaged by divorce.

Go ahead. Guess when the classes were.

You got it. Mondays and Thursdays, right after school. Attendance not optional.

I couldn't have planned it better if I'd been a Mage.

ON FRIDAY NIGHT, I dressed for war.

I chose my favorite black jeans and my black lace-up boots with the heavy soles. My purple hoodie zipped right up to my chin and barely squished under the black leather jacket I'd permanently borrowed from Nick's mom, Alex. I had the ring on my finger and I shoved my rune stone into my pocket. I tucked the last feather of Kohana's into the pocket inside the left front of the jacket, pulled on a pair of acid green gloves, and was ready to go.

My dad didn't seem to notice my departure. He was still in the living room, breathing smoke, his eyes like embers in the dark.

"Going to Isabelle's!" I shouted without looking back.

I raced down the corridor and swung down the stairs of the building, erupting into the night. I could feel the glow of the rising moon and jammed my hands into my pockets as I headed for the cemetery.

To my astonishment, Fish Breath was right behind me, power-trotting through the snow. Maybe he'd heard me say I was going to see Isabelle.

I thought it was a bad idea for the cat to accompany me. He weighed a ton and I had a long walk ahead of me. The last thing I wanted was to need to carry him.

And Isabelle would flay me alive if I lost him.

Furball believed otherwise. We had a dispute in the street, during which I tried to persuade him to go home and he took a swipe at me with those claws of his when I tried to make him. I gave it up and kept walking. He trotted behind me, keeping up and only periodically complaining with a meow or two.

I decided I would not worry about it if he got lost on the way.

I knew it was a lie. I was getting used to His Majesty, watching over me as I slept and flicking his tail at me with attitude in the morning. He sat on the kitchen counter and yowled when he thought it was time to eat, which happened about twice a day.

He had, to his credit, even made my dad smile.

Looked like we were going to Graceland together.

That's an old song, isn't it?

THE CITY WAS QUIET.

Too quiet.

It gave me a sense of foreboding—assuming that I wasn't carrying that along all by myself. This was it, the big test.

And I still didn't have the answers or know what to do.

No pressure.

I shouldn't have been surprised that it started to snow again, much less that it would snow harder with every passing minute. The flakes were as big as my fist by the time I met Isabelle at the subway station.

The cat yowled and wound around her ankles, proprietary and obviously glad to see her. And no wonder—she picked up Ol' Lard Butt right away. We didn't talk much as we walked to the cemetery, although I was pretty sure we were both thinking about Meagan. Could we haul her back from the dark side?

Although the snow had been plowed on the city streets, we sank up to our knees in the white stuff as soon as we entered the cemetery. It was quiet there, and might have been peaceful if I hadn't been fretting about Mages.

We hadn't gone far before I noticed the wolf. It stood on the far side of a gravestone, as still as the shadows, watching us with those unblinking pale eyes.

"Derek?" I whispered, not daring to hope.

His Royal Fabulousness hissed.

I saw, though, that the wolf had one blue eye and one that was gray. So, it wasn't Derek—just one of his kind. Okay. I was encouraged that another wolf shifter had turned up. Would this one follow my lead? Be on my side? Or was he with the holdouts who didn't want to follow a dragon girl?

The wolf turned away, slipping into the darkness just the way Derek did. I wasn't quite ready for him to disappear. It seemed like I should be able to make some argument in my own favor. I leapt after him, sinking past my knees in the snow.

Then I saw that there were dozens of wolves in the shadows. Like the cats in the sewers, they were all heading toward a point of convergence. The moon touched their fur with silver, making them look both precious and ethereal.

Relentless hunters.

I remembered Derek's comment about dogs seeing in black and white. They would decide whether to follow me based on my performance. Deeds over words. I was sure of it. The wolves turned as one and looked toward the far end of the cemetery.

I followed the direction of their gazes and saw the sickening swirl of spell light.

Beckoning.

The wolves were moving toward its vortex with purpose.

Could they see it? Smell it? Or were they just drawn to it?

"That way?" Isabelle guessed and I nodded. "Creepy enough place to eliminate species." She shuddered as we turned our steps in that direction. The wolves kept apart from us, several regularly casting glances our way.

I had the feeling that I was being watched. Not just by occasional wolves, either. I looked around and noticed a monument in front of me. It was a large square block of stone, which wasn't very interesting. The figure standing before it, though, made my heart stop cold.

It was a hooded figure, its face hidden by the shadows of the hood.

It could have been Urd, except the cloak wasn't black. It had the patina of verdigris.

I had the feeling it was the one watching me, like a guardian.

An angel of death, maybe.

But I couldn't see its eyes. I needed to see its eyes. I wanted to know who was watching me, friend or foe.

I swallowed and walked closer to it, seeing the spindle that had fallen in the snow only when I nearly stepped on it. I reached for the spindle, uncertain whether it was real or not. My fingers closed on cold wood. The eyes within the hood glinted.

Relief swept through me. Better the devil you know.

"Hey, Urd, want to come along?" I asked and handed her the spindle.

Isabelle had stopped to watch me. She probably thought I was nuts. I heard her swear for the first time ever when the figure's arm moved. Skeletal fingers reached out to grasp the spindle as

I heard the creak of Urd's bones. She turned it in her hands, checking it. Then it and her hands disappeared beneath the hem of her sleeves.

She abruptly stepped down from the monument. I continued and she followed us, her cloak leaving a trail in the snow. Isabelle's eyes were round and she looked straight ahead, holding tightly to the cat. He stared over her shoulder, watching Urd with obvious suspicion.

Urd began to murmur as we walked. It was a spooky sound, one that made the hair stand up on the back of my neck. I halfway didn't want to know what she was doing. I couldn't see any spell light, but I could feel energy in the air.

A few moments later, I saw one monument from my trip to Trevor's memory. It was the crusading knight, shield planted on the ground, gaze fixed heroically on the horizon. This presumably was where daring deeds were being done. Urd strode to the side of the gravestone, still murmuring. As I watched, she made a gesture, like blowing a kiss to the knight.

He turned his head to look at her.

He lifted his visor.

He gripped his sword more resolutely.

Then he hefted his shield and marched behind us.

I stared. He was stone. He was a carving. But Urd's kiss had him moving like a man of flesh and blood.

Albeit one that was about nine feet tall.

When the monument of the little girl stepped out of her glass box to walk behind the knight, I guessed the pattern. I pivoted to stare over the cemetery, seeing the array of shadows following us. Urd had awakened the stones, turning stones to people instead of the other way around.

The exact opposite of the Mage spell cast at Trevor's party.

"I thought this place couldn't get more creepy," Isabelle murmured, but I was relieved.

We weren't going in alone. We were going in with an animated army of rock.

Couldn't hurt.

THERE WAS NO QUESTION OF our destination. The beat of the spell was insistent. Even if I hadn't been able to see the spell light, I would have felt its allure. It wound into my thoughts and urged me closer, drawing me to certain destruction.

Isabelle was caught in it, too, this time. We didn't have to confer at all about our path. We just trudged along. I didn't doubt that she was trying to keep it from completely claiming her thoughts, just like I was. It was really strong. I fought despair. Futility. A relentless sense of being doomed.

As we walked, the snow stopped falling. I felt the breath of wind and looked up to see the clouds being swept away. They were thinning fast, patches of starlight becoming visible.

We halted when we saw the triple circle of Mages. It was just like my dream. Two circles facing outward and one facing inward. In the middle, I could see Trevor, Meagan at his side, a frenzy of golden light swirling around her. She stared at Trevor with apparent adoration. The guys were there, too, and I was so relieved to see they were still alive that my knees nearly gave out.

They struggled against their spell bonds, snared in human form.

Jessica was there also, although she seemed to be more tired.

Or resigned to her fate.

Derek seemed watchful, caught in a haze of spells and snarling. What did he see two minutes into our collective future?

His Regalness leapt from Isabelle's arms and strode through the snow toward the circle with verve, his tail waving like a banner. Isabelle might have gone after him but I stopped her with a gesture.

The cat Meagan had saved, the gray one she'd named Mozart, was sitting on a stone closer to the circle. His tail lashed as he watched the scene avidly. Fish Breath leapt to sit beside him. They exchanged quick glances, then simultaneously began to clean their paws.

I wasn't fooled. They weren't that disinterested. They would have stayed warm and cozy at home if they didn't care.

I looked to either side and saw that the shadows were alive everywhere. I could barely discern the silhouettes of wolves all around us. Mostly I saw the pale glitter of their eyes.

And incredibly, mingled between them and gathered in smaller groups, there were dozens of cats. Maybe they were survivors from the sewer adventure. Maybe they were other ones.

But they weren't all house cats. I saw black panthers with golden eyes. I saw sleek and spotted jaguars. There were golden cougars with massive teeth watching from the trees. I understood that they were all shifters, all cat shifters, and that was why they'd come. Adrian had shifted to a lion, but lions must be the only cat shifters that the Mages had exterminated.

And Kohana had lied to me about it. Big surprise.

We were all here.

And we were all focused on the Mage circle.

The woman I'd seen in Trevor's memory stepped forward and there was a quickening in the air. Urd exhaled in a hiss behind me. The woman raised her hands just as the last of the clouds cleared and the light of the full moon shone on the circle.

She raised her hands and started to sing.

The ceremony began.

"BEHOLD THE NIGHTBLADE," the woman sang and held the dark blade high. I didn't like the look of it any more than I had in Trevor's memory. The chorus echoed her words, singing them so that they reverberated. "Gift of the ShadowEaters. Carved of a meteorite. Possessed of the power to liberate shadows."

Just as before, she waved the blade, making symbols in the air.

Isabelle caught her breath, so she must have recognized them. The spell light was a vivid frenzy and the light emanating from the blade pounded into my brain. I thought my head might explode from the light show.

"We invoke the ShadowEaters," she sang. "And invite them to our feast. Come, come among us, exalted ones. Come and partake of our offering."

I was sure she would reach for Jessica or one of the guys. I was desperate to think of a way to stop her.

But she turned to Trevor.

He grabbed Meagan's shoulders from behind. I saw her horror. She struggled, but his grip was tight and the spells were wrapping around her as well.

"The ShadowEaters demand a sacrifice for your initiation," sang the woman to Trevor. The light was getting sparkly and I could see those shadowy shapes taking form between the Mages.

"And so it is offered, in good faith," sang Trevor, pushing Meagan forward.

Hey! It wasn't supposed to be this way!

Meagan fought and bit against Trevor's grip. The guys struggled with new force against their bonds, as if they wanted to help her. Even Jessica was writhing in the snow. The wolves slipped closer to the circle and the cats watched unblinkingly, their claws bared.

"The ShadowEaters demand a spellsinger as admission to the inner sanctum," the woman sang, her hands high in the air.

"And so I have snared one. Behold, your humble servant who does only your will." Trevor pushed Meagan forward so that she stumbled. He fell to his knees and pulled her down to hers.

"Blood and shadow," sang the woman as she grabbed Meagan's hair and pulled her head back. "We shall all eat well at this feast." She lifted the NightBlade, its edge gleaming with evil.

She wasn't going to cut Meagan's shadow. She was going to cut her throat.

"No!" Isabelle screamed. She lunged forward through the snow.

And we were revealed.

"Don't touch her!" I cried and raced toward Meagan. Urd hissed and slid behind me, beckoning her army with a bony finger.

The Mages were astonished. The woman looked up in surprise, frozen with the blade an inch from Meagan's throat.

"No!" Trevor roared and pushed his way through the circle to fight me. I shifted shape en route and leapt into the fray in dragon form. It felt good to breathe fire and set a lot of Mage robes alight.

I heard the wolves growl and then they were in, too, biting and snapping. Cats slipped between Mages, slashing and snarling. Figures that had been stone just an hour before beat on Mages, making up for all the time they'd been trapped in rock.

The guys shifted shape, taking their dragon forms, but they were still helpless and bound in Mage light. Jessica became a snarling jaguar, but she, too, was still trapped.

The woman who led the Mages started to work what was obviously a familiar spell. They all joined in, adding their voices to the chorus even as they fought. They weren't going to sacrifice my friend to make Trevor more powerful.

Sacrifice.

The prophecy! I was kicking butt, my thoughts spinning, when I suddenly knew how to get the knowledge and power out of the beryl.

I had to surrender something.

I had to give up the beryl in order to get the rest of my powers. It was elegant, so perfectly logical that I knew it had to be right.

And Urd—Urd had come here to help me. They were like my fairy godmothers, the Wyrd sisters, and they were on my side.

Which explained the stone army.

I SMASHED TWO MAGES' HEADS together, then beckoned to the crusading knight. He came to me, then fell on one knee, his sword and shield outstretched.

I was running on instinct, but then, that's what Wyverns are supposed to do. I shifted back to human form to get this done.

Before I could think about it too much, I took off my ring and pushed it onto the sword instead, jamming it down the stone blade as far as it would go. I pulled the rune stone out of my pocket, focusing on the circle inscribed on one side. That clue had been there all along, looking me right in the eye, but I'd missed it.

And then I smashed the black-and-white glass ring and the rune stone together, shattering the ring against the knight's stone shield.

It broke into a thousand shards and made a sound like crashing glass. The sound stopped the fight, as if a movie had been frozen in midscene.

It was just like the party at Trevor's, except I was the only one who could move.

I saw ghosts rise from the debris of the ring to float above us all. Suddenly I was surrounded by the ghosts of all Wyverns past. There had to be a hundred of them, all in their shadowy dragon forms. They were all white, all glittering like ice. They were ethereal and magical, a long line of female dragons of which I was the newest member.

Urd made a noise of approval. Yup, the past was her territory.

It looked like the snow had started again, falling thickly all around us. On closer examination, though, I saw that it was really an avalanche of feathers, white ghostly feathers shed by the Wyverns. They moved. I stared in wonder. Urd nodded.

This was it. *My* big test.

The Wyverns flew in a circle, making a blur of white and

silver that surrounded me. The circle moved faster and faster. I heard their names like whispers on the wind, each echoing in my thoughts, then immediately disappearing. I felt like I was standing in a cloud.

And then I had it. Traditionally, the Wyvern retreated to the clouds and the mists. They avoided life and its entanglements. I didn't do very well with that worldview. I liked to be in the thick of things.

That was what had to be done differently to change the future.

In the same moment, I saw the flash of one Wyvern's eyes.

They flashed with fear.

On impulse, I leapt. I slipped into that Wyvern's memory. Her memory was like a fog bank, all half-glimpsed images and mysterious shapes. Then the mists parted and I saw her observing a Mage ritual. I tasted her dislike of them. I felt her horror when she witnessed the first sacrifice they made. Her revulsion flooded through me, her reaction the same as mine had been in seeing the mermaid lost.

That sacrifice had been a griffin, a ferocious shifter that screamed and bit until it breathed its last. Its death had not been easy and the Mages had not made a clean job of it.

I felt the Wyvern's horror, her sense that she should intervene.

But I felt her hesitation as well.

She chose to turn away rather than to expel this wickedness.

It was easier to retreat, to decide that what happened in the world was beyond her influence. I knew what had happened next. Unobstructed, the Mages had continued to recruit and slaughter, to grow in power and control.

Because my forebear had chosen to avert her gaze instead of make a difference.

I understood the prophecy with aching clarity. I knew the role I had been born to play. I knew what I had to do to change the role of the Wyvern forever. The fact that I couldn't sit back and watch the view was the good bit, the part of me that could make the difference. That's why it was my job to lead the fight.

I had to make this right.

Now.

It was time to trash the Mages and do what should have been done way back when that griffin had died. The Wyverns fluttered all around me, their eyes bright even as they trembled with fear. If sacrifices were on the menu, I had a bunch of possibilities.

I wasn't afraid.

Or if I was, I wouldn't show it.

I stepped forward and whistled to the Mages, setting the scene in motion one more time. Chaos and fighting surrounded me on all sides.

"I think I've got something you need," I shouted, and held Kohana's black feather aloft. "Want to trade?"

THE MAGES FELL SILENT.

They turned as one to stare at me.

Their spell light flickered orange, as if it too was uncertain how to proceed. The light was agitated, sparking as if calculating new variables.

Then the leader strode toward me, one hand outstretched for the feather and the other holding the NightBlade high. The moonlight glinted off that dark blade.

I stood my ground.

Even though I had guessed what would happen, I was still shocked by how fast he moved. Kohana streaked out of the sky, screaming outrage. He threw thunderbolts into the assembly of Mages, and the earth boomed with their impact. Lightning flashed from his eyes, crackling across the night sky.

He tackled the woman and she screamed as she fell. I saw that he had ripped out her eyes with his claws, then left her writhing in anguish and bleeding in the snow.

Then he leapt for me.

I shifted shape with a roar. Then I seized Kohana and willed myself into the dreaming. He yelped but I didn't let go. With the ring gone, I had to use the view of my left eye again to orient myself. I found the spell light in the dreaming and latched on to it.

I raced down the conduit of spell light, even as Kohana struggled against my grip. He was swearing and spitting and biting, but I didn't care.

We emerged suddenly in the wasteland of the Mages' collective memory.

"Stupid . . ." Kohana began, but I ignored him.

Instead, I breathed dragonfire at the forest. The trees closest to me erupted with brilliant orange flame, their dry wood crackling as it burned.

"What the fuck . . ." he murmured, but I breathed fire in the other direction. I still had a death grip on him, but he wasn't fighting me anymore. The fire danced high on both sides of us, orange and hot, as the smoke rose from the burning forest.

"You could help," I said and cast him aside. "Don't just stare."

He was visibly astounded. "They'll lose their recollection. Of everything."

For once, I could give him a look of disdain. "That would be the point."

Kohana turned to look at the burning forest. "Brilliant. It's fucking brilliant, unless . . ."

I had no time to chat. I didn't know what they might be able to do to retaliate, and time was of the essence.

They still had Meagan and Jessica and Derek and the guys in their grasp.

I flew low over the forest, spewing fire in every direction. The forest was soon aglow with a thousand flames, a raging inferno of light and heat.

To my relief, Kohana quickly decided to join forces with me. He swooped in to throw thunderbolts and heat lightning, his efforts spreading the fire beyond my reach. We flew back and forth, working together, relentless in destroying the hive memory of the Mages.

Far away, I could hear them screaming in anguish.

It worked for me.

And when Kohana and I met over the blaze of destruction we had created, he smiled at me. There was something a whole lot like admiration gleaming in his dark eyes as he surveyed me.

"Not bad, *Unktehila*," he said quietly. "Not bad at all."

"We need to work together," I said. "All of us, in union against the Mages. It's the only way we'll win."

He didn't say anything, just gave me that inscrutable stare.

And extended his claw.

Was it a trick? Or was he sincere?

Tick-tock. We had to get back.

I chose to trust him.

For the moment.

I placed his last feather in his claw.

He laughed and produced the NightBlade from the cluster of thunderbolts in one claw. He flourished it, swishing it through the air.

"You got it!" I cried.

"It's mine to destroy," he said, then shot into the sky. He ascended in a spiral of ebony feathers, seeming to fly straight at the sun. He was faster than ever. I could never catch him.

And really, I didn't want to.

I went back to save the others.

Chapter 16

I closed my eyes and abandoned the destroyed hive mind of the Mages. I willed myself back to the fight in the cemetery and opened my eyes to find a kick-ass fight in progress.

I leapt right into the middle of it, with a roar.

The Mages were at a serious disadvantage. The older Mages—and probably the ones who had been initiated longer—had collapsed on the ground. They writhed wordlessly in the snow, their gazes blank. I could only assume that they had no memory other than what had been in the memory hive. The woman who had led them was only twitching where she had fallen, great bleeding holes where her eyes had been.

Their loss had trashed the ranks of the Mages. I could see Adrian, casting spell light with furious intensity, and Trevor, singing his heart out to cast spells, along with about a dozen other young Mages and Mage apprentices. Their spells cavorted in the air, all golden light, gathering power before they attacked.

The cemetery was full of wolves, all of them leaping and snapping and biting at the surviving Mages. I'd never seen such a furious pack of dogs, and I guessed the Mages hadn't either. Then there were the cats, slashing and spitting and ripping the guts out of anyone they could reach. And there was Urd, gesturing to her stone army, guiding them through the fray as they pounded and smashed fragile human bones.

Some Mages broke rank and ran away, only to be pursued and taken down. Others targeted their opponents with bright spells. There was a lot of blood in the snow, and a lot of fallen bodies. Any ethereal ShadowEater forms had been dispelled, but I doubted that they were completely destroyed.

The amazing thing was Meagan. I could see that she must have talked to Jared. She was standing with her feet braced against the snow, singing defiantly back at Trevor. Her spellsong had purpose as it hadn't before, and it gathered into a ball of furious light in front of her. Sparks flew from that sphere, flattening anyone who was hit.

She was a natural.

I was shocked to hear her singing Jared's song "Snow Goddess." Spell light in a thousand hues of blue and purple emanated from her, forming a barrier between her and the Mages.

I saw then that she stood over Garrett, who was still struggling against his binding spell. He was wriggling and fighting the tight cords of golden spell light, murmuring to himself. Sparks from Meagan's sphere fell on him and I saw one line of spell snap, then sizzle as it burned.

The ends of the broken spell light danced toward each other, like a pair of snakes that would join anew. Garrett glared at them, all fiery intensity, and they burned back several inches. It was enough that they couldn't touch again.

Yet.

I guessed that the spell had been fashioned to repair itself if any of it broke. Meagan saw what he had done and changed her tune, making a whole flurry of her spell sparks fall on the spells that bound him. There was sweat on Garrett's brow, but he laughed as more of the binding broke and he burned it back.

I roared and flew straight to Meagan in dragon form. I helped Garrett free himself, watching Meagan's back as she tossed spells into the crowd of Mages.

"Thanks," he said, then leapt into the air, shifting en route. He lunged past Meagan and attacked Trevor, his dragonfire vivid against the darkness. I'd never seen anyone shoot such a huge plume of flame, and I stared in awe. He was glorious, his garnet and gold scales flashing in the night.

Meagan stopped singing for a moment, her face flushed as she caught her breath. She swallowed, her gaze fixed on Garrett, then smiled when Trevor fled across the cemetery, with Garrett's flames right at his heels to encourage him.

I gave Meagan a thumbs-up, although I'm not sure she noticed. She was focused on singing with all her might.

The other guys, though, were still securely trapped. Derek and Jessica were still trussed up as well, and now apparently caught in human form.

Isabelle, to my relief, was okay; she had a buff guy defending her on either side. One looked like a football player, a seriously large guy. The other was more slim. There was something about the way the first guy beckoned to an approaching Mage, as if daring him to rumble, that reminded me of Fish Breath.

And I understood exactly why we'd been adopted.

Garrett returned to defend Meagan, so I leapt toward Nick and breathed dragonfire at the spell bonds that held him captive. Nick roared as he shifted shape and joined the fight. Then I turned my dragonfire on Liam's bonds.

Nick decked Trevor, silencing his song for a moment. Liam leapt over my shoulder as he shifted shape, too. I barely saw the blur of a malachite dragon rip past me. He seized Adrian by the throat, that Mage having come up behind me. Liam held Adrian as the Mage shifted shapes in rapid succession, breathing dragonfire until he was singed in every shape.

I cut Derek free next. Derek shifted shape in a glimmer of pale blue light, then growled. His pale eyes glinted and then he leapt for the woman who had led the ceremony. She was still prostrate in the snow, but evidently he was taking no chances.

He ripped out her throat with one savage gesture.

I understood his point. She would never again eliminate another species of shifter.

He looked at me, blood on his jowls, as if to acknowledge my help. Then he joined the other wolves, disappearing into their midst.

Far above me, I saw the Wyverns gather in a circle and dared to hope that I had fulfilled the prophecy. A heartbeat later, I saw an orange center, surrounded by the black-and-white circle that looked a lot like Rafferty's ring, then a halo of white that was Wyverns past. I thought I saw the silhouettes of two dragons in the black-and-white part, but it moved so quickly that I couldn't be sure. The circle spun faster and faster, but I couldn't look away.

In fact, we all watched, uncertain what to expect.

Then it exploded in a brilliant blaze of light.

And the circle was gone. There were embers falling in the snow all around, black chunks of ash that sizzled as they hit the snow and then disappeared.

I caught my breath when I saw the ghostly apparition of Sophie high above me. She flickered between human form and dragon form, breathtakingly beautiful either way. *"Thank you, Wyvern new,"* she said in old-speak, then blew me a kiss.

She dissolved then, disappearing from sight like fog being dispersed by the wind. Had I seen the dark shadow of another dragon fly in the mist with her? Were she and Nikolas together forever? I hoped so.

I didn't even jump when Urd put her bony hand on my shoulder and squeezed. "Wyvern made and curse broken," she said with satisfaction.

That was when I knew: I'd passed my initiation test.

THE MOON SLID BEHIND A cloud and the Mages—at least those who had survived—dispersed, running into the night. We let them go. We could tally up later who had survived and hunt them down—as Nick had said before, ridding the world of Mages was going to be a lot like our dads' mission to eliminate *Slayers*. It was going to take some time. And we'd made major progress.

The guys landed beside me, shifting shape when their feet touched the ground. They were giddy with triumph, ready to celebrate our success. We had a kind of group hug going, with Meagan and Isabelle and the guys and me.

But we weren't alone, we dragons and our human friends. The night air crackled with the blue shimmer of shape shifters reverting to human form. Derek shook hands with the guys and introduced some of his wolf friends. None of them had much to say, but they nodded and shook hands a lot.

Wolves mostly became guys, I noticed, while the cats mostly became girls.

Except Fish Breath, who still hovered beside Isabelle, along with Meagan's adopted cat. Isabelle thanked both cat-guys, and both acted as if they were disinterested in what was being said. I could see by the gleam of their eyes, though, that they were pleased.

And they'd continue to stand guard. I guessed that it was similar to my saving Kohana and him feeling that he owed me a debt. Isabelle and Meagan had saved the cats.

Jessica led the cats to us, falling on her knees in the snow. She looked up at me. "I didn't want to hurt you, but Trevor didn't give me much of a choice."

"Us or you?" I guessed.

She nodded, her tears falling.

"You had to swear your loyalty, I'll bet," Meagan said. "After they took the lion shifters."

Jessica nodded again as the burly guy who had defended Isabelle came to her side.

"If we didn't obey," Fish Breath added, "they would have taken the next of our kind."

"They've done it before," Jessica said. "We defied them once, and they eliminated the tiger shifters in retaliation."

"But it doesn't matter now," Fish Breath said, his tone fierce. His hand landed on Jessica's shoulder. "They broke their word by capturing you. All bets are off."

She blinked back her tears as she rose to her feet, and he hugged her tightly. He rubbed the back of her neck as she cried out the rest of her fear and my gaze locked with his.

I had a feeling that Jessica and I were going to get along a lot better in the future, since the secrets between us had been revealed.

And the cat shifters were going to be able to tell us a lot more about the Mages. As slaves, they would have seen a lot. Between us, we would find weaknesses we could exploit to defeat them forever.

"Kohana says he's going to destroy the NightBlade," I told them. "He took it."

Fish Breath shook his head. He was a pretty good-looking guy. "He won't be able to do it. It's a ploy. They'll turn its power against him—you'll see."

"Just like they lied to me," Jessica said.

"Then we have to save the Thunderbirds and destroy that

knife somehow, too." I paused to think. "Maybe that will persuade them to join us." I saw Derek hovering at the edge of the group. "I mean, join our union," I said to him, deliberately using his words, and I thought he smiled a bit.

Fish Breath shrugged. "Maybe. Maybe not."

"You have a name?" I asked him.

He smiled and put out one big hand. "Kincaid. Most people call me King."

"King works for me." I shook his hand and my fingers disappeared in his warm grip.

"Never been much for dragons, but you're changing my mind."

I smiled, knowing that he'd noticed that I wasn't much for cats. "Right back at you." We grinned at each other.

"We're all in this together," Derek said. "Thanks to Zoë."

Everyone nodded agreement and then Derek tipped his head back and let out a howl. It sent shivers down my spine, even more so when the other wolf-guys took up the call.

We had a lot to learn about each other, but I was optimistic that we could do it, and that we could work together to completely defeat the Mages. We were three-quarters of the way to making the union that would save all of us shifters.

There had to be a way to trash that NightBlade. It was just another riddle, waiting to be solved.

I saw that Garrett had taken Meagan's hand and that they had slipped away from the group a little bit. He bent to talk to her, his expression tender. She pushed up her glasses and smiled at him, almost radiant with pleasure.

"Privacy time," Derek murmured as Garrett bent lower and I looked away.

I smiled.

Then I saw Derek smiling and I blushed.

"Good job, Zoë," Liam said, giving me a quick hug.

"Happy birthday, Wyvern," Nick said, punching my shoulder lightly. "Nothing like kicking a little butt to mark the big day."

"But it's not . . ." I began to protest.

Nick tapped his watch. "Five past twelve. You're officially sixteen."

They all hooted and congratulated me.

Then we had the best snowball fight of all time, racing out of the cemetery toward the lights of the city as we lobbed snow at each other. We were all laughing and stumbling over ourselves, loud and having a lot of fun.

I'm sure there were dozens of scandalized humans calling the cops on us, disruptive teenagers that we were.

I stopped on the perimeter of the cemetery to look back. Urd wasn't following me anymore and there was a hooded statue in front of that block of stone again. It didn't have a drop spindle.

The monuments were all just as they had been. Motionless.

I wasn't sure whether the mess of fallen Mages would be there in the morning or not. I didn't much care. They could weave spell light to defend their own secrets. Ours were secure.

The wolves and the cats had taken their own, to celebrate their lives and mourn their losses, which was just as it should be.

"Time to go home," Liam said to me, and I nodded.

"You, uh, want a ride?" Nick said to Isabelle, shuffling his feet a bit in the snow. She looked at him, her expression a mix of caution and hope, but he smiled at her. "Truce?"

Isabelle thought about it for one heartbeat. "Okay."

Garrett turned to Meagan. "One last ride before we meet again?" he offered with a smile, and Meagan lit up.

"Just you and me," I said to Liam, giving him a nudge.

"And one big cat," Liam said. King shimmered and shifted,

standing regally on the sidewalk as he awaited his chauffeur. "Come on, King. I'll give you a lift."

I GOT HOME EXHAUSTED BUT triumphant.

I wondered whether my dad would even notice my return.

It was late, later than I should have been out, so I climbed the stairs to our loft quietly. I didn't want to use the elevator, because it made a ton of noise, especially to dragon ears. When I got to the hallway that led to our door, I even took off my boots and carried them.

I punched my code into the keypad of the dead bolt, hating all the little beeps and whirs. In the daytime you could barely hear the lock.

At night it provided an avalanche of sound.

The hinges even creaked on the fricking door when it opened.

And that was when I knew there was something different.

A trio of candles burned low, perched in their holders on the coffee table. There was an empty bottle of wine and a pair of glasses there, as well as a pile of luggage just inside the door. A witchy pair of black boots with spike heels and pointed toes looked as if they'd been kicked aside.

I recognized those boots.

I also recognized the sweater that had been flung over the back of the couch. I recognized the scent of a familiar feminine perfume.

And the door to my parents' room was securely closed.

I smiled as I flicked the exterior door shut behind me. *My* mom wasn't just home.

She intended to stay.

I hooted as I bounded into my own room, and shouted with joy. I didn't care whether they heard me or not. It was ten past two when I crashed.

I'd gotten the best birthday gift of all.

And it hadn't even made my list of top three.

THAT NIGHT, I dreamed of Urd and Verdandi.

It shouldn't have surprised me.

I felt chilled in the night, and rolled over. It was good to be back in my own bed and my own room. I sighed and opened my eyes, then blinked.

The tree was back, growing out of the floor and through the opposite wall. Verdandi was knitting and Urd was spinning her spindle. They sat on either side of that dark pit of a well, the snow falling lightly all around them. The stars were out overhead, which made no sense, but there it was.

As I watched, Urd put her drop spindle carefully aside. She took the bucket I'd ridden before, the one with a rope around the handle, and lowered it into the well. She let a lot of rope go before the bucket splashed far below.

She glanced up then and I thought I saw her smile inside the shadows of her hood. Tough to tell if someone's smiling or grimacing when she has a skull face. Then she drew the bucket up with her bony hands. When it cleared the top of the well and Urd bent to grab the handle, Verdandi put her knitting aside. She straightened her glasses, then got to her feet. There was a ladle tucked beneath her stool, and it shone as if it was made of sterling silver.

Maybe it was made of moonlight.

She dipped it into the bucket and withdrew a sparkling scoop of water. She poured it carefully over the root of the tree, taking care to dampen all the bark.

She repeated the gesture over and over again, watering all of the tree root that she could reach. When necessary, Urd sent the bucket back down the well for more water. They worked steadily and methodically.

I dozed as I watched Verdandi ladle the water again and again and again. Finally satisfied, she tucked her ladle away and Urd stowed the bucket beside her stool. The pair sat down and began to work again, never having exchanged a word. The spindle spun and dipped, wool gathering on its stem. Verdandi pursed her lips as she knit, the product of her efforts spreading over her lap like a snowdrift.

Just before my eyes shut again, I saw it. A fresh green leaf appeared on one branch of the winter-deadened tree. Urd and Verdandi paused in their work to watch it unfurl. It opened with ridiculous speed, becoming a lushly green and shiny leaf about as big as the palm of my hand.

A second bud erupted farther down the same branch.

The sisters exchanged a glance and then Verdandi began to hum a little. Her needles flashed again and the drop spindle spun. But I saw her wink at me, quickly, just before I closed my eyes.

I smiled as I slipped into sleep. I knew the new growth was because of me.

There was a new Wyvern in town and the sisters liked that just fine.

YES! I WOKE UP READY for the most awesome birthday party of all time. I lingered in bed, enjoying my sense of anticipation. I could smell coffee brewing and heard my mom humming in the kitchen. My dad was on the phone, making last-minute arrangements for something. I felt the *Pyr* coming closer, all of them gathering for my big day. That coppery conduit was all a-sizzle.

This was the good stuff.

I wasn't expecting the doorbell to ring, not so early. But it did, and my mom came to get me. "For you," she said, as if she'd never been gone. "Imagine."

I gave her a tight hug—because she had been gone—tugged on some clothes and ran for the door. I was sure it was Meagan, come to dissect events of the night before, or one of the *Pyr* guys.

But it was Derek.

And he looked awkward.

He cleared his throat when I appeared and didn't seem to know what to say. That my mom was standing there, obviously listening, probably didn't help. Even my dad did a crap job of pretending not to care.

"I, um, wanted to wish you happy birthday," he said. "Before you, um, got busy."

My parents exchanged a look and finally decided they had something to do in the kitchen.

"Thanks." I shoved my hands in my pockets, feeling as awkward as he looked. "I was going to send you a message this morning, and Jessica, too. It's kind of a *Pyr* party, but it'd be great if you could come, too."

"Thanks. I'll do that."

We stood there, neither of us looking at each other, until he cleared his throat again. "Look, about last night . . ."

"What about it?" I thought we might have forgotten something, something keyed to the other shifters, maybe insulted them. I looked at him to find that unblinking stare fixed upon me.

"You were amazing," Derek said. He smiled that crooked half smile. "I told you I always wanted to see a dragon kicking butt."

I blushed then, right to my toes.

To my astonishment, when I could manage to look back at him, he was holding out a box with a bow on it. He couldn't look me in the eye. "For you," he said gruffly. "No big deal. It's just something I thought you'd like."

I was even more astonished. I took the box and shook it a bit—force of habit.

"Open it," he said, sounding more like his usual self.

"You already know what comes next," I accused him, and he grinned.

I opened the box. There was a silver necklace in it, a necklace with a charm. It looked like a woman's hand. I glanced up at him in confusion.

"The hand of Fatima," he said. "It's supposed to avert the Evil Eye."

"Maybe even against Mage spells."

"Can't hurt."

I put it on then, using the mirror in the hall to fasten the clasp. The charm fell into the hollow of my collarbone. Derek took a look and nodded approval. "I noticed you like silver, too."

I do. I love silver. I never thought guys paid attention to stuff like that. He was watching me again, his hands shoved in his pockets, his eyes gleaming. I had a tingly feeling, one that made my skin feel all hot and me a bit dizzy.

I wasn't sure what came next, but I knew he was waiting for something.

"Well, I should go," he said finally. "See you later."

We confirmed the time for the party and he turned for the door. As much as I might fantasize about Jared, it looked like he was gone from my life. But Derek—Derek liked me just fine.

And I liked him, more all the time. Maybe I was finally getting it right.

Maybe I could like guys who liked me for a change.

"Wait." Before I could change my mind, I stepped after Derek. He glanced back, the twinkle in his eyes telling me that he wasn't going to be surprised by anything I did.

And that was okay.

I kissed him, right on the mouth. It was sweet and lingering, an entirely different kind of kiss than I'd had with Jared. Our lips clung a bit and I bumped his nose with mine when I stepped back.

But his eyes shone.

And my heart was pounding.

It was matching its pace to his, making me feel breathless and dizzy and just fine.

"Later," Derek whispered, and then he slipped out the door and was gone.

I leaned back against the door, trying to catch my breath.

Then I knew I had to call Meagan.

THE PYR CAME ROLLING IN throughout the day, and my friends joined us for dinner, too. Derek and Jessica came, and Isabelle and Meagan, after I'd explained to the *Pyr* that these friends were among the trusted humans who knew my secret.

My dad had made it clear that I was in deep trouble and that we would talk about my punishment the next day, yada yada yada. But he'd already added Meagan to his list of humans in the know, and had had a conversation with her, probably about confidentiality. I think she reassured him about her trustworthiness more than I ever could have.

I might not have the gift of foresight—yet—but I had a feeling that he was going to cut me some slack one more time. The Mages, by capturing the guys, had saved me from exile.

And I was the new Wyvern.

Maybe all those victories were what made the celebration of my birthday so completely amazing. We had the most awesome Thai food for dinner—my mom was on a serious cooking spree—and then the best birthday surprise of all was revealed.

My dad had planned a pyrotechnics display just for me. We went up on the roof to watch it over the lake and my mouth fell open in shock when he turned on the music.

The fireworks were synchronized to a song he'd noticed me listening to eighty-seven thousand times.

"Snow Goddess."

It was perfect. Meagan grabbed my hand and squeezed my fingers tightly as we stood there in rapture.

Perfect.

MEAGAN STAYED OVER THAT NIGHT.

We were hanging out in my room after everyone else had

gone, reviewing the events of the night before—well, actually, Meagan was talking about Garrett's deeds of the night before and how hot he was and how relieved she was that he was okay—when my messenger chimed. It was Rox, the tattoo artist and partner of dragon dude Niall. I assumed she'd called with birthday wishes.

"Hey, Rox."

Then I had a wild thought. Was Rox going to offer to do my tattoo, against my mom's objections? My heart took off at a gallop, fueled by crazy hope.

"Hi, Zoë. Happy birthday. Sorry we weren't there for your big day."

"That's okay. Thanks for the good wishes."

"Well, it's more than that. I need to ask you something." Rox sounded distracted, and I could hear music in the background. There were other people talking, so I assumed she was at her tattoo shop. It was open half the night, so it made sense that she was still there.

Working.

Meagan gave me a look, but I sat up, hoping that I knew what she wanted to ask. I sure knew the answer. "What's up?"

"Well, this guy came in tonight," Rox said. I could tell by her tone that there were others around her, and guessed that she would say only half of what she meant. Maybe the guy in question was standing right there. "And he wants a dragon tattoo." She paused, although I wasn't sure why.

"You do good ones. I like Thorolf's a lot."

That was, in fact, why I'd hoped Rox would do my tattoo.

"Yeah, well, that's the thing. He doesn't want one of mine. He insists that he wants one *you've* drawn."

"Me?"

"He says that you have one drawn out to go on and over your left shoulder and that he wants it. And he wants me to start on it tonight, because it's your birthday." Rox lowered her voice. "I know that's true and you know that's true, but how the hell does this guy know that?"

There was only one way any guy could know all of this.

In fact, there was only one guy who did.

I heard her slide her hand over the mouthpiece. "Do you have a stalker, Zoë?"

"Kind of, but it's okay."

"What?"

"I'm pretty sure I know who it is."

"Well, that's one thing," Rox said, sounding firm. "But just because he's seen your work doesn't mean he can just have it. You've put a lot of effort into that drawing and it's *yours*. People think they can just snag stuff because they want it, but artists need to have their rights defended. . . ."

I interrupted her rant, my heart fluttering. "Is he there?"

"You really think you know him?"

"If it's who I think it is, I'm good with this."

"Really?"

"Yeah. The guy I'm thinking of is a . . . a friend."

There was the understatement of the century. Meagan had her "This is good and you'd better tell me now" expression, but I held up one hand.

"Okay. Hang on."

There was a hum of activity, and the sound of Rox's heels on the linoleum floor. I've been in that shop a bunch of times. I could close my eyes and imagine myself there, see it and smell it. I heard Niall's voice faintly, then those of their twin sons. Rox was putting them to work early.

Then someone picked up the phone. I caught my breath and made a wild and crazy birthday wish.

It came true.

"Hey, dragon girl."

Jared.

I felt like I'd been hit with a brick.

And I was just about as coherent as a brick.

There were roughly forty-seven million things I wanted to say to him, but I'd been struck mute.

"Hey, Jared," I managed to say. Meagan gasped and mimed a victory shout, both fists in the air.

"Look, I, uh, thought about what you said," he said, sounding less certain of himself than I could believe possible. "And you know, even though I don't answer to anybody, I could call you once in a while."

"But you let Rox do the dirty work tonight."

He laughed under his breath, and then his words came, really low. "Wasn't sure you'd talk to me, dragon girl."

I was gripping the messenger so tightly I thought it might crack. Of all the thousands of things I wanted to say to him, I chose an easy one. One that didn't sound entirely pathetic, or like my knees had dissolved beneath me. "Thanks for the book."

"You're welcome. It needed to be where it belonged." He cleared his throat. "I always meant for you to have it."

I closed my eyes, hearing the resonance of truth in his voice. I knew Jared was a long shot, but it seemed like there were at least possibilities.

Maybe he just needed somebody to believe in him.

I wasn't nearly sure that would be enough, but I was willing to try.

"You get your beryl?" he asked softly.

"Turned out I had it all along," I said. "I just didn't know it."

"Everything work out okay?"

I heard his worry and smiled. "We kicked ass."

He laughed.

I thought about offering that ride again.

"Look, I need a dragon at my back," Jared said quietly, then continued before I could volunteer. "One who can't get hurt. What do you say to letting me carry a part of you on my skin?"

It was—as I should have expected from Jared—a perfect solution. The ideal birthday gift. I liked the idea of my dragon taking ink and claiming skin. While it was frustrating that it couldn't be on my shoulder—at least not anytime soon—I really liked the idea of my work being on his.

I cleared my throat. "First you've got to tell me about your salamander."

He chuckled a little, the sound making me shiver in a good way. I felt, in fact, tingly and filled with anticipation.

"It's not a salamander," Jared said. "It's a Wyvern. Rox has some ideas about shading it to look white. She already gave it green eyes, just so you know."

I shivered with delight. He already had a part of me on his skin. Or a representation of me.

My heart was thudding because there was only one possible answer to his question. "I'll send her the drawing now. I already have it digital anyway. Are you going to be in New York for a while?"

"Long enough, but don't look for me, dragon girl." He was stern.

Protective.

"But . . ."

"You don't know everything they can do. Don't underestimate them. We can't risk it yet."

I liked him talking about us as if we were already a team. I had a compromise solution of my own. "So, maybe I'll send you a dream instead."

"I'd like that, dragon girl." I heard the smile in his words. I felt warm right to my toes.

And Rox could send me pictures of my dragon on Jared's naked back, to dream on. Uh-huh.

He cleared his throat and I knew he was going to tease me about something. I could close my eyes and imagine the sparkling green of his eyes, that glint of mischief and his troublemaking smile. His voice dropped deliciously low. "Especially since you still owe me a ride."

"Absolutely," I agreed. "All I have to do is finish off the Mages first."

"Go get 'em, Zoë."

FORTUNATELY, I had a pretty good idea how we were going to finally eliminate the Mages. It would coincide perfectly with boot camp, another solar eclipse, the end of the Great Lunar Standstill of 2025, and me taking hold of the future as Wyvern du jour.

Stay tuned.

PHOTO BY MICHELE ROWEN

Deborah Cooke has always been fascinated by dragons, although she has never understood why they have to be the bad guys. She has an honors degree in history with a focus on medieval studies and is an avid reader of medieval vernacular literature, fairy tales, and fantasy novels. Since 1992, Deborah has written more than forty romance novels under the names Deborah Cooke, Claire Cross and Claire Delacroix.

Deborah makes her home in Canada with her husband. When she isn't writing, she can be found knitting, sewing, or hunting for vintage patterns. To learn more about Deborah and her dragon shape shifters, please visit her Web sites at www.deborahcooke.com and www.thedragondiaries.com. Her blog, Alive & Knitting, is at www.delacroix.net/blog.

Read on for a preview of the next Dragon Diaries book,

Blazing the Trail

Coming in trade paperback from New American Library in June 2012.

I dragged my feet down the corridor, trying to delay the inevitable. Suzanne sailed past me with her cronies and snarled her favorite greeting—that would be "Freak!"—and they all laughed their mean girls' laugh. My dread was enough that I didn't even care about Ms. Popularity and her perspective.

You would think that my outlook would be more positive. A bunch of great things had happened in the fall—some due to the efforts of yours truly—and it had been quiet in the realm of dragon shape shifters ever since. We'd kicked the proverbial butts of the Mages when they'd tried to destroy us, we'd formed alliances with the wolf shifters and the cat shifters and I'd been given the blessing of the previous Wyverns as the new Wyvern. Kohana, the Thunderbird shifter, had stolen the NightBlade from the Mages, thereby rendering them pretty much impotent, and we had a plan to help him destroy it on the next solar eclipse, coming to a sky near you in April. All we had to do was wait for the time to be right to completely consolidate our victory—forever.

My best friend, Meagan, had discovered that she had spell-singer powers and was learning to use them. I'd also had the most awesome sixteenth-birthday party ever at the end of all that drama in the fall. My parents had gotten back together after a separation and had even gone away on some romantic vacation, leaving me to stay with Meagan. Things were good. You'd think that a dragon girl would be able to discern the glimmer of gold in her hoard of possibilities.

But no. All I could think about—and dread—was the Valentine's Day dance this coming Friday night.

Derek had asked me to go with him. This wasn't a huge surprise. We'd gone to a few movies and hung out together over the past couple of months. He wasn't much of a talker but it felt comfortable being with him. We'd kissed twice more. I knew he wanted more commitment than that, but I wasn't sure.

Inviting me to the Valentine's Day dance showed he was ready for an answer from me.

I'd been ducking him, avoiding him. It was serious finkdom on my part, but I just didn't know what to do.

The thing is, I like Derek. I even like him a lot. He's sweet and thoughtful and funny once in a while. He's protective of me and pretty quiet, a bit intense. Plus he's a wolf shifter, so he understands the challenge of having two lives and keeping one part of your life secret from the other. We have the shifter thing in common and that makes it easy to be with him. I think it's wicked that he has the gift of foresight, that he can smell the future a couple of minutes before it happens. He calls it his early-warning system. I want some of that, but so far my Wyvern ability to see the future is being coy.

The problem is that I don't think I like Derek as much as he likes me.

And that worries me.

Does it matter? I think it does.

Derek is probably the smart choice. He's probably the guy I should go for. He's the one chance that could work.

Of course, I have this habit of falling hard for guys who don't fall for me. I did it once with Nick, another dragon shifter and one of my buddies, and I'm pretty sure I've done it again.

For Jared. Who is older than I am, elusive, hot, a rebel and a member of a rock band, who rides a motorcycle, is never around when I want to talk to him, and possibly knows more about dragons than I do. He challenges me and dares me and makes me tingle right down to my toes—and that happened even before I scored my very first kiss, from him. He jumbles me up and confuses me—and just the mention of his name makes my dad breathe fire and lock the doors.

I think I could have forgotten Jared—or at least let go of the possibility of seeing him again—until he sent me the only copy in existence of a book about dragon shifters. He had it and at first he said he wouldn't give it to me so that I'd need to contact him regularly. He called me dragon girl then and his eyes were seventy million shades of green, his grip warm and tight on my hand. My heart did somersaults all over my chest.

Then he sent me the book last fall. What was I supposed to think? I thought he was done and gone and that was that.

I was still trying to reconcile myself to the idea of his being out of my life forever when he called out of the blue—then got the tattoo I wanted, the one my mom had forbidden me to get on my back, on *his* back for *my* birthday. I didn't sleep for three nights.

I've spent way too much time checking out the pictures he sent me of the finished tattoo on his gorgeous muscles.

Plus I still owe him a ride on my personal Dragon Air.

So, should I hold to the dream, as crazy and unlikely as it

sounds? Or accept that Derek is my kind of guy and agree to go to the dance with him? I didn't want to be mean to Derek—and maybe love takes time to grow. Or maybe my instincts are right. Or maybe I'm just always going to yearn for guys that don't want me. Maybe that's part of what I like about them.

How twisted would that be? I like to think I'm more emotionally balanced than that.

Maybe Jared just likes the idea of having fangirls, of having me hanging on the line, waiting on him.

That really isn't my style.

At least, it shouldn't be.

I rounded the last corner and saw exactly what I'd wanted to avoid. Derek was leaning beside my locker, waiting on me. Meagan was at her locker, sorting her books, waiting on me.

Derek's dark hair is straight and still a bit too long. It hangs over his eyes, but still doesn't disguise their intense pale blue. They are wolflike, in their color and intensity. I swear he has X-ray vision. He was wearing his usual dark clothes, a combo that the eye slides over easily and lets him blend into the shadows. He's so quiet that he could be made of shadow.

Of course, he wasn't surprised to see me coming or from which direction. His gaze locked on me as soon as I turned the corner, his attention making my mouth go dry.

I'd have to give him an answer before I left today. But what would it be? Heart or mind? I had a feeling that there would be big repercussions from my choice, but of course, I couldn't even guess what they might be. My Wyvern powers could have helped me out here, but no such luck. I was on my own.

No pressure.

"Hey," Derek said, a guy of as few words as ever. His voice is low and rumbly, kind of like a growl. Sometimes it makes me shiver. "How was art class?"

"Best class of the day," I said with a smile. "Makes the rest tolerable."

Meagan laughed as I got to my locker, tapping her messenger to pull up a new message. She was laughing a lot more than she used to and no wonder—she'd finally gotten her braces off. Her teeth looked awesome and she was attracting a lot more attention. People see how cute she is, instead of her mouthful of metal. I'm happy for her.

In fact, I had an idea that I knew would make her happy if I could make it happen.

"It's Jared again," she said with excitement, scrolling through the new message.

"Again?" I asked as I opened my locker. I gave Derek a smile and tried to keep my tone neutral in referring to Mr. Incredibly Hot.

Derek didn't smile back.

He watched me closely. I knew what he wanted and that the moment of reckoning had arrived.

I dodged it just a little bit longer.

I nudged Meagan. "You two have something going on?" I teased, acting as if I did not care.

Meagan laughed again. "He's sending me all these tips about spellsinging. It's amazing. I'm learning so much."

"Oh, so you hear from him often."

"Yeah! Like every second day. He's in Des Moines this week."

My heart stopped. Des Moines was comparatively close.

But he hadn't called me.

Meagan held up her messenger to show the image of some club on its screen. "That's where the band is playing tonight. They're sold out!"

"Great," I said, barely glancing at it. I felt a simmer begin deep in my heart.

She heard from him *every second day*?

And I hadn't had one "hello" since November?

I was so out of his life that he hadn't even told me that he was back with his band.

Even I know enough about guys to understand the implications of that. Jared had been messing with me. We were over. He hadn't gotten in touch, because he didn't want to get in touch, because he did not care.

Just thinking that made me wince, but there was no point in avoiding the truth.

I shrugged into my coat and met Derek's gaze. He was cautious, uncertain what I would do. "You still want to go to the dance Friday?" I asked him, my tone a little more challenging than was necessary.

He straightened. "Only with you." He smiled crookedly and I was struck by just how cute he is. "I thought you weren't sure."

"I'm sure. Let's go."

His smile broadened then and I saw how much I'd pleased him. It is kind of amazing to be able to have that effect on someone. Would it work the other way by Friday? Or after that? "I'll pick you up at seven, talk to your dad and stuff." He was big on the protocol of talking to my dad. Maybe it's a pack thing. A wolf thing. A question of respecting the hierarchy. Either way, my dad likes Derek a bunch.

Probably as much as he dislikes the idea of Jared.

"They went to the Caribbean today. I'm staying at Meagan's this weekend."

Derek nodded. "Okay. I'll pick you up there." He glanced at Meagan. "You coming to the dance, Meagan?"

She pouted. "I don't have a date and I don't want to go stag. I've done it enough and this year, I really want to go with a guy."

"She's coming," I said to Derek and Meagan didn't look that

surprised. There's a casualty of her being a genius—it's tough to surprise her.

"But . . ." she started to protest.

"She's coming," I insisted and slammed my locker. Derek looked between us, amused.

Meagan gave me a stern look. "You're not going to fix me up. I won't be a pity date."

"No, you won't be, but yes, I am going to fix you up." I bumped shoulders with her, the way we always do, and smiled at her. "Trust me already. I have a plan and you're going to like it."

And I did.

I just had to make it work.

ONCE UPON A TIME, ABOUT three months before this, Meagan had gotten her first glimpse of the *Pyr.* That's the name for dragon shape shifters or, at least, our name for ourselves. That's what I am—although I'm the only female dragon shape shifter in existence. There's only one female *Pyr* at a time, and she's the Wyvern. I'm the Wyvern. And being the Wyvern means having a bonus pack of extra powers, some of which I'm still trying to locate.

But my point is simply that all the other dragon shifters I know, all of my buddies and the dragons I grew up with, are all guys. And they are pretty hot guys. I think the dragon business works in a big way for guys: it seems to make them fill out and get buff more quickly than plain old human guys. So any female with a speck of interest in the opposite sex would notice them, even when they're in their human form.

In dragon form, they are breathtaking.

In November, Meagan had been targeted by the Mages because of her innate spellsinging talents. They thought they could turn her to the dark side, then maybe use her against me and my dragon pals. They weren't counting on Meagan the genius figuring out their plan and deciding to go undercover to learn the real deal. It all culminated at a Halloween party at the house of an apprentice Mage named Trevor, who goes to our school. Meagan had been crazy for Trevor forever, until she learned his nasty secret.

And until Garrett, one of my dragon buddies, came to the rescue. Garrett is garnet and gold in dragon form, his scales like jewels, and just about as magnificent as a dragon can be.

I can razz Meagan about Jared because I know she's totally nuts for Garrett.

So that night, when I was supposed to be doing my homework at the dining room table at Meagan's house, I used my messenger under the table and invited Garrett to the Valentine's Day dance. The only problem was that we're in Chicago and Garrett lives in Traverse City. Meagan watched me from the other side of the table, flicking glances toward the kitchen, where her mom was making dinner. Her mom is serious about getting homework done, and if she caught me, she'd confiscate my messenger pronto.

I closed my hands over it in an attempt to muffle the sound as it chimed to signal an incoming message. I peeked between my fingers and grinned.

Garrett was coming.

"That had better not be a messenger I hear," Mrs. Jameson said from the kitchen. "We're going to eat in twenty minutes and I want to see that English homework done."

"*Who?*" Meagan mouthed.

I smiled as mysteriously as I could.

She wrinkled her nose at me, then glanced at her own messenger. It remained silent.

"*Geek*," I mouthed back at her and she wadded up a sheet of paper to throw it at me. We have an old joke that we're not geeky enough to message each other when we're sitting in the same room. (Even though we sometimes do.)

"I am talking to you, Zoë Sorensson," Mrs. Jameson added.

"Just finishing the last two questions, Mrs. Jameson," I answered, apparently the most dutiful student alive. Just so you know, I have nobody fooled on that one.

"Meagan?"

"Done, Mom." Meagan frowned and leaned closer to me, flicking another look at the kitchen. "Who?" she whispered.

"Wait for Friday," I whispered and winked. "You'll love it."

Meagan sat back. Of course she knew. Her mouth fell open and she raised one hand to her lips. "*No!*" she mouthed, clearly wanting me to say yes.

It is so tedious to try to surprise a brilliant individual, you know. Impossible, maybe.

I tried to act like I didn't understand her, but we've known each other way too long for that. I'd been hoping to make her wait for it, at least until we went to bed, but no luck. Meagan was too excited.

She scribbled a note and shoved it across the table at me, interrupting my consideration of math question number twenty-nine.

Her expression was expectant as I read it.

Actually, she was bouncing in her chair, vibrating with such excitement that I knew I'd done exactly the right thing.

For once.

"GARRETT!?!"

I nodded.

Meagan snatched the paper back and scribbled some more. I smiled when I saw what she'd written.

"OMG! What am I going to wear?"